PRAISE FOR

Love You a Latke

"*Love You a Latke* is the Hallmark Hanukkah movie I've been waiting for all my life. Seth and Abby's lovely story of fake dating and meddling parents, small-town Hanukkah festivals, and finding friendship in unexpected places is a cozy delight and as sweet and inviting as a cup of hot chocolate on a cold winter night. I loved every word!"

—Jenna Levine, *USA Today* bestselling author of *My Roommate Is a Vampire*

"One of my favorite reads of 2024, *Love You a Latke* by Amanda Elliot is Hanukkah romance at its very best."

—Jean Meltzer, international bestselling author of *The Matzah Ball*

"*Love You a Latke* is a beautiful story with an unexpected slow-burn romance and amazing supporting characters. But it's also a story about community—the community you're embraced by, the community you make, and the magical miracle of Hanukkah."

—Stacey Agdern, award-winning author of *B'Nai Mitzvah Mistake*

"Amanda Elliot's *Love You a Latke* is a perfect book to cozy up with this holiday season. Come for the unabashed defense of Hannukah not being Jewish Christmas, stay for the tender depiction of love, community, and friendship. You'll be rooting for Seth to win Abby over from the moment he walks into her coffee shop."

—Ali Rosen, author of *Recipe for Second Chances* and *Alternate Endings*

"Reads like a dream of a Hanukkah Hallmark movie. I bet it would make an excellent holiday gift for a reader in your life."

—Deb Perelman, creator of *Smitten Kitchen*

"Enjoy this book with a latke and all the toppings—you won't be disappointed!" —*Oprah Daily*

"This is a fun rom-com that gives great insight into Hanukkah and what the holiday is about. At its core it's about family, friendship, and love. Fans of this kind of holiday love story are in for a treat. And you'll be hungry for latkes by the time you finish the book."

—Red Carpet Crash

"This novel will melt everybody's hearts, but Jewish romance readers in particular will be thrilled to see Hanukkah reflected so authentically and lovingly. . . . This holiday treat is as wonderfully sweet and gooey as the traditional Hanukkah doughnut."

—*Library Journal* (starred review)

"Latkes and jelly donuts (sufganiyot) are a must for this read!"

—*Booklist* (starred review)

"This is a keeper." —*Publishers Weekly*

"Amanda Elliot celebrates the winter holiday season with *Love You a Latke*, a heartwarming exploration of community and human connection set during Hanukkah. . . . This wonderful novel has a well-defined plot and characters with absorbing emotional depth. . . . Elliot's mouthwatering descriptions of latkes, doughnuts, and artisanal coffee will delight readers, as will the rest of her engaging novel." —Shelf Awareness

PRAISE FOR

Best Served Hot

"If you're looking for a real, relatable romance, look no further than *Best Served Hot* by Amanda Elliot! The rivals-to-lovers vibes are delicious, as are all the descriptions of food. Do not read this on an empty stomach—you've been warned!"

—Alicia Thompson, *USA Today* bestselling author of *The Art of Catching Feelings*

"Amanda Elliot is a master of banter and crackling chemistry, delivering yet another winner! This rivals-to-lovers romance is spicy, lush, and addictive."

—Amy Lea, international bestselling author of *The Catch*

"A winning romance that will make your mouth water. *Best Served Hot* features two rivals who come from very different worlds but who are united in their love of food. If only I could eat the meals served in this book."

—Jackie Lau, author of *The Stand-Up Groomsman*

"*Best Served Hot* is a delectably sweet and spicy enemies-to-lovers rom-com from an author who knows the way to a food writer's heart is always through their stomach."

—Washington Independent Review of Books

"Elliot leaves your stomach grumbling and your heart pounding, and it's hard to discern what's more delicious: the elaborate dishes or the couple's simmering chemistry."

—*Kirkus Reviews* (starred review)

"This romantic comedy from Elliot . . . is a sexy slow burn with sizzling chemistry between the well-developed protagonists. Julie and Bennett fall in love over countless meals, and the descriptions of the foods they consume are incredibly described and guaranteed to make readers salivate." —*Library Journal* (starred review)

"This classic enemies-to-lovers plot is a slow burn, but the result is worth the wait and the food descriptions along the way will make readers salivate. Romance fans are sure to be charmed."

—*Publishers Weekly*

PRAISE FOR

Sadie on a Plate

"*Sadie on a Plate* is a joyful, satisfying romp. I loved it—and I'm still hungry!"

—KJ Dell'Antonia, *New York Times* bestselling author of *Playing the Witch Card*

"*Sadie on a Plate* reads like the ultimate cooking-show comfort watch—with the added spice of a forbidden romance. A delicious love story and heartfelt ode to Jewish cuisine."

—Rachel Lynn Solomon, *New York Times* bestselling author of *Business or Pleasure*

"This novel is perfect for any fans of cooking shows who also love to curl up with a beach read. It's fun [and] breezy, and [it's] clear that Elliot did her research into the behind-the-scenes world of *Top Chef*." —*USA Today*

"*Sadie on a Plate* reveals the arduous, exacting tasks of making really good food. Light as a soufflé, it's delicious."

—*The American Jewish World*

"A love letter to Ashkenazi cooking, and food in general, as a means of connecting with one's identity."

—*The Canadian Jewish News*

"Foodies with a hunger for juicy cooking-show competitions will eagerly lap up every last drop of *Sadie on a Plate*, Amanda Elliot's delicious rom-com. . . . Detailed food descriptions, recipes, and kitchen culture—along with a diverse cast—spice up a well-plotted story warmed with romance, humor, and heart."

—Shelf Awareness

"Luke and Sadie are likable characters with magnetic, slow-building chemistry and sympathetic, realistic backstories. The fast-paced, delicious plot is as much about food as romance. . . . Readers, especially those who enjoy shows like *Top Chef*, won't be able to put down this fast-paced romantic comedy."

—*Library Journal* (starred review)

"Elliot's first adult novel . . . has the perfect amount of reality-show high jinks and food innuendos that help dial up the heat. . . . A satisfying debut for foodies and romance lovers alike."

—*Kirkus Reviews* (starred review)

TITLES BY AMANDA ELLIOT

Sadie on a Plate

Best Served Hot

Love You a Latke

Eight Ways to Say I Love You

EIGHT WAYS TO SAY I LOVE YOU

AMANDA ELLIOT

Berkley Romance

New York

BERKLEY ROMANCE
Published by Berkley
An imprint of Penguin Random House LLC
1745 Broadway, New York, NY 10019
penguinrandomhouse.com

Snowflake illustrations by Olgastocker/Adobe Stock

Library of Congress Cataloging-in-Publication Data

Names: Elliot, Amanda author
Title: Eight ways to say I love you / Amanda Elliot.
Description: First edition. | New York: Berkley Romance, 2026.
Identifiers: LCCN 2026007886 (print) | LCCN 2026007887 (ebook) |
ISBN 9798217189618 trade paperback | ISBN 9798217189625 ebook
Subjects: LCGFT: Romance fiction | Novels
Classification: LCC PS3605.L4423 E44 2026 (print) | LCC PS3605.L4423 (ebook)
LC record available at https://lccn.loc.gov/2026007886
LC ebook record available at https://lccn.loc.gov/2026007887

First Edition: October 2026

Printed in the United States of America
1st Printing

The authorized representative in the EU for product safety and compliance is Penguin Random House Ireland, Morrison Chambers, 32 Nassau Street, Dublin D02 YH68, Ireland, https://eu-contact.penguin.ie.

This book is for Jonah.

Eight ways aren't enough to say how much I love you.

EIGHT WAYS TO SAY I LOVE YOU

Prologue

ONCE THEY HIT THEIR TEENAGE YEARS, LEO AND Shira only met at the old swing set back in the woods, where nobody could see them. They'd made this decision after the time in seventh grade when the girl across the street saw Shira running into Leo's house without knocking and went on to tell everyone that obviously the two couldn't be doing anything after that other than kissing, which, thought Shira with indignation, was:

1. Gross, because at twelve, any boys who weren't in famous musical groups still had cooties, and also Leo hadn't quite discovered deodorant yet despite the gentle urging Shira had done by leaving a stick she'd stolen from her parents' bathroom closet on his pillow, where he couldn't possibly miss it;

2. Insulting, because it was the most pedestrian rumor anyone could've possibly come up with—if the girl across the street was going to try to ruin their lives,

she could've at least been creative with it by telling everyone Shira and Leo were secretly siblings or that they were running a counterfeit Pokémon-card ring that could make even the rarest holographics;

3. Annoying, because it led to Shira's friends and frenemies making fun of her to the point where she couldn't even wave to Leo in the hallway without someone making smooching noises at them or asking Shira what she was going to name their baby, which was really stressful, honestly, because every time they teased her, it made her picture kissing Leo, which maybe wasn't as terrible as they wanted her to believe it would be.

People grew up a little after middle school and let it rest, especially once everyone woke up one morning and the other kids no longer had cooties but pheromones, but Shira and Leo kept their swing set meeting place. Partially because Leo had started dating one of the girls who sat in the back of the class with him and Shira didn't want to upset her, and the rest because meeting back there gave her what she'd eventually come to understand as nostalgia. It reminded her of all the years they'd spent racing each other for the slide or trying to do handstands on the swings or climbing up into the little fort so they could pretend they were spies surveilling their New Jersey neighborhood.

And okay, because while Shira knew perfectly well rumors didn't necessarily mean anything, there was one going around that Leo's girlfriend carried a knife in her combat boot. It was true that Shira didn't want to upset the new girlfriend, but mostly Shira didn't want to get stabbed.

On this particular day, they were fourteen, and Shira was the first one there, blowing on her hands to keep them warm in the icy air because she'd run out so fast she'd forgotten her gloves. Usually she would've hopped onto a swing to wait, but this time she paced in a tight circle over the snowy ground, alternating between trying to warm her frozen fingers and checking her phone over and over. Leo's text had been short and to-the-point: 911. So, even though she had an essay for English to finish and a bio test she had to study for, she'd come right away.

She'd gotten a 911 text from Leo once before, when his grandma died, the grandma who'd babysat him as a child, whose house he slept over at every year on his birthday.

Today, Leo showed up before she wore a moat into the snow. Her brows pinched at the sight of him: His dark hair, which he'd cut short for cross-country, was still somehow flying every which way; his tall, skinny form was as tense and coiled as the spring of a garage door, which, fun fact, was among the most dangerous things in a standard suburban house. Thousands are killed and maimed by garage doors every year—people underestimate how tightly they're wound up.

Shira flew toward him, hands fluttering, forgetting the fact that soon she'd probably have to amputate a finger or two due to frostbite. "Who's dead?" she burst out.

Something in that tightly coiled spring of him eased as soon as he saw her. His arms fell to his sides; he looked slightly less like he might strangle the next person to cross his path.

"Nobody's dead, Shira," he said, voice full of venom. "Unless you count dead to me. That fucking *cheater*."

Shira's thoughts leaped immediately to his girlfriend, who she knew mostly as that girl who sat in the back of the classroom and always disappeared with the bathroom hall pass because she was vaping out the window, and who also always got away with it, maybe because of the knife. To be fair, Shira had never exchanged more than a *hi* with her, since they were separated by the honors track Shira was on, which the girlfriend and Leo were not. "Oh my god, I'm so sorry," Shira said. "You deserve better than her. You are such a good guy. The best guy. She's going to regret–"

"Not Livvy," Leo interrupted. Shira grimaced at the flash of irritation that for some reason always ran through her whenever she heard the girlfriend's name. "That asshole formerly known as my father."

Shira gasped. "What?"

"Months. It's been going on for *months*, and we had no idea." Leo threw himself onto a swing, and the story poured out of him in furious fits and starts that Shira had to piece together like a puzzle. His father–his devoted father, the one who'd helped him build a wooden car for the Cub Scout Pinewood Derby and then helped Shira, the non-Cub Scout, build one because she felt left out–was cheating on his mom. And had been for, like, a long time. His mom had found out, and she'd screamed at his dad, and his dad hadn't screamed back but replied that he was in love, and not with his mom; with the lady he cheated with. There was more screaming. His dad was leaving? Maybe? Leo had run outside before he could be sure.

"I've been running ever since," he said, which explained why he was glistening all over with sweat. He jumped off the swing and began pacing in a tight circle, following Shira's tracks. "Around the neighborhood, then back here. So that I didn't have to think. But it didn't work. So I texted you."

He hadn't texted Livvy, Shira couldn't help but note, which wasn't a kind or helpful thing to be noting right now. So she just hugged him, which was allowed when they were hidden here in the trees. "I'm so sorry," she said, her face pressed up against his shoulder as she tried not to breathe. (He'd eventually discovered deodorant, but in the tradition of teenage boys, that deodorant had been way too much Axe.)

"You make it sound like someone died." His voice cracked. He was obviously trying very, very hard not to cry, so she made sure not to look up at him.

"It sounds like the way you think about your dad did," Shira said. Still not looking directly at him, she stepped back, taking a deep breath of air that froze her lungs, and guided him to the other swing. He slumped into it and bowed over like he was about to puke. Shira sat on the one beside him, facing the opposite way, so he could feel free to tear up without her eyes on him. "Okay, let's make a plan. You know that having a plan makes everything better."

"I know that *you* think having a plan makes everything better," he mumbled, which Shira chose to ignore.

"Since you don't know all the details yet, let's think short-term," she said, pumping her legs. Crafting a good plan always got her energized. "Before you can make any decisions for the long term, you're going to want to know all the details. You only know what your parents were yelling at each other before you ran out, right?"

"Yeah." She could barely hear him.

"We want information, not emotion. No, we *need* information, not emotion," she said. "So let's wait out here and let them calm down for a bit. Then we'll go back to your house and find out what actually happened. Maybe it's not as bad as they're making it sound."

"I doubt that."

"I'll come with you," she said. "We'll get all the information, and then we'll go from there, okay?"

He was still all hunched in on himself. She reached over and gave one of those rock-hard shoulders a squeeze. "Hey," she said, trying to sound comforting, which was not her natural state. "It's going to be okay."

But it wasn't okay. They hung out there on the swings for another half hour, until Leo's eyes were no longer red and he'd stopped sniffling ("allergies," he claimed half-heartedly), and then they marched through the woods and into his backyard.

If Shira had known that would be their last turn on the old swing set for an unfathomably long time, she would've . . . she didn't know, done something. Not held a ceremony, because Leo would've rolled his eyes, but at least, like, paused for a moment and laid her hand on the splintery wood and bowed her head while thinking of all the good times they'd had there.

Leo's parents were waiting for him when they approached the backyard, standing out on the deck despite the cold. They could've fit a king-size bed in the space between them, and their arms were crossed, and it was a testament to how much Leo looked like he was about to crumble that they didn't send Shira home. They sat him, and by extension, Shira, on the stiff green velvet couch in the formal living room that nobody ever used, as if to emphasize the importance of the moment. Leo's parents moved two armchairs across from them as if his parents were teachers about to tell them how deeply disappointed they were.

His dad began. Shira focused not on his face but on Leo's hands in his lap beside her, which were twisting at each other so badly she worried he might pull a finger off. "Leo, I'm so sorry you had to find out this way about my affair," he said. "My actions are not a reflection of my love for you, which has never and will never change."

Would it be weird to grab Leo's hand to comfort him and maybe keep his fingers attached? *What would the girl across the street say? What would Livvy say—or stab?* Shira kept her hands in her lap, stealing a glance at Leo's parents. His dad was beet red beneath his thinning dark hair, while his mom's face, normally pale, was whiter than a hard-boiled egg.

She glanced at Leo's dad before turning to Leo. Neither of them seemed to be waiting for a response from their only child. "I'm planning to fly out tomorrow morning to Grandpa's," Leo's mom said. His grandfather, the husband of the grandma whose death had inspired Leo's past 911 text, had moved back to Michigan after the death to be near his siblings and other children. "You're welcome to come with me. If you want."

That got a response. "Why are *you* leaving?" Leo flailed a hand toward his father, who flinched as if he'd been hit. "*He* should be leaving."

"I *want* to leave," said his mom, and Shira turned away so

that she wouldn't have to see Leo's reaction. Her eyes caught on the menorah in the front window, dull brass and streaked with rainbow wax. "The only reason I moved to New Jersey was to be close to your father's work in the city. I no longer want to be close to your father, so I no longer need to be close to the city."

Leo's dad flinched at that, which, good, he deserved it. Shira turned to Leo, whose eyes were sliding between his parents. "Are you coming back?"

"I don't know yet," said his mom. "Obviously, you're the most important part of all this. I want the disruption to your life to be as minimal as possible." Shira couldn't help but snort at that, because fat chance. Fortunately her snort was quiet enough that neither of his parents heard. "I know I want to go out there to be with your grandpa and your aunts for at least a little while, and then we can discuss and decide together what comes next."

What came next would be moving back, obviously. Because Leo couldn't move away. He just couldn't. The thought of living here without him two houses away was unfathomable. Like she'd woken up one morning and found that the sky was now red.

"I want to go, too," said Leo grimly, and he stood, and Shira's chest seized with something like panic. "I don't want to be near him anymore, either."

The room devolved into argument, harsh words swirling around Shira like she was at the center of a tornado. Leo's dad was insisting that he hadn't cheated on Leo, and Leo was spitting back that he'd cheated on the whole family, and Leo's mom was telling them both that Leo was practically an adult and he could do what he liked, and Leo had tears in his eyes again like he was very much not an adult, like he didn't want to be almost an adult, like he just wanted someone to hug him and tell him it was all going to be okay.

Shira's place was definitely not here anymore. She didn't think she could stand it. She slowly began to back out, but Leo stopped midsentence and turned to her. The winds stopped mid-whip. "I'll text you," he said. "Don't worry."

Of course, the second anyone said *Don't worry*, Shira immediately started to worry. "Promise?" she said.

"I promise," he said back, and then the corner of his mouth twisted in a half smile. "By the way," he told her. "Happy Hanukkah."

Outside, the empty, unlit menorah stood stark and alone in the front window. She took a deep breath of the cold air, freezing her lungs again, watching the wind flutter through his dad's hydrangeas. Leo had promised. He'd told her not to worry. Of course he wouldn't leave.

Something pulled taut in her chest like the string of a violin, already mourning.

Because of course Leo left with his mom, and of course he texted Shira, promising that a few flyover states between them wouldn't stop them from being friends. And of course they did their best. But texting every day turned into texting every week turned into texting every month turned into the occasional birthday wish with apologies for being so out of touch. She got so busy with art stuff and school stuff and synagogue stuff that the catch-up phone call they kept promising each other never actually happened. And while Shira held her breath that first summer break, assuming and hoping he'd have to come visit his dad, he didn't. Apparently he was old enough that the judge granting custody took his wishes into account, and while he was technically supposed to come stay with his dad on holiday breaks and for at least part of the summer, he refused.

Leo's dad moved in his affair partner, who lasted about a year before her car unceremoniously disappeared from the driveway. He always waved at Shira whenever she passed his house, and she always pretended she didn't see him. She stayed angry in solidarity with her friend, even if, by the time they graduated from high school, she had no idea what he was up to or where he was going to college or if she'd ever see him again. Their parting of ways had come before the ubiquity of social media, so that wasn't even an option to keep in touch.

Shira never expected to see him again, but still, every time she went home to visit her parents and passed his house, she peeked in his front window anyway. Just in case.

1

Year One

SHIRA WOULD NEVER DARE SAY IT TO ANY OF HER friends in Los Angeles, but she found the holidays in the suburbs superior to the holidays in the city. Or maybe she only found it superior to the way her crowd in particular celebrated the holidays in the city, which consisted mainly of ironic trips to cheesy holiday pop-up bars to make fun of all the decorations and corny drink puns, and visits to art gallery exhibits of "edgy" holiday fare, like last year's series of paintings exploring a crime scene investigation involving the murder of Santa Claus. It turned out the elves had done it in protest of their working conditions, which the artist used as a call for the working class to unionize.

In the suburbs, you can drink eggnog or Manischewitz wine without having to make fun of it. You can express genuine excitement about the first fallen snowflake, because it's not immediately going to turn into a gross gray slush full of fast-food wrappers and needles. You can go for a stroll around your neighborhood with your family to admire the Christmas lights strung on houses or the menorahs beaming proudly from front windows without worrying you're going to get hit by a car when you see Leo for the first time in—

What? She stopped short on the sidewalk in front of Leo's house—well, technically Leo's dad's house; it hadn't been Leo's house in years. It was dark out, and the big front window of the one-story ranch house was bright and uncovered, showing off the glowing electric menorah. Aside from that, it was empty now, except for some ghostly flickering from a TV off to the side.

It took a few seconds for her family to notice she had stopped, which she tried not to feel insulted by. "Shira?" her dad called over his shoulder. He and her mom stopped and turned around, their chins hunched down into their coats, their hands in their pockets. Bundled up like this, they could almost pass for twins: shortish, roundish, their glasses glinting beneath shiny black hoods. "Everything okay?"

She nodded and hustled after them. "Yeah." Her breath came in short bursts, puffing clouds into the air. Talia, her sister, didn't even seem to notice anyone had stopped; Shira could barely see her up ahead at the corner, a lanky teenage outline silhouetted against a horde of inflatable glowing reindeer. "Sorry, I just thought I saw Leo from the corner of my eye."

"Oh, you probably did," said her mom, all casual, as if her words didn't leave Shira breathless. "I didn't tell you he moved back?"

"What?" Shira hustled again to get in front of them so she could turn and fix them with an accusing glare. "No, you didn't tell me!"

"Right after Thanksgiving," her mom said.

"Wow," said Shira, turning back to face the empty street, and it was wild that her first instinct was to think *I can't believe he didn't tell me.* Of course he wouldn't tell her. They hadn't talked in, what, seven years? Something like that. They'd never come back from that first year of falling out of touch, of being busy, of making new friends and getting into new activities, the same way Shira had drifted apart from most of her high school friends after they all went to college. Being in proximity had been most of the basis for those friendships, as it turned out, and though they'd promised to keep in touch and visit each other, those promises had kind of rusted and weakened and broken without hurting anyone.

Shira was twenty-two now, a college graduate. Leo would be, too. She'd wondered where he'd gone, what he was doing now. She'd tried googling him a couple of years ago one night when she was bored but hadn't turned up much of anything besides his high school track rankings. "Huh. I'll have to go say hi."

"I'm sure he'd like that," said her mom. She leaned in and lowered her voice as if she didn't want anyone to hear her. "Joe said he was having a tough go of it."

"You talk to Leo's dad now?" Shira asked. Her parents had been just as scandalized and appalled by his behavior as she had been back in the day.

Her mom shrugged. "He's my neighbor, and it's been a long time. We don't have to be best friends to say hi when he's walking the dog or giving me his doorbell footage so I can figure out who egged my car."

Okay, fine. "So wait, Leo's having a tough time, he said? Why?"

She shrugged again. "Not sure. I didn't get any details." She sounded vaguely disappointed, which meant she'd tried to get some and failed. When it came to digging for details in her phone conversations with Shira, she was like a star paleontologist, able to piece together an entire ancient organism from shards of bone and fossilized skin, able somehow to tell that Shira had had a disappointing blind date from her purposefully vague hints about how the food at the bar she'd gone to the other night hadn't been great. "I got to tell him all about you. How you're living in LA and how you're working at one of the biggest art galleries in the country and how you're getting interest in your own art. He seemed very impressed."

Shira couldn't help it: Her chest puffed up like a proud pigeon's. At twenty-two, she was already living the dream. She'd worked hard, of course, but she'd also gotten lucky when her senior portfolio got noticed by the right person at the right gallery, a big, fancy one that represented a lot of big, fancy artists and that somehow now also represented her. Maybe by next holiday she'd have put on her debut show with them, and—dream big, she always told herself—all her work would receive rave reviews and sell to major collectors and maybe even get her featured in a big museum or a world biennale. And the owner of the gallery where she worked—a different one than the one who represented her, because Shira hadn't wanted to make things awkward with her boss asking if he would be interested in her own work (the thought of him declining and then having to work with him every day gave her hives)—would have to take notice and wonder, *Why is this extremely talented painter doing my admin work when I should be trying to poach her for my own even bigger and more impressive gallery, whose name would get her noticed by even bigger and more impressive collectors and venues?* And then–

"I also told him about your terrace," her mom said proudly.

Shira bit back a sigh. Her tiny studio, which hosted a Murphy bed in the combined living room/bedroom and barely had enough space in the kitchen to open the oven, did indeed have a terrace. It was rickety and always covered in bird shit, but it looked great when properly filtered on social media. "Right, okay," she said. "But did you see–"

"Shira, hurry up!" Talia hollered from up ahead. "It's cold!"

Shira sighed. "Coming."

She stole one last glance into Leo's window before moving on. There was a flash of movement in the corner, maybe a curtain fluttering. Probably the dog had run past and stirred it, but she lingered there for an extra second anyway. Just in case.

THE NEXT MORNING, Shira woke up to a bunch of texts in the group chat; they'd been buzzing deep into the night on West Coast time, while Shira, despite the minor jet lag, had passed out at nine thirty, to Talia's enormous eye roll. She scrolled through the messages she'd missed, knowing that by now it would probably be too late to respond to the political news they were horrified about with anything but an angry emoji, but she was still glad to be included.

Shira had met the three of them shortly after her arrival in

LA. Well, that wasn't entirely true; she'd known Danica fairly well in college, where they'd both taken classes in the art department, but they didn't truly become best friends until they realized they were the most talented painters in their art program (what was the point of being modest when you knew the truth?), and then they'd both landed gallery representation around graduation, a major coup. Ellery had interned at the same gallery as Shira over the summer, and then the three of them had chatted with Nora at a networking event and they'd all just vibed. Now they met almost weekly for drinks and bitching about art, and the group chat was always abuzz.

Shira missed the connection a little bit when she was far away. She texted Danica, I've gotten zero work done this break. It's like I revert to blob form as soon as I get home. Booooo

Danica responded immediately, up early, or maybe still up late from last night. Perfect stunning blob

Shira bit back a laugh, then wondered why she was biting back a laugh in the privacy of her own room, where she could show her teeth as much as she wanted, even the crooked ones on the bottom. But by then the moment had passed, so she didn't try to force the laugh. Sometimes she didn't know what she'd do all the way out there on the other side of the country without her best friends.

Speaking of which. She switched over to the group chat. Guys did I ever tell you that I had a guy best friend as a kid? He moved away when we were fourteen and I haven't seen him since. Apparently he just moved back??

Unsurprisingly, Ellery and Nora didn't respond, considering they were likely (hopefully) asleep. Danica was the only one to answer, and she did so immediately. Have you been teleported into a rom-com?

You know perfectly well I don't have time for either romance or comedy, Shira texted back, cracking a smile.

They'd gone over this several weeks ago when the four of them were having brunch at the local English tearoom, the only one in Los Angeles. It was cozy and always warm, full of mismatched tableware and teacups, and while the scones were usually dry, the servers made up for it with buckets of clotted cream and jam. Shira and her friends had been sitting at their table, elbow to elbow with the people beside them, bitching about the art world and how, despite calls for diversity, it was still a white cis man's world, then sipping their tea and making up the notes of flavor that they found, ketchup and cigarette and grass, when Shira stopped for a moment and looked around and smiled—not just a crack of one, but a real one, a big and toothy one she rarely let loose.

"What's so funny?" Danica had asked, her big dark eyes wide. Though Shira wasn't exactly tall or fat, she always felt she was when compared to Danica, who was tiny and slender as a bird.

"Nothing's funny," Shira said. A lump rose in her throat out of nowhere, and she took a sip of her tea so that she wouldn't unexpectedly cry. She didn't even like tea that much, not even this one, which was supposed to taste like roses, but somehow drinking it made her feel more adult than sipping a glass of wine did. "I'm just thinking about how lucky I am, to be here, at this moment."

"To be drinking tea that tastes like roses instead of cigarettes," Danica said, raising her cup.

"No, I'm serious," she said. "I don't know what more I could want."

"How about to get an exhibit at the Whitney?" Ellery suggested.

Nora added, "Or an apartment with more than one room?"

"Some romance?" Danica said, waggling her eyebrows.

Okay, those were all true. But Shira said, "I don't have time for romance right now, really. But I would like to have a show at the Whitney." She nudged Danica with her elbow. "At the same time as you, obviously. Then maybe you'll tell me what your show is about."

"It's too personal," Danica said, nudging Shira right back. She must have misjudged the force of her elbow, because Shira almost dropped her teacup into her lap. "I'll share when it's ready to go. I'm too superstitious."

"Fair," said Nora. "I wish the artist I worked with felt that way." She was the assistant to a famous contemporary artist whose primary claim to fame was a series he'd done of massive, shiny sculptures of various Happy Meal toys from the nineties. "Sometimes he calls in the middle of the night with a burst of inspiration like, 'Should I try knitting something out of pubic hair?' and I'm like, 'It's three in the morning, I'm half asleep, I do not have the mental capacity to talk you down from your terrible concept while making you think it's all your idea.'"

They all snorted into their tea, and that led into stories of the most outrageous behavior they'd witnessed working in the art world, which, since it was the art world, was extremely outrageous. They'd talked until their tea went cold, until there was nothing left on their tea tower but crumbs and a few sticky smears of jam, until Shira couldn't imagine ever wanting anything else.

Shira's phone buzzed. Danica had texted back, Idk how you say you don't have time for comedy when your face is hilarious

Shira sent back an emoji with the tongue sticking out, then rolled over in her bed and sighed. She'd definitely go say hi to Leo today. Probably. Maybe. She didn't know why the thought was so intimidating. They'd been best friends once! She used to enter his house without knocking all the time, and vice versa!

Maybe that was it. The thought of knocking at the door to say hi just felt too weird. The thought of feeling each other out, trying to navigate their past intimacy with this new strangerhood, too intimidating.

Shira tipped herself out of bed right into her waiting pair of slippers, tuning out the sound of Talia's white noise machine—more "roar" than "gentle whoosh"—filtering through their shared wall. Shira was the second one up after her mom, who was seated on the living room couch with her morning cup of coffee. Her feet were up on the ottoman as she admired the view of the leafless woods through the sliding glass door. "What are you doing up so early?" she said in lieu of good morning.

Plopping down on the couch beside her, Shira shrugged. "Went to bed too early. There are only so many hours I can sleep."

"Imagine telling your teenage self that," her mom said. "She'd never believe it."

"She'd be pretty impressed by me overall, though," Shira said. She imagined it for a moment—that her teenage self was there beside her on the couch. Teenage Shira would be seated at the edge of the cushion, hands clasped at her knees, back straight as if she were at a college interview—not because she specifically wanted to impress her older self but because that was how she sat all the time. Her brow would be a little scrunched from the mental calculations always in progress about what more she could be doing to impress college admissions officers: start another club (she'd already started her school's branch of the Model UN and an art zine) or get another leadership position (secretary of the art honor society, vice president of the literary magazine). Racking her brain about what experience she could try that would look impressive in her college essay.

And it had worked—she'd gotten into Columbia and gone to college in the city, and it had been all she'd ever dreamed of. Once there, since she'd been so good at figuring out what admissions boards wanted, she seamlessly switched to figuring out what her professors wanted in order to give her top grades, then what activities would look best to get her the most impressive jobs in the art world. All the while she'd been working on her own art on the side, trying to balance what she wanted to create with what she knew the market wanted. And again, it had worked. She'd done it. She'd gotten all she'd worked for all those years.

Shira wished her teenage self could know she'd done it. That she could somehow look back in time and thank her for laying all the groundwork. She'd despised Model UN and all the internal politics of dealing with people getting mad at her for giving them some country they deemed boring or insignificant compared to the one someone else got, and covering for the absent president and vice president of the art honor society, while not having their titles, had been incredibly stressful, but she'd stuck it out.

"She really would," said her mom. "I remember when you'd call us crying in college about your internship at the art gallery, how the whole thing was slimy, and how you hated the honors class you had to take to do your thesis, but now you're living your dreams." She paused for a moment. "Thanks for your help with the Hanukkah party, by the way. I know it can't have been easy making all those calls with the time difference."

"It really wasn't a problem!" Honestly, it had been a little annoying but worth it. When her family had first moved to the block fifteen or so years ago, they'd immediately gotten an invitation to the McCormicks' Christmas party. The family around the corner went all out for the neighborhood every year, welcoming everybody in for the merriest food and drink, carols, and a dazzling light show; Shira still remembered being little and standing beside the bonfire, sparks leaping into the air to the jingling of sleigh bells in the background, a marshmallow blackening on the end of her stick. Pure Christmas magic.

When she got home and fell into bed, her hair scented of smoke and caramelized sugar, her first thought was how much fun the evening had been. Her second was *We need to show the neighborhood how great the Jews do parties, too.* And while it probably would have been more fun to go all out for Purim—like, you're supposed to dress up, get so drunk you can't tell the name of your enemy from the name of your friend, and make a racket to drown out Haman's name whenever he comes up in the reading of the Megillah with special rattles called gragers; how could a holiday be any more raucous and fun?—she figured it would be a lot easier to get her mostly non-Jewish neighbors to come out when they were already off work and primed for general merriment than on (to them) some random night in spring.

And thus the annual Levinson family Hanukkah block party was born.

From the beginning, Shira had delighted in her role as the genesis of the party; whenever her parents would tell people, *Oh, the whole thing was Shira's idea,* she'd preen with satisfaction. And then, as the years went on and her specific ideas stopped being things like *Let's give everyone a puppy,* she'd taken more and more responsibility until the whole thing and not just the idea was basically her baby. Or her puppy.

Her mom cleared her throat. "I did see something while I was reading the local paper this morning."

"Did they name it after you, their final living subscriber?"

"That would be so embarrassing," her mom said seriously. "No. Did you hear about the fire at the deli?"

"Fire at the deli?" Shira blinked for a moment, and then it hit her like a flying sack of potatoes. "No, not Mendel's?"

Her mom didn't have to answer. The grim set of her lips was enough.

Shira's stomach flipped the way it did every time she went to get food at the neighborhood Christmas party and smelled the ham (for some reason ham felt forbidden and bad in a way bacon or shrimp didn't, even though none of them were kosher). "But they're supposed to cater the party," Shira said faintly. She put a hand to her chest, then realized how dramatic that must look, then kept it there anyway because this moment deserved drama, damn it. "They're the only Jewish deli within driving distance. The party's in two days." Maybe they could find someone to make salads and sandwiches, but latkes? No way. Jewish delis were the only places making latkes. "Why didn't they call me? That's bad business."

"Maybe they were occupied with the fire," said her mom as Shira pulled out her phone. Oh. She had received a couple of phone calls from numbers with her local area code yesterday, which, as usual, she had declined. In her defense, any call she received from a random phone number with her local area code was almost always spam.

Shira cursed. "There's no way we're going to be able to find someone else in time."

"If anyone can do it, it's you," said her mom.

Usually Shira loved hearing that. Right now it only made her want to run.

2

LEO DAVID HAD HIT MANY LOW MOMENTS IN HIS twenty-two years, but this might have been the lowest one. Both literally, because he was flat on the ground beneath the front picture window of his dad's house, and metaphorically, because he was hiding from his old best friend, who he'd actually very much like to see.

But he didn't feel ready. That's what he was trying to explain to Neptune. "She's going to think I'm a loser. I need some more time." Time for what? To go back to college and graduate, to get a job where his bathroom breaks weren't monitored like he was in elementary school again, to achieve something his parents could brag about? He'd be down here for an awfully long time. "Or, I don't know. It doesn't matter what she thinks, right?"

Neptune responded by licking his face, which wasn't weird, considering he was a dog (it would probably be weirder for a planet or the Roman god of the sea to be licking his face). *Of course it matters what she thinks,* Neptune said with his deep, dark eyes, which seemed to peer right into Leo's very soul.

Then his tongue dipped into Leo's mouth, which ruined the moment. "We are not that kind of close, buddy," Leo said, scooting back on his stomach so that when he stood up, he wouldn't be in front of the window. So that nobody could see how low he'd stooped.

Of course, when he did finally get up, his father was standing there, squinting at him. "What were you doing on the floor?"

Leo's jaw clenched. How was his father able to make even the most basic question sound like an accusation? "I was petting the dog."

"It didn't look like you were petting the dog." Leo's father—Joe, he was trying to think of him as Joe and not as Dad—crossed his arms. Leo fought the urge to cross his right back and stick out his tongue. Something about being back here at his dad's—at *Joe's*—really brought out the child in him. And not in a good way.

"What does it matter?"

Joe opened his mouth like he was going to say something else, then closed it. He sighed. "I guess it doesn't matter. Do you want dinner?"

"I'm not hungry," Leo said just as his stomach growled. *Great timing.* He made himself cough, like that might retroactively cover up the sound. "I'll just eat later."

Joe stared at him for another second. "All right." He ambled back toward the kitchen, and Leo exhaled, his shoulders only now relaxing. He hadn't even realized how bunched up they'd been, almost up to his ears.

He'd moved back here with Joe only because he had no other options. He and his mom had spent his remaining high school years living in Michigan with his grandfather and his new wife, who then both died while he was off at Michigan State (their deaths were both extremely sad and fell at just the right time to excuse him from two separate midterms). Only a few months later, his mom met an Italian guy on vacation who treated her like a queen, which she absolutely deserved after the shit his dad—*Joe*—had put her through. Except then suddenly she was selling the house they'd shared with his grandparents and moving to Italy with her new man and leaving him without a home base, which was fine, he was an adult; he could sublet an apartment during college breaks like an adult would.

Life was happening so fast in general, actually, and he couldn't keep up, or at least that's how he justified withdrawing from so many courses. He'd never been the world's best student, and it had only been by a miracle (and his mom's and grandfather's legacy statuses) that he'd made it into Michigan State. He'd still been managing to keep a fairly respectable grade point average, but without his family there to check up on him, he'd found himself skipping class more and more, and pushing more and more of his work to the last minute, until he pushed it all so far it went off a cliff and he didn't do it at all.

Not that he was trying to use his family's absence as an excuse. He was an adult. He knew that. He was responsible for his own success and all that. It was more like . . . why? Why bother when he didn't like doing any of it and when there was nobody left to hold him accountable?

Anyway, his advisor told him it was either withdraw or fail, and apparently a withdrawal looked better on his transcript than a big fat F, because he could always reenroll later. Except then he found his scholarships and student loans evaporating (because when you'd withdrawn from all your courses, you weren't a student anymore), and he couldn't afford to stay and reenroll. At some point he blinked and he was being kicked out of his dorm, and his choice was between paying all the money he had left in his bank account to make it a few months in a nearby friend's spare room while he found a job or moving in with his dad.

He might not have been a student anymore, but leaving Michigan altogether would have felt like admitting he'd failed. So he ended up using the rest of his bank account on that spare room and getting a local job with vague hopes that he might make enough money to reenroll at some point once he felt more stable and finish his degree. But by the time those few months ended, his waitering job hadn't made him enough money to pay for the next few months of his friend's spare room, and he didn't have the prospects of anything better without going back to school, and he couldn't afford that. So he swallowed his pride, which landed in his stomach in one heavy, solid lump, and called Joe for the first time in years. It was either that or . . . nothing, really. He didn't see how he could stay in Michigan, and maybe if he moved in with Joe and worked while saving as much as he could, eventually he could go back and finish school. When he felt more stable, as if that was something that might magically happen.

It wasn't like he hadn't seen or talked to Joe at all. He'd refused to grace Joe's doorstep during his required custody times, and Joe didn't go to the judge to force it (deciding, Leo figured, that trying to force a teenager to see him would only backfire on him). But Joe did fly out to Michigan a few times a year to take him out to lunch or to a baseball game or cheer him on at his high school graduation from the opposite side of the stands as his mom. The conversation was always stiff and awkward, and Leo usually cut their day or evening short with some blatant lie about wanting to study.

Joe tried. He really tried. But Leo couldn't get over how, whenever he looked at his dad, his insides boiled with anger at his betrayal. Joe had thrown his whole life away—had thrown *him* away—for a woman who didn't even stick around. He'd treated Leo's mother, the best person Leo knew, like the slimy goo left in the gefilte fish jar after all the fish was gone.

But he had an extra bedroom, with Leo's old bed still in it, and he didn't ask for Leo to pay rent, so.

Leo sighed. He was pretty sure he had a protein bar buried somewhere on his desk upstairs. "C'mon, boy," he called to Neptune, but no collar jingled in response. The dog had followed Joe into the kitchen, leaving Leo alone with his empty stomach.

❄

LEO DIDN'T HAVE work the next day, so he resolved to take Neptune on an epic walk in the woods instead of their usual quick jaunt around the neighborhood. Not because he was trying to avoid anyone in particular. Definitely not. Neptune was just a very good boy who deserved the best (despite the fact that, last night, when Leo had gone searching for his protein bar, all he'd found was a torn-open wrapper with beagle-shaped teeth marks in it. It had been peanut butter flavored, Leo's favorite and apparently the dog's as well). And also, because he was off work, Leo didn't need to conserve his energy for the physical labor his job demanded. The main source of employment in the area for people without a college degree was a local warehouse for a huge online-shipping giant. It was easy to get hired there, and so that was what Leo did.

The three loopy streets where Leo's and Shira's families lived sat alongside a state park full of sandy trails and towering pine trees. It wasn't one of the more popular parks, which was perfect for Leo's taste; he preferred seeing nobody on their walks but the occasional equestrian or bounding deer. Neptune trotted along happily at his side, his long silky ears flapping in the chilly wind. In the summer, when it was hot, his tongue would loll out the side of his mouth.

God, no matter how much he loved that stupid beagle, Leo hoped he wasn't still living here in the summer.

The jingling of Neptune's collar and his occasional whuff kept away the birds and deer (though beagles had been bred for hunting, this particular one would make a terrible hunting dog), so Leo focused on the way the sunlight filtered through the trees and left dappled patterns on the ground, on the chill in the air that cut through his puffy jacket. He wished he'd brought a hat. He wished a lot of things, actually. Sometimes he wished he'd told Shira how he felt about her before he moved. Then maybe she wouldn't have gradually faded away like fireworks after they fizzle out.

Or maybe it was better for her that he hadn't. Because Joe had run into Shira's mom the other day on the street, and apparently she hadn't been able to stop gushing about how great Shira was doing. Dream job at a prestigious gallery, making moves with her own work, her own apartment in a major city.

And here he was, spinning his wheels like a car stuck in the mud, unable to move forward and also splattering everyone else around him. Usually he'd just tell himself *Fuck them, what does it matter what they think?*

But he couldn't think that way about Shira. Which was why he just needed a few days to avoid seeing her, or maybe forever, or . . .

. . . nope, that was definitely her running in his direction right now.

He had a split second to decide if he was going to jump into the trees and hide, which seemed crazy but maybe not the worst idea he'd ever had. But then his traitorous dog barked high and excited, wagging his tail and straining at his leash, and that was that. "Shira? Is that you?"

She took out the one earbud she was wearing, her jog slowing into a walk slowing into a crouch before Neptune. She let him sniff her hand before stroking his ears.

Eight years hadn't changed her much, at least that Leo could tell. She still had that prominent nose, her strongest feature, which he knew she'd always hated but that fit her face and gave her gravitas. Her hair was tied back into a ponytail, but he could tell from the way strands of it were escaping around her face that it was just as wild and untamable as it had been when she was a teenager. And he couldn't avoid noticing the curves under her tight running sweatshirt, the way they swelled and nipped and—no, he was a gentleman. She said, "Leonard David, as I live and breathe."

He winced, not just from the sound of his full first name (his mom had really loved Leonard Cohen, which was understandable, as the man was a musical genius, though it would have been nice if she'd loved him more like a middle name's worth) but at what she must be seeing when she looked at him. Old sweatpants with a big hole that was only by chance not on the butt, greasy hair he hadn't washed in too many days. "Eight years and you had to go there right away."

She bounced back to her feet, smile big and toothy. "All of today's babies have old-person names. Your parents were just ahead of the curve."

"Well, I hope baby Gertrude and Milton appreciate it more than I did as a kid." His forced smile turned into a real one, because man, he'd missed her. "How are you doing?"

She cleared her throat. "I'm doing . . . well." His smile went forced again because the Shira he knew—well, the Shira he'd known—would've launched into a list of all her accomplishments. The only reason he could think that she wouldn't was that she was worried about how hearing them would make him feel. Meaning, she pitied him.

Then again, maybe she'd grown more mature since he'd known her back then. They'd lived basically an entire third of their lives without each other. He'd seen plenty of movies that were one thing early on and then had a twist that changed them into something entirely different. Still, he wanted to make sure she didn't pity him, so he said, "I hear you're working at a gallery? An art gallery?" She nodded. "What kind of art?"

Her eyes, still that same dark brown, went wide with animation, and she nearly smacked him in the face with the energetic way she threw her hands in the air. "All kinds! We have painters, sculptors, mixed-media artists, et cetera. There's a guy who makes sculptures of his ex-girlfriends and ex-hookups out of things they left behind at his place."

"That's not illegal?" Leo said without thinking, then winced as he realized he might have accidentally insulted someone she worked with, someone whose art she valued. "I mean, art is art, I guess. I'd just imagine they'd want their stuff back."

Those eyes lit up, and a spark ran through Leo, making him stand up straight. He'd almost forgotten how much he missed that look of hers, that one where she got fired up about something. "Right? I can't say anything at work or to any of my art friends in case it gets around, but it makes me so mad. I kind of want to send them anonymous notes to let them know, but I'd probably get fired."

"Don't get fired," Leo said. "There's got to be another way. Maybe strategically placed advertisements for his shows in their neighborhoods or on accounts they follow."

"Extra-targeted advertising," Shira said, and the laugh that bubbled forth was warm and light, exactly as Leo remembered. "How about you? What are you up to these days?"

His face prickled with the feel of her eyes on his skin. He wondered how she saw him right now, if she was categorizing the changes on his face since they'd seen each other last. "I'm okay," he said, trying to keep his tone light. No need to dump his problems on her. "At least, I don't think any of my ex-girlfriends are creating art shows about me, which is a positive. It's nice to be back in New Jersey. I missed this old guy." Leo gestured at Neptune. "Though I remember him as a fresh-faced little puppy."

"You're still just as cute as you were back then," Shira said to Neptune in a baby voice, though Leo couldn't help but think, for a split second, that the words were aimed at him. Because, yes, they'd changed, but underneath it all they were still the same people. They had their past together. She knew who he was at the core, something he couldn't say for his coworkers or college friends.

That reminder emboldened him, made him stand up a little straighter. Because he knew her, too. "I used to run every day, and if there's something I remember about you, Shira Levinson, it's that you'd only run if someone was chasing you."

"Not just someone," Shira said. "Only someone who made me genuinely fear for my life."

"Right," Leo said. He was the runner. She was the fighter. "So why are you running now?"

She wrapped her arms around her chest and squeezed. "Did you hear the deli burned down? Mendel's?"

"Oh . . . no?" he said uncertainly.

"*Oh no,*" she emphasized. "Well, except maybe for all the chickens who will now get to keep their livers. Mendel's is–was–the only Jewish deli in the area, and they were supposed to cater the big Hanukkah party. There's no way we're going to be able to get someone else to do Hanukkah food in time. My mom told me, and I was like, I need to go for a run and try to think about what to do, but all I've been able to think about while I'm running is how much I hate running." She paused. "Everybody in LA does yoga and Pilates, but yoga and Pilates classes are expensive, so I've been telling people I'm a runner. I figured maybe I should actually do some running."

"Well, your form is good," Leo said without thinking, then felt his cheeks warm. Back when he ran track in school, sometimes he'd purposely run his group by the classroom he knew Shira was staying late in for some activity or another. He'd always made sure to keep his form on point in case she happened to look out the window. He'd wanted her to see him running, fast and sleek, the muscles of his legs flexing, his shoes gliding effortlessly over the pavement or the grass. He felt himself wither a little at the memory, at how she was surely looking at him now. "I mean, for someone who doesn't actually run. You probably won't injure yourself."

"Really?" She sounded almost disappointed, as if she'd been hoping for an injury that would force her to stop. He should've shaken his head in disapproval, but instead he felt himself smile, liking that she was okay bringing him in on such a thought. She smiled back a little in return, which made him smile more. "I mean, it's probably good, because if I was in the hospital, we'd have to cancel the Hanukkah party."

Right, she'd just been talking about it. The neighborhood Hanukkah party. Leo had almost forgotten that it existed. He'd already planned on skipping the Christmas one (he had exactly zero interest in making forced small talk with people he had nothing in common with aside from the street they lived on, trying as hard as he could not to roll his eyes while they told him their opinions on his life), but he couldn't skip the Hanukkah one. Not just because he was Jewish—man, he hadn't thought that in ages, because his dad was Jewish and his mom wasn't, and he'd been far away from his dad both physically and emotionally; he hadn't even thought about celebrating the holidays in eight years. Because he still remembered how much joy throwing this party brought Shira, and he couldn't not be a part of it. "How many people are supposed to come this year?" he asked.

She swiped the sweat off her brow with the back of her hand. Her nails were bare and unpolished, no longer bitten to the quick the way they'd been when she was a kid. "I don't know. Not everybody in the neighborhood shows up. Others are away. We usually have, what, maybe half of everybody turn out? A hundred people?" She took a deep, shaky breath. "I'm sure I can find somewhere to pick up sandwiches and salads, and fortunately the bakery where we always get the doughnuts didn't burn down. But no way are we going to find someone to do latkes for a hundred people, and you can't have a Hanukkah party without latkes!"

He could see the panic bubbling up in her eyes. She'd always been a stress crier. He didn't want to see her cry. "Oh, that's nothing," he said. "Latkes for a hundred people? Not a big deal at all. We can handle that."

One of her hands rose to her mouth. She nibbled on one nail, then pulled her hand away. "What do you mean, we can handle that? That's so many latkes!"

"Trader Joe's and Costco have great frozen latkes," he said. "We get as many boxes as we can carry and stick them in the—" She was already shaking her head. "Come on, frozen latkes are good."

"Not good enough," she said. The finger drifted back between her teeth. She bit down with a sound like a gunshot. "No way am I serving my guests frozen latkes. Supermarket deli sandwiches and salads are bad enough, but latkes are the star attraction. I need fresh latkes. People will think–"

"People will think they're at a great party, and they'll enjoy the free food," he said. Neptune let out a whine; Leo glanced down to see him positively vibrating at a squirrel balanced on a branch above him. He swore the squirrel was smirking. "But fine, no frozen latkes, they're trash, okay. We'll do it ourselves. How hard can it be to make some latkes?"

"Really hard," she said emphatically. "Have you ever made latkes before?"

He . . . hadn't. Even when he'd been living with his dad and celebrating all the major Jewish holidays, his dad was a buy-the-frozen-latkes-and-stick-them-in-the-oven-till-they're-lukewarm kind of guy. "They're basically hash browns," Leo non-answered. "I worked fast food for a year in high school. I can make a hash brown."

Shira had clearly never worked fast food, because if she had, she'd have wrinkled her nose and told him that pulling something from the freezer and heating it up didn't count as cooking. Instead, she cocked her head, bit her bottom lip, and nodded at him slowly. The sight of her lip between her teeth brought a rush of blood to his head, and for a moment he was fourteen again. "You really think we can do this? When? I don't really want to spend the party in the kitchen and come out smelling like oil."

"It wasn't like the deli was going to come to the party and fry the latkes à la minute," Leo said. He'd binged way too many seasons of *Chef Supreme* during his first really depressed months after leaving school (honestly, that was probably helping him out here more than his time in the burger-joint kitchen, where the main thing he'd learned was to be careful putting anything from the freezer directly into the oil, as testified by the big scar on his right arm). "They were going to fry them ahead of time and have you heat them up in the oven. We can do the same thing."

"You really think so?"

Leo nodded. Neptune whuffed as if in agreement.

Shira's face didn't change. "Don't you have anything better to do?"

He knew she didn't mean it in a negative way, but something still twisted in his gut. He pulled in a deep breath, blew it out. "I really, really don't."

She stared at him for a moment, as if calculating something, and then finally, her face relaxed. She smiled, and it was like the sun had come out over the trees. "Okay. If you think we can do it, let's do it."

It had been so long since Leo'd seen a look like that: one of satisfaction, or approval, or trust, or maybe all three mixed into one. Honestly, he couldn't remember the last time someone had looked at him with something other than pity or disappointment. Not that he cared at all—what did it matter what other people thought of him? He just needed some time to figure his life out. He'd do it at his own pace. Even if every day he took to do it meant another day working at the warehouse, a place he left with all his muscles aching and his feet throbbing, his brain filled with resentment over how closely the big boss monitored his work, like he couldn't be trusted to set his own perfectly good pace. "Let's do it," he said.

3

THERE WAS NO WAY SHIRA WAS GOING ANYWHERE without a shower, obviously. She had working nostrils, even if Leo had been too kind to mention her odor. She smiled a bit as she scrubbed herself off, thinking she'd deserve it if she left the shower to find a stick of deodorant sitting on her bureau.

He'd seemed okay, honestly. She'd expected worse when her mom told her he was having a *tough time* of it. Sure, he was living at home and hadn't said anything about a job, but it wasn't like she'd asked; she hadn't wanted to make him feel bad or anything. Not everybody could be her, with everything figured out by age twenty-two.

She pulled off her shower cap and shook out her hair, the endorphins from her run coursing through her. It had been wild seeing Leo again after so many years. She hadn't recognized him when she first caught sight of him in the woods; she'd actually started giving him that polite nod of acknowledgment you give to neighbors you don't really know before doing a double take and stopping. He'd looked . . . grown up; that was the only way to put it. His nose, which had been overlarge for his face as a teenager, much like hers, could now be described as strong, and his jawline matched. His dark hair was longer and shaggier than it had been, but she wouldn't describe it as a mop the way it had been when they were preteens. And those eyes, dark and piercing, had thrown her back into teenagerhood with the flutter they'd given her in her chest when they met her own.

Her fingers had flexed unconsciously as they spoke, wanting to paint him, and eventually she'd stuck them in her mouth to make them stop moving, because that was a weird thing to be thinking, right? She'd paint him in blacks and whites and grays, strong, jagged lines that somehow didn't end up looking overly harsh. Maybe one streak of color somewhere. She wasn't sure where; she'd have to think on it.

By the time she'd thrown on pants and a T-shirt from high school she was pretty sure was originally Talia's, Leo was on the front stoop. "Coming!" she hollered through the door, jamming a fuzzy hat over her ponytail and shrugging on her puffy coat. He'd changed clothes, too, she noticed as they were walking to his car; he'd ditched the nasty sweatpants and put on jeans that were a little loose around the hips—maybe he'd lost weight recently—and he'd covered the too-long, a-little-too-shiny curls with a Yankees baseball cap. Could it be possible he was self-conscious about how she saw him? She shook her head, rolling her eyes at herself. He'd never had feelings for her like that, or that was what his constant string of girlfriends when they were teenagers testified.

When he started the car, metal music came blaring out of the speaker. He nearly dropped his keys in his rush to turn it off. “We can listen to your music,” Shira said, curious. He’d never been a metal guy before.

His cheeks flushed red. “No, it’s fine. I just listen to it to get some of my aggression out after leaving work.” Work. So he did have a job. A job he clearly hated. “I’d rather catch up on the last–how long has it been? Eight years?”

“Something like that,” she replied. It had been almost exactly eight, actually–that specific day she saw him for the last time was seared into her memory, the way she’d gone home as if in a trance and waited for a text that never came, the way her parents finally showed up and dragged her out to light the menorah even though she could barely register the blessings. The next day she’d gone to Sunday school–most kids stopped going to the synagogue for classes after their bar or bat mitzvah, but she’d signed up for continuing classes, loving the calm that studying the Torah and debating Mishnah with other congregants brought her. Eventually she’d dropped out to make room in her schedule for the literary magazine because Sunday school wasn’t impressive on a college application the way editing the literary magazine was, but sometimes she still thought of those days wistfully. “I don’t know, how can I catch you up on eight years in one car ride?”

“I know,” he said. “Maybe we should skip the grocery store and road trip somewhere fun. Somewhere warm.”

“Please not somewhere warm,” she said. “That’s the one thing I don’t like about Southern California. The weather.”

He threw his head back and laughed, which would have been cute, except maybe not while he was trying to make a left turn onto a busy street. *Eyes on the road, friend.* “What could you possibly hate about having sunny, warm-but-not-too-warm weather all year round?"

Her foot crunched on something. She glanced down to find her sneaker resting upon a pile of smashed Doritos. "It's so boring. No variety. No excitement."

"Yes," Leo said. "Nothing's as exciting as waking up one morning and discovering that you have to go outside into the blizzarding snow and shovel until your arms hurt when all you want to do is lie in bed. Or when you want to go take a shower afterward and you can't because the snow means you've lost power."

"Snow days," she countered.

"Okay, true. Though now that we're adults, we don't get snow days anymore. Or at least I don't."

"Fair. Things were better when we were kids." Not just because of snow days; because of Leo. She sometimes felt like she came off as prickly to new people, like a new wool sweater. They'd find that she kept them warm and toasty eventually, but at first she made them itch. And it had been so long since she'd seen Leo, he was basically a new person. But they'd slid right back into their old friendship like those eight years had never even happened.

"They really were," she said. "Our friendship kept me sane. Whenever I was going through something at school or at home, the swing set was always there." A smile twitched at her lips as they turned onto the town's main drag, which was lined by strip mall after strip mall. Bright signs advertising what seemed to be every chain store in existence—Kohl's, Petco, Dressbarn, Applebee's—loomed overhead. Living in LA, she'd thought half these places had gone out of business. It was reassuring to find them still trucking. Just like Leo was still trucking. She hesitated, then took a deep breath before saying, "I was so sad when you left."

He was quiet for a moment. She glanced over to find him frowning at the road. "Yeah," he said, sliding into the right-turn lane without a signal. She'd almost forgotten that, too—how it was almost a point of pride here to make turns without signals. Stupid. "I was, too."

Stupid. Of course he'd been sad. She might have lost her best friend, but he'd lost his home, his dad, his sense of security, and all his friends. Hopefully he didn't feel her stupid comment like itchy wool on his neck. "Sorry, I didn't mean—"

"I hear that in addition to working at a famous gallery, you're a famous artist now." He made a sharp right into a parking space before another car could swoop in; the place was packed, which she probably should have expected, considering it was only a few days before the holidays. "Your paintings are going to be in the Met? Something like that. Your mom had a lot to say."

Shira rolled her eyes as they got out of the car and slammed the doors behind them. "None of that is true," she said dryly. They walked up the row of the parking lot toward the front of the store. "I don't have a—"

Leo flung his arm out, catching her across the front; she stopped short against it. Her mouth opened in a silent O of surprise just as a car flew past, so close the wind blew her hair back. "Sorry," he said, glancing over. "You okay?"

His arm was still there, holding her back from the lane. She blinked and was suddenly thirteen years old again, and he'd slung his arm around her shoulders as he always did, but the feeling of his skin warm on hers was now something new and strange, something that brought warmth flushing her belly from the inside out. "Yeah," she said. "Totally fine."

Inside, she quirked a smile to see the supermarket displays featuring giant hams and bags of cranberries instead of an assortment of organic juices and salad kits. Some things she didn't love about LA, chief among them being the food culture. Sometimes she just wanted a muffin that wasn't gluten-free or sugar-free or full of black beans but in a way you couldn't taste them (you absolutely could taste them). "Okay," she said, clapping her hands together. If they stood here in the entrance much longer, they'd get mowed down by a shopping cart. "So, where to?"

"Potatoes," Leo said. He squinted off to the side. "Over there."

They headed off in the direction of the potatoes, dodging careening shopping carts and people arguing passionately about the difference between white and yellow onions. "How many do you think we need?" Shira asked once the mounds of delicious brown orbs were in sight.

"I don't know, how many latkes per person? Three? Five?"

"Let's say two, because making five hundred latkes sounds like the punishment some obscure Greek god might give you for overconfidence," Shira said. "So . . . let's google . . ." Her eyes nearly popped out of her head. "Sixty to seventy pounds of potatoes?" She blinked hard, as if trying to force her eyeballs back in. "Okay, maybe we can't make our own latkes. Can we even carry sixty to seventy pounds of potatoes? Can we fit that in your car?"

But Leo was already shoveling up potatoes into his arms and piling them into their cart. "Google says that one potato weighs about one pound," he said. "So that's only sixty to seventy potatoes. Not bad."

"I hope nobody else needs potatoes for the holiday. We're about to clear out this store," Shira said. She felt sorry for a second, then not. This was an emergency. A potato emergency. "My parents have matzah meal somewhere in the cabinet. Hopefully it's not expired since it's from Passover. I know they have eggs, too, and it looks like we don't need too many for the recipe, but we should pick up a few onions."

A few onions later, they were steering their cart toward the registers, where the lines were so long they merged into an amorphous blob that almost hit the aisles. They settled in for the long haul. "I'm hoping for a preview at this party, by the way," Leo said. When Shira cocked her head, confused, he clarified. "Of your paintings. Which I'm told have already received a rapturous review from the *New York Times* art critic even though your show hasn't happened yet?"

Shira groaned. "It's not even fully *painted* yet." At his questioning look, she elaborated. "I'm still working on my first show, with input from the gallery that's representing me. Gallery representation is the first step, and once they've helped me refine and edit my vision into something that will hopefully sell, they'll stage a big show that will ideally be a success, in that all the paintings sell and more people want to make shows of my work. They're based on my childhood and my family."

"So they're paintings of me?" He smirked.

"No." She rolled her eyes but not before that picture from earlier, the one she wanted to paint of him, flashed through her mind. A streak of yellow, that was what it needed. Yellow like sunlight, to keep it from being too dark. "This show is about the family side of my childhood, especially the parts involving my bubbe. The paintings are a little dreamlike, but they look at some of the stories she used to tell me and Talia and our cousins about the old country and her family's journey to the US and how it parallels some of the issues American Jews face today." She puffed out a breath. "Sorry, it's hard to summarize it. I kind of babble."

"No, it sounds amazing." His eyes were sincere. "I would say I'd buy one, but I assume I wouldn't be able to afford it. Is it your personal gallery that's putting on the show?"

"Oh my god." She rolled her eyes again, so hard they might roll right out of her head and be scooped up by someone searching for pearl onions. "Seriously, I don't know if it's just normal mom bragging or if this is some kind of delusion. Should I be looking for signs of early dementia?"

"I think your mom is just really proud of you," he said. "Honestly, I haven't seen you in eight years, and I'm really proud of you. I remember when you turned my upstairs hallway into an impromptu art gallery of your work."

"An improvement," Shira said.

"You taped your artwork over all my school pictures."

"Like I said, an improvement."

He gave her this crinkly-eyed, half-smiling look that made something in her chest leap. That wasn't a look she remembered from her childhood. That look was all adult. All new. She said, hastily, "No, I mean, my job is really cool. It starts me on the track to owning my own gallery one day, if that's what I want. I'll make all the right connections." She was quiet for a moment. "It's funny, because that was the dream I never knew I had, while becoming a real artist is the one I've dreamed about for my whole life."

"You've always liked art," Leo said. "It makes sense that you'd want to go into the art world. Even in middle school you started that art club for the elementary school kids at the library, and you would put up their art for display in the halls like a gallery."

Sure, but she hadn't done that program because she'd loved fine art so much; she'd signed up because the junior honor society required volunteer hours, and then she'd kept doing it because all the volunteer hours looked good on her résumé. Still, she found herself nodding. "Right. Yeah."

They finally stepped up to the front of the line. Leo put a divider on the register belt and began unloading their potatoes. "Anything we forgot?"

Yes. She let her eyes linger on him for a moment. Then looked away. "No, we're good."

THEY WERE NOT good. They were weak. That's what Shira realized once they were back in her family's kitchen, had finished unloading, and were beginning to make the latkes. Because the first step of making latkes was to shred your potatoes so that you could mix all your little potato bits up with the egg and matzah meal and salt, and it turned out that shredding seventy pounds of potatoes with the two semidull hand graters they'd dug up from the depths of her parents' drawers required muscles not merely of steel but of diamond. Her biceps were already burning, and she'd shredded—she counted—all of two potatoes.

"Making latkes might be harder than I thought," she said. She wished her parents and Talia were home to help—assuming they'd do anything but point and laugh—but she and Leo had returned home to find them all out. Maybe they'd sensed the potato-scented winds blowing their way. As she and Leo had stepped through the door, she'd gotten flashbacks of middle school, when they weren't allowed to be alone together; if they went into one of their bedrooms, they had to leave the door open, and not just a crack. Now they were adults. No one could stop them.

Not that they'd be doing anything that required a closed door. They'd be getting sweaty, sure, but also covered in potato juice.

Leo was on his third potato, with no sign of slowing down. "You just need to focus on something other than the pain."

She slumped in her kitchen chair. She wasn't a huge cook, and neither were her parents, but she still always felt at home in the family kitchen; it was probably the cheeriest room in the house, with the wallpaper border of chickens going around the top of the room and her mom's collection of vintage and thrifted chicken figurines sitting with pride of place in the china cabinet alongside the upside-down wineglasses and dusty spice collection. Maybe all that a room needed to make it cheery was chickens.

She doubted the room would feel this cheery if the chickens knew how many of their brethren had been nuggeted in that oven.

"How can I focus on anything else when my arm is about to fall off?" Shira said.

"One, think about how buff you're going to be after this and how much fun you'll have telling people that your epic arms aren't due to the gym but to the potato challenge. You'll start a new trend. The whole country will sell out of graters. People will write entire new cookbooks to use up all this newly shredded potato. Celebrities will thank you in their Oscar acceptance speeches. People will be clamoring for your new paintings but only if they follow a plucky new potato who wants to see the world. No, actually they'll want that as a children's picture book."

"Parents are going to love the page where Spud the Plucky Potato gets shredded into tiny bits, screaming all the way."

"And two," Leo continued, ticking off a finger. "Play a game."

She knew he was talking about something they could play while shredding potatoes, but Leo plus the word *game* immediately made her think of Pokémon. She hadn't thought about it for years, other than the occasional nostalgic moment when she spotted a kid's sticker or a surge of horror when one of the gallery's contemporary artists did an exhibition that featured a bunch of Pokémon in flagrante delicto, which, according to the comment cards, had ruined so many childhoods. But now she couldn't help picturing taking out her old deck and giving it a go. She'd always liked the evolutions of Eevee, had shaped her deck more around the Pokémon she thought were cute than any sort of battle strategy. Leo, of course, was the opposite. His deck was full of big hulking beasts. "My Pokémon cards are still somewhere in my closet," she said. Sure enough, the thought almost made her forget the pain in her arm. "Maybe that's the strategy: palm off the potato grating on Talia and hide somewhere with our decks."

He snorted. "The last I remember of your little sister, she was very close to her black belt in karate. I don't know if I want to give her a grater and then piss her off."

Shira hadn't thought about Talia's martial arts career for years, either. She had indeed gotten her black belt, placed at state, and then decided to quit before going to college. Shira had never been able to figure out how her sister could just drop something she was so good at, that she'd won so many prizes for. "Fair enough," she said. "Then what game do you want to play?"

"Karaoke, obviously," he said.

"Boring." You couldn't win a game like that.

"It's not boring," Leo said. "I'll sing along to some of my favorite songs, and then you can do yours, and we'll expose each other to great music. Surely you've always wanted to get into metal, and I haven't listened to the latest Taylor Swift album yet."

"You just assume I'm going to do Taylor Swift?"

"Yes, one hundred percent."

There was no sense arguing when he was correct. "I don't think you want to hear me sing."

He paused for a moment and tilted his head as if considering. "You know, fair enough," he said, and she was insulted before remembering that she'd spent her childhood serenading him with truly terrible versions of various Disney princess songs. "Just tell me your life story, then. Or at least the last eight years of it. Before that, I know everything already."

She'd gotten her period for the first time at his house, so when he said everything, yeah, he really meant everything. "Fine." She bit her lip, trying to remember the important points as her arm moved mechanically back and forth. Somehow the pile of potatoes to be shredded didn't seem to be growing any smaller. "Um. Well, after you left, I made a lot of really emo art. Lots of black and rain and big smears of red meant to symbolize blood."

"Your post-Leo period, if you will," Leo supplied helpfully. His eyes were crinkled at the corners, glinting with laughter.

She dropped her stub of potato before she could shred her fingertips and grabbed another. "They actually got me noticed by the high school art teacher for the first time, and she encouraged me further. I enrolled in the high-level art classes and did some art shows. Painting my feelings out over you felt really good, and winning prizes and stuff was obviously great. But my parents told me I also had to be practical, and they were right, so I ended up double majoring at Columbia in art and economics." She left out the whole college-application process, how high she'd felt after getting into an Ivy League school, like everything she'd done and sacrificed to get there had been worth it. "Then I moved out to LA to try and make it in the art world."

"And you made it," Leo said.

Her cheeks warmed, but in a good way. "I mean, I haven't *made* it made it yet. I'm still at the bottom of the ladder, but it's one I really want to climb."

"And who do you mostly hang out with?"

She tried to catch his eye, but he was studying the potato he was shredding like it was going to bite him. To be fair, he was getting into stub territory, and the grater might actually bite him. He was probably keeping his eye on that, not avoiding hers because he'd basically just asked if she had a boyfriend. Which she didn't. The art world was not exactly crawling with straight, age-appropriate, well-adjusted men. "I have a group of close friends out there. Danica, Ellery, and Nora. We're all in the art scene."

Speaking of which, she should probably check in with the group chat. Nora had woken up in a bad spot; she was supposed to bring the woman she'd been seeing home with her to meet her parents for the first time, but the woman had texted her this morning that she was getting a migraine and couldn't make the trip anymore. Truth, or excuse because she was getting cold feet?

Shira was going to text something encouraging and girlbossy, all like You don't need her anyway if she doesn't see how awesome you are, but Danica was chiming in with her grandmother's wisdom. She'd say not to have feathers in your mouth. It's a Ukrainian saying. Just go talk to her.

Shira's girlbossy thing seemed trite after that, so she backspaced. What Danica's grandma said!! And then the dancing-lady emoji, obviously.

"Sorry," Shira said, putting her phone down and picking her potato back up. Her fingers cramped in protest. "That was them now, actually. They're my entire social life out there, really. Well, aside from the occasional drinks with coworkers or networking wine outing. How about you? Who are you hanging out with these days? Livvy?"

"Who?" he said blankly, and then it dawned on his face. "Oh my god, Livvy. I haven't thought about her in years. I was such an asshole back then. I don't think I even broke up with her. I just moved."

That little part of Shira that was still fourteen years old—because everybody had a little part of them that would always be fourteen years old—felt smug. "You ghosted her before ghosting was even a thing."

"Like I said," Leo replied. "Such an asshole."

"Have you ghosted anyone since then? Or have you been a better boyfriend lately?" she asked, trying to sound as light as possible. She didn't even know why. It was a normal thing to ask someone, right? She was just curious.

He winced. "No, I didn't really date in high school after I moved. Too busy being angry at the world. And then college, I don't know. I dated casually but nothing serious enough where they would've been offended by me disappearing on them."

College. So he *did* go to college. "Wait, where did you graduate from?"

His potato fell apart into shreds. "Nowhere," he said, his tone light, as if he were amused by it. But she'd known him for most of her life, even if the last eight years were a blank spot, and she knew the difference between Leo's real amusement and his fake amusement.

But she also knew what would happen if she put her potato and her shredder down and placed one mucky, slimy hand on his in an expression of sympathy. He'd stand up, drop his half-finished potato, and beat it out of here, probably not even taking the time to close the front door. So she kept her tone light in response. "Did your journey to become a Pokémon master take away from your studies?"

"Something like that," he said, and his shoulders visibly relaxed, as if he'd been waiting for the pity. "The electric gym really energized me, but the psychic one messed with my head."

"What's the conversion rate of gym badge to salary?" she said, tone still light, but this time his smile dropped and he turned away.

"I've been working at the warehouse, you know, the one on 95. It's not so bad for right now. Gives me a lot of time to think." Now his tone was defensive.

"Working at a warehouse isn't bad at all," Shira said. She knew a lot of people in high school who'd worked at the big warehouse nearby because the hours were flexible and they didn't require a college degree. She also knew that all those people couldn't wait to find a job with better pay and better hours that didn't treat them like they were toddlers who couldn't be trusted to go to the bathroom whenever they needed to.

"I could look for something different. I don't want to."

"Sure," Shira said. *Quick, change the subject, change the subject.* "So what else have you been up to? Do you still run? Or paint? We used to have so much fun painting together."

He shook his head. "I twisted my knee in college and just never got back into it. Sometimes walking Neptune feels like running, though."

There had to be *something* she could bring up that wouldn't lead to a depressing response. "How's your mom doing?" Then she realized there had to be some reason Leo was here with the dad he hated. "No, actually, did you see that story about the penguin and the fox that became best friends?"

"I'd imagine that would end poorly," said Leo, and thank god, thank *god*, just then Shira heard the front door open and three sets of footsteps tromp inside.

"Hey," Shira called out toward the front door. One set of footsteps went off down the hallway–Talia, presumably. "I'm in the kitchen. Leo's here."

"Oh, Leo!" Shira's dad was the first to make it to the kitchen, his cheeks pink from the cold, a black knit hat still pulled down to his ears, which might have been due less to the cold than the fact that he was balding and, as Shira had discovered the first time she joked she could see her reflection in his head, sensitive about it. He didn't react to the potato peels strewn all over the floor, the bowls and pans filling slowly with shredded potato on every surface, the potato glop and mush splattered on the stove. "It's good to see you. How are you?"

"Good, good," Leo said. He gestured to the mess around them as Shira's mom appeared behind her dad. "Sorry about all this."

Shira's mom's eyes widened so big they looked like they might pop out of her head. "What are you doing?"

"It was a latke emergency," Shira explained. "With the deli burning down, obviously they weren't going to be able to make the–"

"No," her mom interrupted. "I mean, why are you doing all of this by hand? You do realize we own a food processor, right? With a shred setting?"

Shira had not realized that. She pressed her lips together.

"That would've been good to know before my arm muscles turned to jelly. Where is it?"

It was up high in a cabinet, which meant that her parents hadn't used it recently, either, and it made sense why they hadn't stumbled across it. She sighed as she dropped in her first potato and watched the machine neatly take it apart. Everybody in the art community feared the idea of a machine-learning takeover, but in this moment, she was ready to bow down before her mechanical overlords. "Well," she said, turning to Leo. "We got in a good workout, right?"

"All's well that ends well," he said, and they stood there and stared at each other for a moment. Shira knew her parents were still right beside them, but it felt like they were alone.

And then that moment passed. "I should go take Neptune out," he said while Shira was saying, "I can probably just do the rest on my own."

"Let me know if you need me," Leo said, giving her that crooked half smile again. "I can always come back to help with the frying."

"Thanks," Shira said. He was probably just saying that, though. Nobody actually wanted to spend their day in front of a pan of hot oil. She was already envisioning the gunk that would come out following her face mask later that night. She stepped away from the food processor as if she were going to follow him out. "If I don't, I'll see you tomorrow night for the party, right?"

"Wouldn't miss it," he tossed over his shoulder, and he was gone.

"Never thought I'd see him in here again," her dad mused,

taking her spot in front of the food processor. She went to respond just as he pushed the shred button. He stopped. "Oh, sorry, were you saying something? Go ahead." She opened her mouth once more, and—*BZZZZZZ*.

She rolled her eyes. "Very funny," she mouthed, but she couldn't help smiling. Her dad stopped for real this time, allowing her to speak. "Yeah, I'm glad to see him. Though he's not in a great spot."

"Yeah, we heard just now as we were out walking," said her mom, who was up at the counter slicing onions while looking back at Shira. That didn't seem like it was going to end well. "Working a dead-end job, didn't graduate from college. His dad is worried he's depressed. Apparently all he does is work and play video games."

She'd figured that, but it was still hard to hear about her old friend. Hopefully feeling useful today had lifted his spirits even a little. And she still had tomorrow. Inspiration struck her: She would get him a gift. The perfect gift. Something that would pull him out of his depression, that would give him a path forward, remind him how much he mattered. That wasn't too tall an order for a Hanukkah gift, right?

Okay. She had a lot of work to do.

4

WOULDN'T MISS IT. LEO'S OWN WORDS TUMBLED around and around his head as he walked back to his house to take out the dog. *Wouldn't miss it.* He'd missed so much, though, and talking with Shira had only driven the point home. Usually he didn't care if the person he was talking to thought he was a loser. But Shira . . .

It wasn't even about his job. She'd asked about his running and his art. He'd only done cross-country because his parents had made him try a sport, and then it had turned out he was pretty good at it, so he kept going. And painting? He'd never felt a passion for making art.

Only for the person who'd make art with him.

And the way he'd countered her presumed pity about his job. *I could look for something different. I don't want to.* God, he'd come off like a petulant child. Every morning or afternoon that he went into work, his stomach dropped lower and lower the closer he got to those big warehouse doors. Walking through them made him feel like he'd been swallowed into the belly of some enormous beast, and spending his days speeding around the floor, plucking and sorting the things people ordered, made him feel as if he were slowly being digested by the beast's stomach acid.

It wasn't that he was embarrassed to be working a blue-collar job at a warehouse. It was honest work and nothing to be ashamed of. He had colleagues who seemed to be perfectly happy clocking in and doing the work and clocking out and going home. And there were plenty of others who had plans for what they were going to do next, and they'd taken this job to save money or work opposite schedules from their spouse's, and it was a good option for them for now.

But he resented the tedium of it, and the way the company micromanaged every single step he took, and the way he rarely exchanged words with anyone else over the course of the day, and the way that currently he was on track to be there forever. What else was he supposed to do, though, without a degree or any real knowledge of what he wanted to do? When he pictured choosing something to do for the rest of his life—*the rest of his life*—his heart got all fluttery with panic. The rest of his life was such a long time (hopefully, at least). He wasn't sure he liked anything enough to do it for the rest of his life.

He pushed those thoughts to the back of his mind. He was only feeling this pit in his stomach because Shira was here now, on top of the world, with everything figured out. She'd leave soon, and everything would go back to normal.

He tried to ignore how the pit in his stomach deepened at the thought, so deep now he might fall in and never be able to climb out.

LEO SPENT THE rest of the day and the next waiting to see if Shira would text him for help, but of course she didn't. She had everything down, the same way she always had. The night of the party began crystal clear and calm, not that it mattered, since Leo didn't have to drive. His breath puffed in the air as he walked the two doors down to Shira's house, rubbing his arms to stay warm (why bother bringing a coat when he'd only be outside for two minutes?). He walked quickly, partially due to the chill in the air and partially so that he wouldn't have to make conversation with Joe, who lagged a few steps behind.

No string lights sparkled on Shira's house. In Michigan, one thing Leo had loved about living in a home that celebrated Christmas was the decorations—he smiled, thinking about how excited his mom would get every year when they got to put up their Christmas lights. Most of the setup fell upon him; he'd get up on the ladder and string them wherever she directed.

At Shira's, though, at least five menorahs sat proudly in the front windows, ready to be lit, and bright, cheerful classical music spilled out the cracked-open door. Not Hanukkah music—was Hanukkah music even a thing besides that dreidel song? Leo made a note to ask Shira.

Inside, the house was toasty warm; Leo sped through the foyer, since he didn't have a coat to hang, and went straight for the living room, where several of his neighbors were bunched around the food table. He caught snatches of conversation as he grabbed a pig in a blanket (ironically named, considering the franks were likely made of beef in this household): Mr. Colatrella was annoyed that his property taxes were going up even though the pothole in front of his house hadn't gone anywhere; Ms. Brown was expounding very enthusiastically about a potential conspiracy involving the school board, a local mattress company, and the Peruvian government, which Leo wasn't able to parse despite a solid thirty seconds of eavesdropping. He shoved another pig in a blanket into his mouth just as somebody slapped him on the shoulder.

"Leo! I heard around Thanksgiving that you were back home again." Mr. Colatrella had evidently cooled off about the taxes and the pothole situation, maybe because of the nearly empty glass of what looked like a whiskey soda in his hand (or so his already red cheeks testified). "College didn't work out for you, huh? It's all right, not everybody's meant to go to college."

Leo couldn't help but bristle a little bit. "No, college worked out great for me," he said. "I just felt like leaving a few credits short of a degree."

Mr. Colatrella blinked a few times, clearly unsure what to make of that. "Ah," he said finally. "But you're here working at the warehouse."

"Yeah, that's always been my dream job," Leo said. "Warehousing is my passion."

"Are you . . . Is it?"

Leo bared his teeth in a smile. "It was great seeing you, Mr. Colatrella. Fred." He could use first names now that he was an adult, right? "I'm going to get a drink."

Where the living room had been crowded and dim, the kitchen was bright and cheery and smelled like fried potatoes, which might be the best smell there was. He said that much to Shira's sister, Talia, who was sipping something ruby red with a sour expression. She replied, "There are better smells."

"Like what?" he said, genuinely curious.

She paused, tilting her head back, as if thinking very seriously. "Maybe the first rain of spring, when the ground wakes up and realizes, hey, right, we can grow things," she said. "Or the smell of your childhood home when you come back to it after a long time away."

Hard to argue against those. "Okay, let me amend that," he said. "The best food smell there is. Talia, have you gone from karate to poetry?"

She stared at him blankly. "Why can't I be both a martial artist and a poet?" Then she shrugged. "Though, lo, I am currently neither. I'm double majoring in economics and Russian literature."

"I haven't read any of the Russian masters," Leo said. "Any I should pick up?"

She tilted her head back again for a moment, then tipped it forward and said, as surely as if she'd read the answer on the ceiling, "No."

With that, she wandered off. "Good talk," Leo said, though quietly enough that she wouldn't be able to hear it, because she *was* a black belt.

Someone else had heard, however. Leo smelled her before he saw her, and in the moment it took to register her presence, he thought, *No, fried potatoes aren't the best smell in the world*, that's *the best smell in the world.*

"I still can't believe that the child who wouldn't read anything but my old Baby-Sitter's Club books now exclusively reads books in Russian," Shira said. Leo stepped back, dazzled by the display, and he didn't mean her looks: She was wearing the ugliest sweater he'd ever seen, a blue-and-white monstrosity covered all over with dreidels and sparkly golden gelt and, in its center, a menorah whose candles were real blinking lights. She shrugged, clearly seeing his widened eyes. "It's horrible, I know. I lost a bet with Talia. I only have to wear it for another fifteen minutes."

He had so many questions he didn't even know where to start. She cracked a smile. "Yes, she actually reads the books in Russian. She's really good with languages, apparently? I guess she started learning Russian after she quit martial arts. The sweater is from T.J.Maxx. I know, I couldn't believe they carried it, either, but I guess they needed their one token Hanukkah sweater in the ugly-Christmas-sweater section. And the bet was over how many latkes I'd end up making. I had more faith in myself than Talia did." She leaned in, and Leo got another whiff of her, cinnamon and book pages and paint and some tang that was uniquely Shira. She whispered, "So I'd appreciate if you'd stick to, like, one."

He was going to get dizzy. He stepped back. Cleared his throat. "I can do that."

"Thanks, old friend." She held up a glass. "You can have a latke cocktail, if you want."

"A potato drink?" When he'd said fried potato was the best smell ever, he did not mean when combined with alcohol. He gave her glass, which was filled with a murky brownish liquid, a suspicious look. Then sighed. Because this was Shira asking, and of course he'd say yes. "Okay, fine."

Her eyes sparkled. "Yes! For some reason, nobody else wants one."

Which was a shame for them because, as Leo realized a few minutes later, it was actually really good. Probably because it barely tasted like a latke. Instead, it had notes of apple, cinnamon, lemon, and something a little creamy, all layered over alcohol. "Let me guess—potato vodka?"

She clapped. "You got it in one."

He took another sip. "Did you make it up?"

"No, I found the recipe on the internet." Her eyebrows rose over her glass. "Don't tell."

"I won't," he promised. "Hey—" He caught Joe out of the corner of his eye—he was heading toward them. Thank god, he was stopped by one of their neighbors, an old man who Leo had nicknamed Reindeer Guy after the lifelike reindeer statues that lived in front of his house all year round, dressed as pumpkins and skeletons for Halloween and posed kissing for Valentine's Day. "Want to move back to the living room?"

Shira frowned. "Are you just trying to avoid your dad?"

"No," Leo lied. "I wanted another pig in a blanket before they're all gone. They're really good."

She gave him a pleased smile. "They're Trader Joe's, from the frozen section. Don't tell."

"I won't." The farther they got from Joe, the more Leo's shoulders relaxed. It was like he could breathe again. This probably wasn't healthy, right? Internally, he shrugged. Even if he thought it was a good idea, which he wasn't a hundred percent on, he couldn't afford a therapist right now.

Which was fine because Shira seemed energized about the idea of being one for him. "You can't just keep outrunning your dad, you know," she said, her finger poking his chest. He ignored her, reaching for a pig in a blanket. It was good they'd come here in time, because the hors d'oeuvres were almost all gone. See? Everything was fine. Everything he did made logical sense. "He doesn't just know where you live—he literally lives there, too."

He couldn't respond to that, because he'd just crammed his mouth full of food. He gave her a shrug of faux apology. She didn't buy it, just waited until he'd swallowed to say "It's been a long time. You don't have to be his best friend, but you could open the door. I think it would be good for both of you."

He held back a snort. She hadn't seen him for eight years. How could she know what would be good for him? Besides, it wasn't her business how he related to his dad. It wasn't like she could understand, having two parents who were married and, from what Leo had gathered, never bothered looking at anyone besides each other.

He didn't voice those thoughts, though. He just said, "He's still the same guy who lied to me and my mom. Who had a whole secret life behind our backs. Who betrayed us. Who didn't even treat us like trash, because at least trash you throw away. He treated us like . . . like, I don't know, something that's not even worth being thrown away. He treated us like the empty toilet paper roll someone leaves on the holder because they can't be bothered to make the effort to change it out."

It wasn't like his dad had been a teenager when he'd done it all, with his brain half-developed and zero impulse control. He'd been a fully grown adult man, a husband and father for more than fifteen years. He'd made an adult decision not only to fuck another woman but to carry on an affair in secret. Maybe if the initial night had been an impulse decision but then he'd come clean about it—even if it was to divorce his mom—Leo might have been able to respect him. But he'd made the decision over and over again to hide, lie, betray. Sure, he'd apologized for it, but only after he'd been caught.

Leo was still angry. He didn't think he'd ever stop being angry. And it made him even angrier, somehow, knowing that he was dependent on his dad. On Joe. He both didn't want to look him in the eye and *couldn't* look him in the eye.

Anyway, it was a healthy situation, and all was fine. He said that to Shira in the form of "I don't want to talk about it."

"Okay, okay," she said, but he knew it was only a matter of time before it came up again. Shira was like Neptune when he smelled rotisserie chicken in the Costco bag: He wouldn't stop until he got at least a bite of what he wanted. "Come on, let's make the rounds."

He didn't really want to talk to more of his neighbors, but it was a lot more tolerable with Shira at his side. They fawned so much over her—telling her how great a job she'd done with this party once again, and *honestly* even though they weren't Jewish, they thought the Hanukkah party was more fun than the Christmas party, and *my* she was doing so well out there in LA; they were so proud that one of their very own was going to go so far, and they couldn't *wait* to see her show or not actually see her show, since it was all the way in LA, right, but they couldn't wait to see the pictures that would surely be featured in the local paper—that they barely had time to ask Leo how he was doing. Or maybe that was on purpose. It seemed everybody had already heard from Joe about how *tough a time* Leo was having. Maybe Leo should've been insulted by it, but he was relieved. Besides, not having to talk left him more time to sip on his first and then his second latke cocktail.

The latkes were excellent, at least. And the sandwiches pretty good, too. So Leo trailed Shira around all night, getting steadily tipsier on latke cocktails and filling his stomach with (oops) more than his one allotted potato pancake. Occasionally the thought flitted through his head that, if he hadn't had a couple of latke cocktails and if the person he was following around weren't Shira, he might have felt a bit like a shadow, especially considering that most of the other "kids" his age weren't here. But then Shira would turn his way with sparkling eyes and a snarky comment about Mrs. Kane's hair or Mr. Candido's tendency to say *dagnabbit* over *fuck* and it would all feel okay.

It was almost like he'd never moved away at all. Like he'd seamlessly slipped back into his old life.

After they'd made their way through the crowd, collecting compliments and a few hostess gifts that hadn't made it to Shira's parents, Shira turned to him with those sparkling eyes. He waited for her to comment on the vintage of the wine Benny Thompson's mom had handed her (he'd already decided he'd just nod along, since he knew nothing about wine), but instead she grabbed his upper arm. "Hey, come with me."

His heart skipped a beat. Leo nodded, and she led him through the house and down the hall, past the bathroom . . .

. . . and into her room.

Well, her old room, considering she didn't live here anymore. But it looked pretty much the same as it had back then, not that he'd spent much time in there: the same twin bed with the blue flowered coverlet, the wall-to-wall gray carpet with the stain in the corner from the time they tried the Mentos-and-Diet-Coke trick inside, the walls covered with art posters and magazine pages and photo collages. A lot of the photos were from after his time, of Shira with her high school or USY or art friends, of her posing beside art exhibitions, of Shira Shira Shira. He'd missed so much of her life. He imagined himself in some of the photos, her tucked up against his side, their faces turned toward each other in laughter. Maybe if he'd stayed, that's what would have happened. They wouldn't have drifted apart; they would've drifted closer together.

"Hey," Shira said, her voice low. He felt rather than heard her close behind him, something about the breath from her lips brushing the back of his neck. He swallowed hard.

"Hey."

"Are you having a good night?"

The heat coming off her skin was all transferring into him, into his hot blood and lungs, making it hard to breathe. "Yes," he said. "Yes, I am." *It's the first good night I've had in a while,* he didn't say.

"I got something for you," she said, and she stepped closer, and the heat of her against him was almost unbearable. He turned around as if in slow motion to find her nearly touching him, her face pointed up, eyes serious.

"For me?" he said dumbly. Somehow he knew that if he tried to move his eyes away from hers, he'd feel the physical tearing of it in his chest. His heart throbbed in a new rhythm he'd never felt before. If he died now, he'd die happy.

"For you," she said, smiling a little, and he realized she was holding a box wrapped in sparkly silver paper.

His chest swelled. He couldn't remember the last time anyone other than his mom had gotten him a gift. It was almost all too much: her closeness; her eyes; the gift; the sheer joy of him being here, with her, in this room, at this time.

He couldn't think of anything else to do but kiss her.

5

AS LEO KISSED HER, SHIRA KEPT HER EYES WIDE open. Partially from surprise. Partially because she was so busy thinking about her lips that her eyes were way down on the priority list, and no matter what she'd blustered about dating before, she hadn't been kissed enough recently to make the movement muscle memory.

But mostly it was because she couldn't relax. Yes, she could register that it felt good: the movement of his lips against hers, the familiar smell that made her feel comfortable no matter the situation, the feeling of heat that spread down her throat and pooled into a throb in her belly. She could register herself leaning into him, her lips moving back, into the warmth and comfort and spark that she knew would grow into a flame if she let it. It was that she couldn't turn off her brain. *He's a college dropout, he lives with his dad, he has no career goals, what would all my friends think?*

The thoughts made her rigid. It must have felt like kissing a statue, which had to be why he broke away first after maybe two or three seconds that felt drawn out into eight years. She really hoped he didn't see the wince she wiped off her face. "Sorry,

sorry," he said, and before he could beat himself up, she was saying, "No, no, it's okay," and then he was turning beet red and his eyes were falling away, and she shoved the box at him, mostly to give him something to do with his hands.

He grabbed clumsily at the box, almost dropping it, and they both apologized to each other at the same time, and then there was an awkward laugh, and then he was desperately tearing at the paper, his fingers unable to close on much more of it than a scrap at a time, so he was littering her bedroom carpet with sparkly silver snow.

She could pinpoint the moment when his heart broke. If this weren't Leo, someone she cared deeply about, this might have been a dramatic moment when she recounted the tale to her friends later. But it was Leo, and she did care so deeply about him, and she wouldn't tell anyone this story, because her heart broke a little, too.

"Oh," he said, his face entirely blank as he stared at the present in his hands. "This is a pity gift."

After enlisting her parents' help with the food, Shira had ventured out to the local Barnes & Noble, which said online that it had a whole big section of books meant to help people with their careers. Leo apparently only played video games now? She could work with that. And so could *How to Turn Your Love of Gaming into a Career.* Big black blocky font on a neon-yellow cover, crowning a young man sitting before his outdated computer with an exaggerated scrunched-up, confused expression.

In the store it had seemed so thoughtful. But here, after the kiss, after that blank face, she couldn't help but cringe at it. "No, no, it's totally not," she said hastily but not in time. He was already flipping it over, eyebrows raising.

"For people who need a little help pointing themselves in the right direction," he read aloud. Scoffed a little. "Well, that's me. You nailed it. Congratulations. No, mazel tov."

She couldn't help but be stung a little by his sarcasm. She'd meant well, after all. Surely he could give her a little credit for that? "I was trying to help."

"Right," he said. "Because even though you haven't seen me in eight years, somehow you know exactly what would fix my life. A how-to book. So thoughtful. If I read this book, what, then you'd kiss me back?"

At first she felt like she might shrivel up, and then a spark of anger flared into something more. Like, seriously, how dare he. *He* was the one who'd left. He'd come back to his dad's house now; he could've come back occasionally to see her if she'd really mattered to him. He was the one who was clearly unhappy where he was at, treading water in the house of a man he hated, at a job he hated, no matter what he claimed. It wasn't like she was a lifeguard jumping in after him and hauling him to dry land; she was tossing him a life raft he could choose to grab or not.

But none of that was what came bursting out of her mouth. "'Then you'd kiss me back'? Like you're entitled to my body?"

She felt embarrassed as soon as the anger pushed it out, but it was too late. It caught in his eyes and flared there, too. "Seriously, Shira? Of course not. I thought you knew me." There wasn't only anger there; she could also see hurt. "I just thought we were vibing. I thought it was mutual. It's okay if it's not. It's okay if you're not into me. But . . ." His jaw worked, tightening up so hard she was afraid he might break a tooth. "Did you not kiss me back because, what, you'd be embarrassed to be seen with me?"

"Of course not," she said. "I've been seen with you literally the entire night. We've spent the whole party together."

She opened her mouth to continue her argument, but the words died on her tongue. She couldn't really argue with him—that *was* entirely the reason she hadn't kept kissing him back. Not because she hadn't wanted to. Because she knew that, with Leo, one kiss would lead to another kiss, would lead to something more, would lead to her introducing him to her friends and coworkers and boss as . . . well. The guy who lived at home. The guy with a dead-end job and no degree and currently no hope of anything more.

Her stomach squirmed uncomfortably. Of course Leo was more than that. They had years of history, of inside jokes, and he was funny, smart, kind, all the good things. But she lived across the country in a big city. She was ready to take on the world. How was she supposed to build something with someone on the opposite side of the country, who was content without plans for his future, fine living with his dad? He couldn't afford his own place, and he couldn't exactly share her tiny studio.

"I thought so," said Leo, voice tight. "You were always like this, you know. I thought you might have grown up a little. I guess not."

"Really? Because it seems like, between the two of us, I'm the only one who's grown up."

She could tell immediately that she'd hit him right in the gut. "I meant emotionally," he said. "I don't care what anyone else thinks of me, but that's all you care about. Do you even care that your whole life is basically a performance for other people?"

"That's not true!" she exploded. "Not even a little!" She wrapped her arms around herself like that would protect her, even though she had absolutely zero need of protection. He was hurt, and he was lashing out. That was all that was happening. "Maybe you *should* care a little more about what people think of you, if that means you'll do something with your life."

"Yeah. Sure. Fine." His face twisted, and his mouth opened, and she braced herself for something really ugly to come out—years of history meant they knew where all the bodies were buried, metaphorically but also physically, in the case of all their deceased pets—but then they both stopped at the sound of singing. The crowd. They were singing the blessings for the Hanukkah candles. Or, really, the Levinsons and Joe and the few other Jews in the crowd were singing while the rest of the neighbors were attempting enthusiastic but mangled interpretations from the transliterated Hebrew words on their phones, but that was close enough.

The familiar tune sent calm washing through her; her anger drained right out, leaving her limp and sad. "I can't believe they're lighting the menorah without me," she said. "I threw this whole freaking party."

The tension had left him, too. "We can still make the second blessing. We should go out there."

But neither one of them moved. She huffed out a breath. "Look, I really didn't mean to—"

"It's fine. Don't worry about it." He turned to study one of the photos on the wall: one from college where she, Danica, and some of their other college friends were getting ready for a party. Shira remembered that night well—it was right before winter break, and they were getting ready to part ways, and they were both pouting that Danica's birthday fell between Christmas and New Year's, so they wouldn't get to celebrate it properly together. But then someone had told them to smile for the camera, and while Danica's face was still a little pouty, Shira had automatically fixed her grin on bright and shiny.

Leo cleared his throat. "Go light the candles. You threw the whole freaking party, the least you can do is enjoy it."

And with that, he turned and left the room. She followed him out to the living room, where clusters of people were crowded around each of the menorahs the Levinsons had accumulated over the years: the fancy twisty brass ones Shira and Talia had been gifted for their bat mitzvahs, the dinosaur one they had used as little kids, the tarnished silver one that had been passed down from their grandparents, the stained glass artsy one her parents had gotten as a wedding gift.

She joined the nearest cluster, assuming Leo was doing the same, and opened her mouth in song. The familiar words and the familiar tune poured out of her, joining with all the other people all over the world doing this at the same time on the same day, connecting her with all her ancestors who had sung these same words to the same tune to the same array of shining lights.

Her dad, who was holding the shammash, glanced in her direction and gestured her forward with the hand holding the candle, which splattered wax on the windowsill. The group parted for her, and she made it to his side in time to take the candle and light all six candles before gingerly melting the bottom and fitting it into its holder. (Because it was the sixth night, it was so full of melted wax already that it was like playing a game where if you lost, you burned yourself.)

By the time she was done, Leo was gone. And she didn't realize it until she was packing up to fly home, but so was the book she'd gifted him.

From Shira Levinson's email-drafts folder:

JANUARY: Hey Leo—Hope all is well! Your dad gave my mom your email and I thought I'd reach out. Also, I saw that you have social media now—I hope it's cool that I followed you! I've been thinking about how we left things and I hate that we didn't hash things out before I flew back to LA. I don't know if your dad told you, but I did go by your house twice and you weren't there. Or maybe you were there, just avoiding me. I really don't think that somebody's worth is defined by their job, it's just that, in my field of work, I can't be with someone who doesn't want more from life than oh god I sound like such a tool

MARCH: Hey Leo—Hope you're doing well! I've been thinking about how we left things over the break and wanted to clear the air, because you mean so much to me. I just think you could be doing so much more with your life and I hate to see you oh god I sound like such a TOOL

JULY: Hey Leo—Hope you're enjoying that gross East Coast summer heat. Is it weird that I miss the humidity? Anyway, I just wanted to see how you were doing. It's funny how we place so much importance on what we do for a living, isn't it? It's like the first thing people ask when they meet you. Maybe it should be less important. I just want to make sure you're happy. Ugh no that sounds so condescending

From Leo David's sent-emails folder:

MARCH: To Whom It May Concern: I was perusing the offerings in last semester's Ocean County College course catalog and wanted to inquire about next semester's, as I was considering enrolling in the fall . . .

JULY: Hey Roy—I feel like it's been ages since we were owning the rest of Brody Neighborhood in beer pong, how are you doing? I saw on LinkedIn that you work for Callisto Studios now, that's awesome. They're one of my favorite indie game studios, I loved Blue Blue Sky. I saw that they're looking for an entry-level QA tester. I was planning to apply, and I was wondering if you could put in a good word for me . . .

From Leo David's email-drafts folder:

SEPTEMBER: Hey Shira—Hope you're enjoying that beautiful LA weather while we suffer out here in the mouth of Satan. I just wanted to let you know that I'm moving on up in the world—started taking classes at OCC and also got a new job adjacent to where I want to be in the gaming industry. It's been pretty cool so far. Maybe now that I'm taking steps toward being a Serious Person you might ugh no Leo you're so pathetic, you are not sending this

6

Year Two

IF THERE WAS ONE THING LEO DAVID HATED MORE than anything, it was having to eat crow. Okay, he hated a few things more than eating crow: the taste of cilantro, for one (getting his mouth washed out with soap as a punishment for cursing as a kid had been terrible, why do it voluntarily?) and having to bury a pet (Neptune was going gray around the muzzle, and he was already dreading the day) and forcing himself to sit down for dinner with Joe once a week for omelets or pancakes or steak and eggs (because apparently his dad only knew how to cook brunch food).

But eating crow was definitely up there. And while he'd managed to avoid thinking too hard about Shira Levinson for the past year after their fight at the Hanukkah party, he knew that she always flew home for the holiday. He knew that he could try to avoid seeing her, too, but they'd run into each other at some point, and he'd have to prepare himself for—

Oh, shit. There she was, literally, right there, strolling down the sidewalk all bundled up in her pink wool peacoat and sophisticated navy beanie, her cheeks and the bridge of her nose red with cold, the setting sun making her glow all around as if from a halo. He took a deep breath. She hadn't seen him yet; she was looking over her shoulder at someone behind her, probably her sister or her parents. He briefly considered turning tail and running the other way, but Neptune was not known for his running (more for his skills at napping in the exact shape of a doughnut), and besides, it would be far more awful for her to turn and see his retreating back than his fake smile.

So he geared up that fake smile—shaking it out and hanging it on the line, where it hopefully wouldn't stiffen too much—for when she turned around. Which she did. Her eyes widened in surprise, and for one heart-stopping moment, he wasn't sure whether *she* was going to turn tail and run the other way. But of course she didn't, because she was Shira Levinson, and she had everything together—even her fake smile, which he could tell from her real smile by the lack of a dimple in her left cheek. "Leo!" she said. "Fancy running into you here!" She smiled down at Neptune, crouched to give him a good scratch behind his silky ears. She didn't hunch as she crouched, rather folded elegantly like an origami crane. "Good to see you, buddy." She stood, swinging her arms at her sides as if she were nervous.

There were two ways this conversation could go; he knew that right off the bat. They could exchange a few fake pleasantries, laugh a few fake laughs, and wish each other a good afternoon before they went about their day, and then that would be it. That would be their new baseline.

He'd spent a full year having nightmares about that baseline. He took a deep breath as Shira turned toward him, leaving her face in profile against the setting sun for a moment, outlining the strong lines of her features in gold. "Look," he said. "I'm sorry about the way things ended last year. I was an ass to you, and I shouldn't have been. You were just trying to help." Her mouth was hanging open. "Oh, and also," he said, "hi."

She laughed—her real laugh, the one not just with the dimple but with her crooked bottom teeth on display. "Leo David, apologizing." And she quickly sobered. "I'm sorry, too. Honestly, I've been trying to figure out a way to apologize all year. I was also an ass."

Leo probably wouldn't have been able to apologize a year ago. He certainly hadn't been ready right after their fight, the wounds too red and raw and fresh. He'd walked Neptune in the woods so he wouldn't have to run into her in the neighborhood, stubbornly told himself that she'd clearly changed in the last eight years and didn't know him at all anymore. That he was doing just fine and he'd been doing fine without her in his life for eight years, that he didn't need her at all.

But it was a wonder what a year could do. After maybe a month of pure annoyance in her direction, a doubt cracked through and let in a little light. *What if* . . . And then another couple of months and another few cracks were open, and the light was enough to see that maybe she was right about two things, that his job wasn't a good fit for him and maybe he should start thinking about his future. And then another month and that stupid book was still sitting on his desk, and he had nothing else to do, so he cracked it open.

If they'd tried to repair things immediately, he probably never would have really looked inward and decided that he wanted to change for himself. “No, you were actually right,” he said. “At least about some things.” He cleared his throat again. “I started taking some coding courses at OCC.” The local community college. “They’re not too expensive, and they’re right nearby, so I can live at home and save money.”

“That’s great,” Shira said. “You know, I wasn’t trying to say you were a loser or anything. If you’d been happy, I totally never would’ve said anything, but I could see how unhappy you were, so . . .”

“I was really unhappy.” This might have been the first time he voiced it out loud. It didn’t feel bad, actually. Surprisingly. “But this feels good. A baby step toward something else.”

“That’s great,” she said again. Her eyes crinkled with relief. “And it’s probably easy to schedule shifts at the warehouse around your class schedule.”

“I’m actually not at the warehouse anymore, either.” To be fully honest, that wasn’t entirely due to Shira or what she said. He’d just had it with his boss nitpicking him for going thirty seconds over his fifteen-minute break or telling him that he wasn’t allowed to go to the bathroom until he met his quota. “I found a job as a QA tester. Quality assurance for a game developer. The pay isn’t great, and the hours are long, but it’s remote, so there’s no commute, and it’s a foot in the door for when I’m looking for an internship or something.”

“That’s *so* great,” Shira said, and she wasn’t bullshitting him, either. She sounded more thrilled than his own father had when he told him over one of their now-weekly dinners.

“Yeah,” he continued, a little too loudly, so that she wouldn’t have the opportunity to ask. “A lot of people think that QA is like playing video games all day, but that's a common misconception. Your job is to find bugs in the software, so really you're just sitting there trying to break the game. Like, sometimes I'll be in the same virtual room for hours or even days, running into walls and clicking different buttons on things and trying all sorts of weird stuff during battles, seeing if anything gets messed up."

"That's great," Shira said once more. It was pretty much all she'd said this whole conversation. Because he was blabbering on about himself like an idiot.

"How about you? How are you doing? I heard you finished your paintings and the show is scheduled soon," he said. She smiled at him, her real smile again, and he felt a bubble of hope rise in his chest, knowing that they were okay. They'd reset. Who knew what might happen this year after the party?

"Oh, yeah," she said, and then she turned to greet someone walking up behind her. Leo hadn't even noticed them; he'd been too focused on the way the icy wind brought out the blush in her cheeks and the way tendrils of her dark hair escaping from her hat made her look like the snow queen in that fairy tale. Honestly, she was wasted on the LA weather. "Finally, there you are."

"Had to take a quick work call," the person—the guy—said, and then Leo's heart plummeted to his feet because this guy pressed his lips to Shira's, and she kissed him back. Neptune let out a low *whuff*, and for one moment he wasn't entirely proud of, Leo wished he'd adopted one of those retired fighting dogs instead of a failed hunting beagle.

When Shira and this guy broke apart, breath steaming from their lips in the cold air, her smile as she turned back to Leo was almost apologetic. "Leo, this is William," she said. "My boyfriend. William, my childhood friend Leo."

William extended a hand for Leo to shake. Maybe Leo was just out of practice with handshakes, but William's seemed too firm, meant to break some fingers. "Dr. William Bettany," he said, his voice higher than Leo would've expected for someone taller than him. "Nice to meet you."

Shira's boyfriend must have hailed from somewhere warmer than here, because he was bundled up like he was about to embark upon an expedition to the North Pole. Beneath the fluffy sheep's ears of the boyfriend's hat and above the wool scarf cloaking him up to his lips, Leo could see that he was fine boned and hollow cheeked, like a model or distant cousin of the British royal family, with pale eyelashes Leo could only pick out because of the setting sun's rays; he was definitely older than them, maybe thirty or so, which made sense if he was already a doctor. "Nice to meet you, too," Leo said, pulling his hand away before he could try and smash William's fingers back. "What kind of doctor are you? I have a cousin who's a urologist."

Neptune stepped up to William's foot and sniffed. *Piss on him*, Leo thought, but of course Neptune just stared up with a goofy dog grin. William bent down and gave Neptune a two-fingered scratch that wasn't unkind but that made Leo wonder if the man had ever petted a dog in his life. "I'm not a medical doctor," he said, sounding vaguely annoyed. "I have a PhD in art history."

"Ah," Leo said. "Far more useful."

"Leo," Shira said, and it was amazing how his name could sound like a reprimand in one ear and a friendly call to attention in the other. "William is a curator at the Los Angeles Museum of Art. In the modern art division. He's going to run the place one day."

"Wow," Leo said. *Be nice. Shira doesn't owe you anything. Your friendship is important to you.* "That's cool. How did you guys meet?"

"A museum gala," Shira said. She linked her arm through William's. He smiled fondly down at her, or Leo thought he did behind the scarf. "I don't usually get invited to those things, but my boss couldn't make it and insisted I go in his place."

A neighbor jogged by on the street, her breath puffing out in white clouds overhead. Leo and Shira automatically waved a hand in greeting. "That was lucky," he said. "How long have you been dating now?"

"Six months," said William.

"Seven and a half," said Shira. "Come on, let's get to the Colatrellas' house. They're doing this whole light show synced with music when it gets dark."

"The joys of the suburbs," William intoned, then looked at Leo as if he expected him to laugh. He didn't. Not just because he hated that this guy had Shira nestled into his side but because he didn't think it was funny. A city guy mocking the suburbs. How original. Leo *liked* how excited people got about dressing up their houses for the holidays—their individual displays might not rival whatever big fancy light shows they had in the city, but they were charming all the same. "All right. Come on."

"See you at the party?" Shira said to Leo. "You know when it is, right? Later this week?"

Leo took a deep breath. "Wouldn't miss it."

"Great." And they were off, walking arm in arm, Shira pointing out the different houses and telling him about the quirks of the people who lived within.

Leo watched them go until they were gone, then exhaled the deep breath he'd taken earlier. He needed to breathe. That was probably why he was a little dizzy.

AS SOON AS they turned the corner to the cul-de-sac, a neighbor's red-doored McMansion and its fleet of glowing reindeer blocking Leo from view, Shira puffed her cheeks with relief. "Okay, that went way better than I expected," she said. "Though, honestly, I have no idea how I expected it to go. I'm glad to get it over with, at least."

"He's the one you had a fight with last year?" William's eyes roved over the house's plastic reindeer, then the big blow-up Santas (one normal, one vacation Santa in a bathing suit and snorkel) in front of the house next door. His face betrayed nothing, but Shira's stomach couldn't help but clench self-consciously. She'd already met his parents at their huge, gleaming, all-white home in the Hollywood Hills, where they'd served her a gluten-free dinner that had been cooked by their private chef and cleaned up by a woman William's mother described as *Marta, practically a member of the family*, except that members of the family didn't generally wear uniforms or eat dinner in a different room. Shira hadn't been to his family's house around the holidays, but she suspected their holiday decorations were limited to maybe a string or two of twinkling all-white lights. Perhaps a tasteful, local-plant-life-based wreath.

"Yeah." Shira had told William that much but not about the kiss. Partially because she didn't need her new boyfriend knowing about everything she did with her body in the past but also because . . . well, even after a year, she still wasn't entirely sure how she felt about it.

"Well, I'm glad it all worked out," William said. She heard something buzz. He swore as he pulled out his phone. "Shit, I have to take this."

"Again?" Shira hated the whine in her voice.

"It'll just be a minute." He stepped away, put the phone to his ear. "This is Dr. Bettany."

It was always just a minute. A minute that turned into minutes, plural, that turned into hours. Shira let out a long, low breath as she watched the Colatrellas' lights blink on and begin playing a spirited version of "Sleigh Ride." Almost automatically, she pulled out her phone to take a quick video of the lights to send to Danica, Nora, and Ellery in the group chat—a little Christmas spirit for their day. They'd appreciate it in a way William probably wouldn't. Maybe it was better William was off talking to the head curator at the museum or the assistant director of modern art at Sotheby's or one of his many artists whose hands he needed to hold. He'd probably just nod and smile at the light show and think about how tacky it was.

Danica had warned her. They'd gone to the bar to debrief after their last double date, Shira with William and Danica with her new flame, a waiter-slash-actor (in LA, that *slash* almost went without saying). First they'd dissected the actor, debated whether his wonky nose made him more or less likely to succeed in the business (they settled on more but only if he started pursuing character actor roles over leading man roles). Then the conversation had turned to William.

"He's really impressive," Danica had said, perched on the edge of her stool. She was tiny and thin, almost birdlike in the way she floated through the air, in the dark feathery puff of her hair. "Like, a PhD and a curator job at *the* museum? By thirty? That knocks me over, honestly."

Shira traced the circle of condensation her rum and Coke had left on the wooden bar. Conversation buzzed above and around her; the number of people shouldering in on her to try to catch the bartenders' attention was making her claustrophobic. "I know. Me too."

"And he's quite handsome," Danica continued. Only Danica could say that and not sound like someone's mom. "I'm pretty sure that hair counts as contemporary art."

Shira snorted. He did spend an awful lot of time and attention maintaining that perfect blond wave.

"It was a little annoying how he was on his phone the whole time, though." Danica took a sip of her vodka cran, eyes never leaving Shira's face, probably ready to backtrack and abort mission in case Shira got upset. "I mean, he can't take an hour off for dinner?"

Shira sighed. A particularly eager bargoer elbowed her in the back. "I know." William had gotten up from the table to take two calls and had been on his phone typing out emails or work texts for at least a third of the meal. Danica would ask him where he'd grown up or what his favorite part of Italy was—he'd "summered" there as a kid—and would have to repeat herself two or three times before he looked up, eyes startled and even a little bit annoyed, as if she'd barged into his office and started yelling at him. "The other night we were in bed, you know, in the middle of things, and his phone rang, and—"

"Oh god, don't tell me he got up and took it." Danica's shoulders shook, and she pressed her lips together hard, like she was trying not to laugh.

"No, he didn't get up," Shira said grimly. "He made *me* get up, then he rolled out from under me and took it."

Danica winced. "If I cringed any harder right now, my stool would collapse."

"Right?" Shira slumped against the bar. "I've tried talking to him about it, and he brushes me off. Says he has to live, breathe, and sleep work for now if he wants to advance. And he wants to advance." She slumped harder and considered letting herself slide off. Maybe sleeping under the bar, where nobody could see her. "He says I'll understand when I get to that point in my career."

"Do you want to get to that point?"

Shira sighed. She said automatically, "Of course I do." She and William weren't on the exact same track, but she knew the natural progression of things: gallery assistant, gallery associate, run a gallery. Just imagine everybody's faces when she told them about her own gallery. "I'm just afraid it won't leave me time for my own stuff. If he can't even take twenty minutes to you-know-what, how could he ever create his own paintings?"

"Well, maybe you'll get to the point where you can do your own stuff full-time and not have to do the gallery thing."

"It's so unlikely." And the art world was so unstable. Even if her first show knocked it out of the park, you never knew what might happen afterward, and at that point she'd have been out of her career track for years with no easy way back in. "Fine artists don't exactly make bank."

"Very true, very true." Danica got a gleam in her eye. "Not to change the subject, but my show is finally almost done, so I might be finding that out for myself soon." She held up a hand before Shira could gush with congratulations. "Don't jinx me! But my gallery is saying they have a slot ready for me in mid-March. One of their bigger names might swoop in and take it, so who knows, but I'm hoping it'll be mine."

"Right," Shira said. Her hands fluttered with the urge to hug her friend or throw them in the air in celebration or something. She sat on them to keep them still, but it was tough. Danica had finally let her see her works in progress, and they had been fantastic, of course—her show was about her Ukrainian grandmother and her journey to the US, contrasted with the state of things in Ukraine today, with the inclusion of creatures from Slavic mythology that made it fantastical and eerie and original. "Okay, I won't talk about how great it is, but you'll keep me updated, right?"

"You will know the *minute* after I get a confirmation." She crossed herself. "If I get a confirmation, that is."

"Okay, but how great would that be?" Shira said. Her gallery had scheduled her own show, the one that followed the immigration story of her great-grandmother with a twist of Jewish mythology, for the spring, and it was already popping up on art blogs' lists of things to see next year. No, it hadn't set in yet, and she still got a delicious thrill whenever she got to tell people about it. "Our shows are pretty similar. We could do a show together next! Or a museum exhibit together!"

Danica's face tensed, but just for a moment. Of course. She wouldn't want to do a combination show, she'd want to do her own show. "We don't have to do a combination show," Shira said hastily. "But we could do talks and events and stuff together, since we're working in the same medium with a lot of the same themes."

Danica didn't respond. She just took a long sip of her drink before setting it back down. "I should probably get home. Are you going back to William's?"

That night she had, but she probably shouldn't have, because all she did was wonder if William was right for her. But he totally was, right? They wanted the same thing out of life. They were in the same field and had the same artistic hobbies. Her stomach squirmed deliciously whenever he kissed her. He was proud of her work and liked telling everybody at events that she was going to be the next big thing.

Tonight she sighed, watching the Colatrellas' lights twinkle and dance. She'd zoned out so long that they were now on "Jingle Bells." One of the Colatrella sons appeared in the window, and she waved and nodded automatically. He waved and nodded back. Her phone buzzed a few times with some Santa emojis and reindeer emojis from Ellery. Despite herself, they made her smile.

Shira jumped as William appeared next to her, slightly out of breath. "All right," he said. "What did I miss?"

Shira turned her back. "Nothing too exciting," she said. "Come on, it's cold. Let's go home."

7

THE NEXT FOUR DAYS WERE A WHIRL OF ACTIVITY. Shira introduced William to the local amusement park, which decked out the entire campus in lights and stuck Santa hats on their costumed characters for the holidays. She took him out to eat at the fancy diner, and the diner that made really good breakfast food but mediocre lunch food, and the diner that made really good burgers but mediocre everything else. She took him to the outlet mall, which was on billboards everywhere between here and New York City, where he bought her a surprise necklace from Kate Spade on a deep discount, which thrilled her thrifty heart.

God, she was exhausted. Usually when she went home, her preferred activities were going to bed early, letting her parents cook her breakfast, and lying on the couch so long Talia pretended to try to sit on her because she'd become one with the cushions. And now here she was, putting on real clothes and even mascara.

That meant she loved him. Right?

They lit the first few nights' Hanukkah candles together, William mouthing the English transliteration of the blessings on his phone, the Hebrew syllables awkward on his tongue and in his throat, where he did his best with the guttural throat-clearing *chhhhhh*. "It's like this," Talia would demonstrate, again and again. "Baru*chhhhh*, like you're clearing your throat."

Just leave it, Shira wanted to plead. But she knew William well enough to understand that if she told Talia to knock it off, William's eyes would flash with a challenge and he'd spend the rest of the evening clearing his throat over and over, determined to prove that he could do it.

She was too busy to see Leo. And he was probably too busy to see her, Shira told herself. Surely he had a lot going on. He'd made friends in his classes, she assumed. Or through work. Maybe he was even dating someone, like she was. Good for him and his imaginary girlfriend.

Hanukkah Party Day dawned drizzly and cold; every time Shira went outside, the wind tried to rip her scarf off. It was the perfect weather to stay indoors, wearing fuzzy slippers and luxuriating in how dry and warm you were beside the heater. That's where they all sat, in a circle around the fireplace Shira's family was too scared to light since the time they'd found out a bird had built its nest in the flue (everybody and everybird were fine, just a little smoky), going over preparations.

"Okay," said Shira, consulting her handwritten list. Lists on her phone might be easier to share, but they lacked a certain panache. "Dad, you're going to pick up the food at two. Make sure to count the trays and double-check everything against my order sheet before you leave, and make sure to arrange everything ahead of time so that anything that needs to be refrigerated actually fits in the fridge when you get home."

Her dad nodded vigorously. "You know fridge Jenga is my specialty. I'm glad the deli reopened in time for the party. We can't afford to lose another small business."

"And we can't afford another year of oil splatters and cleaning potato cement off the counter," Talia muttered.

Shira ignored her and moved on. "Mom, you're on drinks duty. Liquor store and grocery store for nonalcoholic beverages and mixers." She fixed her mother with a piercing glare. "Stick to the list this year."

"But the store-brand seltzer was on sale," her mom protested.

"La Croix only," Shira said firmly. "And Talia, you're—" She squinted at the list. "Did you redact your list item?"

Talia said something in Russian. Or Hebrew. She'd started taking Hebrew classes last semester, as if she didn't already have enough languages under her belt.

"I'm going to assume that was a sincere, heartfelt apology," Shira said brightly. "Anyway, you can erase your list item from my paper, but you can't erase it from your heart. Your job is to go pick up the doughnuts. Remember, the bakery closes at one on Saturdays, so you need to get there before then."

"I'm busy," Talia said, in English this time. For context, she was currently lounging so hard she was nearly falling off the couch.

"Yeah, okay," said Shira, fighting not to roll her eyes, because then Talia would pitch a fit and refuse to help her cruel, mean sister. "Just make sure to get there by one. I saved the easiest task for you, all you have to do is give them my name and number. Everything's prepaid. They should have our order waiting in the back."

Talia slouched farther, her fingers brushing the flowered rug as she mumbled something indistinct. "Right, then," Shira said, consulting the list, even though by this point she didn't have to. "William and I are going to decorate and get the house ready. No using the guest bathroom starting now. Not even if it's an emergency."

"I expect the place to look like an art museum," Shira's dad said, standing and cracking his back. Shira's parents had been saying they were going to get a new couch for years now, since she was in high school, and yet somehow every time she came home, there it was, the saggy, lumpy blue beast she'd grown up with. If couches could race, hers would definitely lose to the sleek white sectionals populating William's parents' house. "A Hanukkah art museum."

"I'll do my best," William said seriously.

Shira's dad slapped him on the back. "Great. Well, off to prepare the fridge. No, fridges. For an operation of this size and complexity, we'll need both the kitchen and the garage."

"And I'll get to the grocery store before it gets crazy," Shira's mom said. "Though, honestly, it's probably already crazy. On weekends, all hell breaks loose after eight a.m."

They ambled off toward the hallway. Talia rolled off the couch. Shira winced, waiting for her to hit the ground, but her little sister popped right up like a jack-in-the-box. "Bye," she said, darting after her parents.

Shira shrugged in her direction, then turned to William. "Okay, ignore what my dad said about the art museum," she said. "Our goal is to make the place look like Hanukkah threw up all over it. I try to outdo myself every year, which gets harder and harder because every year I do a fantastic job. I've done most of our ordering online, but we can go stop by the party store in case they got in a surprise Mensch on a Bench or anything that says 'Happy Llamakuh.'"

"I didn't understand any of that, but sounds good," said William. He pushed his shoulders back, which made them look especially broad in his forest-green sweater. "I'll even leave my phone at home."

God, she was weak, because that sentiment actually choked her up. She really hoped no tears would come out when she opened her mouth. "Wow. Okay. I really appreciate it." As a smile spread over her lips, he reached out and brushed the bottom one with a finger, gentle as a butterfly landing. Heat shot through her; the only reason she didn't lean into it and slip it into her mouth was because she could still hear her parents arguing over who was going to take which car in the other room.

"I'd do anything to see you smile," William said. "I know I've had to work a lot over this vacation. We've got that big exhibition inspired by Calder coming up over the holidays, and I need it to be perfect if I want to be in the running for the next promotion."

She tucked her cheek against his shoulder. He smelled like the lavender soap her mom stocked in the hall bathroom mixed with his usual spice and clean laundry detergent. "I know. It's okay. Just think of today like a curation. Best Hanukkah kitsch wins."

"Are there any good vintage stores around here? Midcentury kitsch beats kitsch from any other era, hands down."

"There are, but they're unlikely to have any Hanukkah

stuff," Shira said, lifting her head. Her parents had resolved their argument; her mom had won, as usual, and was taking the bigger car to fit all her purchases. Dad would need to drive home with knishes on his lap. "This isn't a super-Jewish area. There weren't a lot of other Jews in my school growing up. The only other Jew I was ever really close with outside of Hebrew school and the youth group was . . ." She trailed off before she could say his name. She couldn't explain why, but somehow saying his name right now would feel wrong. Blasphemous. "Anyway," she said. "Let's go."

An hour later, they were unloading glittery dreidel garlands and a maniacally grinning Mensch on a Bench from the trunk of their rental car, then stringing those garlands over the fireplace and debating the best place to hide the Mensch to make as many people jump as possible, the coat closet or the bathroom. William didn't check his phone once as they arranged all the family menorahs in the front windows, draped the folding tables they lugged up from the basement in menorah-covered paper tablecloths, set out the chairs, and got all the serving plates and utensils ready.

She was comfortable enough in the work, in their busy hands, to broach a subject that had been on her mind for a long time. Still, she took a deep breath. "Do you ever get frustrated by how much you have to work?"

He shrugged as he strung a Hanukkah garland over the dead fireplace. "Not really. I love my job. It's all I've ever wanted to do."

Well, that answered that. She waited for him to ask her what had prompted such a question, but he was focused on making sure the two ends of the garland were even. She took another deep breath. "I really like my job, but I don't know if I can handle doing it forever."

That got his attention. He taped up the second end of the garland, then turned to face her. "What's bringing this on? Your show?"

"Maybe," Shira said. She'd gone into the art world because it was something she'd always been told she was good at, something that had directly spoken to her passion. She liked helping artists get their day in the spotlight, and working with other arty people was great. It was just that . . . she was getting *tired* trying to do it all. "You used to do art yourself."

"I did," said William. He still had a few of his sculptures on display at his and his family's homes, and occasionally some art student popped up for a "Where Is He Now?" piece. Point was, he'd been quite successful. "And I loved it, but I had to face facts. I wasn't changing the zeitgeist in any meaningful way." He spoke so frankly; she could never imagine speaking so frankly about her art, about something that was at the very core of her. "My talents were best used at a museum, changing the zeitgeist that way."

She got it. She wanted to change the zeitgeist, too. She wanted to be important. She needed to be important. "But you have no time for anything else."

"What are you talking about?" He gave her a funny look. "I'm here, aren't I?" She couldn't argue with that. "Shira," he continued. "Are you okay? You're not considering leaving the gallery, are you? To work on your paintings? When you haven't even had a show yet?"

She shook her head because it was true—she couldn't afford to, even if she wanted to, which she didn't—but it must not have been sufficiently emphatic. "You know how many people would kill for your job, right? You were so lucky to get it. They must've gotten hundreds of applications."

She remembered the fawning congratulations seething with jealousy she'd received from her old classmates when she'd updated her job on LinkedIn. Occasionally, when she wanted to make herself feel better, she scrolled through the profiles of her old classmates who she knew had wanted to work in the industry and run a museum or gallery one day. Most of them hadn't been able to find relevant jobs. She *had* been incredibly lucky, she reminded herself with a pang. She couldn't just give that up. "You're right. You're so right."

By the time they finished up, cars were rumbling in the driveway. Shira sent William outside to help her mom carry in all the heavy beverages. She had stuck to the list this year as Shira had requested, though she did make a point to tell Shira an entire eleven times that they would've saved eighteen dollars with the store brands. And then they helped her dad haul in all the food from the deli. "Okay, so now we're just waiting for Talia to get back from the bakery, and we'll be all set," Shira said and then squinted outside, because wasn't that Talia's car parked on the street?

"Talia?" Shira yelled down the hall. Her sister's bedroom door was closed. "Hey, Talia!" She stormed down the hall and threw open Talia's door. Her sister was sitting at her desk, big headphones over her ears, laughing at someone on the monitor. "Hey!" Shira shouted. Talia didn't move, just said something in

Hebrew to the person on the screen. Shira lifted one of the earphones. Talia rolled back in her chair and shrieked. "Talia!"

"What the *fuck*," Talia said, glowering from beneath her thick dark brows. "I'm in a *meeting*."

"Did you not go to the bakery?" Shira asked. The girl on the screen was saying something into her mic, maybe asking what was going on.

Talia shook her head. "No, I didn't go to the bakery. I told you I couldn't go to the bakery."

"It doesn't count if you tell me in Hebrew," Shira said, fists clenching at her sides. She struggled to remain calm only for the sake of William or, really, for the sake of their relationship; she didn't need him to see his normally confident, on-top-of-everything girlfriend red-faced and shrieking like a banshee. "Or Korean or Russian or whatever."

"I told you in English," Talia said sullenly. Without turning around, she reached behind her back and flipped off the person on the screen, who was now laughing. From the way she kept laughing, Shira assumed they were friends. "I said I was busy. And I am busy. Talking to Yael."

Shira scowled at Yael, who was clearly on Talia's side. "I didn't think you were being *serious*."

"Well, that seems like a you problem." Talia turned back to the screen, slipped her headphones on again, said something guttural and vaguely mocking. Shira took a breath so deep she thought it might explode her lungs.

"Talia." She drew her sister's name out into its full three syllables. Then stopped. Because what was she going to do, sit here and argue with her useless sister when the bakery was getting closer and closer to closing? She shook her head. "You're the worst. Zero doughnuts for you tonight." And backed out, slamming the door before Talia could say something else scathing to Yael that Shira didn't understand.

Her skin was boiling. She wanted to punch the wall. So that she wouldn't, she pulled out her phone and texted the group chat. It would be bad to kill my sister for ruining my party, right?

Nora responded immediately. The three of us combined don't have enough money to bail you out of jail. Please don't make me give up my life savings trying.

And Danica: Can't do artist talks from a prison cell. Or bask in the admiration of everyone at the gallery.

And Ellery, who had two younger sisters: Don't kill them, torture them. It's way more fun that way.

Okay, now Shira was a little calmer. Even cracking a smile. God, she loved her friends.

William had retreated to the living room, where he was sitting on the armchair, brows creased as he stared down at—was that his phone? "Okay," Shira said. "My useless sister didn't do what she was supposed to do, so we have to go to the bakery ourselves. They're like twenty minutes away, but it shouldn't be too . . ." She trailed off as she noticed the time on the cable box. One oh seven. "Oh, shit."

"Shit is right," William said grimly.

Well, he might be dooming about the situation, but she appreciated that he at least understood its gravity. She pounced on her own phone and slammed the dial button, holding her breath as the bakery's line rang. And rang. And rang.

When it became clear nobody was going to pick up and the

line was never going to click into a voicemail box or answering machine, she tried again. And again. Maybe the third time would be the charm?

The third time was not the charm. She let out a long whoosh of breath, ticking through her options. She'd already ordered and paid for all the custom doughnuts and pastries—it had been expensive. Too expensive, honestly! Expensive enough that Shira had put it on her own credit card because her mom's eyes would have bugged out of her head at the price and going to the doctor to pop them back in would be more expensive than the doughnut order. So she didn't really want to pay for a second order somewhere else, even if they could do such a perfect order in a short time period. Most bakeries weren't even open right now. Probably the only place that could pull it off was, like, Dunkin' Donuts. They weren't even good. She could never serve their doughnuts to guests.

But she couldn't not have *any* doughnuts. Hanukkah was all about fried food, and any Hanukkah party *required* latkes and doughnuts. She set her jaw. "Okay, let's figure this out."

"I can't." William was typing furiously into his phone with one hand and digging around in his sleek white leather laptop case with the other. "I had my phone off too long and missed a crisis. One of the artists is threatening to pull out because he found out that another artist in the exhibit has worked with the government in the past in some capacity? I'm not entirely sure what's going on, but it's escalated. I need to deal with this."

"Okay," Shira said faintly. It wasn't like she could argue with that—his career potentially blowing up was a higher priority than the lack of doughnuts at her party. And he *had* spent the morning with her, his phone off. Still, she couldn't help but feel a little wounded as he turned his back to her and hustled toward her bedroom. He'd soothe artists' feelings and make difficult decisions at the same wobbly IKEA desk where she used to struggle through her algebra homework.

So she had to do this alone. That was fine. *Think, Shira.* She could research other bakeries and doughnut shops for a rush order and just eat ramen for the next few weeks, or she could try to find the personal info of the owner or an employee of the bakery and plead her case. A "tip"—aka a bribe—to get them to open up long enough for her to get her doughnuts would surely be less expensive than a whole new order.

Time to consult the ultimate authority: Google. A quick search showed that the bakery was owned by the Kanelos family, which sounded vaguely familiar. Hadn't she gone to school with a Theo Kanelos? They clearly hadn't been friends, not if she didn't remember him for sure, but a quick search on social media wouldn't hurt. She didn't follow him, and he didn't follow her, and the account was private, so she couldn't see much more than a small out-of-focus picture of what appeared to be Theo on top of a very tall mountain.

They did have a few friends in common. Some high school classmates she hadn't talked to in years . . .

. . . and one person she had.

8

IT WAS EMBARRASSING BUT ALSO PROBABLY TIME TO admit it: Leo's sixty-year-old mother was undeniably much cooler than he was. He came to this realization upon receiving a flurry of texts from her "on holiday" (as she now referred to it) on an obscure Greek island with her boyfriend, or as she liked to refer to him, her *life partner.*

The first couple were simply pictures of the land and the sea—sparkling white sand, aqua water Leo could tell by sight was the temperature of a warm bath, craggy hills covered in ancient trees and goats. He managed to tamp down his jealousy. Then the next one dropped his jaw because it was his mom and her life partner beaming in between two of the most famous faces on the planet, a singer whose new Christmas song was currently playing from every speaker everywhere and her boyfriend, a famous athlete. As if that weren't enough, the final two were snaps of them all partying on a yacht bigger than Leo's dad's house, champagne toasts raised toward a sky full of stars.

The only words his mom texted with them were This champagne cost more per bottle than my car but honestly I couldn't tell the difference between it and the kind I used to get at the supermarket LOL

How was he even supposed to respond to that? He settled for ??????????

Oh, right, she texted back. It's a pretty funny story actually! We ran into each other on a nude beach and she was shy about the nude part, so I gave her a pep talk and told her that if I can let these babies hang low she should appreciate hers while they're high LOL. Leo had not needed quite that much detail, but okay. I didn't realize who she was until somebody came over to take a picture of her and she told me that was why she didn't want to take her top off, but we were getting along so well by that point she invited me and Giorgio on her boat. It's very nice though the bathrooms are small. If she was single I would try to set her up with you! I showed her some pictures of you and she agreed that you were very handsome.

Oh, god. Leo snorted, setting his phone down on the kitchen table next to his sandwich before he could respond. "I'm glad someone is having a good holiday," he said to Neptune, who was perched on one of his feet beneath the table, the very picture of a vigilant good boy. Though Leo knew perfectly well the only thing the beagle was vigilant for was any piece of deli turkey that fell off his plate.

"Who's having a good holiday?" asked his dad, taking a seat across from him at the table. Though it had been several months since Leo resolved to change things, he still had to fight the instinct to make an excuse and get up from the table.

Today, Leo would not. He would tell his dad the truth. They

usually avoided saying anything about his mom or their marriage or, god forbid, the divorce, but Leo thought his dad deserved to hear how great his mom's life was now. So he told his dad who his mom had met and that she was currently partying on a mansion-size yacht off the Aegean Coast with some of the world's most famous figures. His dad's eyebrows rose higher and higher the more Leo told him, finally hovering so high they nearly touched his receding hairline. "Wow," he said when Leo took a break. Leo assumed he thought he was done. "How exciting."

An awkward silence settled on the table, as smothering as a blanket. Of course, his dad hurried to change the subject. "How about that Knicks game, huh? They really bungled it at the end."

Leo had agreed, but as usual, he automatically took the opposite side. "I don't think that's fair. They had a lot to contend with that day."

They argued back and forth for a while as Leo took bite after bite of his turkey sandwich, his heart not really in it; he could tell his dad's heart wasn't really in it, either. Was this what their relationship would be now? Talking about light, surface-level things while all the resentment continued to simmer underneath?

Leo supposed it was better than the active avoidance their relationship had been before, but it still wasn't great. Yet now he had a path forward. Eventually he'd graduate, and he'd get a job, hopefully with the same studio he was at now, and he'd finally make enough to move out, and then he'd see his dad on holidays and for the occasional baseball game or whatever.

He didn't know why the thought made him sad, so he fed

Neptune a small piece of turkey. The beagle gobbled it up. At least one creature in this room could be happy.

His dad cleared his throat. "Ah, er . . . are you dating at all?"

An unwelcome subject change. Leo forced a smile. "Not really. Kind of hard to date while living at home." That awkward silence settled back between them. Leo could say something more, something serious and real, maybe talk about how he felt insecure trying to match with someone on a dating app and not being able to bring them home. Or that every time one of his classmates convinced him to install a new app (there seemed to be a new one every week, sprouting up like mushrooms after the rain), he'd swipe half-heartedly because all the girls looked perfectly nice, but none of them were Shira, and it was awfully pathetic to be hung up on her still, wasn't it? Had his dad ever been in a similar situation?

His dad cleared his throat again, and the moment was lost. "Ah, yeah. It's okay with me, though, you know." Yeah, that was just what Leo wanted: for some girl he'd just met to be here at the table with them, sweating through this uncomfortable conversation.

It wasn't all on Leo. His dad could push deeper, too. Maybe that was why Leo never wanted to, because the fact that his dad never pushed made it clear he didn't want to. That he was happy, or at least content, like this.

Before Leo could think about it too deeply, his phone buzzed. He grabbed for it with a sense of relief, not even caring if it was a spam text trying to trick him into sending money to someone in Pakistan for tolls he didn't owe.

But it wasn't a scammer. It was Shira. "So much for not

dating," his dad said wisely, or in a way he thought was wise, at least. "That's definitely a girl you like."

Leo's cheeks warmed. He was glad for his olive skin tone; it wouldn't betray him with a blush. "It's just Shira. From down the street."

"I know Shira," his dad said. "The party's tonight, right? You're coming?"

"Of course," Leo said. He turned his attention to his phone. She was calling, not texting. Which took him by surprise. People didn't really do that anymore. "Hello?"

SHIRA WAS AFRAID he'd be busy, but Leo picked up on the third ring. "Oh yeah, Theo Kanelos," he said into her ear, and her whole body went slack with relief. "He was my buddy back in elementary school. We did soccer together. I was better."

"Oh, thank god." Shira sagged against the wall of the living room and wicked some sweat from her forehead. "So you can get us into his family's bakery, I assume?"

"Sure," he said. "Right now?"

"If you're free," she said, her whole body clenching with thanks for her old friend. "Thank you. I really, really appreciate it."

"Okay," he said. "I'll be right over."

"You don't have to take the time to come over," she said. "It's okay if you just DM him and ask him to . . ." She stopped when she realized Leo was no longer on the line. By the time she'd gone to William to mime that everything was going to be okay—she couldn't speak out loud, since he was talking into his

Beats to someone while emailing someone else on his laptop, a feat of multitasking Shira still felt a little bit in awe of—the front door was opening.

"Hello?" Leo was calling inside.

Shira wondered if he'd knocked and nobody had responded, or if he was popping in the way he used to. She slipped out of her bedroom, closed the door gently behind her, and tiptoed a few steps down the hall before daring to shout "Hey!"

She hadn't really looked at him in detail during their first run-in of the year—too nervous—but now that she knew they were still friends, she couldn't help but think, *He looks good*. He wore his hair a little longer than it had been last year so that the curls showed themselves, and while his switch from the warehouse job to QA meant that he'd exchanged lifting boxes and running around for sitting, he was clearly keeping fit, because his chest had filled out and the biceps flexing from underneath his black T-shirt were toned and tight. He grinned at her, and she couldn't stop the warmth that rushed through her. "Thank you again," she said. "I really appreciate it."

The corners of his eyes crinkled. "What would the neighbors think of a Hanukkah party without doughnuts? I could never bear it."

She knew he was making fun of her, but also it was true. "What a great point, I didn't even think about it," she said with a mock gasp. "So did you already message Theo?" Theo and Leo. They rhymed. Maybe that was why they'd been friends as kids. "Have you heard back?"

But he wasn't listening. "Hey, can I borrow a sweatshirt or something?"

That was weird. Why didn't he just bring his own? "Um, sure, I guess?" she said. "My dad has a bunch of sweatshirts and old jackets in the coat closet if you want to grab one."

He opened the coat closet and immediately rocked backward on his heels, almost knocking his head into the wall. "Jesus Christ!"

For a moment Shira was confused, and then she let out a burst of laughter. "Oh, right," she said. "I almost forgot about Uncle Moishe. He's shy." She stepped up so that she could see the Mensch on a Bench, who was not actually on a bench but perched atop the hanging rod, his big white teeth luminescent in the dark, like a shark's, and his fists balled, as if he might spring out and punch whoever was hanging up their coat. "Also a tad insane."

"Who isn't these days?" Leo grabbed a black coat off the rod, then bowed elegantly to the creepy stuffed man. "Very nice to meet you, Uncle Moishe. Now back into the dark with you. Ideally forever." He shut the door, shaking his head. "Where did you even find that thing? Why did you buy it? Or was it thrust upon you by some kind of curse?"

Her cheeks couldn't help but warm from Leo's word choice. "Come on, like Elf on the Shelf isn't just as creepy," Shira said. "It's just normalized in our society."

"The surveillance state," said Leo. "Right, it's much better to normalize locking your creepy uncle in a closet."

"Better than letting your creepy uncle loose at the party," Shira said. "Come on! No time to waste."

The bakery was a good twenty minutes away, down winding roads lined with pine trees that were obstacle courses full of deer whenever the sun wasn't high in the sky and sometimes even when it was. Fortunately Leo was a safe driver, calm and slow and not quick to jerk the wheel whenever a squirrel darted across the road, which had been the source of Shira's one and only car accident. The squirrel had lived to climb another tree, but alas, her car's hood had ended up crumpled. Shira propped her chin on her hand as she gazed out the window. Last year, he'd driven more recklessly. Maybe now that he was happier in his life, he was calmer behind the wheel. She couldn't help but note the lack of metal music, too; she'd entered the car to a podcast about sports playing. She glanced back at him. "So how are your classes going?"

His eyes lit up. "Pretty good! You know, I took a bunch of classes in computer science before I dropped out of college in Michigan, so I had the basics down already, and now I'm taking some specifically in game development. I have some great professors, and I'm making connections through my QA job. My one professor, he's an adjunct while he makes indie games, and he says I have a lot of promise. He's actually been helping me with this game I've been working on for my final project—well, it started out as a final project, and then it turned into more . . ."

Leo spent the rest of the ride telling her about his game, which seemed to be set in a fantasy world but didn't involve fighting or war or boss battles—players could advance or level up by fixing up their homestead or running errands or making connections with other characters.

"It sounds so fun," Shira said. "Very gentle and chill."

"Exactly," he said. "But it's in a big sweeping fantasy world like a *World of Warcraft* or *Lord of the Rings*, and there is this big overarching story, and you find out as you play that there is a world-ending catastrophe and a climactic battle against a dark lord coming, and there are people fighting it, but you're not one of them. You're just trying to live your life against the backdrop of the world ending."

Sounds depressing, Shira didn't say. But Leo was her oldest friend, so didn't she owe him some honesty? If he wanted it? "Do you want feedback?"

"Sure," he said, glancing over at her as he coasted to a stop at a red light.

"Obviously I'm not a big gamer or anything, but I was thinking, what if you don't realize that you're helping with the big battle, but maybe you actually are without knowing? Like it turns out that two of the people you fix up are the two people who need to combine their powers to defeat the Dark Lord. Or in your garden you grow the powerful herbs the hero needs to heal themselves after a critical moment. You know, something like that."

Fortunately, he didn't roll his eyes. He wrinkled his brow thoughtfully, eyes trained ahead on the road, and mused, "Interesting. So you are helping, just not in the traditional way." He flipped on his turn signal, which wasn't really necessary, considering there was nobody behind or ahead of them on this side road, but perhaps that was just the suppressed New Jerseyan driver in her speaking. "Maybe it turns out that every little task you do is a help in some way or can be made to help."

"Yeah," she said and then realized they were in the bakery's parking lot. It was empty, the small bakery shuttered and dark, no cakes on display in the picture window. "Is Theo meeting us here?"

Leo turned off the car. "No." He reached behind him for the coat he'd borrowed from Uncle Moishe's closet and shrugged it on as he got out of the car. It was black, so now he was wearing a black jacket over black jeans, which was funny because it looked kind of like how a burglar would dress.

And then Shira realized he was holding lockpicks.

Honestly, her first thought was not to put it all together. It was to marvel at the fact that she apparently knew what lockpicks looked like. Maybe she'd seen them in a movie? Or a TV show where the characters were breaking in somewhere? She gasped as it finally hit her. "Leo! We are not breaking into the bakery."

"It's not really breaking in," he said, and now he had *gloves* on, too, also black, tight, and flexible, like the ones she wore when she used to go running in the cold. "It's not like we're stealing anything or vandalizing anything. We just need to pick up what you bought and paid for." He flashed her a devilish grin. "Just think of it as an ice-cream heist."

Well, those were words she hadn't heard together in years. Despite the fact that she was apparently about to be dragged into breaking several laws, her cheeks cracked open in a wide smile.

They'd been . . . nine, maybe ten? Old enough to have some semblance of independence, old enough to know better but not to care. Leo's dad had ordered so many special Popsicles and ice cream bars and fancy treats for the neighborhood Fourth of July cookout that he'd needed to store them in the extra basement fridge of the house next door.

From the way Leo had explained it, it sounded logical. "When the ice cream comes out tomorrow night, it's going to be madness," he said from his seat on the swing beside her, both their legs kicking in solemn agreement. "People everywhere, little kids grabbing for dessert. We need inside information, or who knows what could happen. People are going to be in there grabbing for something, anything. We could end up with a root beer bar or something else gross." They both stuck out their tongues. "We need to taste test everything beforehand so that we can make sure to get something good at the party in the madness."

"But they're in the Smiths' basement," Shira had said. "How are we supposed to taste test anything in there?"

Leo's eyes had gleamed. "They're both at work all day, and Curtis and Lucas are in day care till five. We'll have a full two hours from when we get home from camp until they all do. Plenty of time."

Thus began Shira's very first (and honestly, only) foray into lawbreaking. Leo's dad had an extra key to the Smiths' house in case of emergency, and so all they had to do was swipe it, sneak through the Smiths' back door so that no neighbors would see them, and then enjoy their ill-gotten treats on the Smiths' cracked leather basement couch. The Oreo Fudgsicles, it had been unanimously decided: That was what they'd aim for in the madness the next day.

"I remember that day very well," Shira said now, the shadow of this bakery looming over her. "Do you? Because I remember being screamed at by Mr. Smith when he came home early from work."

"Yeah, but he didn't tell on us after we threatened to tell his wife, so it all worked out," Leo said sunnily. They both hadn't understood why that had worked; they'd only learned later that Mr. Smith had been fired and neglected to let her know.

"Didn't the Smiths take their key back from your parents without telling them why, and your mom thought they hated them?"

"So?"

"Why can't you just DM Theo and get him to let us in?"

"I did check out his profile first," Leo said. "He's currently hiking his way up Mount Kilimanjaro. Not much signal atop Africa's tallest mountain." He paused. "And no, before you ask, I couldn't find either of his parents online. This is our only option."

She sighed. Damn Theo and his very impressive hiking goals. "I really don't want to get arrested," she said. "I can't imagine many galleries would hire a felon."

"We're not going to get arrested," he said. "We'll be in and out in ten minutes. And remember, we're not stealing, since everything's already paid for. We'll even lock up behind us. Come on, the longer we stand here, the more chance there is of someone catching us."

And so, Shira found herself pressed against the back of the bakery, sweat dampening her underarms and pearling on her forehead, keeping watch as Leo fiddled with the lockpicks. "How do you even own those, let alone know how to use them?" she asked, trying to distract herself from the thought of celebrating Hanukkah tonight in a prison cell.

Though he didn't turn her way, keeping his focus on the task at hand, she knew his glancing half smile was for her. "My grandparents had one of those beautiful old houses where every room had its own French doors. The keys were lost long ago, probably before they even bought the house. After my grandpa's wife died, dementia started setting in for my grandpa, and he'd constantly be locking himself into or out of rooms, so . . ."

"I'm sorry," she said. Words felt useless here. She almost wished she could show him her feelings in a picture, something quickly sketched or painted: You'd think blue would be natural for sadness or sympathy, but she'd go yellow, a washed-out, almost-golden yellow, one strong in its central line and fading to fuzziness toward the outside of the page.

He shrugged. "It is what it is." His hand sprang back toward him, and her heart jumped, afraid, absurdly, that he'd activated some high-tech security system and been electrocuted. But all he did was tuck the picks back into his pocket and turn the door handle, his half smile turning into a full-on sly grin. "Let's go."

She inhaled deeply, taking another wide look around her. All she could see besides the crumbling asphalt of the nearly empty parking lot were trees. No movement—not even the flash of a bird or scamper of a squirrel. If the police showed up now, she could be okay. She hadn't actually done anything illegal. But the second she crossed the threshold of that building . . .

Don't think about getting arrested. Think about throwing a Hanukkah party without any doughnuts. It's basically an affront to God.

And also—she didn't want to think about it, because it made her feel like a bad person—there was a tiny little part of her that was reveling in the delicious thrill.

Another deep breath. Her foot crossed the threshold, landing on worn tile. There. Officially a lawbreaker. Her stomach squirmed with all sorts of things. She wouldn't be painting in yellow now; she'd be painting in purple, one that was a little trembly around the edges—she'd always seen purple as a nervous color for some reason—and darkening close to black in the middle to symbolize the unknown. "Okay. Let's do this."

Going inside was anticlimactic after all that: They closed the door behind them, turned on their phone flashlights to avoid flipping on a light that might be seen from the front of the building, and that was that. No alarm started wailing. No masked paratroopers stormed the building, guns drawn. They just walked down a short hallway, opened a door, and literally, there was her order sitting on a gleaming metal table, her full name stickied onto it with a Post-it. Very professional. "All right," Leo said, hefting the plastic bags of white boxes like they weighed nothing. "You already paid for them, right? So we're good to take them and go?"

Like she thought, anticlimactic. She'd spent so long building herself up and talking herself into doing the thing, she couldn't just take her order and go. She looked from side to side, her stomach jangling with nerves and terror and also excitement. "Yes. But doesn't lockpicking make you hungry?" There was a clear glass refrigerator door, through which she could see little cakes and tarts lined up on shelves. A big shelving unit was stocked with day-old croissants and pieces of banana bread, probably waiting to be tossed or sold at a discount. "I could go for a snack."

His eyes widened. "We're already breaking and entering, you want to steal, too?"

She couldn't tell if he sounded impressed or aghast. "Of course I don't want to steal," she said. "I've got cash, we'll leave whatever the items cost on the table."

And then—a creak.

From the direction of the door.

Someone's coming. Shira's heart jumped into her throat, and her body jumped, too. In Leo's direction.

He dropped the bags of doughnuts and caught her before she could collide with anything. It was a statement to her panic that she didn't even react to the sound of her precious doughnuts hitting the floor. "Did you hear that?" she whispered with barely more than a breath, and it was only then she became aware of how close they were to each other.

As in, she couldn't really separate where she ended and he began. She was tucked flush against him, her rabbit-fast heart against his hard chest, his reassuring arms wrapped around her, strong on her back. When he whispered in return, goose bumps erupted all over her arms at the brush of his words on her forehead. "Yes."

She drew in a deep breath, trying to slow her racing pulse. She didn't think anything would be able to calm her down, but he smelled familiar, of coffee and the pines behind his house. And now, because they were in a bakery and he'd just been carrying doughnuts, a little bit of sugar. It was that smell that eased her breathing, made her heart slow just enough that she thought it might not give out on her. "It was just one creak. Maybe it wasn't—"

Creak. She went to jump closer to him, only she couldn't possibly get any closer, so it was her cheek that nestled into the center of his chest, his chin tucked into her hair. She fit perfectly, she realized a little inanely. And pointlessly. Because William wouldn't like her being this close to Leo, his warmth and his strength sending waves of heat through her. Understandably.

She broke away, taking in a deep shuddering breath, and was immediately seized with panic again. Fighting the urge to dive back into him, she squared her shoulders and called into the hallway, "Is someone there?"

No response. She went to take a step toward the hallway, steeling every nerve she had and telling herself that maybe getting arrested could be good publicity for her show—because there was no such thing as bad publicity, right?—but Leo stepped in front of her, taking the lead. "We're not supposed to be here, but we don't want any trouble," he said, and his voice was deeper and more sonorous than Shira had ever heard it. It would've made her quake in her boots if she weren't already quaking in her boots. "We just came to pick up our prepaid order. We'll go right now."

Still no response. Leo took another few steps toward the hallway. She couldn't let him go alone—she followed.

They saw it at the same time, and he huffed out a breath as her shoulders relaxed. A squirrel. Nothing but a stupid squirrel who'd ventured a few steps in through the open door, probably drawn by the smell of all these baked goods, but who froze upon seeing them and darted outside before they could even say anything. "At least we scared it away," Shira said faintly. "What if we'd locked it inside the bakery?"

"That squirrel would've thought it won the lottery," Leo said, and she let out a breathless laugh. "Didn't we close that door?"

"Clearly not all the way." The only thing she wanted to do right then was flee, but they'd left the doughnuts behind, so they backtracked to the kitchen, where Shira was relieved to find, upon checking a few of the boxes, that their drop to the floor hadn't damaged the goods too badly. She'd tell her family that they had to stick to the damaged ones and leave the pristine ones for guests. "Okay, let's get out of here," she said, but Leo stopped her.

"I thought you wanted some banana bread or something."

She couldn't admit that she was a chicken now. But her daring only went so far after her near heart attack; she didn't take the time to scrutinize everything on offer, just grabbed a few of whatever was in front, tossed what was probably way too much money on the counter in exchange, and beat it down the hall, ready to get the hell out.

Once they were outside and Leo had relocked the door behind them, she let out another breathless laugh. "We did it!"

"I feel so alive," he said dryly, though he was still smiling as he placed the order for the party in his back seat.

She was, too, and the feeling didn't fade even after they pulled away.

9

LEO'S HEART WAS STILL POUNDING AS HE DROVE away, but not because of the crime they'd committed, or even the moment when they thought they'd been caught. No, it was that moment when Shira had been tucked up tight against him, heart thumping so hard he could feel it vibrating through him like an earthquake, her hair up against his face smelling like lavender and something else that was quintessentially Shira.

She had a boyfriend. She didn't have feelings for him the way he had feelings for her. That was okay. He had to accept that if he wanted to keep their rekindled friendship, which he one hundred percent did.

It was just hard to think that way when the scent of her hair was still in his nose.

He knew the best thing to do for his own sake was probably drop her home to her boyfriend, but the smell of banana bread was hard to resist, so when she said, "Can we please pull over somewhere and eat our spoils?" he replied, "Yes, of course," and he pulled the car off into the parking lot of a drugstore.

As she unbuckled and turned to reach over the console into

the back seat, her hair brushed up against his cheek again. He held his breath until she'd turned back around, brown paper bag clutched in her tight little fingers. "Should we start with the lemon thing or the banana bread?"

"The lemon thing," he picked at random. He couldn't stop watching her fingers as they flexed and cupped, pulled off a chunk of lemon tart. She didn't need to make art. She *was* art.

Stop it, Leo. That's not a friend-like thought.

The lemon thing, as he'd called it, was delicious, tart and bright, with a sweet buttery crust. They wolfed it down in about three seconds. "Banana bread?" he asked, then realized she was staring down at her fingers. Hopefully not thinking about licking them, because that might make him lose his mind. "You okay? You didn't develop a lemon allergy in the last nine years, did you?"

Her eyes were pointed at a woman doing her hardest to detach a shopping cart without paying the twenty-five-cent fee, but Shira was clearly staring somewhere beyond her. "I think this is the first dessert I've eaten since last year."

"What are you talking about?" Shira had always loved sweets—brownies, ice cream bars, whatever else was full of sugar and would make your dentist shake their head.

"My boss would never say it, of course. That would be highly illegal," Shira said. "But if you spend all your time in an art gallery, you should look like art, too. Your clothes, your hair, your body. People should want to look at you."

Leo hadn't noticed before, but her hair did look smoother and shinier and straighter in a way it had always refused to as a kid. "I would think the opposite. That you would want your employees to blend into the walls so that people would pay more attention to the art."

Shira's bark of a laugh was short and tense. "I would think so, too. But it's still a man's world at the top, and what they want goes." She was quiet for a moment. "I'm due for a promotion in the new year. Probably next month."

"Wow." Leo wasn't sure what to say to that. "Uh, congrats?"

"Thanks," she said in a monotone. She raised one hand to tuck a lock of hair behind her ear, leaving a crumb or two on her cheek. "It'll come with a small salary bump, of course, but more pressure. More hours. Part of my new job description will be fraternizing with emerging artists, so I'll be scouting them out at smaller galleries and traveling to other cities in search of someone my boss can break out big."

Leo wasn't sure what to say to that, either, so he just said nothing. Waiting.

"And it'll be cool, of course. I know how many people would kill to have my job," she said in a rush, almost like she was trying to convince herself. "But it's going to mean a lot more hours, and I don't know what that means for my own career. For my debut show." She was quiet again. "William used to be an artist, too, you know."

"I didn't know," Leo said, which, to be fully honest, was a lie, because of course he'd googled Dr. William Bettany (there was only one of them, apparently, an honor he himself did not share, thanks to three other Leonard Davids; the other Leonard Davids were all over sixty, so Leo supposed that in thirty to forty years he'd probably be the only one, for what it was worth). Dr. William Bettany talked in interviews about how working on his own wire sculptures and showing in a few galleries had inspired him to work in museums. The wire sculptures had looked, Leo thought, like the tangled snarls his headphones turned into when he fell asleep wearing them, but he didn't really get modern art.

"You wouldn't know," Shira said. "He doesn't do it anymore. He doesn't even talk about it. He doesn't have time for art now. Too busy working with other people's art." A shadow crossed her face. "I just . . . I don't know what to do. I like my job now. It's fulfilling. It's a really cool career track that I've worked toward for practically my whole life. I kind of don't know who I am without it. But is it worth doing at the expense of everything else?"

He was quiet again, assuming the question was rhetorical, but then she turned and looked at him from beneath pinched eyebrows, as if she were waiting for his response. He hesitated. "I'm probably the least qualified person to tell anyone what they should do."

"That's exactly why you should be telling me what to do," she said. "You knew me before this version of me. A different Shira than William knows or Danica knows or Ellery and Nora know. You're not in deep in the art world, where we're all trying to one-up and top and impress one another."

That sounded miserable, honestly. "I don't know," he said. "To me it's really simple. Do it until you aren't happy anymore, then find something else. What about your own art? From what your mom's been telling me, you're going to be swimming in money."

Shira snorted. The woman with the cart finally gave up and

stalked away, cartless. "That's really, really not how being an artist works. If the show gets good reviews and my paintings sell spectacularly well, I might get more shows, and I might make enough to live on. Maybe live on comfortably if I do some teaching on the side or freelance work. But no, the vast, vast, vast majority of artists do not get rich off their work. And I wouldn't even dare to try it until I have a schedule full of shows at places people have heard of and pieces on back order."

"You could try and find something that's a little more low key to do full-time," he suggested. "That way you'll have time to work on your art but also enough money to breathe."

She winced. "But I've spent all my life so far working toward this goal, and if I leave now, I'll never be able to get back in. And also, what would people think?"

He could see the specific moment when it dawned on her what she'd said, what she'd meant. Her mouth twisted as if she'd bitten into something sour.

Leo wasn't sure if he should say something or stay quiet, let her marinate in the realization. For a moment he watched her chew on the inside of her cheek, twist her fingers together as if she were trying to imitate one of her boyfriend's sculptures. In the end he couldn't resist. "Your whole life can't be a performance for other people," he said. "You have to live for yourself first."

"I *know*," she spit out. "I know that. Of course I know that. It's just all my life, I've been hearing about my potential, and I can't . . . I just . . ." She shook her head, slowly at first, then more vigorously, as if trying to physically shake the idea out of her brain. "What about you? How is everything besides your classes and your game? How's your dad?"

He couldn't help but flinch at the way she'd said it so casually, at the way she'd used it to get away from the subject she herself didn't want to discuss. "He's fine. Still at his same job. Still living in the same place. Still the same guy." God, he was being so boring. "You know, nothing new."

"Banana bread?"

He held out a hand automatically to take some, and crammed the chunk of cake she'd passed him into his mouth. He appreciated it not because it was especially good (it was a little dry, maybe because it was beginning to stale) but because it gave his mouth something to do other than respond to Shira.

Almost a year ago—not long after last December's Hanukkah party—he'd gotten a call from his mom. "Isn't it, like, the middle of the night in Italy right now?" he said in lieu of hello or ciao.

His mom let out an airy laugh. "This is how I live now, darling."

That was new. So was the old-timey movie-star *darling* thing. But you know, honestly, good for her. She deserved to spend her nights on yachts and wear giant sunglasses that made her feel glamorous after a life of raising him, where she never woke up any later than seven and lived in athleisure. "Very fancy," he said. Much fancier, much more interesting, much more fulfilling than his own life. Something struck him in the gut as he realized that. "What's up?"

She gusted a heavy sigh into his ear, and he could almost see her: perched on the edge of a beach chair, deeply tanned beneath the light of the moon, a gauzy swimsuit cover-up blowing in the gentle Mediterranean breeze. "It's been a long time since the divorce," she said. "And the divorce was the most devastating thing that had ever happened to me, but if not for that, I wouldn't be here where I am, very happy. I'd still be back in that same old rut."

A pang at the thought that the life he was leading was literally in that same rut, one he tried to cover up with righteous indignation at the way she referred to Joe's betrayal as "the divorce." It wasn't like they'd fallen out of love and mutually decided to consciously uncouple, he'd– No. She was allowed to define what happened to her however she wanted. And he was happy for her; he really was. She'd spent so long making him the center of her life, and she deserved to be the center of it now.

"I'm glad for you," he said, voice measured. "But I still feel betrayed."

She sighed into his ear again. Someone else murmured in the background–the boyfriend? Leo had only met him a few times; he was a retired finance guy, very boring, but it had been clear from the way his eyes lit up in her presence and how he constantly turned to face her like a moth to a flame how crazy he was about her. "Your dad called me for the first time in years. Asked for my help with . . ." She took a deep breath. "He did a horrible thing, but it was to me, not you. I officially forgive him and give you permission to let him back in."

"I think that's my decision to make," said Leo, the anger simmering under his skin cooling just the tiniest bit.

"Of course it's your decision. It's your life," she told him, which made it cool a little more. "You only get one, and so does your father. Even if you're angry at him, you can let him in. Whatever else he did, he's still your father. Who knows how many years any of us have left?"

Leo's mom might not have been Jewish, but she'd clearly absorbed enough of it from him and Joe that she was pitch-perfect at guilting. It was his turn to sigh in her ear. "Would it make you happy?"

"It would make me happy," she'd said.

How could he argue with that? While he and his dad had been living together for a couple months at the time, they were basically roommates who talked as little as they possibly could, and rarely ate together. So he'd gone to Joe and told him through a clenched jaw that he'd like to start having dinner together once or twice a week. Usually they made conversation about work or Leo's classes or how much they hated the current president or whatever neighborhood gossip they'd picked up while walking the dog. The Fels husband seemed to have moved out; the teenage LaTessa daughter was obviously pregnant. Joe had actually made him laugh a few times, and Leo had to admit, it was freeing not to have to stonewall him every minute of every day. It was like Leo had put down a backpack full of rocks he hadn't realized he'd been wearing.

He swallowed the banana bread in one solid lump. "You'd better not say I told you so."

"I would never say I told you so," Shira said, eyes dancing. He'd shared the latest on his and Joe's relationship, and of course, she blurted, "Told you." She clapped her hands over her mouth. "Whoops." It came out muffled.

"Technically you didn't say the *I* or the *so*, so does it really count?"

She pulled her hands away, a tiny grin still on her face. "Very true."

"Yeah. So that's a positive of the last year, I guess." He shrugged. Hesitated. Debated whether to go on. Decided why the hell not. "I've been enjoying my classes. I've been enjoying making my game. But I still don't know if it's what I want to do with my life."

"Really?" Shira tilted her head, stuffing another piece of banana bread into her mouth. "But I thought that was your passion."

How to explain it? Sure, he enjoyed playing games, and he was enjoying working on them too. But . . . "I see you with your passion for art and the art world, and I just . . . I don't know if I have that passion for *anything*," he said. Then looked at her and reconsidered. "At least not anything work related."

"Hmm." Shira pursed her lips. He wondered what she was thinking. *What a loser? What a directionless loser? What a pathetic directionless loser pining away for me even though I don't feel the same way back?* When she finally said, "Maybe you just haven't found it yet," it came as a relief. "Can you try taking other classes while you're there? Maybe you'll discover a passion for . . . I don't know, archaeology or meteorology or woodworking?"

"Sure," Leo said. "Maybe." But he didn't think so.

Her eyebrows raised. "How about passion for a person? Are you dating anyone?"

It was good he hadn't taken a bite, because he would have choked. "Uh, not seriously." Did that make him sound like he was a weirdo hung up on someone who wasn't hung up on him back? "I mean, I'm on all the apps. But nothing's stuck."

She smiled mischievously. "You could always move to LA. I

know a bunch of single women." She paused. "Who are great. Mostly artists. Actually, you probably don't want to date an artist. We're difficult."

"Noted," Leo said, pretending to scribble an imaginary note in an imaginary notepad, then flushing with how stupid he must look.

Shira didn't seem to notice, however. "Lots of women still live at home. It's not weird. Housing is so expensive. Especially if you're still in school."

His cheeks warmed further. Oh, good. Great to hear that it wasn't weird and sad and pathetic. He hadn't been thinking that in this particular moment, but *now* he was.

Shira must have noticed this time because she added hastily, "Sorry, really stuck my foot in my mouth. I wasn't trying to say that . . . I mean, I don't mean that . . . ugh." She closed her eyes and winced before opening them again. "You know I meant well, right?"

He nodded. *Quick, change the subject.* They'd run out of treats, so he pivoted to her other favorite topic of conversation. "How's party prep going, other than the doughnuts? Everything ready for tonight?"

Her face lit up as she launched into a detailed explanation of everything from the new kitschy decorations to the chopped liver appetizer the deli had convinced her to try, and he nodded and smiled every time she paused while allowing his mind to drift.

Seriously, was there something wrong with him? It wasn't even that he didn't know what he wanted. He knew plenty of other guys in his classes (it was mostly guys in his classes) who weren't sure what they wanted or how they wanted to get there.

But they knew they wanted *something*.

Maybe he'd bristled so much at what other people thought of him because he knew, somewhere deep down, that there was something wrong with him.

". . . and I'm really excited to see what people think of the drinks this year," Shira was saying. "I looked up some new cocktail recipes that are cheesy but sound like something people might actually want to try, unlike the latke cocktail. Do you think adults would voluntarily drink something bright blue?"

He smiled and nodded automatically before realizing what he was saying yes to. Hopefully she wouldn't hold him–

"Okay, I'm holding you responsible if people hate it," Shira said, elbowing him gently in the side. The car trembled from the force of a big rig zooming past. He trembled a little bit, too. "You know, being serious for a second, I'm really glad to be friends again." Pause. "I mean, I know we're only friends again because you're stuck living at home, and I'm not trying to say that I'm glad you're stuck living at home. I mean, not that living at home is a bad–"

"I get it," Leo said before she could spiral again. "I am, too."

He did want something. He wanted Shira in his life, and if she wasn't going to be in his life romantically, then he wanted her in his life as a friend. They really had to do a better job of keeping in touch. He told her this, and she beamed. "I was totally thinking the same thing."

That night, at the party, he landed at the dinosaur menorah, across the room from where Shira was lighting the abstract-art menorah, surrounded by her parents, a less-surly and suspiciously blue-tongued Talia, and William, who'd draped his arm over her shoulders. Leo held the shammash, and the blessings poured out of him, unremembered for so many years yet somehow still there in his mind, and surrounded by so much love, his heart was calm. This was good. This was *good*.

He made a Hanukkah resolution. Was that even a thing? Either way, he made one. By the next time he saw Shira, he would have quashed any feelings for her other than friendship, and their friendship would be great.

Texts between Leo David and Shira Levinson, April:

Leo: Hey, congrats on the show! Wish I could be there for opening night but all the pictures look amazing. I ordered a print of one of the paintings. I think it was called New Country

Shira: Thank you!! Excited but nervous

Leo: This is what you've been working toward your whole life. It's going to be great

Shira: Ugh thanks for reminding me

Shira: Sorry for the ugh. It's just that so much rides on this one show

Leo: You're an amazing artist. Even if this one doesn't go perfectly, you'll have more in the future

Shira: . . .

Shira: . . .

Shira: Sure.

From the May issue of *Artlight Magazine*:

Painter Shira Levinson makes an ambitious leap in her debut solo show that sometimes sparkles and sometimes falls flat. . . . While the works shimmer with whimsy and color, they don't always hold the gravity invited by the subject matter, and the inspiration comes off as a bit trite . . .

From the June issue of *Artlight Magazine*:

A must-see! Painter Danica Chaika's first solo show is an absolute triumph. . . . The story threaded through her paintings is heartfelt and beautifully told through spectacular brushwork and use of color, and the subtle inclusion of magic will leave visitors poring over each canvas, desperate to catch every deliberate detail . . .

From Leo David's email inbox:

Dear Mr. David,

After reviewing more than 700 applications, we are very pleased to award you the Emerging Game Creator grant for $50,000 to help you continue production of the game you submitted to us, *Washing Dishes at the End of the World*. We were so impressed by the inventiveness and skill you demonstrated in your application, and we cannot wait to see more from you . . .

Dear Mr. David,

I'm a recruiter from SpiralCraft Studios. We recently learned that you obtained the extremely competitive Emerging Game Creator grant from Tiny Elephant Studios, and we wanted to reach out to make sure we're on your radar when you start looking for a job . . .

Texts between Shira Levinson and Leo David, September:

Shira: Happy birthday! Hope you have a great day!

Shira: You doing anything fun?

Leo: Thanks! Not sure yet, but probably not. Maybe someone will bring cupcakes to the break room haha

Leo: Work has been pretty crazy lately

Leo: How about you? Are you working on your next show? I'm already excited

Shira: . . .

Shira: . . .

Shira: I hope they bring chocolate!

10

Year Three

THIS YEAR, THE LATKES WOULD BE BROWN AND LACY and perfectly crispy around the edges and made to order. Why had Shira ever tolerated latkes made in advance and heated up in the oven? That wouldn't do now. And the music? Why had she ever thought that a random playlist of classical music was enough?

This year, she would create her very own playlist, full of not only kitschy Hanukkah tunes but wintry non-Christmas songs and Jewish artists with Hanukkah-adjacent music, like the Maccabeats or Matisyahu. She would feed it through speakers via her phone so that every time someone asked how her career as an artist was going, she could press a button and turn the volume up, up, up until she could no longer hear them. No, better yet, nobody would bother asking about her art, because they'd be so busy having a *fantastic* time at this *awesome* party.

She was going to hurt her cheeks smiling this hard.

"Shira, food's ready," her mom called from the kitchen. Shira groaned from where she'd flopped on her bed. She still had airplane on her, and now airplane germs were on her pillow. Usually that would make her freak out, but today—tonight? was it night already?—she couldn't be bothered.

Her phone buzzed once, twice, three times. She couldn't be bothered about that, either.

"Shira!" her mom called again. Shira flopped herself over the side of the bed, landing dramatically (and painfully) on one knee.

"Fuck," she said. Nobody responded. She shouted, "Fuck!"

Her door opened. Talia poked her head inside. "Are you dead?"

"Yes," said Shira.

"Cool," said Talia. "I call your computer." She shut the door.

Great. Fine. Everything was fine. She gritted her teeth and forced herself to reach for her phone, trying to avoid the rising tide of dread in her stomach. Two of the pings had been emails from work; a third was a text from her boss asking why she hadn't yet responded to the emails. None were from the group chat. The group chat had been silent for months at this point, yet she always instinctively looked for it anyway.

The next notification came from Leo, which was the first to make her smile. The only to make her smile, at least in the past month. Hey! You home yet? Then another ding. Can't wait to get my print of New Country signed.

The smile dimmed. Right, he'd purchased a print of one of her paintings from the show. She went to tuck her phone away, then hesitated.

"Shira!" called her mom. "We're going to eat without you."

"One second!" she hollered back. "It's work!" She quickly

typed out responses to the work emails—they weren't even that urgent! It was already close of business in LA!—and then turned to Leo's. Yup! See you soon, I hope?

She tossed her phone on her bed and ran away before anyone could get back to her. Then returned to shove her phone into the pocket of her sweatpants because if her boss called, she knew she had to be able to pick up.

At the table, she kind of wished she could take her phone out without getting a reprimand and scroll so that she didn't have to look anyone in the eye. She sat across from Talia, her mom on her right and her dad on her left, and all were watching her cautiously like she was a piece of old ordnance they'd dug up in a field. "What?" she said, bristling.

Talia said something in Hebrew. She'd become nearly fluent in the past year; she was planning on studying abroad next semester at her university's partner campus in Tel Aviv.

"I'm going to start spraying you with water like a misbehaving cat when you speak Hebrew to me," Shira said. "You know I can't understand it. It's extremely annoying. I wouldn't speak French to you."

"Yeah, 'cause you can't speak French," Talia said. Fair point. Shira had taken French to the minimum level needed to pass her school's language requirement and only really remembered how to say the colors and parts of the body. "You used to understand Hebrew."

"I mean, not really." She'd known maybe a hundred words back when she was in Hebrew school, mostly related to prayers and the ancient Israel of the Torah—so if Talia had been talking about olives or fruits or numbers, maybe Shira would have understood. She used to be able to read Hebrew pretty well, though. Could she still? When was the last time she'd tried? It wasn't like she'd been able to make it home for the most significant Jewish holidays where she'd need to, Passover or Rosh Hashanah or Yom Kippur, in years.

An unexpected pang hit her in the chest. *That's what the party is for,* she told herself. She'd get more involved in Judaism again when she was older and had more time. For now, she'd throw a great party and that would be her connection.

"We're just worried about you," said her mom, and it took a moment for Shira to realize that she wasn't talking about her lack of Hebrew knowledge. "You seem very . . . stressed."

"You hesitated before you said stressed," Shira said. She couldn't argue with the fact that she was stressed, so she'd pick something else to argue about. "What were you actually about to say?"

Her mom and her dad glanced at each other, eyes widening and narrowing, and Shira had to bite her tongue to keep herself from snapping, *Stop having telepathic conversations about me.* Dad was the one to turn to her this time. "Unhappy," he said. "You seem very unhappy." He paused. "And also stressed."

She stabbed her pasta with her fork, wishing a tiny bit that it was a person and not a piece of rigatoni with Broccolini and garlic sauce, which was unfortunately very good. "I don't know what you're talking about."

Talia actually spoke up in English this time, which, to Shira, made things feel really serious. What was this, an intervention? "It hasn't been that long since you and William broke up."

"It's been months," Shira said frostily.

"Still," Talia said. "You were together a long time."

"Not that long." Queen Elsa of Arendelle had nothing on Shira's iciness right now.

"Still," said Talia, but Shira had had enough.

"I'm the one who broke up with him, remember?" Though, admittedly, that did understate how hard the decision had been. She'd loved showing up at galas on his arm, enjoyed running into colleagues at restaurants or bars and having their eyes widen when he introduced himself.

But he'd ultimately forced her hand. It wasn't the fourth time he'd left her on the verge of orgasm to take a call, or the umpteenth time he'd flaked on a friend's birthday party or a dinner date or work lunch.

No. It was the day her show debuted. Everybody she knew was there, from her best friends (a lance went through her heart at the thought of Danica standing before her paintings with her plastic cup of wine, flanked by Ellery and Nora, beaming so proudly) to coworkers to random acquaintances she hadn't seen in years but who happened to be in the LA area. And William was there, too. He showed up ten minutes late, but he came. And the first thought Shira had when she looked out at the crowd and saw him wasn't *I'm so happy to see him* but *Wow, I can't believe he's actually here*. It had taken a few months for her to finally pull the plug, but that was the moment it started easing free.

She would always feel like he loved her second to his job. And if she'd ever worked up the nerve to ask him if that was true, she was pretty sure he wouldn't be able to respond, which was a response in itself.

"Seriously," Shira said. "I'm seriously fine."

Her family nodded and exchanged a glance they probably thought she didn't catch. "The pasta is delicious," said her mom, taking a delicate bite from the end of her fork. Obvious subject change. Her dad made this pasta all the time. They knew it was delicious.

They didn't even mention Danica, Ellery, and Nora. Which was kind of funny. Because in her admittedly limited experience, friend breakups were a hundred times more devastating than romantic ones. She couldn't stop glancing at her phone whenever it buzzed, assuming it was the group chat. Every time she passed her and Danica's bar, the one neither of them particularly liked but was cheap and near both their workplaces, she stared at her feet and hurried past so that she wouldn't cry.

Breaking up with William had been like cutting her hair. Maybe like giving herself bangs. Yes, she'd cringe every time she walked by a mirror and was reminded of what she'd lost, and she didn't feel good about it right now. But it would grow back, and it would look good eventually, and even if it was never exactly how it was before, she'd still be able to throw it up into a ponytail without thinking too much about how bad she'd looked with bangs.

Breaking up with Danica and Ellery and Nora had been like chopping off half her fingers. Their absence hurt every time she tried to type a text or button her shirt or got a reminder of something they'd done years before, reminding her that *this used to be done another way, a better way*. And, even if she eventually got high-tech prosthetics—like, advanced prosthetics controlled by her mind—her fingers would never, ever work the same.

Why were there no angsty songs about friend breakups? Maybe she would write one, she thought as she jammed a bite of pasta into her mouth and chewed with such ferocity that she could feel her family's worried eyes on her again. She couldn't sing or write music, but she could learn. She could learn.

Her phone buzzed in her pocket again. Despite the family rule of no phones at the dinner table, Shira took it out. Sure enough, it was work. An artist her boss wanted to poach was going to be at a party in New York City the next night. She'd gone to Columbia and graduated in the same year, the same program, as Shira. Shira must know her, right? Could she go and schmooze her? It wasn't that far from Shira's family's house, right?

Without even seeing the artist's name, Shira could respond that she'd know her. The art program wasn't that big, and she'd known everyone in her year, if not well. And it wasn't like she could tell her boss she couldn't go because she needed to prep for the Hanukkah party. Gritting her teeth, she typed back, Of course. Clicked on the event link, and her stomach plummeted to her feet, then through her soles and into the basement and down, down, down until it burned up in the molten core of the earth. No. Oh, no.

"Shira?"

She glanced up to find her family studiously not looking at her, which was almost as bad as when they were all looking at her. "What?" she snapped, wanting to actually literally snap something in between her teeth. "Something to say?"

"Nooooooo," said Talia. "Except that the pasta is delicious."

So after dinner, when Shira snuck a bottle of wine from the basement—she didn't need to sneak alcohol at her age, she knew that, but force of habit—and met Leo at his house with a few plastic cups, she felt like she deserved it. "You didn't need to bring cups," he told her, shutting the door against the winter chill. "We do have cups."

"I felt like drinking the wine out of a plastic cup," Shira told him, bending down to give Neptune a good scratch between the ears. She still felt like she might vomit up her pasta. "It's a whole mood."

"Ah." Leo took the bottle, grimacing. "It's warm, too. Is that part of the mood?"

"Yes."

His dad wasn't home—he was out on a date, apparently?!—but sitting at a legitimate venue like the dining room table did not fit the whole mood, so they went down into the basement, where the musty smell and old cracked leather couch and spidery boxes piled in the corners completed Shira's vision. She slumped into the couch, feeling it sag in the middle under the cumulative history of too many butts. "Thanks for letting me come over. I desperately needed to get out of the house."

"Ah." Leo had declined her warm wine—fine, more for her!—but had deigned to accept one of her plastic cups for his cold orange soda. "One of those nights? Family getting on your nerves?"

Shira sighed. She felt the anger draining out of her like the wine draining from the bottle. "No, they're just worried about me, and I guess it's better than them not caring about me, but god, sometimes it feels suffocating."

"Well, you're used to being on the other side of the country." He'd clipped his hair shorter this year, not quite to his head but close enough where the curls didn't tumble anymore, and it made everything he said sound somehow more logical and serious.

She took a sip of her wine. It had started the process of turning into vinegar. She winced but gulped it down anyway. "Maybe."

"What were they so worried about?" He rested his elbows on his knees. His wardrobe had changed a bit, too. He was still in a T-shirt and jeans, but the soft gray T-shirt fit him well, had clearly been purchased for the purpose of him wearing it to the office or to see friends rather than having been found crumpled in the back of a drawer. The jeans were dark and distressed, baggy in an intentional way but the exact perfect length despite his tallness. Maybe tailored.

One of his socks had a hole in the toe, though. That cheered her. He clearly hadn't changed *that* much.

"They think I'm unhappy. Mostly because of the breakup."

Leo didn't show any surprise, which made sense because they had indeed done better at staying in touch over the year, mostly via text. They hadn't texted constantly or anything, but maybe once a month or so Leo would text her something that reminded him of her, or Shira would send him a link to something she thought was funny, and they'd have a little conversation about what was going on in their lives. "*Are* you unhappy because of the breakup?"

She wrinkled her nose. "No. William was a good guy, and I

don't regret dating him, but he wasn't the one." She knew that mostly because, once she'd done what needed to be done, she'd been sad, yes, but also relieved. She'd thought about the future and didn't feel lonely without the thought of him by her side. "It's . . ." She couldn't even get into all of it. So, as her family had, she went ahead and changed the subject. "Did you hear that the deli's shut down again for some kind of infestation?"

"What, locusts?" Leo said. "It's Hanukkah. Do they think it's Passover?"

Shira snorted. "But it's okay. I'm going to do all the food myself this year, and it's going to be spectacular."

Leo furrowed his forehead. Without all his hair getting in the way, his eyebrows, thick and dark, were extra expressive. "What do you mean, you're going to make the food yourself? Won't that be a lot of work?"

"Sure, but I can handle it!" She waved her arms in the air, nearly knocking over the plastic glass of wine on the end table. "I'm going to go all out. Homemade latkes with sour cream and smoked salmon and caviar. I'm going to make the smoked salmon, it's not that hard."

"I'll do the caviar," Leo said seriously. "Finally put my scuba certificate to use."

She rolled her eyes. "I'm serious. And I'm going to make a big brisket and noodle kugel and some vegetable sides, and I'm going to make some of those big doughnut cakes for dessert. Do you have any Bundt pans? I need more Bundt pans."

"I don't know what a Bundt pan is," Leo said. He lifted his arm and took another sip of his orange soda, grimacing. Maybe it had gone flat.

"They're those big round doughnut-shaped cake pans with ridges inside," Shira said, drawing the shape of one big in the air. She went to take a gulp of her wine. The cup was empty already. Well, it was a very small cup. "Though do you think that's enough? I mean, they won't actually be fried. They'll look like big doughnuts, but they won't actually be doughnuts. Do you think I should make my own doughnuts?"

"Shira," Leo said slowly, leaning forward so that his elbows met his knees again. "Don't take this the wrong way, but are you okay?"

"Yes," she said, but her body was a traitor, and evil little tears sprang to the corners of her eyes. She viciously swiped them away. "*Yes.*"

"Okay, but you nearly took your eyes out there," he said. "Are you sure you're okay?"

She drew in a deep breath. "I need this party to be perfect."

His face was solemn, those thick brows pinched. "How come?" Now that she looked closer, she could see that his elbows were actually hovering just above his knees, as if he were ready to spring into action. To do what? Keep her from smashing her plastic glass and trying to slit her throat with it?

Another deep breath. *Don't be overdramatic.* She burst out, "Because it's the only thing I've got left!"

Not overdramatic at all. She braced herself for Leo's tone to get all pitying and sad.

His eyebrows jumped up. "Wow, okay." His arms fell open, going palms up. "Tell me about it."

No judgment in his tone. No reassurances about how he was sure that wasn't true, or a list of her accomplishments. Somehow that made it feel easier to talk to him and tell him all the things she hadn't quite been able to make herself type out over text. "One, my show flopped." That was the big one. She pushed on through the tremor in her voice, the lump in her throat. "I worked on those paintings for so long. It was such a personal show." Talia had flown out for the opening, had marveled at the paintings and told her that some of them had been like looking through a window into a magical version of their childhood. "And I thought it was really, really good."

"It was really, really good," Leo said. "It was great, from all the photos I saw. I loved it."

She hoped he wasn't about to ask her to sign the print he'd special ordered. Looking at the paintings from the show now made her feel some insidious mixture of pride and hope and also embarrassment and shame. Because this work had poured out from her heart and her soul, however cheesy that sounded. And people had rejected it. The bloggers and reviewers were wishy-washy about it, ultimately deeming it fine but nothing that stood out from the crowd. Only a few of the paintings had sold, even after the gallery had reduced the prices. They'd parted ways with her soon after, and now she no longer had gallery representation, just a bunch of useless paintings stacked against the wall of her kitchen.

What did that say about her heart and her soul? And her life in general? She'd worked her entire life to create that show, and she'd done it, and she'd just . . . failed. She wasn't good enough.

"Well, the public didn't agree," she said, her voice shaking more now. "And since my paintings didn't sell well, my gallery dropped me, and none of the other big galleries are going to be interested with my record. So . . . that's that for my painting career, I guess."

"You never know," he said loyally.

She really didn't need to hear this from people outside the business, who didn't know anything about how it worked. "And at least I've got my job, except I hate my job now." That was an understatement. Sometimes she woke in the middle of the night in a cold sweat after a nightmare about having to woo a new artist, only she'd forgotten he was coming over and she was naked in the shower. "It turns out the job at this level is a 24-7 commitment, and I don't like having to schmooze and flatter all day. It feels so insincere, and I'm not good at it."

She drew in another deep breath, one that almost made her dizzy. "And before you tell me again that I should just quit and find a new job, it's not that simple. A thousand people would kill for my job."

"But if you're not one of the thousand anymore, what does that matter?" Leo said.

It made sense theoretically, but she dismissed the idea out of hand. What would all her classmates and coworkers and artist acquaintances think about her if she let such an opportunity go? She'd worked her entire life for two things, and one of them was now out—she had to hold on to the other. Now that she couldn't introduce herself with pride as an artist, at least she could still raise eyebrows with her job title. And besides, if she just left, what were all those years of work for? She'd sacrificed sleep and parties and classes in things she could've been interested in in pursuit of a career path like this.

If she left, what was the point of it all?

She didn't want to fight about it with Leo, though. He would just tell her again that she was too worried about what people thought of her, and . . . and . . . okay, maybe that was a little bit true, but it didn't matter.

"But neither of those is the worst part." She paused, letting the gut-twisting pain and shame and sadness pour back over her. She'd already marinated in it for so long you'd think she wouldn't feel it anymore, but no, that wasn't how life worked. "My best friend—my whole friend group—they . . . I got . . . They're not my friends anymore," she finished lamely.

"What happened?"

Shira hesitated. The way Danica had dumped her . . . well, she'd won the group chat and the friend group. Ellery and Nora had said they'd still be friends with both of them, that they didn't want to take sides, but in practice, Danica had won. Because you couldn't have two group chats discussing all the same things where only one member differed. Not unless you were using one of them to talk shit about the other. And Shira would rather have no friends than fake friends. "I . . . It doesn't matter. It matters that it really hurt, and that I miss them, and I'm also furious at them, and also—" She swallowed the urge to scream the next sentence, then drowned it in another swallow of wine. God, that was terrible stuff. "We're all in the same circles, art world and college and friends, and there's this party in the city I know they're going to, because before everything went down I was going to go, too, but now of course I wasn't going to go, but then my boss told me I had to go because it's an art party and apparently this artist he wants is going to be there, and I *can't* go. I'd rather *die*." She stopped talking only because she ran out of air. She gulped in another breath, but Leo spoke before she could expound upon exactly how dead she would be.

"I'll come with you."

It was the simple yet authoritative way he said it that did her in. If he'd asked her if she wanted him to go, she'd have instinctively shaken her head, not wanting to be a bother. If he'd couched it in a bunch of excuses about how much he really wanted to go, she'd have known immediately he was lying for her sake, and she would've shaken her head, still not wanting to be a bother. But those four words. *I'll come with you.* No pretending that he was doing it for himself. Meaning she'd have to tell him *No, I don't want you to come,* and that, she realized, wasn't true. "Thank you," she said, and that was true.

"We'll go in, fake laugh and fake smile and act like we're doing great and having a wonderful time, we'll connect with your artist, then we'll make up an excuse and get the hell out of there," Leo said. "Sound good?"

She nodded. "Thank you," she said again. She could fake laugh and fake smile and pretend she was doing great. She could totally do this.

11

SHIRA COULD NOT TOTALLY DO THIS, BECAUSE HERE she was, down the block from the event venue—an art-gallery-slash-bar—heaving big gulps of air, leaning against the bricks of a New York City building caked with at least a hundred years of accumulated New Yorker grime and urine, trying not to cry, because that would ruin her makeup.

"Take a deep breath," Leo said, which was not helpful, because she was already taking lots of big breaths.

They'd taken the train in, the same train Shira used to take into the city every time she'd go back to Columbia after a weekend break or visit home. She watched the same trees flash by against the same sunset and listened to the same robotic voice announcing that they were approaching New Brunswick and Metuchen and Newark Liberty International Airport. She squirmed in her seat against the too-tight confines of Talia's borrowed little black dress and cursed herself one more time for not bringing a cocktail dress home with her.

This might have been the first time she'd seen Leo all dressed up in nice pants and a button-down, though that wasn't saying much, considering he moved away as a teenager and then she'd only seen him a couple times since. What if he hadn't moved? Maybe they'd have gone to prom together, and he'd have slipped a flowered corsage on her wrist while wearing a full-on tux. She gave herself a moment to imagine it, and it sparked something in her. She wasn't sure exactly what it was, because her heart was beating too hard in her ears for her to feel it.

When they'd gotten off the train at Penn Station, Leo stepped into the street and called them a cab without asking if she wanted to take the subway in her heels, which she appreciated. The cab had let them out on the end of the one-way block so that the driver wouldn't have to take the time to circle around, and from their spot on the corner, Shira spied Danica entering the art gallery, not encased like a sausage à la Shira but cradled in a knee-length red dress that flattered her olive skin and feathery dark hair, her head thrown back mid-laugh as the light from inside bathed her in a golden glow.

Shira's feet rooted her to the dirty sidewalk. Which was probably good because otherwise she might have fallen over, thanks to her blinding panic at the thought of following Danica inside and having to face her. This would mark the first time she saw her since the breakup, and Shira had no idea what the etiquette for such a situation was. Were they supposed to catch each other's eye or pretend not to see each other? What if they both descended on a mutual friend at the same time—were they supposed to fight over them? Had Danica told her version of events to any of the people here? Did all Shira's old friends think she was a bad person?

"Okay, forget about the deep part. Try to take regular breaths," Leo said, and his hands clamped down on her shoulders and squeezed. Somehow they didn't hold her down any further but anchored her flailing thoughts in one solid place. With them in one spot, she found she had more room to focus on her breathing. "It's going to be okay. You can do anything for a half hour, right? We're going to go in and put on a good show for a half hour, then make an excuse and leave."

"Okay. Okay." It suddenly occurred to her that "They're probably going to think we're together, you know. Like, together. Is that . . . okay with you?"

He smiled at her. "That's fine with me. I'll make sure to make you look good, okay?"

She nodded, suddenly so grateful for him she could cry. She took a deep breath. *Do not cry.* Steeling herself, she turned toward the door. "Okay. Let's do this."

The gallery was, like most spaces in Manhattan that weren't outrageously expensive, too small for the event it was holding. Shira had always been the worst at that guess-the-number-of-jelly-beans-in-the-jar game, but she estimated there were somewhere around fifty people here so far. Many of them familiar. Sweat broke out on her forehead, and not just from all these people crammed into a small space surrounded by paintings and sculptures they couldn't get too near.

From a side table she grabbed a plastic cup of wine or seltzer or something. She didn't care—she just wanted something to do with her hands. "I need to find the artist, talk to her, and then we can go," she said, head on a swivel. "She's South Asian, with a black pixie cut and gauged ears. I can't imagine she'll be that hard to spot." The art world had made a lot of progress in recent years, but it was still extraordinarily white.

"On it." Leo slouched a little as he looked around, almost as if he were bored, and she sent him a silent thank-you for the body language. He was already doing a great job blending in with the art crowd, who sometimes made Shira wonder if there was a competition she didn't know about over who could look the most jaded and blasé.

"Shira!"

Shira was looking at the other side of the room, squinting at someone's back, so she hadn't realized Ellery was approaching until her (former?) friend was already there, giving her air-kisses. Ellery shook Leo's hand next, looking him up and down in an extremely obvious way. Shira mechanically gave her air-kisses back, reminding herself over and over not to sniff herself beneath the underarms. If she was stinky, it was too late to do anything about it. "Celery!" Shira said, striving for enthusiasm. She touched Leo's arm, hoping for some of that strength he'd imparted earlier by touching her shoulders. "This is Leo. Leo, this is my friend Ellery. We call her Celery because—"

"Because it rhymes with Ellery?" Leo said, eyes glinting.

"No," Shira and Ellery said together, and Shira almost cracked a smile. Almost. She continued, "Because she did this art project once using a bunch of celery where she let it sit in a jar of water for way too long to see what happened to it."

"It was pretty gross by the end," Ellery said. "I think Nora threatened to make her next art project a ceremonial burning of my art project." She paused and thought for a moment. "You know, the reason I did that art project in the first place was because my name rhymed with celery, so you're technically correct."

Shira's heart was racing. She could see Danica out of the corner of her eye—what if she came over to assert her dominance, to make it clear to everyone that Ellery was *her* friend now? "How is Nora, by the way?" she said, this time striving for casual. "I feel like it's been forever since I've seen you guys."

"I know, right?" said Ellery. "We live in the same city, and yet we had to come to the opposite coast to actually talk." She turned to Leo. "Nora's our other friend. The fourth one in our—" A faint grimace crossed her face, one Shira didn't think she'd have noticed if she wasn't looking for it. "Well, she's our other friend. Her family is from SF, so she's there for the holidays, while I'm from Philly, and Danica's also—" She stopped short, red blooming on her cheeks. She gave a short laugh. "Sorry. Anyway, yeah, we need to hang out. I saw you got promoted. That's amazing! I'm still floating around trying to break in. I'm so jealous."

Simply touching Leo's arm wasn't working. Shira slid her hand down his arm and grabbed his hand, squeezing hard. He squeezed back, sending a jolt of strength and calm through her. Shira took a deep breath, trying to forget that Ellery had once been one of the people she texted first when anything big happened; that they used to have a list of all the new LA restaurants they wanted to try together, categorized by how bad the traffic would be getting there around dinnertime; that she knew the exact boniness level of her shoulder because of the number of times she'd cried on it.

It was like mourning someone who'd died, only they weren't dead. The grief was a splinter in her heart and a stone in her belly at the same time, but she had to pretend she didn't feel it, that everything was normal. A performance. Hadn't Leo said that thing about her life being a performance? It wasn't, he was totally wrong, but she could put on a performance now if she had to.

She let out the breath. Squeezed Leo's hand again. Turned to him with an adoring gaze. "Leo, tell her about the game you're working on." She hadn't asked him about it since she saw him last year—she hated it when people asked about her art projects; so many times she worked so hard and so hard and so hard and ended up with nothing to show for it—but here he didn't need to tell the truth. "It's going really well, isn't it?"

"Oh, wow!" Ellery said. Her enthusiasm was well acted but definitely fake—Shira knew she hadn't played a video game since *Pokémon* in middle school. "Where do you work?"

The enthusiasm that lit up Leo's eyes, on the other hand, was clearly real. "I'm not at a studio currently, I'm an indie developer. I've been working on this cozy RPG for a while now, and it's really gaining traction—it's gotten funding from a few major investors, and it's been short-listed for an award that would take it to the next level, so fingers crossed."

"Oh, cool," said Ellery. "What does that mean, cozy RPG?"

Leo launched into the description of his game, the same one he'd told Shira about last year, where the player had to perform everyday tasks in the shadow of a looming world-ending catastrophe, but this time—she was pleasantly surprised to hear it—he'd added in her idea about making their small, relatively unimportant tasks ultimately responsible for the heroes saving the day. A nice touch, she thought. Even though Leo might have been exaggerating his accomplishments to make himself look like an excellent catch (he had to be, right? because she definitely would have heard if all this was real), he'd made sure to throw her a bone. He finished, "I'm still in school, doing my final internship, but a few studios have reached out to see if I'd be interested in joining them, so I'm trying to decide whether I want to finish my degree or go right to work."

"Oh, cool," Ellery said again. "Well, you probably can't go wrong either way."

"Yeah, probably. It's interesting talking to art people about gaming, though. It's really an art form on its own."

Shira's attention wandered as Leo and Ellery went back and forth about art and gaming and what exactly constituted art (spoiler: literally anything could be art). Part of her tracked Danica, making sure she didn't get too close; a second part of her was fruitlessly seeking out the artist, who was still MIA; and the third was clocking the rest of the room, seeing who was getting close and who else she might know.

Her attention jumped back into the conversation at the sound of Ellery saying the artist's name. "Oh, there's Neena."

"She's here?" Shira couldn't see her. "Where?"

"Over there." When Shira still couldn't see, Ellery clarified, "With the bright red hair. It's new."

That explained why the dark pixie cut was nowhere to be seen. Shira's heart leaped. One conversation, one photo taken to prove her attendance to her boss in case Neena blew her off, and then she could fake frown and tell Ellery that she was getting a migraine and beat it. *One conversation.* "My boss asked me to come here and talk our gallery up," Shira said. "I'm going to go do that before Neena's all talked out. It was great seeing you!"

"Likewise!" Ellery's fingers wrapped around Shira's wrist before she could pull away. "I mean what I said about hanging out. Nora and I want to be friends with both of you."

And yet somehow that amounted to only talking to her if Shira reached out first, hence the tumbleweeds blowing through the group chat of the three of them Shira had created before realizing she'd lost them to the other. Shira had to stop the sharp laugh from leaping out of her throat and stabbing Ellery in hers. "Sure. Okay." Ellery's fingers felt like they might leave stripy burns on Shira's skin. Shira yanked her arm away, and Ellery let it go.

Shira threw one final grimace in her direction before pulling Leo—whose hand she was still holding, she was almost surprised to find out—toward Neena. "Are you okay?" Leo whispered in her ear as she blazed a path across the room, shouldering through bare sweaty arms and stiff sprayed hair. Shira couldn't fall apart before doing her professional duty. So she nodded quickly over her shoulder and steamrollered on. Honestly it was all kind of a blur now.

So much of a blur that Shira didn't realize Danica was also plowing toward Neena until they were both there at her side.

Danica's gaze met Shira's, and it was like someone had poured a bucket of ice water over Shira's head. Like she was suddenly drenched to the bone, the fabric of Talia's dress clinging to every lump and bump and exposing them to the room, teeth chattering and hair sticking to her forehead and *god*. Danica pressed her lips together in acknowledgment, an expression that was polite enough but wasn't anywhere near a smile, like she was girding herself to eat the dry, overcooked chicken she'd been served for dinner.

Shira tore her eyes away first. She was suddenly fiercely angry, as if the imaginary cold water had woken something in her. She was allowed to be here, too, damn it. She wasn't going to slink away with her tail between her legs as if she'd done something wrong. *Let Danica slink away if she doesn't want to be around me.* "Neena!" Shira said brightly, leaning in for cheek kisses. Neena's cheeks were sweaty, but she smelled like cinnamon and wine. "It's been so long!" She pulled back and gestured toward Leo. "This is Leo. Leo, this is Neena, the star of the night."

"Nice to meet you, Leo. And I know, I can't believe how long it's been!" Neena leaned back, her big dark eyes luminescent with interest. "I heard you were working at the Michael Spiro Gallery. That true?" Shira nodded, and Neena clasped her hands together. "And you got promoted recently, didn't you? Most of the people I know who even managed to get a job at a gallery, which is hard enough, washed out as an assistant." Was that jealousy in her eyes? "Amazing."

That familiar glow of pride washed through Shira. See, that was why she couldn't "just quit"—what would people say if she talked about her job then? A polite nod with glazed eyes? *All that work, wasted. All that potential, wasted.* Heads shaking behind her back.

"It's an exciting place to work." Danica's presence was like a spider crawling on the back of Shira's neck. Shira fixed her smile on, focusing on Neena and the feel of Leo's hand strong in hers. "Not to jump right to business, but my boss is really intrigued by your work. I know he'd love to set up a call with you."

"Okay, wow," Neena said, breathless. Shira wished she could focus only on the artist, but Danica was still hovering there at their side, a small polite smile on her face, and Shira could read her mind as clearly as if her thoughts were written on her forehead, because they were the same as Shira's. *Can't slink away. Can't let her win.* "Yeah, totally. Though I am working with a different gallery right now. I don't want it to seem like I'm unhappy with them or anything."

Shira kept that smile pasted on her face, hoping it didn't look as strained as it felt. *Just don't look at Danica, don't look at Danica.* "Of course. And I don't want to make it seem like we're trying to poach you or anything." This was why her boss had sent her to open up this delicate avenue of conversation: a former friend and classmate, in person, casually bringing it up. Nothing formal or in writing. "It's just a talk."

"Absolutely. Do you still have my number?" Shira probably did somewhere in her phone, but she shook her head, allowing Neena to slip her a business card. "Looking forward to it!"

"I know he is, too." There. Her task was done. She couldn't just run off now, though, or it would look like the only reason she'd come was for this. "I love this show, seriously. The lacework motif is so gorgeous and meaningful. I love how you combined sewing work with your painting."

"It's based on my grandmother's work." Neena beamed, then looked between Shira and Danica. "Seems to be a trend nowadays! Weren't your debut shows based on your grandmas' stories? I loved seeing your posts pop up on my timeline!"

"Yes!" Danica said. "I've been working on my show for years and years, practically since I was a kid. It's really my whole heart."

Like she'd put more of her heart into her show than Shira had? Or that the fact that Shira had only started working on her show after college made it less authentic or important? Shira gritted her teeth. *Don't do it. Don't do it.* But she couldn't resist. Keeping her eyes firmly fixed on Neena, she said, "How funny that you also based work on your grandma's life! It's almost like more than one person can make art about their grandma at a time."

Neena laughed, but Shira could feel Leo tense up behind her. He knew her well enough to hear the blade in her voice.

"Yeah, I'm happy with how well mine's been selling." Danica's voice was icy cold. She was also staring determinedly at Neena, a muscle ticcing in her angular jaw. "Great reviews, too. And I don't want to jinx anything, but since the show's been so successful, my representation has been in talks for some *really* exciting things."

"Moving onward and upward!" Neena said with an airy laugh.

Shira might actually grind her teeth into sand. "I've been so happy with the reception for mine as well!" Neena's smile was now beginning to falter. "Especially from my family, since so much of the show is drawn from my family history and my childhood. That's what my sister told me, actually, after she saw it. That it was like looking through a window back into our childhood."

Neena was now glancing back and forth between the two of

them, her brow furrowed in confusion. *Stop it*, Shira told herself sternly, because if she upset Neena, then her boss would be furious. "Well," Neena said uncertainly. "It sounds really good. Both of them do. I wish I'd gotten to see them in person instead of just online."

The sound that escaped Shira's throat was a little bit maniacal, and this time, she turned right to Danica as she spoke. "Oh, I don't know. It's hard to tell much about a show from a few shots online or a few words about it, right?"

"It's enough to know the basics," Danica spit back, and Neena shrank away, and Leo's arm draped itself over Shira's shoulders with the calming power of a purring cat.

"Hey, Shir," he said casually. "We should probably head out. We don't want to miss the book party."

There it was: an excuse. She seized it with both hands and held it tight to her chest. "You're right," she said, turning to Neena and leaning in for a brief hug. "It was so good to see you! I'm glad I made it tonight. Your work is amazing. And I'll email you or text you to set up that phone call."

Neena murmured much the same in response. Shira turned to Danica. "Bye," she said flatly, because it felt weird to walk away without saying anything, and then turned her back. She didn't exactly flee, but she walked away fast enough that she was quickly swallowed up by the crowd and couldn't hear if Danica said anything back.

Outside, the cold hit her like a slap in the face. It took a second to shrug on her coat. She'd done it. She'd faced down Danica and survived. She was done.

Why didn't she feel good about it? She felt vaguely dirty, like she'd stepped in something gross and wiped it off on her coat. For the first time in a million years, she felt the urge to go to synagogue. She suddenly missed the sense of peace it used to give her, the way it calmed her and made her feel like she'd taken a shower on the inside.

She had the Hanukkah party, at least.

But what was that other than one more performance?

She shook the thought away. "Thanks for the last-minute save," she said to Leo, though her cheeks burned a little bit that he'd seen her lose control like that. She wasn't sure what she would've done if he hadn't been there at her side—probably cried. "What is a book party, anyway?"

"No idea," Leo said. He was frowning down at his phone. "It sounded good while not being close enough to what we were doing that they might ask about it. Hey, how expensive do you think it would be to take an Uber home?"

"Absurdly expensive," Shira said. "The next train is in a half hour. We should make it in time." He was still frowning down at his phone. "Is everything okay?"

"Yeah. I think so. I don't know." He tucked his phone in his pocket, stepping to the curb and raising his arm to hail a cab. "My aunt just texted me that I should get home as soon as possible. My aunt never texts me. I messaged my dad to ask what was going on, and he hasn't answered. I don't know, it's all very weird."

A cab with its lights on whizzed by without stopping. Shira took a step farther into the road, narrowly missing getting knocked over by an e-bike, and flung her arm out into the street. The next taxi skidded to a stop in time for them to clamber in the back. "Penn Station, please. The NJ Transit entrance." The cab peeled away, and Shira shifted to the far window seat, leaving Leo on the other side of the sticky leather. Advertisements for dental work and Shake Shack blared from the little screen before them; she stabbed at the mute button, but it didn't work. "Should I call my parents to have them check in?"

Lights flashed over Leo's face. "No, don't worry about it. I can't do anything until I get home, right?"

He'd given her so much strength before and during the party. Now it was her turn. His hand was resting palm up on the middle seat. She grabbed it and squeezed. He squeezed back, and for one moment, the two of them were all there was in the world.

12

LEO'S MIND WOULDN'T STOP WHIRLING AS HE AND Shira made their way through the city to the train. He kind of wished she'd start talking about something stupid, anything trivial, but she seemed too focused on getting them where they needed to go, which was fair, as Leo's head was useless with all the whirling.

First the taxi driver dropped them off in the wrong spot, and they had to go around asking people to figure out where they were, and then they had to wait in line to buy paper tickets at the glitchy machine because the even glitchier app was malfunctioning, and then she was pulling him along in a run for the train, which they hopped aboard just as the warning bells were clanging. Leo's heart was racing as they finally sank into their cracked brown leather seats. That was one blessing, at least: The train wasn't crowded, so they got a whole three-person bench to spread out on. Small luxuries.

Leo held his breath as he checked his phone again. No service, but he'd received a few notifications while they were running for the train. He swiped past a couple of work email alerts—the video game world never slept—and a suggestive text from a girl he'd dated briefly a month ago who he'd been positive had ghosted him. Nothing from his aunt or his dad. He lowered the phone into his lap and stared out the window, which was blurry with the smears of a thousand fingerprints, into the dark tunnel beneath the river.

"Hey, I don't want to forget to thank you for coming tonight," Shira said, her tone so light it was obvious how hard she was trying to distract him. "You did a bang-up job as my fake boyfriend."

"Bang-up job?" he said, amused enough that he was actually distracted from his phone, just for a moment, and then the train rattled out of the tunnel, and the signal bars came back, and he refreshed. Nothing. "Are you British and forgot to tell me?"

"Righty-o I am," she said in the worst British accent he had ever heard. "Seriously, though, thank you. I don't know how I would've made it through the night alone."

She could've just left it there. He would've felt all warm inside, knowing that whatever was going on with his dad, at least he'd always have his old friend.

But she had to continue. "You made yourself look so good for everyone. It was great how you spun that whole story about your game."

He could feel his whole face go blank. A "story"? That's what she thought it was? Because, what, it couldn't possibly have been true? The idea she'd thrown at him last year had made everything click, and it had gone really fast after that: He'd submitted it for a grant, where it had gathered a lot of attention, and everything had snowballed from there. He was getting offers from studios both to acquire the game and to offer him jobs, but he wasn't sure if he was going to take any of them. The whole thing was a little overwhelming, to be honest.

But it probably made her feel better, considering all that was going on in her life, like she wasn't the only person with everything falling apart. Maybe he should just be a good friend and let her believe whatever she wanted to believe.

She continued before he had to decide whether to speak up. "It was especially good that you told it all to Ellery, because she's the gossip of the group. She'll definitely tell Danica everything."

Here, something that could distract him from jumping every time his phone vibrated, only to find an email from L.L.Bean or REI. "Are you going to tell me what happened between you and Danica? There was so much tension between the two of you I don't know if I could've cut it with a machete."

She pursed her lips, letting out a long, slow stream of breath. "I have integrity. I would never steal someone's work."

"I know," Leo said. She might care way too much about what people thought of her, and she might have a habit for blurting out the worst thing at the worst moment, and she was also at least a little elitist, and—no, he was not going to sit here and mentally list out her flaws; that wasn't what a good friend did. The point was, she might have a whole list of flaws, but dishonesty wasn't one of them.

"It was wild." Her lips were barely moving now, like her whole body was resisting the topic of discussion. Despite the stress of the situation, his eyes couldn't help but linger on the little indents in her bottom lip where she'd chewed off her lipstick. "Danica didn't like talking about her work and the paintings she was working on, which, okay. Plenty of people are worried talking about it will jinx it or ruin their creative energy or whatever. But finally she got to the point a year and a half ago where she wanted to share some of her sketches and early work for feedback, so I went through them and gave her my thoughts. It was really good! She'd also based it on her family history and had incorporated some creatures from Slavic mythology."

"Your work is also based on your family history and has creatures from Jewish mythology." It wasn't like he was an expert, but he'd loved Shira's paintings. Loved the way he could see her and her voice and her soul in the way lines arced on the canvas, in the smirky expressions the supernatural creatures held.

"It does! I told her about it, and told Ellery and Nora about it, and I kept rambling about how we could do shows together and do talks together and blah blah blah, and I didn't realize until after how her face would go blank whenever I talked about it."

That tracked. Shira had a habit of putting her foot in her mouth and then wondering why everything tasted like toes.

"It wasn't some big moment where we had a showdown, she just finally snapped after months of us being compared to each other. Maybe it was the roundup that came out in *Arthouse* that called her work similar to mine, since mine came out first." Her eyes were shiny. "She ended up doing it over text. We were friends for years, and she dumped me over *text*. Somehow that's almost the worst thing of it all. Like, I thought of her as one of my best friends, and I didn't even matter enough for her to tell me with her voice and her face that she couldn't believe I'd stolen her ideas. At first that was all I kept asking for. I was like, Danica, can I call you? Can we meet up and talk about this? Because surely you'd see in my face that it's not true.

"And it's *not* true. She hadn't even seen my work! All she knew was that it was also about my great-grandma and had some fantastical elements! Like, does she own the topic?" Her chest was heaving now with righteous indignation as her finger jabbed the air. "And I literally had work I'd done before I'd seen her own, so there was actual *proof* I couldn't have stolen her idea, and she didn't even *care*.

"I really spiraled after that. Like, was there some kind of chance I'd overheard something and subconsciously decided to use it in my own work? Or was it because I'm Jewish? Because she didn't accuse Neena of stealing her idea, even though Neena obviously didn't start her show until after Danica's show came out. People are always accusing us of stealing things. Like Jewish and Israeli food! Jews have been in the Middle East and North Africa for thousands of years. So yeah, when we got kicked out of all those countries, we took our food with us wherever we ended up. It's our food, too."

Her eyes were now blazing with righteous anger as she continued. "So then I obsessed about what the real reason could be. Did she just not like me? Did she not like the two of us being compared? But, like, it didn't matter." She shook her head. "She'd already gone out there spitting fire, and it didn't matter if it was really about something else. And then it was awful because I didn't just lose her, I lost the whole friend group."

"I'm sorry," Leo said. And he was. If there was anything

losing Shira as a teenager had taught him, it was that friend breakups were incredibly hard. If she were sitting closer to him and not on the outside seat, he'd offer her his hand again for strength. "Your other friends believed Danica?"

Shira slumped in her seat, silhouetted by the Newark skyline glowing outside the window. "I don't know how much of it was that they believed her and how much of it was that they just chose her. Ellery and Nora told me that they weren't taking sides, but they chose to continue the group chat with her instead of me. I see on social media that the three of them still hang out all the time. So that's been a real mindfuck, too. Like, why not me? Is she so much more likable than me? Am I a bad friend?"

Leo had to admit to himself: Honestly, sometimes she was! (Case in point: He was still stinging from the assumption she'd made about him before.) But the good outweighed the bad over all these years, so he answered honestly. "No. You're a good friend."

She slumped against the window. Trees, nothing but dark skeletons at this time of night, whizzed past on the other side. Lights flashed over her face, highlighting the movement of her cheek that came from her chewing on the inside. "The mindfuck didn't end there. I kept spiraling. Like, so much of my life is outward-facing, and this was something that was internal, only mine, if that makes sense. And she was telling me that even my innermost self wasn't me, that I'd stolen it from her. And even though I knew it wasn't true, I *knew* it, this was my friend, and I believed everything she'd told me before, and it was hard not to believe something she told me now." Shira drew in a deep, shuddery breath. "People only seem to like the performances I put on. They don't seem to like *me*. And it made me think, do *I* even like me?"

"I like you," Leo said.

She didn't seem to hear him. "The whole thing has just . . . sucked."

"I'm sorry." Leo jumped in his seat as his phone finally buzzed with something relevant: His aunt was calling. He slapped it to his ear on the first ring. "Hello?"

"Hi, Leo," said Aunt Ellen. His dad's older sister. She didn't sound like she was crying, which was good, right? If something really bad was going down, she'd probably be crying? "Do you want to meet us at County? The hospital? Your father's just been admitted." Leo's heart nearly stopped before she hastily added, "He's alive, he's okay. They think he had a heart attack. It was scary for a minute there, but he pulled—"

For one second, all Leo felt was a pure, empty, gasping horror, and it threatened to make him fall apart. He had to fill the space with something else. "Why didn't you tell me?" he shouted into the phone, suddenly full of righteous fury. Someone in front of them turned to glare in his direction, but Shira outglared them back.

Aunt Ellen was irritatingly calm. "You were rushing home anyway. It wouldn't have helped you to know your father was getting shocked back to life while you were far away. Now you have somewhere concrete to go."

"You should've told me anyway." He was still shouting, and more of the people in the surrounding seats were starting to look over, probably gauging whether or not to flee to the next car.

"Well, I'm sorry, then." She didn't sound sorry at all. "Just come to County as soon as you can, okay? I love you."

"Love you," he grumbled back automatically, and she hung up. He lowered the phone slowly into his lap, eyes trained straight ahead at the scarred leather seat back. Someone had scribbled a heart, and then next to it someone had scribbled a dick. He found it hard to believe someone hadn't added the *I* yet. Maybe he should do it. He felt suddenly like he was back on the school bus, snickering with his friends as they poked holes in the seat with pencils. Everything smelled like erasers.

"Leo?" Shira said, placing her hand on his. He jolted back to this time, this place. "What happened?"

He told her everything he knew, which wasn't much. She kept her hand on his, squeezing his knuckles occasionally. "So I need to get to County right away," he finished. "I know I drove us to the station. Can I call you an Uber home from the train? If there's no one there, I'll wait with you until the car comes. Or a car home from the hospital? It's not that far away."

"I'll come with you to the hospital," she said immediately. "If that's okay. It's also okay if you don't want me there, but . . . I'd like to be there for you."

"Oh," he said, surprised. "Oh. Sure. I guess. Okay."

They were quiet for the rest of the train ride. Shira kept her hand on his the whole time; he never flipped his over to hold hers, but he liked knowing it was there in case he needed it. Mostly Leo stared out the window. Instead of the trees and buildings flashing by, he saw a movie playing out again and again on the smeared glass. Leo arriving to the hospital. Aunt Ellen in tears in the waiting room, barely able to form the words

You didn't make it in time, he's gone. Leo standing there in shock, realizing that the story of him and his father would end here, with years of grudging silence and then a tense dinner once a week, and he'd never get to have an actual adult conversation with him. That things could never, ever change.

Somehow he'd thought he'd always have time. Which was stupid. Every year his dad's hair was a little grayer, the skin on his throat a little looser, his belly a little rounder. What if his time had run out?

He should text his mom. Let her know. He reached for his phone again, then stilled. Last he'd heard, she was in Morocco, vacationing in a riad with a crystal clear pool in its courtyard and an assortment of eclectic guests, one of whom she thought might be a Hapsburg. He didn't want to disturb her vacation. She would probably have zero interest in rushing home to care for his father, but she might want to rush home to take care of him. And he was an adult. He didn't need someone to take care of him.

The train screeched to a stop. Shira tugged Leo to his feet, then into the aisle. "We parked over here."

Somehow he blinked and he was at the hospital, everything around him white and gleaming, his nose filled with the odors of disinfectant and urine. Hopefully he hadn't been the one to drive here. Shira was towing him by the hand, periodically stopping to speak with people at desks to make sure they were going in the right direction.

And then they were in a waiting room, chairs hard and orange, TVs overhead playing some talk show where everybody seemed to be laughing the entire time. Aunt Ellen was there, clasping his shoulders and pulling him in for a hug that threatened to squeeze all the air out of him. "I'm glad you made it." She was older than his father by a few years, short and stout as a teapot, with a blocky gray bob and a raspy voice she swore she hadn't gotten through smoking. "They asked me to step out for a minute so they could do a test or change a bedpan, I don't know. I just listened to them."

"So he's okay?" Leo said, blinking hard as if he were coming out of a dream. Everything around him felt surreal: the bright white lights overhead, the sound of someone crying in the distance, the smell of baked beans on his aunt's shirt, the women on TV laughing laughing laughing with too many teeth.

"He's okay." Aunt Ellen stepped back. "They're going to keep him for observation for another night or two, and then he's going to have to start seeing a cardiologist, but they caught it in time. He's going to be okay." She fixed him with a squinty glare. "So you might want to see your way to forgiving him. Who's this?" She turned to Shira before Leo could even process what she'd said. "Your girlfriend? When did you get a girlfriend?"

"I'm Shira," said Shira, extending a hand and then wincing as Aunt Ellen crushed it with one of her signature handshakes. "Just a friend. It's nice to meet you."

"Sure," Aunt Ellen said gruffly, very obviously looking Shira up and down. Shira shifted from foot to foot, tugging down the hem of her dress. "You meet at school? Incredible what this kid's done in so short a time, right?"

"What?"

"With that game of his," Aunt Ellen said. "Getting all those investors, those awards, those job offers? Kid's incredible."

"Wait," Shira said, glancing back and forth between the two of them, something beeping in the background, and he could see the moment where she realized her blunder. "Wait, it was all true?" She clapped a hand to her mouth with clear mortification. Red roses bloomed on her cheeks. "Oh my god, why didn't you say something? I feel like such an asshole!"

You were *kind of an asshole,* he didn't say. But the cringe on his face must have spoken on its own. Her arms crossed so tightly it looked almost like she was hugging herself. "Oh my god, you felt sorry for me. You pitied me."

He didn't respond. She bit her lip, and he wondered if she was thinking about the day he'd tried to kiss her. Not that it mattered, of course. That day was a long time ago, and he had no interest in kissing her. Especially not right here, right now, while in one direction someone was sobbing like their heart might break and in the other it sounded like machines were trying to take over the world.

"Yes? Good. Okay," Aunt Ellen was saying to a nurse, and then she was grabbing Leo by the shoulder, maybe a little more roughly than she had to. "This is the son. He'll go with you." To Leo, she added, "Your dad's ready. Go. Be a good son."

Instinct told him to reply, *Well, maybe if he wanted a good son he should've been a good dad.* He even opened his mouth but managed to stop himself in time. Was this what it meant to grow up?

He was glad he didn't say it when he saw his dad. He again managed not to blurt anything mean out, but Joe looked *terrible.* Against the stark white background of his hospital bed, surrounded by metal grab bars and hooked up to various beeping tubes, he appeared as if he'd shrunken by half since Leo had seen him earlier. His face was grayish and his eyes red. The hospital gown fit him so awkwardly that his chest seemed shrunken and his legs like sticks.

Joe cracked a smile. "Looking good, huh?"

Leo closed his mouth. He hadn't even realized it had fallen open. "I've seen worse," he said gruffly. He stood there for a moment, the two of them staring at each other, before Leo moved gingerly toward Joe's side and perched on the foot of the bed. He noticed, too late, a chair on the other side of the room. "How are you feeling?"

"I've been better." He sounded exhausted. "Glad I don't have a roommate, at least. And also glad they caught it in time. You know, I'll start on a diet, take some drugs, hopefully I'll head off the big one."

Leo could have made a joke about the drugs, but he was suddenly also exhausted, as if all his energy had puddled at his feet when he'd sat down. So he settled for "Hopefully."

They stared at each other for a moment again, the silence broken by the sounds from all the machines monitoring Joe's body and keeping him alive.

And then they spoke at once. "Listen—" "Hey, let me—" Then each gave a snort, and Leo realized, with a start, that the way Joe's mouth twisted at one end was just like his own.

"Listen," Joe said, and this time Leo nodded for him to go on. "I always figured you needed time to process and stew and sort through your feelings after the divorce, and that I'd give it to you, and maybe in the end I gave you too much time, because as I was lying there thinking I might die, that was all I could think about. That I might die with you hating me."

"I don't hate you," Leo said weakly, but it was as if Joe didn't hear him.

"And then I realized, hey, I gave you time, but I didn't give you much to process. I never wanted to talk to you about the divorce, because I knew I'd been in the wrong, and so I took the coward's way out. But listen, Leo." Joe struggled to sit up, the hospital gown drooping over his collarbone. "I'm sorry. Hell, I'm sorry. I'm sorry for what the divorce did to you and how it made you feel toward me. I didn't want to be a husband anymore, but I sure as hell still wanted to be your dad."

Leo suddenly felt that maybe he might also be having a heart attack. Well, he thought this was the place for it, at least. How exactly were you supposed to respond to something you've been wanting to hear for years, without even knowing how badly you wanted it? "Thank you," he croaked. "I wish I'd let my guard down even a little bit. I don't know if I'll ever fully forgive you for what you did to me and Mom." Joe's face fell a little bit, but it was the truth. "You're still my dad, though. And I want to try to make it feel that way again."

"We could start by actually talking at those dinners your mom made you do," said Joe.

Leo snorted. "I'll do my best."

"Or," Joe said. "You could start by telling me about your life. Are you still in love with Shira Levinson?" He clearly noticed Leo's surprise. "You were never subtle about it."

Leo cleared his throat. "Definitely not," he said. He was over

Shira. For good. He changed the subject. "How are you . . . You were out on a date the other night, right? How was it?"

They talked about it, actually talked about it, for the next however long, only breaking at a gentle knock on the door. It was Aunt Ellen and Shira—his dad raised an eyebrow at Leo, who shrugged a little bit sheepishly—and, strangely enough, they were holding a menorah. One of the plastic electric ones, with those blue ombré bulbs that screwed in and out. "It's the first night of Hanukkah," Aunt Ellen explained. "Shira kindly reminded me, and it turned out they had this menorah at the nurses' station. We asked if we could bring it in here to 'light' it."

"We thought it might be nice," Shira said, her voice as bright as her smile. She bobbed her head at Leo's dad. "Sorry about your heart."

"Thanks," said Leo's dad, bemused. "Sure, let's light the menorah. Why not."

Shira scuttled forward to put the menorah on the windowsill, which overlooked the parking lot. Then she paused for a moment, hands on hips, to take it in. Leo said, "My dad really got lucky with the view, didn't he?"

She spun, her smile brilliant. "I know you're kidding, but for Hanukkah, yes. The whole point of the menorah is for people to see it burning so that they can all share in the light. What better place for that than the parking lot everyone is using?" Her smile faltered, and she added, so quietly Leo could barely hear her, "Maybe a party to show everybody how great you're doing."

"What was that?" Aunt Ellen asked.

Shira shook her head, her smile back on. "Nothing. Come on, let's do the blessings."

Leo hung back on the bed with his dad, but his dad nodded him toward the window. Sure enough, there were lots of little people scurrying around the parking lot. None of them were looking up—probably, since they were at the hospital, they had more than enough to worry about down below—but Leo liked the idea of the menorah's light shining down on them.

Shira tucked one of her arms through his, leaning her head on his shoulder. Gladness filled his heart. He was lucky to be here, in this place, with his living father and his aunt and his friend. He was lucky to be here, alive, period.

Next year, he vowed, he'd do a better job at showing it.

He opened his mouth and sang his feelings out into the dark night.

Texts between Shira Levinson and Leo David, April:

Shira: Well, I did it. I quit my job

Leo: Wow! Congrats! I think?

Shira: I don't know. I'm just walking out of the office now and I don't know how to feel yet

Leo: Wow, so it's fresh

Shira: Fresher than a salad

Shira: I realize that was a terrible metaphor, but that's about all I have in me right now

Leo: You're going to be okay

Shira: Easy for the rising indie star to say.

Leo: That's also currently fresher than a salad

From Shira Levinson's email inbox:

MAY: Shira! We miss you so much here at the gallery. The new assistant has no idea how your organizational system works and keeps fetching us the wrong files. No way she's getting promoted. Any chance you remember where you left the permission agreements for the upcoming Flower exhibit? We can't find them anywhere and we're starting to panic . . .

AUGUST: Excuse me, you charge what for a character sketch? I can make something almost as good with Photoshop myself.

SEPTEMBER: How dare you threaten small claims court on me? I'm only sixty days past due, which is nothing. And the book cover you sent me wasn't even that good. I'm going to call small claims court on YOU!

Texts between Leo David and Shira Levinson, November:

Leo: My dad ran into your mom while walking Neptune and heard that there's not going to be a Hanukkah party this year. Everything okay?

Shira: Life is madness right now. Just don't have time

Leo: Well, we can't not have a neighborhood Hanukkah party. What would people think?

Shira: . . .

Leo: I'll do it

Shira: Seriously? You're going to throw the Hanukkah party?

Leo: What, like it's hard?

Shira: . . .

Shira: . . .

Leo: Okay, you've been typing a long time. I was kidding. I know it'll be hard. But we can handle it

Shira: We?

Leo: See you there!

13

Year Four

HAVING NEGLECTED TO PAY THE TWENTY-FIVE-dollar seat-selection fee, Shira ended up, of course, in a middle seat on the plane. She grimaced as she slid her way in past the woman on the aisle, who seemed to have bathed in mothballs before boarding, and settled into the cramped space next to the teenage boy by the window, who was furiously mashing buttons on his Switch. This was going to be a long six hours from LA to Phil–

Her jaw dropped as she realized that the teenager wasn't killing monsters or fighting war battles on his screen but . . . picking litter off a cobblestoned path. She blurted, "Hey, is that *Washing Dishes at the End of the World*?"

The kid shot her a glance. His screen beeped in celebration. She was so excited to see it that she didn't even take a second to pray that he'd brought earphones. "Yeah?"

Pride swelled her chest. "My friend made that game!"

"Yeah?" The kid's eyes slid back to his screen. "Cool. Tell him he did a good job and that he'd better not kill off Antley."

Shira cringed inside because Antley did indeed die a glorious death, depending on the player's choices, but on the outside she only smiled, a master at avoiding spoilers. "I'll pass that along."

She settled into her seat, sticking her headphones in and letting herself be washed away by the sound of the latest hit historical Broadway musical. Or trying to let herself be washed away, at any rate. Every time she closed her eyes, she was jostled in the side by the teenager furiously jabbing buttons, in the elbow by mothball lady annoyed that Shira was using their shared armrest (come on, plane etiquette said that the middle seat got the armrests), or in the mind by the approximately one thousand deadlines she had coming up. *If you close your eyes now, you're going to get behind.*

Her eyes popped open. She sighed. She pulled out her headphones–she couldn't listen to music while drawing; it impacted her lines–and pulled out her tablet. Got to work. What was up next on the docket? The cover for someone's self-published young adult book, due next week. She'd already gotten approval for one of her sketches–a scene that pulled from *The Little Mermaid,* with the book's mermaid heroine sitting wistfully on a rock by the shore and the book's hero staring wistfully at her from the beach–and now had to do a finalized version with full color.

The odor of mothballs grew bigger and stinkier in her nostrils. The lady on her left was leaning in, looking curiously at her tablet. "Wow, that's really good."

"Thanks," Shira said wearily. She wished she could say the same about the book. Though she'd promised to read the whole thing, she'd barely managed to plod through the first third.

"What do you do? Are you an artist?"

A ghost of a smile stretched out her lips. "Yup. Full-time artist."

"Wow, that's the dream," Mothball Lady said admiringly, pushing her bleach-blond hair out of her eyes. "Lucky you."

Shira allowed herself to feel it for a moment. Not the luckiness. But the feeling of impressing someone, that golden glow that came whenever someone thought she was really cool.

It faded within seconds. It was like a drug, kind of. The more she'd felt it, the more she needed to feel it again. And, sometimes, it no longer even felt good. It just felt like she needed it to avoid the crash.

"I've always wanted to be an artist, but it's just a hobby currently." Mothball Lady clicked her long red nails against her lowered tray table. "Do you have any tips for me?"

Any tips? Well. She wouldn't recommend her current path. She still heard that conversation with her boss sometimes in her stress dreams, the ones she awoke from gasping in a cold sweat. *I'm afraid we can't offer you a raise this year.* The most annoying thing was how sympathetic he'd sounded. The man had complained to her last year about how frustrating it was to be in the highest tax bracket. *Typically, by this point, people at your level have started bringing in their own artists to work with and are earning commission that will take them to a higher salary level.*

But she couldn't bring in her own artists, she wanted to say. Because she was already staying up late exhausting herself working on her own stuff, trying desperately to get something in shape to submit to galleries. To prove to herself and to everyone else that there was more to her than who she was on the outside, the performance of Shira. She didn't have time.

"Well," Shira said carefully. "When I left my full-time job, I found that I had to earn money taking on freelance projects that I'm not super passionate about."

Mothball Lady's eyes widened. "Like monster sex?"

Shira choked on air. "Excuse me?"

"I mean, it's not something I have experience with personally." She examined her long red nails. "But I hear it's booming business online. Kraken and giants, oh my."

Shira hated that, for a split second, she wondered if she should try it. But that would definitely *not* fit her brand. "No, I started out as a painter and I worked at a gallery, so I have a lot of connections through my old workplace with other painters and people looking for painters," she said. "One of the painters does a lot of book covers and freelance illustration work, so he's sent some of those projects my way when his own schedule is packed."

"Oh, how cool," she said. "I love going on gallery tours. I saw that show recently that everyone was talking about at LACMA, the one with the creatures from Ukrainian mythology? The artist has a show at the Whitney soon. I'm hoping to see it while I'm in New York. Ah, what was her name?"

Shira was suddenly grateful for the vomit bag in the seat back. "Not sure," she said, reaching for her headphones again.

Mothball Lady raised her eyebrows. "If you're really tuned-in to the gallery scene, wouldn't you have heard about another young artist getting a solo show at the Whitney? Isn't that one of the biggest honors an artist can get, and this one is so young?"

"I'm sure you can google it," Shira said, sticking her earbuds in and staring down at her tablet, though the sketch blurred before her.

The woman kept talking, oblivious, and since Shira didn't actually have anything playing in her headphones, she could hear her words as clearly as the flight attendant's safety announcement. "Wasn't she, like, the youngest artist in history to get her own solo show at the Whitney? I think the show I saw was her first one."

That was enough. Shira had to make it stop. "Sounds like you're already an expert," she snapped. "You don't need me." And now she hit play and tried to lose herself in the music.

She wished she could say the rest of the flight *flew* by, but she might as well have crawled from LA to Philadelphia: Mothball Lady kept dozing off on her shoulder, and the teenager played his game without headphones the entire trip, despite the seven times the flight attendant stopped by to offer him a pair. By the time her dad met her in the arrivals parking lot—rental cars were for people with salaries and health insurance—she felt like she'd traveled to a whole different year.

She hadn't even finished the stupid cover.

"Thanks for picking me up," she said after she'd thrown her luggage in the trunk, leaning over the central console to give her dad a kiss on the cheek.

He nodded. "You're welcome." Someone beeped at them from behind. He rolled his eyes as he shifted into gear. "So impatient."

She kind of felt like reaching over and laying on the horn in response to the beeper, just to let out some aggression. "How was the drive?"

Their house in central Jersey was actually closer to the

airport in Newark, but her parents had asked her to fly into Philly instead if they were going to be picking her up. "Nice and easy," said her dad. They pulled out of the airport and into the dark night. All Shira had seen today was the dark: Between the flight, the time difference, and having to leave early to beat LA traffic, she'd missed any trace of the sun. "You could stay, you know."

Shira's teeth ground together. She'd thought she'd get at least one good night's sleep in before her parents tried to convince her to move back. She should've known they'd pounce on her while she was tired and weak. "I still have eight months left on my lease."

"You could break it." Cars whizzed by them on the highway while Shira's dad stayed comfortable in the right lane. "If you want to get another art-world job, you could come back to the East Coast. Start over in New York. If you're worried about the gap on your résumé, that would explain it."

"I think I'm going to close my eyes." Shira rested her head against the window, the cool glass soothing against her skin (the juddering from the road, less so).

Her dad didn't fully take the hint that she wanted to stop talking, but he at least got that she wanted to stop talking about moving back, which was a win. "Leo seems to be doing a good job planning the Hanukkah party," he said. "He's borrowing all our menorahs. Apparently he only has one."

"Great," Shira said. Leo had been peppering her with questions through the planning process, half of which she thought he only posed to get a rise out of her: *Can I just go get a bunch of french fries instead of latkes? What about a little Hanukkah tree with ornaments on it?* "I can't wait to see what he comes up with."

She hadn't totally told Leo the truth about why she wasn't throwing the party this year. It was true that her life was madness; somehow freelancing took even more time and hustle than her job at the art gallery had, which was the exact opposite of what she'd wanted when she quit. And it was more stressful. Any hint of a fallow period left her panicking that she wouldn't be able to cover her rent, which led to overworking herself to make sure she was saving enough for the inevitable downtime.

It was more that she'd realized she was a fraud. She hadn't meaningfully done anything Jewish in years besides throw the Hanukkah party, which was a performance showing other people how Jewish she was. And she was sick of performing. Life was too short to spend it performing for other people, right? That's what she'd decided.

It felt like she'd been born onstage and had spent her entire life wearing theater makeup and reciting the lines of a script, and now she didn't know how to improv. How to just . . . be.

If there was anyone she could learn from, though, it was Leo. He seemed to have it all figured out.

She discovered quickly that Leo's dad agreed. Pretty much as soon as Shira got home, she kissed her mom and sister hello, lugged in her baggage, rebuffing her dad's offers to carry it all, and told them she had to go take a walk or she was going to go insane. Talia didn't tell her she was already insane, which meant Shira must have looked really bad. That was fair, she consoled herself, because she'd spent the entire day in transit.

All she needed was to stretch her legs and enjoy the . . . howling wind and bitter cold. Nice.

The only other person crazy enough to go out in this weather was, of course, the guy who didn't want his dog pooping in his house. With the way Shira held her head ducked against the wind, she didn't notice him until she'd almost bumped into his chest. "Oh, hi," she said, leaning down to give Neptune a scratch with her gloved hand. "Not a very nice night."

"Not at all," said Leo's dad. "I wish I could trust this dog to go do his business on his own and then come back inside instead of tear off after a squirrel." He shook his head at his furry son in disappointment. His furry son was busy trying to eat frozen grass. "How are you, Shira?"

A few years ago, Shira would have mumbled something indecipherable and moved on. But if Leo could forgive his dad and talk to him, she could, too. "I'm okay," she said gamely. "It's nice to be home for the holidays." She paused for a moment. It wasn't like she was going to stand here and spill her guts to this near stranger. "I hear Leo's doing amazing. You know, the kid I sat next to on the plane was playing his game."

Leo's dad's eyes lit up. The pride he clearly felt on behalf of his son radiated through him, brighter than the streetlamp shining ghostily above them. "He's incredible. He's come so far in only a few years. I can't wait to see where he'll be in a few more."

Shira let herself picture it. Leo, another blockbuster game under his belt. Maybe heading up a studio or division at a studio—she had no idea what the hierarchy in video-game land looked like. Successful. Happy.

Where would she be in a few years? Treading water, like she was now? She didn't want to think about it. "And you're not too lonely living on your own?" she joked. Leo had texted her with pride when he'd moved out to his own place—an apartment closer to New York City, on the train line, where a bunch of game studios were located. Not too far away, though. He'd told her he still came back frequently to see his dad and probably make sure he hadn't had a heart attack and died.

Leo's dad laughed. "Far from it," he said. "Having a grown son living at home really cramps your dating life, as it turns out."

Shira did not want to hear details about Leo's dad's dating life. "Good for you," she said, then hoped he could tell she wasn't being sarcastic. "I mean it. I'll see you at the Hanukkah party, right?"

"It's at my house, so yes," he said. "And Leo, too, obviously." He hesitated, and somehow Shira knew to tense up before he spoke again. "I'm glad you two reconnected over the last few years. I think it's been good for him."

Shira didn't know how to respond. She didn't like thinking of friendship as something transactional. "I'm glad we reconnected, too." She left it at that.

The other night she'd dreamed about Danica, Ellery, and Nora. In her dream they'd been at a conference together, and she'd been stuck in the audience while Danica got up to give a speech, and it turned out Danica's speech was about the huge mistake she'd made in dumping Shira as a friend, and Shira had sat there crying in the audience until Danica came down and pulled her up out of her seat and hugged her, to everybody's applause.

Over a year since they'd dumped her and Shira still wasn't over it. Especially now that she had to see Danica's stupid face in every industry trade magazine, every museum and biennale newsletter talking about the hot new thing, everybody's enthusiastic cross-posting of her on social media.

When Shira had first perused Danica's work, she'd told her she saw the Whitney and the Venice Biennale in her future. And now Danica had actually done it, so much sooner than they could ever have dreamed, and Shira couldn't even congratulate her. Or say "I told you so."

Shira loved saying "I told you so."

"Well, good seeing you," Leo's dad said, snapping her back to the present. "I'm going to get this dog back inside before both of us freeze." He hesitated, then, maybe unable to override dad instinct, said, "You should get back inside, too. You're uninvited to the party if you get frostbite."

Shira rolled her eyes. "Okay, okay." And yet she turned around and went home. Leo had figured everything out; maybe she could, too.

❄

LEO DAVID HAD nothing figured out, nothing at all.

About the Hanukkah party, that is. (And other stuff, too, but he didn't need to focus on that right now.) How had Shira pulled this off every year on her own?

"The caterers are asking if crème fraîche is okay instead of sour cream," he read aloud from his phone, which was way too close to his face. When had he gotten so old that he couldn't read without glasses? He slumped back into his leather couch, biting back a sigh. "Do you think that's okay?"

Emily gave him that soft chuckle that always managed to twang some string deep in his chest. She was sitting atop one of the barstools at the counter that separated his living room area from the kitchen, eating yogurt and granola. "Christian-slash-agnostic, remember?"

"Right." Leo's eyes dropped back to his phone, mostly because Emily was wearing a spaghetti-strap tank top with no bra and he couldn't afford any distractions right now. "Shira would know. I guess I could text her."

"Then text Shira." Emily's voice was mild, a little curious. She'd been waiting to meet Shira ever since Leo had told her Shira had been his best friend in childhood, probably to beg her for embarrassing childhood-Leo stories.

"Okay. I will," he said, as if he'd been waiting for permission. He tapped out, squinting, Is crème fraiche acceptable for latkes in place of sour cream?

Due diligence done, he tossed his phone aside with a sigh. Though it had been nine months since he'd moved out into his own place—not coincidentally the same amount of time since he'd met Emily; there was no way he could've dated while living with his dad—he still instinctively flexed his fingers as if scratching Neptune on the head. He missed that old guy.

Though he was glad his dad had the company. Leo had felt bad about moving out after the heart attack, and it was his dad who'd finally forced his hand. "I'm not some frail old man," he'd said, though he said it while wearing reading glasses in his recliner with his graying hair sticking up all over his head, which didn't help his case. "I want you to live your life."

A conversation like this wouldn't have been possible the previous year. But they'd done the work, week by week by week, forcing themselves to talk about their feelings and their hopes and their regrets, and while Leo couldn't say he'd entirely forgiven his dad for what he'd done years earlier, he could say that he at least had some empathy for the man he'd been then and love for the man he was now.

"What if you have another heart attack?" Leo had asked.

His dad waved a hand in the air, stirring up a dust cloud. Leo should probably book someone to come by and clean the place a couple of times a month. He could afford something like that now. A little thrill ran through him at the thought. "So I'll have another heart attack," his dad said. "You'll find me eventually."

"Great," said Leo. "That won't be traumatizing or anything."

"Well, I'd hope you'd find me before Neptune started eating me." They both swiveled toward the dog, who was lying on the ground at Leo's dad's feet. At the sound of his name, his ears perked up and his tail started thumping.

"Neptune would never eat you," Leo said, more out of loyalty to man's best friend than anything else, because, truth be told, Neptune probably would. Beagles were food driven. He'd probably let a kidnapper cart Leo off, screaming while having his fingernails pulled out one by one, if he got a hamburger in exchange. "Anyway, you need me. I can't move out."

"You're going to move out. That's actually what I was doing. Looking for rentals in the paper." Leo's dad frowned down at his pen. "Not finding many."

"That's because you're searching in 1995. Rentals are all online now." Leo took a seat on the couch across from his dad, still focused on the dog. (He might have gotten better at talking about his feelings, but it didn't mean he liked to look people in the eye while he did it.) "Seriously, what happens if you have another heart attack?"

His dad folded up his paper, then frowned down at it. "Don't you remember the doctor telling us how lucky we were that we caught the first one early, because that meant they could treat the problem and hopefully avoid another one in the future?"

"Sure, but–"

"So my odds are better than they were back then," his dad said, slightly louder. "What if I slip in the shower and hit my head? What if you do stay and live here, but I have the grand one while you're in Italy with your mother or out on a date? Are you just never going to leave the house because something bad might happen?"

It was hard to argue with that, so Leo didn't try. Because, honestly, he was ready to move out. Sometimes, when he thought about having his own space where he controlled the temperature and the decorations and nobody was there to judge him if he just wanted to rot on the couch in holey sweats for a day, he physically itched with how badly he wanted it. "I'm going to call you every day," he said. "And if you don't pick up, I'm coming to check on you."

His dad grimaced. "You could just send a text."

"Or I could get you one of those necklaces that really old people wear," Leo had mused. "The ones that send an alarm if it feels you fall."

"Yeah, I'm not wearing that."

Leo's phone dinged. Not from a Life Alert notification—his dad steadfastly refused to wear any form of jewelry—but from Shira's response. He didn't have to squint to read it, because it was in all caps. ARE YOU KIDDING? NO, CRÈME FRAICHE IS NOT AN ACCEPTABLE ALTERNATIVE TO SOUR CREAM WHEN IT COMES TO LATKES. FIRE YOUR FANCY CATERER.

Emily's soft auburn hair brushed his cheek. "She has very strong feelings about latkes."

"And Hanukkah food in general." Leo grinned and typed back, Got it, thanks. So I'm guessing Cronuts in place of doughnuts is also a no?

Typing bubbles arose, then fell away, then arose again, then disappeared again. Probably because it was hard to type while your head was exploding. She finally responded with You're dead to me.

"Period and all. Harsh," Emily commented over his shoulder, but her tone was light.

Leo lowered his phone, grinning. "Shira takes her food very seriously. You know, a couple years ago, we broke into a bakery together and stole doughnuts."

"What?" Emily spun to face him, her wide green eyes shocked. "And here I had no idea that I was about to move in with a career criminal."

"It's good you found out now." Leo strove to keep his tone light, to match hers. "You can still back out."

Emily plopped down beside him and rested her head on his shoulder. "Just call me Bonnie," Emily said. When he stared blankly at her, she clarified. "As in Bonnie and Clyde. I'll call you Clyde."

Leo snorted. "Leonard is bad enough."

Emily smiled up at him. "I'm going to start calling you Leonard in bed."

"Then I'm going to start calling you Aemilius," he said. "Which is where the name Emily comes from."

She rolled her eyes and changed the subject. "Have you thought more about the offer from Tiny Elephant?"

He immediately tensed and pulled away. "No."

"I'm not trying to get you to go one way or the other, you know that," she said. "But you've got to respond to them. You don't want to snub one of the biggest gaming studios in the country."

He groaned, closing his eyes and leaning his head back. "I'm not trying to snub them. I genuinely don't know the best thing to do."

"There's no right or wrong," she said. He felt her fingers stroke through his hair, and immediately relaxed into the couch like chocolate melting in the microwave. "Do you want to sell your game to them and become its head developer there, or do you want to keep doing it on your own? I know you've been stressed lately."

"I'm living the dream," he said automatically, because he'd learned that was what people wanted to hear. He'd made it. That was what they all thought.

He couldn't help but think of Shira every time he said it. How people got that same admiring and slightly jealous look in their eyes when they spoke with him now, and how it made him a little uncomfortable because he knew he was a fraud. She'd gotten addicted to it, though, and who could blame her?

"Well." Emily kept stroking his hair, turning him into butter on a hot piece of steak. Okay, continuous food similes meant he was ready for dinner. "You've got time. Sleep on it. And if you really don't want to get back to them, maybe that's an answer in itself."

Maybe. Maybe not. Leo drew her forward for a kiss, and that was better than any chocolate or steak. Work situation, whatever, at least he had this figured out.

14

THE MENORAHS WERE SET UP IN PLACES OF PRIDE near the front windows. The caterers were bustling in and out, setting up their steam trays and crisping up some latkes on portable griddles. The bartender Leo had hired was practicing his pours in the den. Neptune was trotting around, his beagle ears scrunched about his face in confusion, probably wondering why all these people were in his peaceful home and also if he could snatch a latke off the griddle without burning himself.

Leo was ready to take a nap. He was barely doing anything on his own—Emily had yoinked the task of decorating from him after she'd seen the few sad garlands he'd picked up from the dollar store—but just getting everything done and organized had really taken it out of him. He stood in the corner of the living room, taking direction from his girlfriend about what to hang where. Hold this here while she tapes it up, help her straighten this paper dreidel tablecloth.

At least he wasn't the only one hovering around: He had his dad for company. Leo had insisted he sit, though, and not worry about helping with the decorations. "Exercise is good for me, you know," his dad kept grumbling. "You're going to send me to an early grave."

"Don't even joke about that," Emily chided.

Leo's dad smiled absently at her as she stood on her tiptoes to place a Mensch on a Bench on the highest shelf of their bookcase, ready to startle anybody tall. *I like her, she's very nice* was what he'd told Leo after they'd met for the first time. *She's not Jewish, is she?*

Leo had no idea if he was saying that in a positive or negative way. A few years ago, he would have assumed the worst and picked a fight. A couple of years ago, he would have just rolled his eyes and not asked any follow-up questions.

But now, he felt free to ask *No, but what do you mean by that?*

His dad was evasive with the follow-up. *Nothing. I just always thought you'd end up with someone Jewish.* Which didn't even make sense. Technically, according to Jewish law, Leo wasn't considered Jewish himself, since his mother wasn't Jewish. Reform Judaism considered him Jewish, but Leo didn't belong to a synagogue. Truthfully, he felt more Jew-ish than Jewish.

Though being around Shira had always made him feel like part of the tribe. She'd never treated him like anything less, even though he didn't think she'd grown up Reform.

As the guests began to arrive, Leo stationed himself near his dad's front door, Emily on his arm, his cheeks already aching with a constant smile. Since Leo had moved out almost a year ago, he hadn't seen most of his neighbors in that time, and he was surprised by how nice it felt to greet all these familiar faces he was used to seeing on Neptune's walks. There were a few new faces in the mix, too, young families, some people not much older than Leo but with a kid or two in tow. It made him a little queasy, to tell you the truth. Not the kids; he liked kids and wanted one or two of them someday. But people his age with kids? He didn't feel even remotely ready, not even when he saw how naturally Emily cooed at the baby and made it smile.

Talia was the first Levinson to show up, though it took him a second to realize it. Gone were her black hair and heavy bangs, the constantly rolling eyes lined in thick black goop. Apparently graduating from college had shifted her style to a brown bob (Leo had no idea if it was her natural hair color; she'd been blond as a kid) and either no or natural makeup—Leo could never tell. Once he'd told Emily how incredible she looked with no makeup, and she'd laughed and told him she was wearing mascara, foundation, and some other stuff he couldn't remember. The only person he could for sure tell was or wasn't wearing makeup was Shira, because he'd seen her face in so many states of dress and undress over the years. He'd literally watched her face form into its current state, from childhood to teenagerhood.

Why did he keep thinking of Shira tonight? Probably because he was about to see her for the first time in a year. It made total sense.

"Happy Hanukkah, Talia!" Leo said, and she glowered at him. At least that would never change.

"I've decided to go to rabbinical school," she told him.

"Wow." He blinked. That had certainly come out of nowhere. "Nice. Congrats. Or mazel tov, I guess."

"Thanks," she said, and swept inside. Her parents came after her in a flurry of "Congratulations on your game, we've heard all about it" and "How nice to meet you, Emily" and "Ooh, is that brisket?" before they ran in to nab the good end pieces, as they put it.

And then there was Shira. She was wearing a dark-blue dress that flared out around her knees and fit much better than the black dress from last year had; she'd thrown her hair up in a messy bun, and her hands were clasped before her, holding each other tightly, as if she were trying to stop herself from biting her nails. (She clearly hadn't been doing a great job at it–Leo could see the gnaw marks from here.) "Shira, hey, happy Hanukkah," he said and turned to Emily. "Emily, this is Shira, my neighbor and old friend. Shira, this is Emily. My girlfriend."

Was it Leo's imagination, or did Shira's whole body do a stutter stop before her smile turned on? "Emily, hi," she said, extending her hand. Emily shook hers back. "It's so nice to meet you."

"You, too," Emily said. "I've heard so much about you."

"Only good things, I hope." Shira beamed with all her teeth. "You guys met at school?"

"Yeah, after Leo transferred to Rutgers. We were both the old people in our psychology elective." She laid her head on Leo's shoulder, arm twining tighter through his. "I swear you could hear all the eighteen-year-olds groan whenever we asked a question. And I'm pretty sure they had a class Google Doc we weren't invited to."

"Joke's on them because we set the curve for the final," Leo added. Somehow it seemed important that Shira knew how well he'd done.

"Wow, good for you," Shira said, mostly sincerely. She glanced over her shoulder, as if she were worried she was blocking other guests from entering, but no, she was the last one, at least for now. Her earring swung with the movement, an earring shaped like a menorah, tiny jewels glinting in place of candles. Of course Shira would own menorah earrings. "And did you see my text about how the kid next to me on the plane was playing your game?"

"Yeah, that was so cool," Leo said without a lot of enthusiasm. Which was probably weird, right? He should be enthusiastic that his game, the thing he'd crafted with his brain and his hands and his time, was reaching so many people and striking so many chords.

But he knew better than to try and inject false enthusiasm into his voice, because it just made him sound insane. So he took the coward's way out. "What's new with you?"

"Oh, well, you know." She sounded a little too bright herself, verging on the edge of insane. "I'm sure you saw that Danica was not only the youngest artist to have a solo show at the Whitney but was also the US's exhibition in the Venice Biennale. So she's been everywhere, and that's been fun."

"What's the Venice Biennale?" Leo and Emily said at the same time. Emily snickered and elbowed him. "You owe me a Coke."

"There are plenty of Cokes over on the beverage table that I purchased. Help yourself," said Leo. She rolled her eyes.

"You guys don't know what the Venice Biennale is?" Shira said. "It's basically . . ." She trailed off, shaking her head. "Never mind. It doesn't matter."

"I love that print of yours that Leo has hanging up!" Emily said cheerfully. "He said you're doing your art full-time now? That's so cool!"

"I am indeed doing my art full-time now!" Shira said, matching Emily's level and then going all-in on the cheer. "Had a tiny little breakdown earlier this year and left my job at the gallery to hustle on my own stuff. What better time, right? Being young and single and sans mortgage?"

"The perfect time!" Emily said, and if she was going to add any more exclamation points into the conversation, Leo couldn't handle it. He didn't think Shira could handle it, either. Her smile was so huge it took over her face, and yet somehow it didn't reach her eyes.

"Hey," he said, leaning in. "I should probably warn you that your creepy uncle's made an appearance."

Nothing but confusion on her face for a few seconds, and then it clicked. Her eyes lit up. "Can I get a hint so that I don't jump out of my skin?"

"He's not a mensch, and he's also not actually on a bench. And he's very tall this year," Leo said.

"I see." She looked up. "I'll keep my eye out. He'd better not try to look down my shirt."

"I'll stomp on him if he does that," Leo promised, and Shira laughed.

"Okay, thanks for protecting my honor. I hope that your fancy caterers are doing my latke cocktail?"

"I wouldn't have it any other way," he said.

"Great. I'm going to go get one." And there she went, shouldering her way into the crowd. For a moment he wanted to go after her, serve as her shield. Because she'd spent years telling everyone about her art and her job and her life, they'd certainly start asking her about all that, putting her on the spot.

But of course he couldn't go be her shield; he had to introduce Emily around. Not *had to*; that had come out the wrong way. He had the privilege of introducing his beautiful, smart, kind, funny girlfriend to all the people he'd grown up around. Right. That was better.

The next hour-ish passed in a flurry of introductions and snacks. The latkes from the catering company were good, but the ones Shira used to make were better. The latke cocktail the bartender made was better than Shira's, but Leo would never let those words pass his lips. Some of his neighbors actually patted Leo on the back upon meeting Emily, which honestly made him feel a little gross, but everybody seemed to like her and she seemed to like everybody well enough that she didn't run screaming out the door.

Emily was ensconced in an actually fascinating conversation about a scandal recently uncovered by the local paper (apparently the school board had been taking bribes from someone high up in the Peruvian government for years, the money laundered through a local mattress firm). And then: disaster. He noticed Talia sitting by herself in the corner, which in itself wasn't unusual, since whenever she'd come over in the past she'd spend at least some time cloistered in the corner giving Neptune belly rubs. As if she were thinking the same thing, she said in a way that sounded as if she were accusing him of theft, "Where's your dog?"

Where *was* his dog? He wasn't in the kitchen begging for

food or trying to jump up on the table when nobody could see him, which was the only other place Leo would have expected him to be. "If he gets too annoying around the food"—the specification was necessary because beagles were always at least a little annoying around food—"sometimes my dad sticks him in the bedroom so people can eat in peace." But then they would've heard him howling with displeasure, and Leo didn't hear anything except the Maccabeats rapping about Hanukkah.

Neptune wasn't in the den. He wasn't in the dining room. Half-panicked now, Leo found his dad holding court on the living room couch, drink in the air, clearly about to toast to something. "Dad," Leo said, and his dad turned to him, lowering his glass. "Have you seen Neptune? I can't find him anywhere."

He wasn't on the deck, which was Leo's last hope. Leo cursed as Emily shook her head and his dad pressed his lips together hard. "He must have gotten out," said his dad. "There were people going in and out all night. We should've taken better precautions."

It was too late for that. No sense in wasting time on the *could'ves would'ves should'ves*. "He's not chipped, is he?" Leo said.

His dad shook his head. "Unfortunately not."

The words hung there in the cold air for a second, then dispersed into white mist. Again, no point in wasting time on wishing it had been done. "Okay," Leo said. "Let's split up and find him. Emily, you go up the street toward the cul-de-sac. Take some food with you, he'll come running if he smells food. Chicken, ideally. Dad, you go toward the main road." God, hopefully he didn't find Neptune on the main road. "And I'll go back into the woods. Text immediately if you find him, okay?"

Emily nodded, eyes resolute. His dad didn't even nod, just turned and hustled away.

A few seconds later, Leo had a hunk of chicken in hand and his coat thrown over his shoulders—no time to put his arms in the sleeves—and was striding with his flashlight into the dark trees behind his house. The cheerful music coming from the lit windows faded the farther away he got. His stomach flip-flopped—there was a reason so many horror movies started with people camping alone in the woods at night. His tiny light barely penetrated the thick blackness ahead. Trees loomed above, branches silhouetted against the moon like skeleton fingers. Anything could be lurking behind them.

"Neptune? Here, boy," he called out, partially so that the silence wouldn't get overwhelming. In the summer the woods were thick with sound at night—the thrum of crickets and frogs, birds chirping at one another—but in the winter everything was bare and quiet. "Neptune, I have chicken."

His feet crunched on dead pine needles and ice crystals, and he was about to admit defeat and head back—he couldn't see anything, anyway—when he heard a tiny plaintive howl. "Neptune?" he called in its direction, hoping it was a beagle howl and not a wolf pup who would at first seem disarmingly cute and in need of help but whose mother would pounce upon him and tear him to shreds for daring to go near her baby.

"Leo?" *That* certainly wasn't a beagle howl, no matter that his dad always insisted Neptune knew their names. Leo swung his flashlight in the direction of the voice. Light flashed over creaking ropes, ladder rungs, the plastic curve of a slide. The swing set, Leo realized, and then the light landed on Shira.

SHIRA SQUINTED INTO the beam of the flashlight, shielding her eyes with one hand. She clutched the leash with the other, of course. She wasn't going to let Leo's dog run off.

Out of the darkness stepped Leo, a much gladder sight than the other things she'd worried might step out of the darkness and swallow her whole. His white button-down—which really should have been an ugly Hanukkah sweater, as was his right as party host—practically glowed from under his jacket. Neptune whuffed with surprised delight, his tail thumping the dirt between Shira's feet. "There you are, boy." Leo crouched before her to scratch the beagle's head, setting the chicken before him, where it was downed immediately in one gulp. "We thought you'd run off."

Oh, crap. Shira hadn't thought to tell anyone where she was going when she found the poor dog pawing at the back door, tail between his legs, clearly needing to pee. "Sorry, sorry," she said. "I should've told someone. He just looked like he needed to go out, and I really needed to get out too, so I figured we'd kill two birds with one stone."

"No worries," Leo said. "Let me just text my dad and Emily that I found him." Emily. Of course Emily would've been out looking with him. He hesitated, glancing up from his phone. "I assume that when you say you needed to get out, it wasn't to pee."

"I'm a free woman," said Shira. "I'll pee wherever I want to."

Leo hesitated again. He shrugged his coat, which was draped over his shoulders, down over his arms, then fully on. He took a seat on the swing beside her. It creaked in a way it never used to when they'd been kids. "Talk to me," he said.

Over the past year, he'd grown his hair out a little more so that the curls were back, and a short beard, too, which she'd never seen on him. It didn't quite fit him somehow, made him look both older and younger at the same time, depending on the angle. Something clenched inside her. It was like all the fears, worries, and pains of the last several months had clogged some vital tube in her chest, blocking the blood flow, and she didn't know how to dislodge it. "It seems that I didn't have everything figured out at twenty-two after all."

"I don't think anybody thinks twenty-two-year-olds have everything figured out," Leo supplied. He sounded faintly amused, his tone deadpan. "Except maybe other twenty-two-year-olds."

She swallowed, her throat dry. "I really thought I did, though. I had the dream job that I'd spent my whole life working toward. I had my painting, and I was really starting to succeed there. I had my group of friends, I had my city, I had everything."

"You can still have the Hanukkah party," Leo said. "I'm just keeping it warm for you."

"But that's the thing," she said. "Every year I told myself, you have the Hanukkah party, that's how you're connected to your Jewishness. But I stopped doing everything else. I haven't belonged to a synagogue in years. I haven't been to a Passover seder since I moved out to LA, since it's too expensive to take time off work and fly home for a few days. I could've gone to a seder with a colleague or at the local Chabad, but I didn't. I haven't even fasted on Yom Kippur. Hanukkah isn't actually an important holiday, you know, it's just that non-Jews think it's the most important holiday for us because it's right around Christmas. And yet I turned it into my most important holiday. What does that say about me?"

He stayed silent. Which was good, really. She didn't think she wanted to hear him answer that.

She dragged her toes through the dirt. Even after all these years, the soil beneath the swing was still shaped like a little valley. It hadn't forgotten them. "That's the real reason I didn't want to host this year," she said quietly. "Because it was just one more performance for the rest of the world. Beautiful on the outside, rotten on the inside. Like me." She immediately felt silly. "That was just a metaphor. I'm not trying to say that I'm beautiful or—"

"You are, though." He said it simply, just as a breeze brushed her cheek. Her heart skipped a beat, and she tried to tell herself it was the chill of the wind, but it didn't work even for a second.

Leo David telling her she was beautiful. She touched her lips, remembering the feeling of his on hers so many years ago. She hadn't thought about their kiss in ages, and to her surprise, the memory didn't bring back the mortification she remembered feeling. Or had it been mortification right away? Hadn't she lost herself in it for a moment, sunk into him, before her brain yanked her out of it and told her he wasn't good enough?

A bitter laugh huffed through her lips. Look at the irony now: She was the one who'd fallen apart, and now he was the one with everything together. If she tried to broach anything now, she'd be such a hypocrite. She wouldn't broach anything anyway, because he was happy with Emily, and she wasn't about to break up somebody's relationship. To be the other woman. No.

Besides, what if she only wanted him now *because* he had everything together and she didn't? If she only wanted a taste of what she'd had before everything fell apart?

"When my friends dumped me," she said quietly, "it rocked my world. No, it rocked *me*. It made me realize that work wasn't enough. That even if I had the best job ever that impressed everyone around me, it still wasn't enough, and where did that leave me? What was the point of it all?" She shook her head. "And then Danica got that Whitney exhibit, and that fully broke me. Because nothing I could ever do would be more impressive than that. She'd won the image war. Forever. Even if I somehow eventually got one, which I won't, she'd still be the youngest artist ever to do it. So again, what was the point? It really made me look inward. Think about what actually mattered."

The woods were silent and still. Even Neptune was quiet, his ears perked for whatever came next. She continued, feeling each word like ice melting in her mouth, "I think that I don't know who I am. I think that I've lived my life so far in pursuit of what other people want. First college admissions boards, then trying to get the dream job, then . . . I lost sight of myself. I don't know what I actually want. I don't know who I actually am."

She let the words hang in the air for a few seconds in a cloud of fog. Her eyes had adjusted to the point where, when it cleared, she could see Leo looking at her not with pity but compassion. Her fingers flexed with the want to hold his.

Somewhere in the process of her thinking all this through, Leo had swiveled to face her, twisting the cords of his swing the way they used to when they were kids and they'd want to spin

spin spin until they were dizzy. "I know the Shira Levinson that was there before you started joining clubs to impress the admissions committees at Harvard and Yale and Princeton." *And Brown*, she thought, her first choice, which had rejected her. "She loved art, and she loved sharing art with others. None of that was made up to impress people. She's meant to share art with the world. Maybe not in a high-pressure gallery but somehow." He reached out as if going to grab her hand. She held her breath, but his arm fell before they could touch. "And she wanted to throw a Hanukkah party for her neighborhood so that she could share the joy of being Jewish with everybody, not so that she could show off."

She felt like she might burst into tears. "It's true. When did you get everything figured out?"

"I don't have *everything* figured out," he said softly, and she could hear the words he didn't say. *Just you, Shira.*

She loved him, she realized suddenly. She'd always loved him.

How had she never realized it before?

Maybe this was the stripped-down core of her, or part of it, anyway. As a kid she'd loved Leo before she knew what romantic love even meant. And now, as an adult, with everything stripped away from her, this was still who she was. She still loved Leo David. She wanted Leo David.

And she couldn't tell him that. He'd moved on.

Her stomach twisted. She'd figured the first bit of herself out, and that was good, she told herself. It gave her some sense of peace because it meant that there was still a Shira Levinson in there to find.

She didn't burst into tears, but her eyes did well up. "I'm really happy for you," she said, swallowing over the lump in her throat. "Genuinely, I am. I'm really happy that you're doing so well." That harsh laugh again. "You've really found your thing. Your passion. You're living and breathing your game, right?" He was staring at her like she was leaking out of the ears instead of the eyes. "I cared too much about what people thought, and you didn't care what anyone thought. You really had it right."

He was quiet. His tongue darted out to lick his lips, then slipped back into his mouth. "Shira." His voice was nothing more than the whisper of wind on trees. "That's not true. I cared what one person thought." He met her eyes, and his were soft now, like the carpet of pine needles underfoot in the summer. "That first winter I saw you, I was ready to rot at the warehouse forever, miserable and angry, and I didn't care what my dad thought or the neighbors thought or my old classmates thought. But then you were here, and you were disappointed in me, and I could live with their disappointment, but I couldn't live with yours." She realized she was holding her breath. "I did this all for *you*."

For a moment it was like the rest of the world faded away. The only two people in existence were Shira and Leo, sitting on their swings, their legs kicking into gray nothingness, the ropes reaching up into the endless sky above. For a moment she let herself imagine it could stay this way forever. No having to figure out her life and who she was. No dating apps. Only the swing set and Leo and his hands and his lips and the way her head fit perfectly into the crevice between his chin and his chest.

And then the bubble broke. "Leo? Neptune?" Emily's voice echoed through the woods. "Are you guys still back here?"

Shira allowed herself a moment of wild, crazy hope that Leo would ignore his girlfriend, grab Shira's hand, and—what? They would run away giggling madly into the dark woods, which eventually ended at the highway? Of course he didn't. He had a whole life without her, one with a job and a girlfriend and friends and activities, that existed entirely outside this bubble. He stood, holding Neptune's leash—when had he grabbed it?—and called back. "Yeah, we're here."

Dead leaves crunched softly as Emily approached. Her flashlight beam blinded Shira for a moment before she stood, too. "Oh, cute," Emily said, squinting at the swing set. "I didn't know this was back here."

"Yeah, all this is technically my dad's land." Leo stepped closer to Emily and gave her a quick, casual hug. Shira hated how her heart squeezed to see it. "We didn't get the swing set until I was older, and I begged for it to be back here, where we'd have more privacy. I think by then my parents knew they weren't having another kid, so they were more than happy to have the screaming of older kids on a swing set farther away."

"Nice," Emily said. "Privacy." She smiled at Shira. "I hear you found our runaway friend?"

Why did she have to be so nice? Why couldn't she be stiff and snobby toward her boyfriend's female childhood friend so that Shira could dislike her in peace? Shira forced a smile. "I didn't find him so much as run away with him," she said. "I should've let someone know I was taking him for a walk. Sorry."

"All's well that ends well," Leo and Emily said in unison, and they laughed, her head resting on his shoulder—where, Shira hated to see, it fit perfectly. "Anyway," Emily said. "They're about to light the candles but didn't want to do it without you. And by *they*, I mostly mean *me*, because I've been studying up on those blessings and you need to see the way I am going to rock them even though I don't know any Hebrew."

"Yeah you are," said Leo, and the two of them, plus Neptune, pulled ahead of Shira. "By the way, I think I made my decision about Tiny Elephant."

"You did?" Emily said. "What are you going to do?"

The rest of their conversation about a tiny elephant—Shira wanted a tiny elephant, honestly, because then people would ask her only about her tiny elephant and not about herself, and also it would be extremely cute—was swallowed up by the noise from the party. Even with the cold, the back windows were all flung wide open to let out some of the people steam inside.

Leo and Emily, still talking, disappeared through the back door. Shira stood there on the deck for a moment, watching them go. They didn't notice her back there, and that was fine. Because you know what? Shira didn't deserve Leo, anyway. Not the Shira she was now. Leo knew the Shira she'd been back then, but she wasn't the same person now. She couldn't be. And she couldn't try to blow up his whole world without knowing if that new person would be worth it. Would deserve him.

A sense of peace spread through her as the sounds of the blessings poured out the window, bathing her in light. This was what she wanted. This was what she needed. By next year, she wouldn't just have outer peace—she'd have inner peace, too.

From Leo David's sent-emails folder, January:

Hi Eric—I really appreciate you reaching out. The idea of Tiny Elephant buying Washing Dishes and also bringing me on to head the department is an exciting one, and I'm thrilled to accept. As I'm sure you know, doing this on my own has been quite the undertaking—all the marketing, all the developing, all the storyboarding—and I'm ready to have a team to take on some of that work in the future . . .

From Shira Levinson's email inbox, February:

Hi Shira—Thanks so much for coming by yesterday for a synagogue tour! I loved meeting you and getting to introduce you to our rabbi, who I know enjoyed meeting you too. As we discussed, we have a vibrant, active Sisterhood chapter with members of all ages that makes volunteering in our community and doing social events a priority, and we have space available in our adult Torah study class if you're interested in pursuing that . . .

Texts between Shira Levinson and Leo David, October:

Shira: Bad news, bucko: the bitch is back

Shira: And by the bitch, I mean me

Shira: And by back, I mean the Hanukkah party is mine again. But don't fret, you can still be the guest of honor

Shira: Along with Emily, of course!!

Leo: . . .

Leo: . . .

Shira: Uh-oh, the typing bubbles of doom. Don't tell me you're going to fight me for the party

Shira: I will lose

Shira: I'm weak

Shira: I have noodle arms

Leo: Don't worry, I'm not planning to eat your delicious arms of spaghetti. But bad news, bucko: Emily and I won't actually be around for the Hanukkah party ☹ Neither will my dad. We're traveling for the holiday break to go see my grandparents in Florida, the land of sun and alligators

Shira: Aw we'll miss you ☹

Shira: Try not to get eaten!!

Leo: It'll be easier for me considering my arms are not made of edible material ☺

Shira: Bad news, bucko: to an alligator, all of you is edible material

Shira: But seriously, hope you guys have a great trip!! ☺

15

Year Five

LEO HAD BEEN IN FLORIDA FOR FOUR DAYS AND HAD already seen three alligators. He had fortunately been eaten by none (so far), but his guard was up. Sure, an alligator probably wouldn't try to eat him, but you never knew. And his grandparents were weak and slow and fragile. Likely too bony to make a decent meal, but an easy catch.

It was undoubtedly for the best they'd boarded Neptune back home. Those juicy chops and plump belly would've made him a prime alligator target.

Not that there were alligators at Disney World, where they were currently strolling down Main Street, Cinderella Castle looming above like a benevolent overlord. Was it true that Walt Disney's cryogenically frozen corpse was hidden somewhere inside? He kind of wanted to sneak in and find out.

"Do you even *see* how clean it is here?" Emily said enthusiastically, and he couldn't help but smile at her. She'd never been to Disney World before, so Aunt Ellen, of all people, had insisted on taking her. The two women plus Leo and his dad had started the day at Epcot (because even though Leo had tried to convince her it was the most boring park, Emily was determined to see the giant golf ball that was Spaceship Earth) before heading over to Magic Kingdom for the afternoon. The park was decked out in holiday finery, garlands decorating all the lampposts, Christmassy music tinkling over hidden loudspeakers.

"It is very clean," Leo agreed.

Emily spun and jabbed her finger at his chest while walking backward—awfully confident of her, considering the crowds ahead. "No, I'm serious. When's the last time you've been to a place with this number of people milling around that didn't have even a single piece of garbage on the ground? It's incredible."

"Some might say . . . magical."

She didn't even roll her eyes, just spun back around and gasped. "Cinderella!" She dashed off into the crowd, followed closely by Aunt Ellen, who, upon walking into the park, believe it or not, had pulled out a pair of Minnie Mouse ears bedazzled with her name in pink crystals. Leo hung back to walk with his dad, who'd been following with a bemused expression.

"You don't want to meet Cinderella?" Leo asked.

His dad snorted. "I'd rather meet the Fairy Godmother." He jutted his chin at one of the benches lining the street. "Want to sit down for a few?"

Leo followed him to the bench and sat. You know, it was true. The park was incredibly clean, something he hadn't appreciated during visits as a kid. "If Emily is this impressed by the cleanliness, wait till she meets the moving, talking garbage cans," he said. That had been his favorite part of his Disney

World trip with the Boy Scouts in elementary school. He and his friends had followed one around for half the day, rides be damned.

His dad snorted again. "I still can't believe I paid for you to go on that trip and the one thing you couldn't stop talking about was the garbage can."

Leo smirked, and then his dad's words from before caught up to him. "Wait, why would you want to meet the Fairy Godmother? Have some wishes you want to make?"

His dad cracked a smile, but he didn't laugh. "Who doesn't?"

"Huh," Leo said. Honestly, he'd never really thought about it. Life was just life. You got what you got. The thought of making a wish and your life changing was a little disconcerting somehow, like it was too easy. He supposed this explained why he never bought lottery tickets, something Emily did every time the jackpot rose over a billion dollars. It was worth the few bucks to see the pink in her cheeks as she romanticized over the places they'd buy homes and the palaces they'd stay in overseas. "What wishes would you make?"

His dad scuffed the bricks below with one toe. Leo half expected some maniacally frowning Disney peon to pop up from an underground trapdoor and reprimand him or, more realistically, for some maniacally grinning Disney peon to pop up with a mop and polish any evidence of a mark away. "I think I'd ask to go back in time," he said, a little moodily. "I've told you I don't regret the divorce."

Leo's stomach clenched, and he swallowed hard, but he didn't follow his instinct to change the subject to something airy and light. His mom (currently staying in one of those ice hotels in the Arctic North and dancing beneath the northern lights, hopefully clothed) would have approved.

"But I do regret how it happened," his dad continued. "I wish I could take the opportunity to go back and be honest before I got caught. Tell your mother I wasn't happy and hopefully make things less difficult for you. Keep you in my life."

There was no sense in wishing things were different. No point. But Leo understood that wish at least. His dad had spent a lot of years being lonely and sad, and yeah, it had been his own fault, but he was only human. He wasn't perfect. None of them were. And he'd done the work to change and grow and become a better man. "I'm really proud of you," Leo said. He kept his eyes trained on the ground because, again, eye contact while sharing feelings was not his strong suit. "You've come a long way. And I'm happy you did. I'm glad we're . . ." He trailed off because he didn't know what to say. Friends? That didn't really capture the relationship. "Close again."

"I'm not the only one who's come a long way." His dad's voice was gruff. "Look at you. I couldn't be prouder."

Leo might choke on the lump in his throat. Okay, now he had to change the subject because no way was Mickey Mouse going to catch him crying. "I was thinking of proposing. To Emily."

This time he looked up because he didn't want to miss his dad's reaction. The older man's eyebrows raised. His jaw didn't quite drop, but it did fall slowly. "Here? At Disney World?"

"No, no, no," Leo hastened to say. "I don't even have a ring yet. It's just something we've started talking about."

His dad blinked at him for a moment. "I suppose it makes

sense," he said finally. "You've been together for a while now. You live together. It's the natural next step."

Leo waited for his dad to tell him how great he and Emily were together, how he was definitely making the right decision, but nope. Silence. "I love her," he said, and it was true.

"I know you do," his dad said. "I love her, too. As a daughter-in-law. I just . . ." He laughed a little, shaking his head. "I don't know, Emily is wonderful. I have no doubt that you love her. Just, the way you light up around Shira . . . I guess I always thought . . ."

It hit Leo like the Fairy Godmother's wand thumping him right on the head. When his dad had said that thing about how he'd always thought Leo would end up with someone Jewish—an incongruous enough statement that it had stuck in Leo's mind for a year, like a burr on his pant leg—he hadn't been thinking of any random Jewish woman. He'd been thinking specifically of one Jewish woman.

Leo cleared his throat. It almost felt blocked, for some reason. "I had a crush on her for years, but I never told you."

"You didn't have to," said his dad. "It was obvious."

It wasn't like Leo could argue with that. He *had* been in love with Shira. A long time ago. Not anymore. And it probably hadn't even been love, just a crush. He wondered how Hanukkah party prep was going. If she was insane enough to try to make latkes from scratch again for everyone. He smiled at the thought, then banished the smile just as quickly. "Well, me and Shira are clearly not happening," he said. "Because I'm with Emily. I love Emily." He paused for a moment, the curiosity nagging at him. "You know, I was also in love with Gal Gadot as a kid. But you weren't convinced I'd end up with her. Why did you think I'd end up with Shira?"

His dad was quiet for a moment. "If you're going to marry Emily, I don't want it to come off like I'm trying to convince you otherwise. Like I said, she's wonderful, and if she makes you happy, then I'm happy."

"I promise I won't take it like that."

"Okay," said his dad. "Are you familiar with the Yiddish word *bashert*?"

"I'm familiar with zero Yiddish words," said Leo.

"Not true," said his dad, his face lighting up, which–groan–meant he was probably about to lecture Leo about something nerdy. "Don't you know how many Yiddish words have made their way into the English lexicon? Klutz. Schlep. Chutzpah. Kvetch. Bagel, Leo, *bagel*."

"Point taken," Leo said before his dad could really get started. "Turns out I know at least several Yiddish words. But *bashert* is not one of them."

His dad looked away, as if ensuring Emily was nowhere in hearing distance–she wasn't; Leo could see her and Aunt Ellen in the distance still waiting in line to meet Cinderella–then turned back. "It's not an exact translation, but it means something like *soulmate*," he said. "The two of you always just . . . balanced each other out. Your attributes balanced her flaws, and vice versa. The two of you together . . . I don't know, it seemed like you could do anything. Maybe it's silly. You were just kids."

Leo was at a loss for words. Deep inside him, he felt something like a spark. Old feelings coming back to life.

No. Stop it. You love Emily, and talking about another woman like this isn't fair to her. You're only feeling this way because your dad brought up your old crush. Leo shook his head and stood, then extended a hand to his dad. "I think I'd like to meet Cinderella after all. Want to come?"

His dad grimaced as he stood, a little hunched over, like an old man. "Lead the way."

Later on, after they'd met not only Cinderella but Belle and Aladdin and Jasmine and some of the characters from *Toy Story*, and after they'd gone on Space Mountain twice and It's a Small World one godforsaken time, which Emily had insisted on because she wanted the "experience," and after they'd eaten an extremely overpriced yet admittedly tasty meal and watched fireworks explode above, Emily's head on Leo's shoulder the whole time, they arrived back at his grandparents' house exhausted. Leo was young and able-bodied and still ready to collapse; he couldn't imagine how his aunt and his dad felt.

Emily excused herself almost immediately to take a shower, and Aunt Ellen left shortly after to pass out, probably. His grandparents were already in bed, so that left Leo with his dad again, alone for the first time since their awkward conversation earlier. Leo really hoped he didn't want to continue it. "Any interest in a nightcap?" he asked.

His dad shook his head. "I'm exhausted. I'm going to go straight to bed. See you in the morning."

Leo would blame himself later, even though logically he knew he shouldn't. They were all exhausted, after all. There was no way to know.

16

SHIRA WAS TIRED. NOT (ONLY) FROM THE JET LAG; IT was a good tired because she'd been up late the night before sketching. Sketching some concepts for what might become future paintings or what might just be something fun for her. She wasn't entirely sure yet, but she'd been invigorated enough by it to stay up late working and even to stop in the middle of the sidewalk the next morning to email herself an idea that had suddenly popped into her mind upon seeing the way the sun reflected against the icy sidewalks, which was not serving her well with her sister the drill sergeant.

"Shira, stop lollygagging!" Talia hollered from half a block away. Shira jumped, squinting into the bright reflection of the sun, then stuck her phone back into the pocket of her big down coat and slipped on her glove again. Talia was standing on the snowy sidewalk outside the Davids' house, probably glaring impatiently from under the wooly rim of her hat, though it was pulled down too far to tell. You'd think they were running a relay race in the Olympics. "You're not working, are you?"

That was one thing that had been freeing about the past year. Once Shira had gotten her new job, she'd finished up her outstanding freelance projects and declined to take on any more. "I'm not working," she said, not having to yell as she'd already closed half the distance between them. Ice crystals crunched under her boots. "The office is on West Coast time, and it's nine a.m. They won't open for another few hours."

"Then what are you doing?"

"Doesn't matter," said Shira. Her project still felt too new, too vulnerable, to share at this point. "I'm off this week anyway. Don't you have a flock to herd or something?"

"You're the flock I'm trying to herd right now," Talia said and then hollered behind Shira. "Dad! Did you fall and break a hip on the lawn?"

Shira shook her head, bemused, as she passed her sister. Somehow this family walk got harder and harder to corral every year.

Still, she wouldn't miss it for anything.

Her eyes lingered for a moment on the Davids' dark front window. She was sad to miss Leo. She'd grown to look forward to seeing him every year. Now she probably wouldn't see him until next December, and who knew where they'd be then. He'd probably be engaged to Emily.

She pushed away the pang in her chest. Mostly she was missing Neptune, she told herself. Poor doggie, in a kennel for the holidays. Hopefully the boarding people would slip him some turkey or ham for Christmas.

Leo or not, this party wasn't going to plan itself. She asked Talia, "Anything I should be sure to include at the party tonight that I've forgotten, Rabbi?"

"I'm not a rabbi yet," Talia told her. "And you know the basics.

Hanukkah isn't even that important a holiday anyway." She paused and then went on, more quietly, "I'm glad you're throwing the party again, though. It wasn't the same last year."

Shira patted her heart, oddly touched, unused to receiving any sort of compliment from her sister. "Aw, thanks. I love you, too."

"I didn't say that," Talia grumbled, which was much more like her. Still, Shira had seen the way her eyes lit up whenever she talked about her schooling and the congregation she was hoping to be placed in as an assistant rabbi one day, in a rural town whose congregation size had been shrinking over the years and that could no longer justify the cost of a full-time rabbi. If she needed to save all her loving-kindness for her flock, so be it.

She glanced again at Leo's dad's dark window and pulled her phone back out, quickly, keeping it cupped in her gloves so that Talia wouldn't see. She told Siri to text Leo, Happy first day of Hanukkah! Thinking of breaking into your house to keep my skills sharp, anything in particular I should look for?

He responded immediately. Happy Hanukkah. My dad keeps his secret chocolate stash in the cabinet above the refrigerator, but it's protected by a fleet of lasers and pits of spikes. Proceed carefully

She snorted. And here I thought I was free to go since the guard dog isn't here

Welcome back to your life of crime, he replied.

She tucked her phone away, sighing deeply. The moment she'd gotten that text telling her that Leo would be away with Emily and his whole family, she couldn't help but think a proposal was coming. They were in their late twenties. Leo and

Emily had been together almost two years, living together for half of it. She'd prepared herself, putting on the armor so that when she officially got the word, it wouldn't pierce any vulnerable organs.

Not that she'd crumble or sob or anything like that. She'd be happy for him. He was her friend—maybe the best friend she'd ever had. They might have been a good couple, but life had never lined up for them. She'd been an ass when he had feelings for her. Then, by the time she'd gotten her shit together and was no longer an ass—or at least less of an ass—he'd moved on.

Two of the older women in the Sisterhood at her synagogue had been clucking to set her up with their sons. Both sons were supposedly doctors. Medical doctors, not doctors of art history. Maybe she should finally give it a go

That night, the Hanukkah party came and went in a glitter of silver and a blur of candlelight. The neighbors complimented the decor, the kitschy garlands and shiny tablecloths; they said the food was good, too. This year she'd officially given herself permission to be easy and buy everything from the deli, even though it would've tasted better to have made her own latkes again. The doughnuts came from the bakery. She went to pick them up herself and felt a pang of something both sad and amused to see that they'd upgraded the lock on the back door so it was now all big and shiny and silver, beside a sign warning that she was on camera. She impulse-bought some extra pastries out of guilt—banana bread, something with guava and cream cheese, an ube hand pie—and ate them in the car while she drove, smiling at how dry the banana bread was.

Being with her old neighbors felt a little bit like being with the people at the synagogue. None of them knew Danica; none of them knew exactly what it meant to put on a show that didn't do well or the difference between all the art galleries in LA. All they knew was that she'd had a show of her art exhibited by a professional gallery and had worked at an art gallery and now she worked at a marketing firm, and that was all cool.

When the party had ended and she'd made a half-hearted attempt to clean up before swearing to her parents that she'd do it the next day, she went to bed. Showering was less necessary without latke grease to scrub out of her hair, but she did it anyway, even treating herself to one of those bead-rub things that were supposed to tenderize her skin like a baked chicken.

It took a good long time, long enough for Talia to bang on the door not once but twice. When Shira emerged in a cloud of steam, it was good and late, and she was ready to throw on her coziest sweats and fall into bed. Which she did, and she slept like the dead.

When she woke up, she immediately grabbed for her phone—yes, she knew it wasn't healthy and she should probably start the day with a peaceful meditation and analog breakfast or whatever, and yes, she would keep doing it anyway—and found it full of notifications.

Which was weird. She blinked at it, and it blinked back, another text popping up. This never happened, not since she'd gotten kicked from the group chat with Danica and Ellery and Nora—she was in a few new group chats with the synagogue and with some other artists she'd befriended, but she limited notifications on those.

Her phone buzzed again. She hated the spring of hope in her

chest—*maybe, years later, Danica would realize she'd been an idiot and add her back in.* Of course that wasn't the case. They were never going to come back. It had been years—why did it still sting?

She picked up her phone to find that all the notifications were from . . . Leo? Her heart quickened. *What in the—*

Her phone buzzed in her hand. A call. She answered it before she could read any of the texts. "Leo? What's up?"

"Shira." There was a sob caught in his throat. "My dad died."

The dust motes swirling around her slowed and sparkled, then stilled in the air. The sound of her neighbor running their snow blower dulled and became muffled like she'd pressed her pillow around her ears. "What?"

And then immediately felt like the cold, soggy, shredded latke remains in her trash for making him repeat himself. "My dad died?" he said, like it was a question. "He's dead? He didn't come down to breakfast this morning, and I went to check on him, and . . . and he was gone."

Shira plopped down on her bed, cold spreading through her body from the chest out. "Oh, god. Leo, I'm so sorry. I don't . . . I don't know what to say." She felt a swell of grief, not so much for the man himself, but for Leo.

"I was hoping you could help," Leo said, and Shira sat up straight at attention, nearly vibrating. Yes. She could help. She was good at that. "I don't think my dad personally would care, but my grandparents and my aunt are insisting everything is done according to Jewish tradition. So—"

"So burial should be the next day, right," Shira said, her mind racing. "And you're going to want to sit shiva here?"

"Yeah. At my dad's house. I'm swamped trying to contact the funeral home and figure out how to get the . . . how to get him back, and book our new flights, and I just . . . I can't do it all. Could you prep the house for the shiva? Maybe order some food and get things picked up? I'll pay you back, of course."

Like that was the biggest concern of the day. "Of course," she said. "Of course I will, Leo. And don't worry about the money at this point." She wished she could just say don't worry about it at all, but being an admin didn't exactly rake in the big bucks. "Do any of our neighbors have an extra key?"

"I'm sure somebody does, but you'd have to go around knocking on doors and asking, and then you'll have to tell everyone why," Leo said. The sob had trickled out of his voice, and now he only sounded thoughtful. Having a concrete task to focus on at this moment was probably useful for him. "So you can do that, or you could harness your history of crime. If you're caught, I won't press charges. And once you get inside, there's a spare key on the Rutgers lanyard hanging from the leash rack by the front door."

"Thank you," Shira said, her mind already busy with how she could do it. "Okay, I will make sure your house is clean and set up for a shiva, and I'll get the food ready, too. Oh, and what about Neptune? Do you want me to pick him up?"

"Oh. Oh, yeah," Leo said, sounding startled. The poor dog. "I'm going to call the boarding place and give you permission to pick him up. You don't mind, right?"

Talia would definitely not love getting dog all over her car, but she owed Shira this one after not picking the doughnuts up a few years ago and forcing her sister into a brief life of crime.

Shira could've gone to jail! *Which would give you something interesting to paint about in a new show,* whispered a small hidden part of her.

Shira didn't immediately banish the idea. That voice, which she'd crushed down after everything that had happened with her last show and with Danica, had started popping up again now that she wasn't so busy with freelance work or at the art gallery. Had started whispering ideas again, a few of which she'd actually written down to noodle on further. This one was not getting written down.

She'd been quiet for too long. "Of course I don't mind," Shira said. "Neptune's my buddy. Text or call me if you need anything else, okay? I'll make sure you're patched through do not disturb."

"The ultimate honor," Leo said wryly. Shira waited for him to hang up, but he stayed quietly breathing on the other end, so she stayed, too.

After what felt like ages, he finally said, "It doesn't feel real."

She was definitely not qualified to talk him through this. She'd been fortunate enough never to lose anyone close to her aside from grandparents at the end of their lives, when it was really more of a mercy than anything. But he was her friend. She would do her best. "I can imagine," she said. "I mean, I can't imagine. It happened so fast. But you don't have to process everything right now, right? One step at a time. Get things sorted with the flights, then the funeral home, okay? Let Emily and your aunt help." She had no idea what shape his grandparents were in. "Let other people help. We all want to help."

That was all she could do. She couldn't hold him while he cried; that was Emily's job. But she could help.

"Thanks, Shira," he said quietly. "I appreciate it."

The funny thing was that preparing for a shiva really wasn't all that different from preparing for a party. "Is it tacky to use the Hanukkah garlands as decorations?" Shira said to Talia, brandishing the glittering silver-and-blue decorations.

Talia rolled her eyes. "Isn't it tacky to joke about this?"

Shira had enlisted her sister's help to prep Leo's house, mostly so that she wouldn't have to do it alone. When Talia had found out that prepping the house required breaking into it, her eyes lit up with enthusiasm. "I knew those years practicing how to pick locks with bobby pins would come in handy," she'd rhapsodized as they crept through the darkness, by which Shira meant an overcast sky at eleven a.m. "Do you think we'll need to break a window? I brought an extra shirt to shield my hand with as I punch through a pane."

It was extra funny hearing Talia say this given how she looked now: like an assistant rabbi in a rural area, with her sleek brown bob, no black eyeliner or heavy mascara, orthotic sneakers instead of combat boots. Sometimes Shira looked at her and blinked and saw the version of her sister that had been there most of her life, like a shadow overlay, but that wasn't her anymore.

"I think that's the last thing Leo needs to deal with right now," Shira said, slightly concerned for her sister's future flock. As it turned out, no picking locks or breaking windows would be required, as one of the kitchen windows had been left unlocked. Talia neatly popped out the screen; Shira hoisted her up so that she could shimmy through the opening, then circle around to open the back door.

There was a chill to the air inside. Maybe because the home's owner was dead, maybe because the heat had been set at fifty-eight degrees, maybe both. The first thing Shira did was turn up the thermostat. She didn't want Leo shivering when he stepped through the door.

Then they vacuumed, dusted, brushed dog hair off couches. The house was in pretty good shape. Probably Leo's dad hadn't wanted to return to a dirty house. Shira felt her first stab of grief for him, the man who'd left his house fully assuming he'd come back to it. "I still have all the chairs rented for the party," Shira said, surveying the living room. "So we'll bring them over. Mom and Dad can help." Another pang at the thought that the chairs that had been sat on to celebrate would now be sat on to mourn. "I'll call the company and see if we can get the rental extended, otherwise I'll just pay the late fees. Let's clear space now." They moved couches and tables, made room. "Okay, that should do it for now. I'll call the deli in a bit and order some sandwich platters. Is there anything else we should do?"

"Cover the mirrors," Talia said. "You're supposed to cover all the mirrors at a shiva."

They found sheets in the hall linen closet, then moved through the house draping them over all the reflective surfaces, even the one in Leo's dad's bedroom. Shira paused in the doorway of Leo's old room. It had been scrubbed of much of its personality—no more posters for the *Pokémon* movies or the classic-rock bands he claimed he'd loved as a kid but that Shira was pretty sure his dad had convinced him to say he liked, no more baseball bedding with little men hitting little balls—but the bed was roughly in the same place on the far wall, the desk on the near one, the pull-up bars in a conspicuous spot by the closet where visitors couldn't help but clock them, though Shira couldn't help but clock that they couldn't be used very much if he'd left them behind.

"This Leo's old room?" Talia appeared beside her like a ghost. Shira started, leaping forward to drape one of the old sheets she'd gotten from the linen closet over the mirror on the back of Leo's door.

"Yup." Shira stepped back, her face now blazing hot for no reason.

"Shame you two never worked out," Talia continued, breezy as usual. "Always thought you would be good together, but you never liked each other at the same time."

"It's none of your business," Shira said brusquely, backing down the hall. She stopped when she realized she was about to fall down the stairs. "He's too good for me now, anyway."

"Oh, would you stop doing that?"

"What, putting myself down?" Shira was oddly touched in a way that made it tough to meet her sister's eyes. She took one step down the staircase, fingers tracing one of the dusty photographs hanging along the side. "Should we take some photos of Leo's dad down to put on tables or something?"

"I think we can let Leo decide if he wants to do that." Talia pushed past her and clomped down the stairs like a clog dancer, which, given her eclectic list of hobbies, maybe she'd actually won a few championships at. "No, I mean, would you stop acting like someone's achievements define what they're worth? It's one of the reasons I quit martial arts."

God, how had Shira almost forgotten Talia had been a karate

champion back in the day? The years really flew by. "You could've gone pro, I bet," Shira said. "It would've been really cool, telling people my sister could beat them up. 'No, like, seriously, my sister could really beat you up.'"

And then Talia's skill at languages. How many languages did she speak fluently? Five? "And what about your language skills? You could be a professional translator."

"Not everything has to be about work," said Talia. "Some things can just be about personal fulfillment. I like speaking all these languages. It's going to help me as a rabbi because I can use those skills to help people in the community. It's why I decided that's the path I wanted to pursue, actually. Becoming a rabbi. I don't want to be some shiny trophy in a silver case that people are jealous of. I want to be out helping those people."

Shira absorbed her sister's words, a fire alarm light blinking silently red above them. "I don't think I ever realized that's why you quit martial arts."

"Yup," Talia said. "It's better for you if you define your worth by what you can do for other people, versus how you look to other people. Anjali's really been helpful in that regard."

"Who's Anjali?" Shira asked in order to avoid engaging with her really very astute point, because accepting that her younger sister was wiser than her was an impossibility.

"Oh, my girlfriend," Talia said. "Did I not tell you about her?"

"I have literally never heard the name Anjali before in my life." And yet, somehow, Shira wasn't that surprised. She'd always kind of figured she'd learn she was an aunt when Talia one day showed up at some family event with a baby in her arms.

"Oh. It's been maybe . . ." Talia squinted at a photo of Leo smiling painfully before a neutral school backdrop. "Eight months?"

"Eight months and I've never even met her?" Shira cried, now a little insulted.

Talia shrugged. "Well, you do live in LA." She was quiet for a moment. "You don't have a job now that can't be done here. Do you think you'll ever move back?"

"I . . ." The words stuck in her throat. Her mom delicately broached the subject every few months on the phone, but Shira always moved quickly to quash it. Somehow moving out of LA, even though she had no concrete reason to be there anymore, felt like losing. She'd been the girl who'd moved to the big city to follow her dream. If she left the big city, didn't that officially mean she'd lost the dream?

Or did it even matter anymore? "I don't know," Shira said honestly. "I really like my synagogue that I found. But . . ." But it would be nice to have met Anjali after a more normal two or three months. It would be nice to see her parents more than twice a year. It would be nice to experience seasons again. "I don't know. I should probably stay at my job for two years, right? Then I can reassess."

"Hmm," Talia said, as if she were too nice to call bullshit even though she was definitely not nice at all.

Shira took a deep breath. "Okay. We got the mirrors. I'm going to go put in an order for the food." And she marched off, having made at least one decision.

17

LEO WAS NUMB. ENTIRELY NUMB. LIKE HE'D GONE IN for dental work and instead of a small anesthetizing needle in the gums, the dentist had pulled out a giant needle and plunged it into the middle of his sternum.

It was affecting his hearing, too. Every time Emily said something to him, she had to repeat it two or three times before he even realized she was speaking. Like he was always standing in the middle of a wind tunnel.

To her credit, she didn't let it bother her, or at least she didn't show that it did. "We can go all together on a ten eleven flight," she said quietly, and somehow the expansive gesture she made with her arm told him that by *all together* she meant them and his grandparents and . . . the body.

The body. His dad was a *body*.

He almost crumpled at the thought, no matter how many times he'd already had it that day. He landed on the couch, Emily's hand resting on his shoulder as if she'd tried to catch him and failed. "Is that okay?" she asked, brows wrinkling with concern. He leaned into her in response, closing his eyes against the softness of her belly.

They'd had a pregnancy scare about a month ago. Emily realized her period was late, and she'd been feeling nauseous in the mornings, and Leo had just about pulled out all his hair in the twenty minutes it took to drive to the drugstore, pick out a first-response pregnancy test, go pick out another first-response pregnancy test when she decried him for picking the generic brand, and then wait for her to pee on it. In the end, she hadn't been pregnant. It had been maybe the biggest relief of his life. *I'm free,* he'd remembered thinking, which didn't make any sense, because Emily was his girlfriend and he loved her and they'd been talking about buying a ring, so having a baby with her would happen anyway and simply be out of order now, right?

He didn't know why he was thinking about that at this moment. He'd considered raising the subject with his dad but hesitated before he could. Didn't want his dad to think poorly of him, to think that he was irresponsible. *I'll tell him with the one that's on purpose,* Leo had decided. *When he'll be a grandfather.*

If he weren't already sitting, that thought would have made him buckle again. *He'll never be a grandfather.*

The rest of the morning and his flight were a blur. He drank whatever Emily put to his lips and mechanically chewed whatever she told him to eat. He blinked and he was in an Uber to the airport, the Uber driver asking him how he liked Florida, and then he blinked again and he was on the plane, in a window seat, Emily asleep on his shoulder. The shade was closed. He considered opening it, then thought all the sun dazzling on the ocean might hurt his eyes. He slept, too, maybe, because at one point he was talking to his dad about their shared hatred of the TSA, and that could only have happened while he was asleep.

He didn't stop at his apartment, though Emily decided to. "You're sure that's okay?" she said, hovering anxiously before him in the airport parking garage. "I can take an Uber, or I can take the car and you can take an Uber if you don't want to drive." She wanted to pick out an appropriate funeral dress and maybe take a shower. Were you supposed to shower before a funeral? Some rule lurked in the back of his mind that you weren't supposed to shower when you were sitting shiva. Or shave or brush your teeth. Or was that Yom Kippur? And did the rules apply when you had plane germs all over you? Surely the ancient rabbis hadn't accounted for that.

His dad would probably know. His dad would probably want him to know.

Shira would know. Shira would know, and then maybe he would feel less alone for it.

"Yeah, no problem," Leo said. "I want to go right to my dad's house." The funeral home had come directly to the airport to pick up . . . the body. Leaving Leo with nothing to do until the funeral. He couldn't do nothing, though. There had to be something he could do at home.

He'd dreaded the thought of opening the door to his childhood home and finding the air stale, everything dusty and unchanged from the moment his dad had left—the house confused, wondering why Leo was there and not his dad. "I'm sorry," Leo said to the house, which seemed to be holding its breath. "I'm sorry it's me and not him."

A whine. Leo nearly jumped out of his skin, thinking the house itself was responding, and then he heard the nails click-clacking on the wood floors. He crouched instinctively and let the dog throw himself into his arms. "Hey, boy," he whispered into the smelly fur on his head. Neptune sagged into him in response. "I'm sorry. I'm sorry."

Another footstep because, of course, Neptune wasn't here alone. Shira stepped into the foyer, keys jingling from her fingers. "I just picked him up," she said. "I was looking for his food, but I couldn't find–"

"The bottom shelf of the china cabinet next to the kitchen table," Leo said. "I know, it's not intuitive. I don't know why my dad put it there."

"Got it. Thanks." And Shira disappeared back into the kitchen. Leo gave himself another minute to extricate himself from the dog, who was shaking with how happy he was to see him. How would the rest of this go? Would Neptune even care that his dad was gone?

As if proving his point, Neptune was gone in a flash at the sound of kibble hitting his bowl. Leo followed slowly, reaching the kitchen as Shira was putting the kibble back on the shelf. "It's a pain to reach it here," she said, standing up and wincing. "I think I twisted something in my back."

"Yeah," Leo said. It was honestly comforting how she'd moved the furniture around and covered the mirrors, because it was like he'd entered a slightly different universe from the one he'd left. "Hey, thank you so much for breaking in and setting things up. I really appreciate it."

"Of course. Anytime," she said. She wore her hair in a long, loose ponytail down her back that swung with every movement in an almost hypnotizing fashion. Her pale blue sweater looked softer than a pillow. "Talia helped, too, but she had to go home for some video call. Oh, I ordered sandwiches and salads from the deli. They said they'd be ready by the shiva. I'll pick them up."

"Thanks," he said. He felt the sudden urge to ask if she'd gotten roast beef, because that was his dad's favorite, then realized that his dad wouldn't be here to eat it so it didn't matter. The combined weight of all these thoughts and feelings meant that there was nothing else to do but sink down to the kitchen floor, his back up against the cabinet where all the cleaning supplies were still secured behind a child lock despite the fact that his dad had more trouble with it than Leo did now, and try not to fall through the floor.

Neptune ran to him, of course, and sat alert by his side, as if watching out for threats. Shira sat on the other side of the dog, her back against the cabinet with all the random doodads and cords that had accumulated over thirty years of kitchening. "Just tell me if you want to be alone and I'll go," she said. She didn't extend her hand toward him as she had years ago on the train. He didn't know why he was thinking about that now. Maybe because that was the last time he'd been in such a dark place. "Or if you want to sit in silence or if you want to talk."

He didn't know what he wanted. All he knew was that if she left him alone, he might sink into the floor, his mouth filling with fake wood and cement and dirt and magma and whatever else lay below him. He took a deep breath, trying to keep himself upright. "Are you working on any new paintings?"

If she was surprised by his question, she didn't let on. "Not seriously. I've been jotting down ideas here and there, making sketches." She was quiet for a moment. "I've been thinking about trying something different than I'm used to. It'd be new, but the freedom in failing at one thing is that nobody wants you to keep doing that thing."

"Ah," said Leo. She'd hit upon the opposite of how he'd been feeling lately. At the beginning of the year, he'd sold *Washing Dishes at the End of the World* to Tiny Elephant Studios and accepted a position with them. They'd wanted to put him in charge of the department handling his game, which seemed only fair, since he was the one who'd created it, so he agreed. Only now they wanted a sequel, which was good, but also he had no ideas. Creating the first game had been fun and challenging, and the second one was . . . work. Which was expected.

But he didn't love doing it. He was beginning to dread the hours stuck at his desk, sending Slack messages and bouncing ideas off the crew. He'd sit there and picture himself back in the warehouse, which of course wasn't where he wanted to be, but that job hadn't held the pressure and the stress of this job.

He wasn't going to be an asshole and complain about having the exact same thing Shira was missing, but she'd given him the key once before. Maybe she could do it again. "Did you play *Washing Dishes at the End of the World*?"

"Of course I did," she told him, tipping her head back against the cabinet, exposing the long pale line of her throat. *I want to bite it,* he thought nonsensically, before flushing hot and turning away. What was he, a vampire? Grief was really messing with his head. "Granted, I don't play a ton of video games, but it was my favorite one." She paused, a smile tugging at her lips, and he realized he was looking at her again, that his face had gravitated back toward her without him even realizing it, the way a flower turned toward the sun. "I was thinking of it yesterday, actually, when we were talking. An entire world had ended, and there we were, scheduling flights and ordering sandwich platters. I think that's why it resonated so deeply with people. Because it's really about life, isn't it? Genocides happen and entire cities break off into the ocean and our brains are all full of plastic, and yet we have to keep washing dishes and arguing with coworkers about who keeps burning popcorn in the microwave."

He took a deep breath and held it. It was true, and somehow it made him feel a little better, the knowledge that other people had lost loved ones and kept muddling through. "What do you think about a sequel?"

She turned to him, eyes bright with interest. "Ooh, are you planning one? Maybe set after the world's been saved but there's all sorts of dirty work to do to clean up from the great battle and everything the Dark Lord left behind?"

He blinked, processing. Duh. He couldn't believe he hadn't thought of it before. Someone would have to go and disperse the Evil Miasma that cloaked the Elven Forest, and sort out the magic land mine situation underground so that the dwarves could obtain enough ore to rebuild all the cities the Dark Lord had destroyed. Someone would have to go make the world livable again while the heroes were on their grand victory tour. Someone would have to make it possible to live in the world again.

Someone would have to sort through his father's things and

keep some and sell some and trash the rest. Someone would have to get the house ready to sell. Someone would have to take care of Neptune. Did Leo's apartment even allow dogs? It had to. He couldn't give Neptune away.

"Breathe," Shira said, and it was only then Leo realized he hadn't in what was probably too long a time. He sucked in a big gulp of air and immediately got light-headed. "One step at a time. You don't have to worry about any of it yet. Just get through today."

Today. Right. The funeral. He still felt faint. They were going to bury his dad in the ground. According to Jewish tradition, which meant no embalming and no wake, just a plain pine box and the ground.

Leo would never see his dad again. He'd always thought of wakes as kind of creepy—both his grandparents on his mom's side, along with his grandpa's second wife, had had one, and their waxy faces and unnaturally posed hands had made him want to run away. But it was technically one last time to see them. His dad was gone forever.

Eventually, probably, that thought would break through and stick and stop hitting him so hard every single time.

"Have you eaten anything lately?" she asked him, and he realized he hadn't at the exact same time his stomach growled so loudly Neptune jumped away, ears pricked, as if some beagle-eating monster were approaching. Shira snorted. "Okay, there's my answer. I've got some time before I have to go get the sandwiches. Let me fix you something."

"You don't have to," Leo said, but she was already opening cabinets and grimacing at whatever was inside the fridge.

"Of course I don't have to. I want to." She shook her head. "My god, your dad really has the most stereotypical old-bachelor cupboards. He's got olives, boxed mac and cheese, sprouting onions, and several bottles of hard alcohol."

"He wasn't supposed to be drinking after his first heart attack," Leo said, a flash of anger lighting in his chest. Maybe this second heart attack was his dad's fault.

Maybe he could be furious instead of sad. That seemed like a small improvement.

But Shira was already shaking her head. "They're pretty dusty, see?" she said, showing him the bottle of vodka, which actually looked like the exact same bottle Leo used to take the occasional hit from back in his warehouse days. Her fingers, closed around the neck of the bottle, showcased unbitten nails. Her stress levels must have lowered over the past year. "Oh, we have some canned soup here. I could go all *Chopped*. What do you think about fried mac-and-cheese arancini with a velvety cream-of-mushroom-soup sauce and an olive-onion crumble?"

His mouth actually watered. "Not bad."

She laughed. "Well, I'm not making that. Sorry." She pulled out one of the boxes of mac and cheese, flipping it over to read the expiration date. It apparently met her satisfaction, because she didn't grimace at it, just put it on the counter. "Though it was always fun when we used to play *Chopped*. Right? Remember that time you gave me a basket of black licorice, hard-boiled eggs, blueberries, and bologna?"

His turn to grimace. "I set you up to fail with that one."

"Yeah," she said, reaching to the rack above the stove for a pot. She was too short to reach the small one; without asking,

Leo stood and snagged it for her, then set it gently on the stovetop. "I didn't have to make hot licorice deviled eggs with a blueberry-bologna sauce, though."

He stuck out his tongue, pretending to gag. "I'm pretty sure my dad actually puked."

"And not even from eating it, remember?" she said. "It was just from the smell."

His laugh was genuine, and it felt good, though he sobered quickly when he remembered the whole reason they were here. Shira didn't seem to notice, or if she did, she didn't let on, only put water on to boil. "And he wasn't happy when we used his frozen crab legs for another *Chopped* round," she said. "Remember, he'd been saving them for some special occasion? Maybe for when he got a promotion. But we thawed them, and then we couldn't even break them open for the meat, so we just used them as swords."

"Not swords," he said, remembering. "We were monsters, I think. They were our claws."

"But it turned out that the licorice eggs were poison and burned out our esophagi before we could finish the battle."

"Unfortunate," he said, the memory tickling his brain, how he and Shira had writhed around on the grass, gagging and clawing at their throats. "It was lucky they grew back in time for us to have lunch."

"Very lucky," she said. The sound of falling rain as she poured the box of macaroni into the boiling water. "Set a timer for six minutes."

He set a timer for six minutes. It ticked away as she rooted around for milk in the fridge, then wrinkled her nose at the smell of the open jug and pulled out a stick of butter. "I'll add extra butter. It'll still be good."

"Extra butter is always better," he said. "What was it your mom used to say? There's no such thing as too much butter?"

"Until you ate an entire stick plain on a dare."

"Oh man, I almost forgot about that." Something about bringing back these old memories was making him breathe a little easier, helping him remember that there was a world out there beyond what was happening right now. "I don't think my intestines knew what to do with it. I might as well have eaten a sock."

"Please, keep the rest to yourself." Shira dumped the pasta into a strainer. The water swirled down the drain while the steam rose to cloud around her hair. "Okay, one more minute." She added the butter to the pan, let it swirl around until it melted, then added water and cheese powder. "Mmm, orange." She stirred it with the one wooden spoon his dad owned, then dumped in the pasta and stirred again. It made a squelching sound that could've either come from a horror movie or a sex scene. "Okay, get a plate."

It was easy to listen, so he did. Well, mostly. He got two, holding one out in each hand. She glanced over her shoulder at him, wielding the wooden spoon before her like a wand. "Is Emily coming?"

He'd almost forgotten about Emily. Which was understandable, he told himself, given that his head was full with thoughts of his dad and how he was going to survive the day. "I got the other plate for you." He immediately felt silly standing there holding the empty plate. "If you want some. If not, no worries."

She blinked at him, then smiled. A spark of something lit in his belly—not happiness, exactly, but the thought that the feeling might eventually exist in him again. "You know what, sure. Why not." She slopped a few big spoonfuls of mac and cheese onto each plate with more horrible squelching noises, then gestured at the table. "I know we used to eat on the floor, but I'm old now."

"I'm old, too," protested Leo.

"Not as old as me."

"By three months!"

"That makes me three months wiser," said Shira.

"Whatever you say." Leo took a bite of his mac and cheese, and hell, it might have been the best thing he'd ever tasted. He'd needed creamy, cheesy comfort, and that was what she'd given him. A homemade mac-and-cheese casserole wouldn't have accomplished the same thing, no matter how many fancy kinds of cheese it used. "Thank you. For this."

She took a bite. "Anytime."

They reminisced as they ate, bringing up more memories, and it felt good to think about something other than his dead dad. He did have to keep stepping away to field calls—his mom, who was hopping on a flight despite how many times he'd told her he didn't need her, but he was grateful for it, honestly; the funeral home, who needed a time and a place and a grave site, and thank god his dad already had a little plot purchased; Emily, asking what she should bring him from their apartment—but was glad each time to come back to his plate, no matter how cold and congealed his food was becoming.

As he was chasing the last few noodles around the plate with his fork, the doorbell rang. At the same time, Leo's phone buzzed. Emily. I'm outside. He texted back that the door was open, and in she came. "Oh, hey," she said, her eyes flickering back and forth between Shira and Leo. She tucked a strand of auburn hair behind her ear, revealing one of the shiny diamond earrings that Leo had gotten her for her birthday. "Shira, right? Nice to see you. Thanks for helping set up the house."

"Nice to see you, too, and no problem," Shira said. "Hey, you should've just broken in."

"What?"

"Nothing," Leo said hastily. "Did you bring my suit?"

"I brought both your suits," Emily said. "They're in the car."

"Did you bring any ties?"

Emily smacked her forehead with a palm. "Oh, crap. I knew I forgot something."

Borrow one of mine, he heard his dad say, clear as the sodium in his mac and cheese. Maybe it was a good thing Emily had forgotten the tie. He could bring a bit of his dad to his own funeral. His dad would appreciate the dark humor of it all. "No worries," said Leo.

"Well, I'd better go," said Shira. She gave Emily a quick hug, then Leo. Her hair brushed his cheek, and he almost clasped his hand to it to keep it there longer. A weird thing to do, probably because he was still craving the comfort all their childhood memories had brought him. But she stepped back and nodded. "I'll leave you to it and go get the sandwiches. Let me know if you need anything else, okay?"

He nodded back, unable to reach the words he needed. A simple thank-you didn't seem like enough. But it would've been better than nothing, which was what he ended up with, and then she was gone.

"That smell is so familiar," Emily said, sniffing the air. "What is that?"

"Boxed mac and cheese," Leo said. "A real blast from the past. Probably literally, since I have no idea how long that box was in my dad's cabinet."

"Oh, man," Emily said. She was already dressed in her funeral attire, a knee-length black dress that covered her shoulders and collarbones. It had been so clearly purchased for a funeral that Leo couldn't help but wonder whose death had spurred it. "I can't even remember when the last time I had some of that was. You save any for me?"

"Sorry," Leo said. He had to go pick out a tie. And yet, now that Shira had left, the thought of going up there into his dad's closet, which still smelled like him and held all his clothes waiting patiently to be worn again, was overwhelming. "Will you come upstairs with me?"

"Of course," she said, and her presence was a comfort as he climbed those stairs and entered his dad's room. His dad had made his bed before leaving, Leo couldn't help but notice. He closed his eyes and could practically hear his dad crack, *Something happens to me, I don't want anyone thinking I'm some schlub who doesn't make his bed, you know?* "Oh, the mirror's covered up. That's weird. Did your dad do that?"

Leo opened his eyes with effort. "No, it's a Jewish thing. Shira or her sister must have done it." And it came as a relief, honestly, as Leo opened the closet and picked out a burgundy tie covered with navy-blue flowers, because he didn't have to look at himself and think about how much he looked like his dad. How much of his dad he carried in him.

He cleared his throat. "Did you know I didn't talk to my dad for years? Like, almost ten years?"

Emily's eyebrows shot up. "I knew you'd had your issues after the divorce, but wow, I didn't know it was that long."

"Yeah." It felt important to voice this all out loud, somehow. Maybe because this was the truest eulogy he'd get to give for his dad—he certainly couldn't get up and say all this at the funeral. "I actually moved back here and didn't talk to him while I was living in his house, which was pretty disrespectful and ungrateful, right? I was an angry kid. But he had patience with me and waited me out." He cleared his throat again; a lump kept trying to block his words. "I wish we had more time, but I'm glad for the time we had. I'm glad we worked things out before he died."

Emily rubbed his arm up and down, as if she'd just given him a shot. He had to force the next sentence out, but somehow it meant the most. "I'm glad he was proud of me when he died." Because it did matter, sometimes, what people thought of you. It was okay to care, it was okay to feel like your actions mattered, and it was okay to cry, finally, in the room of your dead father, knowing that he'd be glad you were there at all.

From Shira Levinson's email inbox:

Dear Shira, Thank you so much for applying to the Green Leaf Residency. While we appreciated the opportunity to consider your work, we had an enormous volume of talented applicants, and so we regret to inform you that you have not been accepted this year . . .

Dear Shira, I'm so glad you've started painting again! In our classes, I always thought you had tremendous talent, and thought it was such a shame that things didn't work out after your debut. Of course I'd be delighted to write a recommendation for you . . .

Dear Shira, Thanks for signing up to make hamantaschen for this year's Purim baskets! We have some nut allergies among the kids, so please steer clear of marzipan and peanut butter, and we've also got some of those almond moms who freak out if their kids eat chocolate, so maybe stick to fruit fillings. We'll need about . . .

From Leo David's sent-emails folder:

Hey Rashid, How've you been? I feel like it's been ages since we were developing games side by side at Rutgers, it's awesome that you've been at Storm for so long now. Question—I was looking at their open positions and thinking about applying, because things have been so crazy at Tiny Elephant, but was wondering what your work-life balance is like? I hear that there isn't much of one anywhere in the industry, but maybe there's some magical Eden I haven't found yet . . .

Hi Frank, My plumber, Benito, passed along your name. He and I have been working together to remodel the bathrooms in my dad's house that I'm planning to put up for sale soon, and he told me that you're not just great at refinishing floors and tiling, but that you'd be willing to let me work with you so that I could learn . . .

Texts between Shira Levinson and Leo David, March:

Shira: Thinking of you today. How are you doing?

Leo: Why are you thinking of me today?

Shira: It's . . . your dad's birthday, right? I put it in my calendar after the funeral.

Leo: Oh, shit

Leo: Yes, it's my dad's birthday

Leo: I can't believe I forgot. He's going to be so mad I didn't get him a present

Shira: . . .

Leo: Kidding. Obviously

Leo: I'm allowed to joke about that kind of stuff

Shira: That's a very Jewish mentality, you know

Leo: Is it?

Shira: Yeah. Black humor. We're hated so much everywhere all the time that you just have to laugh about it, you know?

Leo: Huh

Leo: I'm surprised by how much I like hearing that

Leo: I bet my dad would like hearing that too

Leo: You know, if he wasn't dead

Shira: I'm not sure if I'm allowed to laugh or not

Leo: I give you special permission to laugh at dead parent jokes

Shira: Wow, something I've always wanted. Thank you, Leo David

Leo: You're welcome, Shira Levinson

18

Year Six

THOUGH THE EMAIL HAD BEEN SITTING IN HER INBOX for several weeks at this point, Shira still felt a warm stirring of pride every time her eyes caught the subject line. Congratulations! You've been selected . . . The rest was cut off by her phone's small screen, but she could recite it in her brain like the Sh'ma. Congratulations! You've been selected for admission to the Residency at the Grossman Center for Jewish Art.

It wasn't one of the big residencies that people knew by name: MacDowell or Yaddo, single words that produced dropped jaws and intense surges of jealousy. When she told people about the Grossman Center, they'd probably say, "What?" It wouldn't receive a glowing write-up in *The New York Times* like Danica's exhibition in the Venice Biennale, written by one of their childhood artist idols. Shira hadn't gone seeking it out, but she hadn't been able to resist reading it after Ellery had reposted it with gushing words of praise.

But it was hers. She'd earned it. The Grossman Center was an offshoot of a synagogue in LA, and they would pay her to come paint in their hall and show her work and teach some classes at the synagogue. The judges had looked through her work in relation to other people's and decided that hers deserved a reward. That the people at their synagogue wanted to learn from her. And that was enough to keep her ember of a new show idea alive and glowing, hopefully ready to catch fire.

She'd considered not telling her coworkers at the marketing firm, almost as a test—could she be happy about something even if it didn't impress other people? But she'd decided to do it. This residency wasn't about impressing people. It was about furthering her work, and it was okay if it impressed people along the way. She could still care about what people thought, as long as it wasn't the only thing she cared about.

She did really want to tell Leo, though. And not over text. In person. Because the new idea she'd been workshopping, that she'd submitted for consideration for this residency, was a play on memory candles, which were staples at her and all her friends' and classmates' bar and bat mitzvahs back in the day. Basically, one of the b'nai mitzvah kid's friends would swipe a glass from the venue, usually a fancy wineglass, and they'd gather with a group of other friends, usually the b'nai mitzvah kid's closest ones, and fill the glass with mementos of the day: personalized ribbons, little toys, favors from the DJ, et cetera. Then the glass got filled with water. Somebody always brought crayons, and they'd melt the crayons using a stolen candle over the top, with the idea of creating an airtight seal so that the water couldn't evaporate (it never worked—Shira's had evaporated long ago). Then a candle was plopped in the middle of all the melted wax, and the whole weird, beautiful thing was presented to the b'nai mitzvah kid in front of everyone. They were supposed to burn the candle one year later, but Shira had never lit hers. She'd wanted to keep it forever.

Even though Leo hadn't been part of her Hebrew-school/Jewish-youth-group crowd, who were usually the ones who made the candle, he'd taken part in making hers. She'd directed him to bring blue and green crayons so that the candle would fit with her bat mitzvah theme of Under the Sea, where each table didn't get a number but a different species of fish. Shira had been seated at the Mermaid Table, of course.

She found herself standing outside Leo's old house almost on instinct, squinting through the dark front window, poised to go barge inside the way she had when they were kids. Of course she didn't. That was silly. And he might have sold the house, anyway. She knew he was working on it, and he'd mentioned talking to a Realtor.

"If you want to break in again, I recommend the back window."

She jumped, cheeks heating as she turned around. "No challenge," she said to Leo, who was standing on the driveway, one eyebrow quirked with amusement. "I've already broken in here before. Boring."

"Got it. So you won't mind me just unlocking the door." He gestured her forward. She followed automatically. "I'm coming from the unveiling."

"Ah," she said. According to Jewish tradition, graves were not carved and permanent until a year after death, when the headstone would be unveiled. He was clearly dressed for the occasion—he wore a black button-down over dark jeans, and while she assumed he hadn't cut his hair for the unveiling, the way it was cropped close to his head felt sober and serious. He'd also lost a bit of weight over the last year—not a lot, not enough that maybe anyone other than Shira would even notice, but enough to make his cheekbones jump out and his dark eyes look larger. "Just family, I assume?"

He nodded. "Just me and my aunt. It would've been difficult for my grandparents to make it up. Traveling is hard for them these days. I'm going to fly down and see them in the new year." His key clicked in the lock. Shira regretted that his back was to her, that she couldn't see his face. Because shouldn't Emily have been there? Assuming they were still together? She'd posted a photo of them together just a month ago, and she wasn't a big poster, so it wasn't abnormal for her not to have posted anything more recently. Not that Shira made a habit out of analyzing Emily's social media or anything. "Come in and nose around to your heart's content."

Most of the furniture was gone, was the first thing she noted. Just a few pieces remained: some nesting tables in the living room, a silver-framed painting of a stylized world map on the wall, a wooden bed frame in a guest room. "We held an estate sale a few months ago," Leo said. Her parents had mentioned that. They'd purchased Leo's dad's unused ice cream maker, which would probably continue to sit unused in the Levinson kitchen. "When I could finally bring myself to do it. I took some things back with me to my apartment and put some more in storage. A few things got left behind. I have to figure out what to do with them."

He'd clearly done work on the house, Shira couldn't help but notice. The ratty carpet on the second floor had been ripped up and that flooring that looks like wood but isn't actually wood laid down; the bathrooms on the first and second floors had been totally modernized. "Wow, it looks great," she said. "Who'd you have do the work?"

He shrugged a little self-consciously, or at least that's how it looked from the back as he showed how the primary bedroom closet had been expanded out into the hallway, swallowing up one for linens. "I did it myself."

"No way!" she exclaimed. "For real?"

He nodded, turning while leaning against the wall. She couldn't help noticing how his biceps flexed with the movement, more prominent than it had ever been before. The buttons of his shirt were tight against his chest, and his thighs really filled out his jeans. "That's why the house hasn't been up for sale yet," he said. "I've been kind of practicing with it. The more I do, the better I get. I started mostly with YouTube, honestly, and one of the guys I knew at the warehouse got into contracting, so he helped me out with some of the more technical things and sent me some guys who didn't mind me following them around. I still can't do wiring or anything like that by myself, it's dangerous. I have to call an electrician for that. But the hall bathroom upstairs I did entirely by myself. Had to rip up the tile a couple times and redo it, but I think it turned out good in the end."

"You know, when I was looking at that bathroom, I was thinking about how straight and even the tiling was," Shira said. "It must take a lot of your time." *Time you should be spending with Emily?*

He shrugged. "I actually left Tiny Elephant this year. I have a lot of savings to keep me afloat while I figure out what to do next."

"You left Tiny Elephant?" Shira had seen the announcement for the sequel to *Washing Dishes at the End of the World* recently—*Mopping Up After the End of the World*. She'd thought it sounded fun, and of course it always flattered her to see her thoughts in the text. "You don't want to work on *Mopping Up*?"

He shrugged again. "A lot of the work on *Mopping Up* is already done. They wanted to talk another sequel, and honestly, I'd already moved on mentally to the newest thing. I've been working on a new game on the side. It's about grief—you start off fighting all these grief monsters, and fighting and fighting, but they get overwhelming, and eventually you have to learn that you can't kill them. You have to figure out other ways to work past them. By the end you're walking side by side with them, like they're your friends or your pets or both, though sometimes they'll still jump on you and try to rip you to pieces. You just know better how to handle them by that point."

That sounded so profound. And yet . . . Shira couldn't stop thinking how he was crazy for giving up a job heading his own work at a major game studio. Though wasn't that what people had thought about her, too, when she left the art gallery? Sometimes dream jobs weren't dream jobs once you started doing them. Sometimes you didn't have to dream of labor, per James Baldwin. Sometimes it was enough to lead an unassuming life that was happy and fulfilling in ways other than how you made money.

"Anyway, I've really enjoyed working with my hands," said

Leo. "And having the freedom to set my own schedule. I think that was one of the things I hated about being at the studio—I enjoyed making the game a lot, when I could do it on my own time on my own schedule, but liked it less when I was bound to a desk. I'm thinking maybe of trying to do this full-time. Work on houses, I mean."

"Like flipping them?" Shira asked.

Leo was shaking his head before she'd even finished speaking. "I wouldn't want to call myself a flipper, because they often do such shoddy jobs. They go in and add white subway tile to the bathrooms and paint everything gray and put in air-conditioning and hike the price a few hundred thousand dollars while hiding old wiring and plumbing problems. I'd want to do a good job. Like, really make the houses places where people would want to live. Preserve the character of the current house—no tearing out glorious 1950s bathrooms to put in cheap white sterility, or removing crown molding to make everything look the same."

"That sounds great," Shira said. And it did. But he wasn't speaking like he'd found a passion, something that lit up his life and made him want to wake up every morning. He sounded excited about his work, like it was something he enjoyed doing and found challenging and was proud of, but not like it shaped his life.

She didn't know where else to go from there. She just knew it was what she wanted, too. To spend her workdays doing something she liked and found fulfilling, but to live her life in the other hours of the day. For her job to give her that space to work on her art without the stress and pressure of her art having to support her.

"Yeah," he said. He ran a hand along the hallway wall, which Shira was pretty sure had once been covered by striped paper and was now painted a neutral matte eggshell. "I just have to put this guy on the market, and then I'll have capital to start. I was thinking of finishing like I began and handling the sale myself."

"Is that allowed?" she asked. She didn't know much about buying and selling houses—hell, she'd probably never be able to afford one—but from what she understood, real estate agents had their claws deep into the industry.

"Of course it's allowed," he said. "Is it wise? I don't know." He chewed on his lower lip. "I was thinking about going to some open houses today to get an idea of where the market is so I know how to price it."

She perked up. "Ooh, can I come?" One of the traits she'd inherited from her mother: irredeemable nosiness. She hadn't been to an open house in a while, but she used to like going in LA, especially to ones in relatively fancy neighborhoods, since the REALLY fancy neighborhoods didn't have open houses. Walking through those big airy homes with in-ground pools and six-burner stoves while she imagined what it would be like to live there in that life was both fun and a little depressing. She didn't think she'd ever been to open houses around here, though.

"Really?" he said, sounding a tiny bit surprised. "You don't have anything else to do?"

She had plenty she could do. But nothing, she realized now, that she wanted to do nearly as much as tour houses with her old friend. "Let's do it."

"Okay," he said. "But just so you know, I've been to some of these open houses before, and the brokers don't like it if you're there to compare features. The first time I went, I asked the agent for tips on how to sell my own house, and you'd think I tried to burn the place down."

Understandable, really. Sometimes people used to come to the shows she'd put on at the gallery and tell her that their paintings were way better than the crap on her own walls and did she want to see? It wasn't exactly the same thing, but she didn't think anyone who liked their profession wanted to help someone else take them out. "That's fine," she said. "We can pretend to be looking for a house. No big deal."

And it wouldn't be. Friends looked at houses together all the time, right?

19

THE FIRST HOUSE THEY WENT TO WAS A COLONIAL revival—a term Shira heard for the first time today from Leo's mouth and that she nodded at, pretending it meant something to her—from the 1970s located across town, a few minutes away from the main road, which wasn't an elegant little Main Street but a four-lane highway lined with strip malls and gas stations. "So the size isn't all that different from my dad's house," mused Leo, standing on the sidewalk outside the house with his hands on his hips. Shira imagined this was how he evaluated all the issues he'd work on in each house, like a teacher ready to lay down some discipline. "The landscaping is nicer here, though, even though it's winter. My dad kind of let it go, and I can't do much with it unless I want to wait for the summer. Which I don't."

"Hmm," Shira said, trying to evaluate it herself with a real buyer's eye. "It's definitely closer to civilization, too. Our house is in a quieter area." The words *our house* had just snuck out—she stole a peek at Leo to see if he'd react, but he seemed lost in his head. "It is the same school district, though."

"That's a good thing to remember. School district counts for a lot." Leo dropped his hands from his hips and strode up the driveway, leaving her to follow. "Windows are new but the roof looks old." He flashed her a smile. "I can tell these things at a glance now."

"Very impressive," she said, and actually meant it. To her, the windows just looked like windows, the roof like a roof.

Inside, they were greeted in the foyer by a real estate agent pulled straight from central casting: middle-aged; white, with dirty-blond hair in that mom cut where it's longer in the front and shorter in the back; caked-on mascara that turned her eyelashes into spider legs above an overly lipsticked smile. "Welcome to 566 Brookdale Road," she said. There was a smear of magenta on one of her front teeth. "Please sign in on the sheet over there and let me know if there's anything I can help you with. Are you working with a Realtor already?"

Leo was already in the corner squinting at the fireplace mantel, so it was up to Shira to respond. "Uh, no," she said. "We actually just started looking. Kind of getting an idea of what's out there so far."

"Oh, wonderful," said the agent. "Well, your husband seems to like the fireplace. It's a wonderful feature of this house—the current owners put in the gas line, so it's convenient to light at the flick of a switch whenever you want some coziness."

Shira made a mental note to remember that. Gas fireplace. She didn't think Leo's dad's house had a gas fireplace. How much did that add to home value? Leo would probably know.

She was busy enough with her mental note that it took her a moment to realize the agent was speaking to her again. "So, how long have you two been married?"

Panic flared through Shira. "Oh, uh . . ." She should tell the agent they were just friends. That they were just browsing.

"Almost a year." Leo came up behind her, his smile calm and assured. "Should we check out the kitchen, dear? We should make sure there's enough stovetop space for your latke marathons."

Shira snorted. "And enough surface area for all the shredded potatoes."

"I love latkes," the real estate agent said brightly, in that overly cheerful way Shira sometimes took to mean *I do not hate Jews*, or maybe Shira was just paranoid. "You'd be very welcome in this neighborhood."

Shira felt it was pretty safe to take that as *The neighborhood does not hate Jews*, though how exactly could the real estate agent know that? Just because there weren't any swastika bumper stickers or Klan rallies happening on Sundays didn't mean she had any idea what prejudices simmered behind closed doors.

But she meant well. That was what mattered. Probably what she actually meant was that she'd sold houses in this neighborhood to other Jews, so they wouldn't be the only ones here. "Great," Shira said, trying to match her brightness.

She didn't know what made her go on. It was probably because Leo's dad's house had a big backyard. It was because, just for a moment, she could actually see it, her and Leo, sitting on a green couch across from the gas fireplace, Leo complaining it was too hot and Shira volleying back that it was never too hot to be cozy. "How about the backyard?" she asked. "Is there room for a swing set?"

"Oh, the backyard is lovely," said the agent. Shira kept her eyes studiously on her. "Come on, let me show you. You get a great view out of the kitchen windows, too, so you can be cooking up lunch while watching your kids play!"

The thought made Shira's chest ache for some reason. She'd always thought of kids as something she'd have one day in the future, but now the future was kind of here. Thirty was looming in the not-so-distant future. Her friends from high school and even some from college were posing for pregnancy shoots, cupping their big bellies in flowery meadows and in front of waterfalls.

Her arms weren't exactly aching to hold a baby, but she was starting to feel the lack of a plan there, because having babies wasn't something you just *did*. Not if you were Shira Levinson, anyway. First you had to find the right partner, and you had to date them for an appropriate number of years, and then you had to get married, and then, only then, could you try for a baby. And because she was Shira Levinson, she'd worried about the amount of time it might take to get pregnant. It could take a perfectly healthy and fertile couple a year to get pregnant! What if she wasn't perfectly healthy and fertile and needed to pursue reproductive treatment?

"Are you okay?" Leo asked her. Shira realized that as she was looking out into the backyard into the unremarkable frozen space where a swing set could theoretically go, she was dabbing at her eyes.

"Yeah, I'm fine." She cleared her throat. Banished the inappropriate thoughts. "I was actually thinking about a playground for us. An adult play set."

The real estate agent was too professional to blurt out *What the fuck?* but her eyebrows did raise. "Ah. I see. Well, as you can see, there's plenty of room in the backyard for whatever kind of play set you're looking to add." A delicate cough. "Though I should inform you that regulations in town only allow for fences up to four feet, so your neighbors will be able to look in on your activities."

Leo erupted into a series of coughs that was anything but delicate. When they cleared, his face was redder than a steamed beet. "I don't think my wife meant that kind of adult play set. I think she just meant . . . a kid's play set but adult size. So that we can swing and slide to our heart's content."

"I see," said the real estate agent skeptically.

Shira linked her arm through Leo's. "Shall we go tour the rest of the first floor, darling?" She felt rather smug as she steered an extremely flustered Leo around the eat-in kitchen, the mudroom, the living room.

By the living room, Leo had recovered somewhat. From the way he cleared his throat before speaking, Shira knew she was in for something fun. "This gas fireplace is indeed very nice," he said, as if responding to the real estate agent earlier. "But I'm not sure it's big enough for us."

Shira had no idea what he was getting at, but she played along. "I agree. We need a fireplace large enough for an entire cow."

She could hear the real estate agent start their way from the other room, then stop. Probably she'd decided it wasn't worth it to tell them they were unlikely to find any house in the area with a fireplace large enough for an entire cow. Leo said, innocently, "Are we the actual size of a cow when we're in our doubles cow costume? We might be able to go a little smaller."

She said, her poker face stone, "Might be time for a new double cow costume, ours is starting to smell a little like old milk. Maybe we should go horse?"

She hadn't even been that funny and she knew it, but Leo broke anyway. Shoulders heaving, tears welling as he snorted a laugh that actually sounded very much like a horse. She smirked, even more smug now, and led him upstairs. Behind them, she heard the real estate agent greet another couple; the relief in her voice was audible from here.

Though the agent wasn't there to listen, Shira kept the game going in the primary bedroom. "I was really hoping for one of those bathtub-in-the-middle-of-the-room situations," she said, mock frowning as she paced around the (king-size, she noted for their comparison file) bed. "Though I guess you only really find those in old buildings in New York City."

"Maybe we should scratch the house hunt and buy one of them," Leo said. "For you, at least." He gave her what felt like an overly long look, or maybe she was just imagining it because she was still feeling all tender and vulnerable after thinking about him as a father. "Have you thought about moving back? You know, since you're not working in the art world anymore?"

Shira sighed. Ever since Talia had raised the subject last year, it was like her family had decided together to put on the pressure. Her parents had been relentless with the guilt trips, reminding her how old they were getting, and Talia had been subjecting her to random, poorly punctuated, weirdly religious threats (e.g., *move back or ill instruct hashem to put you in the book of death on yk*). "I've been thinking about it, but it's a big decision. I've lived in LA my entire adult life. It's not easy to just abandon that and move across the country."

"I get it," Leo said, even though how could he possibly, considering he'd—oh. He actually had been in a similar situation, in high school, when he'd abandoned his entire life in New Jersey to move to Michigan with his mom. And then again, when he'd left Michigan and moved back here. He took a seat on the edge of the king bed. Shira winced, having to physically stop herself from yelling *no outside clothes on the sheets.* "It's a hard decision. But I can tell you that, at least for me, it was a relief to make it and to be done with it. Once my mom left Michigan and my friends graduated and moved around the country, I didn't have much left there that I couldn't have here."

That made sense. Shira had her synagogue community that she loved, but being fully honest, she wasn't so close to them there that she felt she couldn't leave them. She'd miss them, but she could be just as happy with another synagogue community. She had her residency coming up, but that was temporary. And while she'd made friends out there since the blowup with Danica and Ellery and Nora, they weren't as close. Sometimes, at night, when she closed her eyes, she could admit to herself that she purposely kept any new friends at a bit of a remove because she was so afraid of it happening again.

But that wasn't healthy, was it? It was like those people who got a divorce and never let themselves fall in love again. She should go out there. She should let herself get close to people. And it would be really, really nice to be near her family once more, if only to stop her mom calling her to tell her that she had another strange ache in her side and it was probably cancer or something equally as horrible. "I'm going to do it," said Shira, and just like that, she could breathe a little easier. "I'm going to move back."

"Yeah!" Leo touched her on the shoulder in a gesture between a clap and a pat. The force of it, the touch of his palm, sent a zing through her arm. Energized, she clapped her hands together.

"But you have to find me an apartment with the bathtub in the kitchen."

"Shouldn't be too hard," Leo said confidently. "And now that I know how to do a lot of this house stuff, if I have to, I can install one. So that you can bathe while your boyfriend cooks."

Boyfriend. Why did he say it like that? "He'll have to be careful not to mix the pasta water with the bathwater," she said, eyeing Leo carefully. "I wouldn't like that. I bet Emily wouldn't, either."

It was the stupidest way possible to slip Emily's name into the conversation, and Shira immediately felt like an idiot. But she *had* to know.

Leo let out a delicate cough. "Emily and I actually broke up," he said. "A few weeks ago." He was ducking his head, so Shira couldn't read anything in his face, or his tone, which was decidedly neutral. "So she won't feel any type of way about it."

She wanted so badly to barrage him with questions. *Who broke up with who? Why did you break up? How are you feeling about it?* But only that last one seemed appropriate to ask, so that's what she did. "Are you okay?"

He shrugged. "I'm fine." Of course he would say that—he was such a guy. Footsteps sounded up the stairs, and Leo turned at the noise, his face slackening with what appeared to be relief. When he spoke, his voice was back to its previous game-playing heartiness. "I think this bedroom is smaller than the primary in my dad's house, but it's hard to tell without checking. I should've brought my tape measure."

Damn it. Back to business. "I think there's an app you can use to measure somehow with your phone," Shira offered, but Leo was already walking out of the room. She went to follow but was stopped trying to get around the other couple; by the time they'd finished their awkward step dance, Leo was somewhere else in the house, the attic, maybe, or the basement. She couldn't know.

THEIR DRIVE TO the next house was silent, aside from the occasional assessment of how similar that house had been to Leo's dad's. Shira spent most of the ride turning over every possible scenario for Leo and Emily's breakup in her head, trying to read into the tiniest of things. *Leo must have been the one to do it, because otherwise why would Emily have posted a happy photo of the two of them only a week or two before they broke up? But he doesn't want to talk about it, and doesn't that mean that it probably hurts?*

"I wonder what it'll sell for," Leo mused about the house, putting on his turn signal so he could coast to a spot on the curb and pulling her back to the present. He'd driven exactly the speed limit all the way here. "My guess is not as much as my dad's, with less usable space in the house and older bathrooms. But we'll see."

"We'll see," echoed Shira.

The next house was definitively nicer than Leo's dad's, with two more bedrooms and an extra bathroom and a really high-end kitchen, everything shiny chrome and gleaming granite. "This one will definitely go for more than my dad's," he said, scrolling through some of the photos on his phone, holding it up so she could see. "But it's still a good data point. Not every single house we see can be an exact comp."

"Right. Of course," Shira said. "It's not like we're going to find an exact copy of your dad's house up for sale." Except maybe in their own neighborhood, where the houses seemed to have one of four different blueprints. But none of the houses in their neighborhood had recently sold.

This time, as they greeted the real estate agent, Shira smiled at her and tipped her head in Leo's direction, as if in fond exasperation. Something about the gesture felt freer, knowing that he was single. She wasn't worrying about accidentally going a bit too far and stepping on someone else's territory. "I don't think we need the extra bedroom and bathroom, but he wanted to take a look anyway," she said. "It's two more bedrooms than we need, really. But thinking about resale value, what do you think those two extra bedrooms and that extra bathroom add to the value of the home?"

The real estate agent's eyes lit up as he began rambling about added value, home offices, blah blah blah, basically trying to convince them that more space equaled better. Shira nodded along, hoping Leo was gaining something of value from this speech, and letting her mind drift. Maybe she and Fake Husband

Leo would need home offices, Leo to work on his games between houses and Shira to work remotely at least a few days a week. That would leave room for kids. One, two, even three if two shared a room. Kids could share rooms and be fine. Sure, she'd never shared a room with Talia, and that was probably good because they might have killed each other, but Talia was a rare breed. Surely she wouldn't birth a Talia.

"Thanks," Leo finally said, cutting off the agent. "We'll keep that in mind. I'm just not sure if we can afford the extra space right now."

"Well, of course it doesn't hurt to look," said the agent.

"Of course," said Leo. "Come on, dear. Let's take a look at the upstairs."

They trooped upstairs, the sleek wooden staircase washed in light from an opening up above. The bedrooms were spacious, the bathrooms redone without being too modern and sterile. Shira opened the closet in one of the kids' rooms to find dolls shoved into shelves, little dresses dangling over tiny sparkly shoes. She closed it, something sticking in her throat. "This house is really nice, but I don't know if it's me," she said.

"Oh, yeah?" Leo said, still in character. "Tell me, what would please the missus?"

He probably expected her to launch into a speech about ensuring there was enough room in the backyard for her cage of tigers or a high enough ceiling in the basement to hang her sex trapeze, but something about her stilled. It was like those few thoughts about Fake Husband Leo and the knowledge that he'd broken up with Emily had nudged a switch from the *off* into the *on* direction, and this time she couldn't flip it back with enough determination.

She walked over to the window, giving him her back. It seemed to be the only way to get the words out when he was looking at her with those soft eyes, pretending she was his. "Years ago, even a house this nice probably wouldn't have been enough for me," she said. "I'd probably want one of those flipped houses. I wouldn't care if everything was shoddy underneath, if I was risking a fire from faulty wiring or things were put together on a slant that would make all my furniture roll, as long as when my guests came by they shook their heads and were like, all quiet where they thought I couldn't hear them, 'Wow, look at this place. All these bedrooms and that view, she really made it.'"

He didn't make a joke in response. Beneath them, faintly, the footsteps of another couple echoed. Probably a real one, really looking to see if they wanted to make this their home. "But that's not what matters to me anymore," she said. "I want a sturdy build and safe wiring and maybe one fun, cool feature that I can point out when I give a house tour, like a stained glass window or an original doorbell from a hundred years ago. Three bedrooms and bathrooms with character. A safe neighborhood. A garden I could grow over the years." She stopped and considered. "Okay, and the stained glass window. I've actually always wanted a stained glass window."

He was quiet for long enough that she couldn't bear it and glanced at him over her shoulder. He met her eyes as if he was waiting for them. "Houses like that are expensive, and stained glass windows around here are extremely rare," he said, and she realized he had no idea what she'd actually been saying. "You usually find them in really old houses, and most of the houses around here aren't that old. The few that are would probably take a lot of work to restore properly."

"I know," she said, and even though he didn't know what she was really saying, she couldn't stop herself from saying it anyway. "But I'm ready to do the work. I wasn't before, but now I am."

"Do you think you want to buy when you move back?" he asked. She shook her head. She didn't want to live around here; she'd move to one of the cities nearby, New York or Philadelphia, where the jobs were. "Me, I like renting for now. I'm still not entirely sure what I want in a forever home."

"Yeah." Shira looked away. "It's not like I can afford a house, anyway."

"Come on, you're Shira Levinson." He gave her a friendly nudge with his shoulder, and she had to fight the urge to relax into it. "Like you haven't been saving money for a down payment practically since birth."

She couldn't argue with that. Most of it was still in a savings account, earning a paltry amount of interest, because she was too afraid the stock market would crash and take everything with it. "I just don't know if I deserve a house like that." She blinked back the sudden sting of tears. "I had my chance with a good, sturdy house, but I didn't appreciate it back then. I was so immature."

"Hey." He slung a friendly arm around her shoulder. This time she couldn't resist leaning into it, closing her eyes, pretending like she belonged there. "Maturity has nothing to do with buying a house. Most of our peers aren't going to be able to buy houses until we're old, anyway. It's depressing but normal. Are you sure you're okay?"

No. "Yeah," she said, lifting her head, opening her eyes, blinking into the light like she was a new thing, just emerged from the dark. "I'm fine."

"Okay," he said, squinting at her like he couldn't see, either. "You up for another house?"

No. "Of course."

20

LEO WAS HAVING A GREAT TIME TOURING HOUSES with Shira, honestly. Such a great time that he dragged her to an extra one that wasn't even a good comp for his dad's, just to see how she'd charm the real estate agent and embellish their fake marriage even further. By the fourth house, they'd gotten married two weeks after they'd met on a hot-air balloon tour of the American Southwest. "It was a shame how many of our fellow riders perished due to the cactus needles," Shira had said somberly as Leo fought off a laugh. "You could say it was fate that neither one of us wanted to get that close to the ground."

"Flying high with love," Leo said solemnly. The agent nodded along, blinking furiously, unsure how much bluff was worth calling when his commission stood in the balance.

It was an excellent distraction from everything else that was going on in Leo's life, namely the breakup with Emily and his dad's unveiling. Watching that cloth come off that stone and seeing his dad's name etched permanently in the rock had made Leo's knees weak. The plastic marker that had sat there until then was impermanent. It was small. Leo could've fooled himself that it was anybody's name there. But the stone? Leo could've been blind and still felt the ridges on the rock and known that his dad was buried under there.

And it had been even harder standing there in the freezing cold wind, his jacket whipping all around him because he couldn't find the strength to uncross his arms, as Aunt Ellen patted him brusquely on the shoulder. (It wasn't her fault. She did pretty much everything brusquely.) "I never thought I'd see my little brother's name there first," she said, her voice fragile as an old metal radiator cover that was rusted on the edges, which was about as fragile as he'd ever heard it. "He shouldn't have filled in the first spot."

The grave was large enough for four sections, the family name DAVID written big at the top. Leo's grandparents had purchased it after the divorce; Aunt Ellen had never married or had kids, and the presumption was that Leo's dad wouldn't again, either. So it was one macabre way that Leo's grandparents as parents could take care of their children. "Well," Leo said, rubbing his nose and coming away wet. "You'll be there soon enough."

Aunt Ellen's surprised cackle warmed him sufficiently to stop his shivering for a moment. "Sure will," she said, though her face dropped as she said it. "What about you, though, Leo?"

He knew what she meant: He was an only child, relationship status undetermined. He pretended he didn't, though. "Surely there's enough space here to tack on a fifth name," he said, gesturing at the expanse of grass beside the grave. "I'll try to die of something wasting so that I don't take up too much room."

He wasn't looking at his aunt, but he could feel her roll her eyes. Something about the vibrations in the air. "I have no regrets," she said. "Singledom is my gladdest state. I have a lot of friends and a lot of solitude, and I'm very happy with my choices. I know you, though, and singledom isn't yours." She let the words hang there the way she had when they'd first met up at the grave. *Where's Emily?* And him, bracing himself for her to tell him how sad she was, how much fun she'd had with Emily at Disney World. "So I hope you don't end up in the ground next to us."

"Thanks?" Leo said. They'd recited the Mourner's Kaddish clumsily from their phones. Then he'd stood at the grave with his aunt as long as he could bear it before making an excuse and getting the hell out of there.

So now, in the car with Shira, given that he'd exhausted his list of open houses in the area, he didn't want to go home to Neptune, who was happily sleeping without him anyway, and stare at his empty walls. There was no excuse for his empty walls—he'd lived there long enough, and Emily had lived there long enough. They'd just never bothered to find anything to hang up. "Are you hungry?" he asked. "We could stop and get something to eat."

She was staring out the window, watching pine trees and dirt driveways zip by. "We're going in the wrong direction from all the food, unless you want to break into the bakery again," she said. "We could—ooh!" She pointed, but they'd already flown by whatever she was pointing at. "Was that a sign for a Hanukkah light show? There are never Hanukkah light shows, they're always Christmas! Oh my god, if I read that sign right, I'm going to be so excited."

It was already starting to get dark even though it wasn't even four thirty, the joy of an East Coast winter. He could go for a light show, especially a Hanukkah one. It was the Festival of Lights, after all. Why weren't there more Hanukkah light shows? (He knew the answer perfectly well: because there weren't enough Hanukkah celebrators in most areas to make having one worth it.) "Hold tight," he said, slamming on the brakes so that he could turn into the jughandle, swinging around. Shira squealed, holding on to the sides of her seat.

"You know, it's not an emergency," she said. "We could've just taken the next one. It's New Jersey. We've got more jughandles than jugs."

"It is an emergency." He wasn't stupid. He was still a cautious driver; he wouldn't have slammed on the brakes or made a wild turn if any other cars had been within striking distance. But hitting the brakes like that, even in a no-stress situation, made a thrill run through him. "The light show awaits!"

"I wonder what it even is," Shira said once they'd located the sign, which was glossy and bright, made to stand out against the darkness. "The theme park always has one, but obviously this isn't at the theme park. What else is out here? It couldn't be held at the military base, right?"

"If the military base had a light show, it would probably blow up our car." The road they were driving down now was narrow and bumpy, the occasional house looming suddenly on the side of the road, their headlights ghostly circles in the dark. "Do you think it's an anti-Semitic serial killer preying on people who want to see a Hanukkah light show?"

They rounded a corner, and there it was, all of a sudden: an explosion of light surrounding a small ranch-style house. And there, another sign, bigger: **HANUKKAH LIGHT SHOW**.

Theirs appeared to be the only car there. Leo coasted to a stop, but neither one of them made a move to get out. "If it is a serial killer," Shira said, "they put a lot of effort into it."

"Yeah," said Leo. "Maybe we should just let them kill us. They've earned it."

Before either of them could work up the nerve to get out, the door to the house burst open, and children poured out. Four of them, at least, though they looked like mere outlines against the lights in the yard. "Someone's here!" Leo could hear one of them squeal. "Our sign worked!"

Okay, fine. If these children were serial killers, they could have him. Leo swung open the door and stepped out, Shira close behind him. "We couldn't resist," he said. "We'd never seen a Hanukkah light show before."

"Oh boy, oh boy," one of the other kids said. Leo was beyond abominable at picking out children's ages—shout-out to the second cousin he'd infuriated by asking if he was seven when he was actually nine and three-quarters—but he thought they probably ranged from around five to preteen. "Come on, come on."

Leo glanced around. "Is there an adult here or something?" Following a bunch of random children into dark woods seemed like a good way to get in trouble.

One of the smaller kids pointed. "Back there. On the porch." Sure enough, barely illuminated by strings of white lights, Leo could make out an older couple standing and watching. Upon seeing him looking, they waved. Leo waved back, Shira echoing him a second later. "Okay, see? Now come on."

"We don't pay you or anything?" Shira asked, feet beginning to drift after the kids as if compelled by some outside force. Leo remembered as a kid hearing Shira tell him stories she'd heard in Hebrew school of Jewish demons and monsters and goblins. *On the fourth night of Hanukkah is when the veil between the worlds thins,* she might have said, though she probably hadn't, it was probably just Leo's imagination. And why was his imagination now remembering that story about the corpse bride from the old country, about the man who accidentally placed a wedding ring on the bony finger of a dead woman and ended up entangled in the world of the dead? *Just don't try to marry anyone tonight, Leo,* he told himself, and he blinked, and for a moment he saw Emily, face stricken, hands over her mouth. His heart twisted. *Just don't try to marry anyone at all.*

Shira didn't look like a corpse bride, even in the shadows as they were. She was healthy, vibrant, full of life, practically bouncing with every step. Every so often she'd look over her shoulder as if to make sure he was following, and a flash of worry ran through him that she'd trip over a root or walk into a tree.

"You can tip us at the end if you think we did a good job," the kid was saying to Shira up ahead, almost too far off for Leo to hear. That stirred Leo's boots into motion; he wasn't going to let Shira walk into a tree (more likely), or allow a dead man to slip a ring on her finger (less likely).

He was surprised by the flash of jealousy that went through

him at the thought of anyone slipping a ring on Shira's finger. Anyone but him. But then he blinked, and there was Emily's face again, her chin now trembling with tears. He shook away both images and hustled after the group.

Like Leo's dad's backyard, these kids' backyard was mostly trees; the small house bordered the pinelands as well. Except, unlike Leo's dad, who'd done nothing with the trees behind his house other than take walks back there and hide away the swing set, these kids had turned theirs into a winter wonderland. A Hanukkah wonderland, specifically. "Start here," the oldest kid directed, motioning him and Shira to a circle of rainbow lights. "And follow the rainbow throughout. If you get lost, yell for us. We'll be waiting." He smiled, and was it extra toothy, or was that just Leo's imagination working overtime in the dark?

But Shira had grabbed Leo's hand already and was tugging him forward. They were both wearing gloves, so there was no actual skin-to-skin contact, though a jolt ran through his arm as if there were. "Thank you," she called over her shoulder. They turned a corner, and everything disappeared except for the lights.

Their first light scene ahead was, inappropriately, centering Santa Claus. A big light-up Santa stood over a crowd of lit-up—Leo had to lean in to verify—action figures and Barbies. "Wait," said Shira, also leaning in. "It looks like someone tried to color in Santa's hair and beard with marker. And there's a Burger King crown on his head."

"Hmm," Leo said. "Do you think Santa Claus is supposed to be God here?"

"I mean, you can't exactly go buy a light-up figure of God, right?" Shira said. "They were probably working with what they had."

Leo and Shira continued on, much amused. They passed some Stars of David designed in string lights and some small light-up animals before stopping at the next scene, where light-up Jesus was conferring with some light-up Wise Men. "Jesus is wearing a yarmulke," said Leo. And there was an inflatable hammer leaning against his side, one of those used for carnival games. "Is he supposed to be Judah Maccabee?"

"The Three Wise Men are wearing kippahs, too," Shira said, a laugh caught in her voice. "I think these *are* supposed to be the Maccabees. Maybe Santa Claus wasn't God, he was supposed to be King Antiochus?" Probably catching Leo's blank stare, she clarified, "You know, the evil king who wanted to ban Judaism and sparked the whole rebellion that became the Hanukkah story?"

"Right," Leo said. "And it turned out the whole time that Santa Claus was his twin. What a coup."

"They're doing their best," Shira said, whapping him lightly with her wrist. "We live in a Christian society. It was probably all they could find."

With that in mind, they admired the next scene of an assorted group of reindeer (wearing kippahs) who were trying to light a menorah with empty bottles of olive oil that each contained a battery-operated candle inside, probably so you couldn't miss that they were supposed to contain olive oil. "This is from the next part of the Hanukkah story, after the rebellion," said Shira. "After they sent the king packing and celebrated that they could continue to practice Judaism, the temple was still destroyed and desecrated. They needed to light the sacred menorah, but they could only find enough sacred oil to last one night, even though it would take eight nights to make more. But then the miracle of Hanukkah was that–"

"The oil that was only supposed to last one night lasted all eight nights, until they were able to make more, I know," said Leo. "I remember that much from all your elementary school presentations." As one of the few Jews in their elementary school, Shira had been tasked with telling their class every year about Hanukkah, a task she took to with great enthusiasm and bags and bags of gold-foil-wrapped chocolate gelt, which made the class enthusiastic about it, too. Leo wondered, not for the first time, what it would have been like if his parents had enrolled him in Hebrew school. If he'd gotten bar mitzvahed, and if he'd gotten up in front of the class every year with Shira to tell his class about all the holidays.

If maybe she hadn't had to be the only one to perform.

Shira was still talking about the Hanukkah story, something about the morals and the meaning and the fact that it wasn't a very important holiday after all, that general American society just thought it was important because of its proximity to Christmas, and people felt bad that only the Christian kids got presents. Leo did his very best to pay attention as they neared what seemed to be the final light display, since they'd circled back around enough that he could see the house in front of them. They passed more light strings looped in patterns that were probably supposed to evoke something Hanukkah related, a few menorahs and dreidels, and then there they were.

The kids had put the scene together with a bunch of elves, though the kids had looped glittery Hanukkah garlands around their necks and placed kippahs on their heads (they must have raided their synagogue's stores, unless their parents had been popular enough to have attended a million bat mitzvahs and Jewish weddings). Two larger elves, probably the parents, were standing in the middle before a glowing light-up menorah. Their–Leo counted–twelve smaller elf children were arranged in a semicircle around them, their faces all turned toward the fake candles. "Aw," Shira said, her voice for some reason a little froggy. "It's a Hanukkah party."

The figures were surrounded by scraps of glittery wrapping paper (pinned to the ground so that it wouldn't blow away) and scattered plastic dreidels and bits of gold foil (also pinned down) from gelt that Leo assumed the kids had eaten themselves. It would have been irresponsible to leave chocolate outside; chocolate was poisonous to dogs–who knew if it was poisonous to deer and squirrels and whatever else lived out here as well?

That's what he was thinking when Shira kissed him.

21

SHIRA LEVINSON WAS *KISSING* HIM.

The shock was almost too much to keep Leo from kissing her back. Almost.

It was as if, five years after their first kiss, they were continuing what they'd started. Like they'd hit pause, and there were her lips moving once more against his, there was that little sigh escaping her throat, there was her body pressed warm and tight against his, and *oh god* he was going to get hard right here in front of this maniacally grinning elfin family.

That thought was almost enough to make him pull back, but he couldn't stop. Not now. Not with her hand tangled in his hair and her tongue slipping through his lips and her melting into him like she wanted to become one.

He closed his eyes, surrendering to the kiss, and then she popped up. Not Shira. Emily. Her chin was trembling; her arms were crossed, her body turned slightly away as if she couldn't bear to face him full-on.

That thought was enough to make him pull back. Not easily. Not smoothly. The kiss broke like something smashing, a light suddenly going dark.

They stood there for a moment, almost nose to nose, breathing in sync. She spoke first. "Is it Emily?"

Hearing her name out loud was like a bucket of ice water drenching his head. He took a step back. "Emily and I broke up. I told you that."

Shira touched her lips, then shook her head. "But you're still hurting over her." Even though the only light out here was emitted by cheerful elves and a plastic menorah, he could still see how crimson her cheeks were. "Fuck. I'm sorry. I thought . . . I don't know, I guess I didn't think."

He couldn't help himself. "This is the one time in your life that you choose not to think something through before doing it?"

Little spots of red bloomed on her cheeks. "What are you talking about?"

Honestly, he wasn't totally sure if he was talking to her or to himself. "Everything was great in our relationship, until I started thinking about things too hard. She wanted to get married and have kids," he said. He took a deep breath. "And we'd been together for almost three years. We're almost thirty. She wasn't rushing things or being unreasonable, and that's what made it so hard. I thought about it for way longer than I had to, and she got really mad at me for stringing her along." Which he hadn't been. He'd loved Emily. He'd loved her the whole time. He just . . .

He hadn't been able to stop thinking about Shira during all the wrong moments.

"What?" said Shira. "You don't want to get married or have kids?"

"I . . ." The words stuck in his throat. It wasn't that he didn't want to get married or have kids. When he thought about himself five, ten, fifteen years in the future, there was a kid or two there, learning how to hit a ball off a tee or painting a picture of a smiling family beneath a shining sun. He heard someone calling him Dad, and he felt a woman standing there by his side.

He just didn't think it was Emily.

He'd loved Emily. He cared deeply about Emily. But when he thought about everything he'd go through in the future, he didn't see her there next to him. He saw Shira. And that made him furious because Shira had made it so clear that she didn't see him there with her.

So to have her kiss him like this out of nowhere, right now, now that he had everything in his life together? When she hadn't wanted him before?

It felt shitty. So shitty.

And even shittier to have her admit that she hadn't thought about the kiss at all, that she'd just kissed him on the spur of the moment. Like she could just play with his feelings and those feelings didn't matter. When he'd spent all this time thinking so hard about his future and his relationships and she could do this to him with a snap of her fingers, it wasn't right and it wasn't *fair.*

"I'm sorry," Shira was saying now. "It wasn't cool to kiss you without asking. Especially since you're still hurting over Emily. I shouldn't have made things about you and me right away."

She sounded so calm about it, like she assumed he'd spent plenty of time thinking about the two of them, that it almost made him want to stomp the head of an elf into the dirt. "What are you talking about?" he said, an incredulous laugh bubbling up in his throat. "What do you mean, you and me?"

Her eyes were wider and rounder than any chocolate gelt coin he'd ever eaten. "Well, you kissed *me* before–"

"Five years ago," Leo said. "And then remember what happened after that?" He spit out the words like he was trying to rid his mouth of something bitter. "You didn't think I was good enough for you." His stomach bubbled. "And now, what?" In a flash, that whole speech she'd given him while "house hunting" about only wanting a sturdy three-bedroom took a whole new light. "You're ready to settle, so I should still be at your beck and call?"

"That's not at all how I feel," Shira said, and now her eyes were shiny like gelt. *Well, too bad, Shira.* Leo refused to feel sorry for her. "I had to change and grow up and mature and realize those shiny status symbols didn't matter to me anymore. It has nothing to do with–"

"So if I was still at the warehouse, you'd want to kiss me."

She reared back like he'd slapped her. "You hated the warehouse," she said. "You were miserable."

"Yeah, but did you actually care about that, or did you just care about being seen with a guy who works at a warehouse?"

"I was immature," she whispered, then raised her voice. "That was five years ago! People are allowed to change in five years and decide that they care about different things than they used to."

Sure. Sure they were. But he wasn't sure if he'd ever be able to get over the lingering feeling that she'd never think he was good enough. He'd quit his fancy job at the studio. He was going to work on houses, and then what? Maybe he'd decide to do something else. Maybe he'd make another game. He was a grown-up, and he'd always make sure he had enough to pay the bills, because of the whole grown-up thing, but he wasn't done growing and changing. He didn't know who he'd be next.

But he knew he'd never be the kind of guy Dr. William had been, because he didn't want to be that kind of guy. He didn't want to work work work and never do anything else. He didn't find his passion in a job. He hoped he'd find it somewhere else, but maybe not. Maybe he just wasn't one of those people with a great all-consuming passion anywhere in his life. Maybe he'd just be content. That didn't sound so bad.

For him. He wasn't convinced it didn't sound so bad for Shira. He turned away, feeling the temperature drop. "Sure. Okay." A beat when she could have said something. Anything.

But she didn't. So he continued, "We should finish up. I bet the kids are waiting." And he set off without checking to see if she'd follow.

Sure enough, the kids swarmed him as soon as he set foot over the strings of light marking the boundary. "Did you like it?" the oldest one asked, breathless, eyes sparkling.

Leo forced a smile. "Sure did," he said. "We were really impressed with how you repurposed all the Christmas light-up figures. Right?" He glanced over his shoulder. Shira wasn't there. Without meaning to, he reached back for her, like he could somehow sweep her into being. The space where she should be was cold and empty.

"Right," she said, and he felt like an idiot because she was just on his other side. "Really smart."

The kid positively vibrated with delight. "Can you believe we looked for light-up Maccabees and King Antiochus and couldn't find any?" Leo shook his head, bemused. "I mean, we found some online, but they were really expensive, and Mom and Dad said we had to work with what was on clearance at the dollar store, so those were our options."

"Well, you did a great job," said Leo. He reached for his wallet and peeled off a twenty, then hesitated. Would Shira think he was cheap?

Who the fuck cares if Shira thinks you're cheap? He handed over the twenty. Shira followed up with a twenty of her own. The kids cheered. "We're rich!" Their parents waved from the porch as if apologizing as Leo and Shira cleared out.

Back in the car, Leo turned on his headlights, which drowned out the scene before him. He was careful to check his rear mirror and windows about a thousand times to avoid running over an errant kid before pulling onto the lightless street.

Shira was the first to speak once they'd made it back to the main road and Leo was waiting to turn right. "Will you still come to the party tomorrow night?"

Honestly, he couldn't think of anything less appealing. Going over to Shira's house, to the party he always used to go to with his dad, having to awkwardly accept all the neighbors' condolences for his dad and deflect all the neighbors' questions about Emily, while putting on a happy face for Shira and dealing with the surge of complicated feelings in his gut every time he circled around to face a photo of her on the wall or on a table, which, in the Levinson house, was literally everywhere? It sounded awful.

So he took the easy way out. "I wish I could, but I can't," he said, eyes on the road, the yellow line streaking into the distance. "My aunt is having a little gathering."

"Oh."

Leo slowed at the sight of two eyes gleaming like coins on the side of the road. He caught the brief swish of a tail before whatever it was turned and vanished into the dark woods. "Yeah."

Quiet fell over the car again, but this wasn't the comfortable silence of two old friends happy to exist in each other's company. It was thick, uncomfortable, like an itchy wool sweater you were forced to wear even though it wasn't even that cold out.

Shira was the first to break it again. "I hope this doesn't make things too weird," she said. "I wish I could take it back. The kiss."

"Don't say that," Leo said, then immediately felt awkward because that made it sound like he was happy it had happened. He fumbled, trying to recover. "I'm serious that my aunt is having a thing. Otherwise I would go." Otherwise he would have to think of a better excuse, he meant. But, here in the dark, glancing over at Shira, it was hard to know what year they were in. The darkness softened everything, reducing her face to a flash of cheek here or a gleam of eye there, and she could've been twelve, lying on his floor bemoaning the starters in the new Pokémon expansion; or she could've been fourteen, crying that he was moving away; or she could've been twenty-two, back in his life and the most beautiful sight he'd ever seen. Or she could've been thirty, older and surer and still new and uncertain, because weren't they all new and uncertain no matter how old they were? What would she be like at thirty? What would *he* be like at thirty? Thirty was getting closer and closer, which felt wild and a little mean. "Spending time on regrets is pointless. You can't go back in time."

"I guess you're right," she said quietly.

He continued, "If my kissing you five years ago didn't ruin our friendship, this won't ruin our friendship, either. We're even. Okay?"

"Okay," she said. "I just . . . once your dad's house sells, you'll have no reason to be in the neighborhood anymore."

"We'll text each other," he said. "Okay?"

She didn't respond, just turned to look out the window. It was fine. She didn't need to respond. He knew exactly what was going through her head: *We said we'd text each other the first time you moved.*

But this time would be different, he vowed. This time, he'd actually lost her, and he knew what it was like to be Shira Levinson-less. And that wasn't a world he wanted to live in.

Texts between Leo David and Shira Levinson, June:

Leo: Happy birthday!

Shira: Thanks!

Leo: . . .

Shira: . . .

From Shira Levinson's email inbox, September:

Dear Shira, Your lease application for **105 Glenbrook Ave, Unit 501**, in **Philadelphia, PA** has been approved! Please find enclosed the amended document, whose term begins on **January 1st**. You can pick up the keys within a week of your lease's start date at the management office, whose address is . . .

Dear Shira, Thank you for submitting your work to our gallery! We've reviewed your work and loved it—your take on the memory candle is startlingly bright and original and like nothing we've exhibited before. We would love to discuss representation and an exhibit with you—are you available for a Zoom chat next week? Or, if you happen to be in person in the Philadelphia area (I know you mentioned you were moving, but I'm not sure when) we'd love to take you out to dinner . . .

From Leo David's email inbox, September:

Hi Leo, We never met in person, but my name is Elizabeth Arnold—my husband and I purchased the home you renovated at 118 York Street. When we were looking at home listings, we were always wary of homes that had been flipped, and yours was no exception, but our real estate agent persuaded us to take a look anyway, and I'm so glad he did! The work you did really brought out the historical character of the house, and I love the little touches you put in . . .

Texts between Shira Levinson and Leo David, September:

Shira: Happy birthday!

Leo: Thanks!

Shira: . . .

Leo: . . .

22

Year Seven

SHIRA HAD ALMOST A WEEK BETWEEN QUITTING HER job and boarding her flight across the country, so she decided to use those six days as a kind of farewell to Los Angeles. She met her old work friends and art friends for final rounds of drinks, giving one another toasts and promises to stay in touch that she knew even as the glasses clinked were probably going to be broken. She went for final walks in Griffith Park and waved farewell to the California condors at the LA Zoo. She took final trips to the Getty and the observatory and the La Brea Tar Pits to marvel at all those creatures whose skeletons had stood the test of time. Goodbye, goodbye, goodbye.

One of her last farewell trips was to LACMA, the art museum. She'd loved coming here as a gallery assistant, taking a break from the dog-eat-dog gallery world to listen to her footsteps echo in these grand halls, taking in works that had stood the test of time, even if it was not quite as much time as a mammoth skeleton had endured. For some reason, she'd always liked the way museums smelled. Pristine, clean, not like the paint and turpentine of her studio. Art divorced from the messy processes of creation.

And then, of course, it got really messy. She rounded the corner away from Jeff Koons's *Balloon Dog* (overrated, she'd always thought) and came face-to-face with a rotating exhibition. Staggeringly big, gloriously beautiful paintings, explosions of color and light and hope and despair. At first they looked abstract, but then, as you focused, you could see the people in them, their bodies contorting into impossible positions, wings and beaks and feet bursting forth as they finally, finally flew.

One of the reasons Shira had liked working in the art world was that feeling when a piece of art spoke to her, when she looked at something and it was like the something was looking back into her, pulling out a feeling or an idea she knew but hadn't known she knew, and putting it on a canvas or a stand. She took a few steps closer to read the name on the exhibit card.

Danica.

She blew out a breath of air, taking an instinctive step back. It had been long enough since their friend breakup that she was beginning to suspect seeing Danica's name, especially when unexpected, would never not feel like a small electric shock or a light kick in the stomach. But that was it for now, she was surprised to realize. No wave of pain or anger. No—

"Is this piece speaking to you?" someone said, way too close to Shira's ear. She turned, expecting to see a docent or tour guide, someone excited to share everything they knew about the art and the artist, but no.

It was the artist herself.

Danica clearly hadn't recognized Shira from the back,

maybe because Shira had let her hair go curly after leaving the gallery; her eyebrows jumped up nearly to her hairline upon seeing Shira's face. Shira knew this game well: Sidle up to someone looking at your work; figure out how they're feeling about it; cry if they hate it, but reveal yourself as the artist if they love it and bask in the glow of their praise.

No basking here. Danica looked a little like she might throw up. Shira remembered that look well; she'd held Danica's hair back over the toilet multiple times in college. It felt a little bit like she was doing that again now, like she was hunched over on the floor and something was compressing her chest, and okay, maybe it wasn't anything like that at all, maybe it was like a heart attack.

It wasn't like they could pretend they hadn't seen each other. Shira nodded with some effort, fighting back the ingrained urge to *smile, smile, don't forget you have resting bitch face*. "Hi."

"Hi," Danica said back. Shira stared at her. She stared at Shira. Shira wondered if this was the beginning of a staring contest, one with mortal consequences for the loser.

What should she do? Part of her wanted to tell Danica right here, right now, that she'd never stolen her idea and she wished Danica had given her the chance to tell her that when it mattered. Another part of her wanted to yell at her, to tell her how much Shira hated her for grabbing the wheel and crashing her life into a wall for a stupid reason. And another part of her, the part of her that still wished they were friends like they'd once been, wanted to pull her into a hug and tell her old friend how proud she was, how excited she was, that she was reaching heights they'd once only ever dreamed of.

Shira could, if she wanted to. Danica was still staring at her, frozen, lips slightly parted as if she were trying to play dead.

Shira turned away first. Forfeited the staring contest. Because what would be the point of any of it? What was done was done. And Shira was surprised to feel a great big breath of air entering her lungs, filling her up, making her light. Freeing her. "The painting is beautiful," she said, and then she turned on her heel and walked away. Those would be the last words she'd ever say to Danica, she thought. And that was okay. She was okay.

She didn't wait to see if Danica called her name. She didn't care. And, on the way out of the museum—which wasn't right away; she still had exhibits to see, and she wasn't going to let Danica scare her off—she unfollowed Ellery and Nora on social media and deleted their numbers from her phone.

It was just getting dark as she exited, which meant the light installation was beginning to sparkle outside the museum, guests oohing and aahing at the way the lights glittered like the stars that light pollution kept them from seeing. Shira let the light blaze in her vision, blotting out everything else, and then she turned to go home.

Not home. Home wasn't here, not anymore. Because the next day, before she flew out, she left her apartment key on the clean, bare kitchen countertop, taking a deep breath as she surveyed the expanse of empty space that had once been cluttered by furniture she'd picked up off the curb and piles of books stacked all over the floor in lieu of bookshelves. Most of it had been unloaded on Facebook Marketplace for a couple of bucks; the few things she couldn't bear to part with were making their very slow, very expensive way across the country toward her parents' house. That included her work clothes: She hoped their trip wasn't too slow, because she'd need them in January when she started the new marketing job a member of her synagogue in LA had helped her procure.

"Excuse me." She shook the thoughts out of her head, returning to the present, where she had to stand up from her aisle seat to allow the middle-seater in. The plane air-conditioning hummed overhead, already making her shiver. Once the person next to her sat down, she followed suit, glancing over at him. He wasn't playing *Washing Dishes at the End of the World* or its less well-received sequel; he was swiping a dating app on his phone. Shira hoped her profile wouldn't pop up. She hadn't opened it in ages. Too busy. Way too busy.

She pulled out her phone, though. Considered opening up the dating app and presetting her location to Philadelphia. Opened up her messages app instead. Scrolled down, down, down. Her thumb hovered over her last message with Leo, which was a Thanks! from him after she'd wished him a happy birthday back at the end of September. Nothing since then.

"Excuse me," someone said. The window seat person had arrived. Shira stood, using that as an excuse to put her phone on airplane mode and stick it in her pocket. She would text Leo later.

Only she didn't. Her dad picked her up and presented her with a bouquet of colorful dyed daisies he'd clearly purchased from the grocery store. "Aw," she said, clutching the flowers to her chest. They smelled like plastic. "Best Uber driver ever."

"Welcome back to the East Coast," he said, gesturing her

inside with a flourish and then closing her door gently behind her. "I'm glad you're here."

"Me too," Shira said, and watched the lights of the airport recede behind her. She had to text Leo eventually because he had to come to the Hanukkah party this year. He had to. There was no other option.

It was just kind of hard to express that type of urgency in a text without making the other person want to run the opposite way. But she would figure out the best method to say *Your attendance at this party is mandatory,* and she would text it to him. Soon. Very soon.

Only she didn't. She kept putting it off. Because what if she texted him and things stayed weird and awkward? What if he didn't listen to her when she tried to tell him how important it was that he listen to her, the same way Danica hadn't? Maybe she'd done all the work changing herself and growing and maturing, and it still wouldn't be enough. It could be fun when an old friend couldn't see you as anything but your old self, but it could also be hard and sucky not to be able to move beyond that previous version of who you were.

"You can't expect a relationship to fix you," said Talia frankly at the dollar store where they were trawling for Hanukkah decorations. Shira rolled her eyes. Her little sister had gotten irritatingly wise since she and Anjali had moved in together. "You have to fix yourself."

"I already fixed myself," Shira said. "He just couldn't see it."

"It's been a year," said Talia. She stood on her tiptoes and pulled a glittery blue-and-silver tinsel garland from a top shelf.

The benefits of being tall. "Maybe he can see it now. Especially now that you're moving back to the area."

Shira still couldn't quite believe it. It was scary, honestly. She'd gone to college in New York City and then had moved right to Los Angeles. Lived there for her entire adult postcollege life. Built her identity in an environment of sunshine and traffic and green-juice places.

It was freeing, though, the thought of starting over new. Not entirely new—her synagogue had connected her to another synagogue here, and they'd helped her find a job, too. So she'd be meeting people and hopefully making friends who were already vouched for. She'd actually planned at first to go back to New York, before crunching the numbers and realizing that she'd probably have to get roommates. Roommates were great in college, but after years of living alone, there was no way she was going back.

And Philly was nice. Good food. Not too far from her family. Culture. A much lower cost of living.

"I want to show him my new paintings," Shira said. The paintings of the memory candles that . . . well. That had so much to do with him. "No, I *have* to show him my new paintings."

"So show him your paintings." Talia made it sound so easy.

"You're a genius," Shira said, deadpan, but her mind was racing. She used to create art galleries out of their hallways . . . and over there were plenty of art supplies that had to do with Hanukkah. Stickers. Stencils. She might have been a professional artist, but she was a sucker for a stencil. There was something sweet and childlike about them, and she could always dress them up.

"Obviously," said Talia.

Shira gathered a bunch of the Hanukkah art supplies in her arms, then leaned in to give her sister an impromptu hug. Leaned back. Smiled. "You know you have a dreidel sticker on your forehead."

"I know," Talia said without missing a beat. "It's a sign from above that I'm the messiah."

Shira nearly choked on air. "Can't you get kicked out of rabbinical school for that?"

Talia grinned. "Not without offending the messiah. Hey, is that a female Hanukkah Harry?"

God, Shira hoped so.

23

EVERY SO OFTEN, LEO TOOK OUT HIS PHONE AND scrolled down in his messages app until he hit his last conversation with Shira. They hadn't communicated in months, and then she'd texted to wish him a happy birthday. Nothing elaborate, no inside jokes, no regular jokes. Just two words and an exclamation point, the same exact message he used to get before he deleted social media from old middle school friends he hadn't talked to in years and distant cousins he still wasn't entirely sure how he was related to.

So he'd responded the same way he'd always responded to them, the people who would have no idea it was his birthday if the site hadn't alerted them. Thanks! One word, one exclamation point, too impersonal. She hadn't responded to that, not even to like the message. It was hard to think how to follow that up, so he hadn't. And now it had been months, and it seemed too weird to come out of nowhere and be like, *Hey, you having a Hanukkah party this year? Can I invite myself?*

"Whatcha doing?" His mom suddenly loomed over where he was stretched out on his couch. He jumped. For an old lady, she moved with supernatural silence and speed. Then again, she was so deeply tanned and had done such a skillful job dyeing her grays brown that she easily looked ten years younger than she was, so it wasn't so surprising she moved that way.

Leo grimaced, tucking his phone into his pocket and hopping to his feet, nearly bumping into his mom. "Nothing. Looking up what to get for lunch. Directions. Are you hungry?"

She fixed him with a beady stare. It had probably been too much to hope that would work. "Were you on one of those dating apps? Can I help you? I know what you should be looking for in a woman."

There was nothing he'd like less than having his mother pick out his future mate. Ugh, that sounded gross. Then again . . . arranged marriages had worked for years around the world. Maybe he *should* let her give it a try.

Though that would involve joining one of the apps again. He'd deleted them all after he'd met Emily and hadn't been able to bring himself to join back up.

As if contributing to the conversation, Neptune nudged Leo's dangling hand with his wet nose. "We should probably actually take the dog for a walk," Leo said. "You want to come?"

"Sure." They slipped on shoes and headed outside. There weren't many places walkable from Leo's condo complex, but there was a nice little gravel path that ranged around the property, past the amenities Leo paid for in his monthly fee but rarely used: the dog park (Neptune was too nervous around other dogs), the playground, the swimming pool, the courtyard. Their feet found a crunchy rhythm, and they relaxed into a comfortable silence as Neptune sniffed at everything and then peed on everything.

This was the first time his mom had actually come to stay with him; usually he'd gone to visit her in Italy, or they'd taken a trip together somewhere and stayed in a hotel. She'd surprised him this year by asking if she could come visit—apparently her boyfriend would be staying with his daughter for a few weeks after the birth of her first child, and the daughter wasn't entirely comfortable with Leo's mom tagging along. "Which is totally understandable," she said, seeming unbothered. "I imagine that when I come stay with you after you have your first child, you'd probably be weirded out to have Giorgio there, too. I know you two are friendly, but there's a gap between 'friendly' and 'roommates while postpartum.'"

It was amazing how she said it so matter-of-factly—*after you have your first child*—as if they both assumed it would happen. Leo almost snorted, but he didn't want to deal with the consequences of snorting at something his mother said. It was weird, their relationship—he'd spent every day with her for years and years, she'd been the central figure in his life, and then suddenly she was just . . . gone. Like she'd done her duty and then it was time for her. But this woman he heard from in Italy, going on wild adventures and romancing foreign men (well, *man*, though she'd dropped hints about swinging that Leo always shut down right away because he did *not* need to hear that) and spending so much of her time on boats that she claimed to be landsick with her feet on solid ground, was someone totally different from the woman he'd known back in New Jersey and then in Michigan.

He took a deep breath. He and his mom didn't talk about deep things; they talked about pasta and video games (she'd resolutely played the entirety of *Washing Dishes at the End of the World*) and the sights of wherever they were seeing. But there were no sights to see here. "Do you think the person you are in Italy is the same person you were back when you were in New Jersey?" Maybe he just hadn't seen it then. He'd been a kid, after all. Kids didn't actually see their parents as people. But maybe she was going out late then, having affairs, eating bucketloads of pasta with men who had different accents.

No. He would've noticed that, right? Even as oblivious a kid as him would've noticed all the pasta on her breath. She never ate pasta back then; he remembered that much. She'd always been on some kind of low-carb diet to stay slim, while now neither she nor Giorgio seemed to mind that her hips and belly had grown round, her cheeks full.

He was surprised by her belly laugh. Bigger belly, bigger laugh. "I want to say no," she said. "I did all I could to leave her behind when I went to Italy. But you can't really leave a version of yourself behind, can you?"

"So you're still the same person," Leo said. "You just . . . changed. A lot." He felt silly saying it aloud like that, but somehow he felt the need to voice it. To hear himself say it and maybe to hear his mother, who'd spent so long as his ultimate authority on things, say it back.

"I changed a lot," his mom said, and he got the feeling she'd make a joke about it because that was what they did—they didn't talk about serious things—except then her face changed. He didn't even know how; all he knew was that one moment her expression was light and the next it looked as if she might be ready to share the nuclear codes. "Your father and I had a lot of trouble getting pregnant with you. It took a long time, and we weren't sure if it would ever happen."

Leo had never known that. He'd never thought to ask, he supposed. He had asked at least once why he was an only child, if they'd never wanted to have more, and his dad had said something about how Leo was enough for them. He'd never pushed harder, maybe, thinking back, because his mom had looked like she might cry.

"Even my pregnancy with you was touch and go," she continued. "I'd lost pregnancies before you at different stages, so I didn't truly believe you'd be mine until you were actually crying in my arms. And I don't know, therapy wasn't really a thing back then, and I punished myself for not being able to have more kids. I thought that maybe if I was the perfect mom, the perfect wife, then I'd be able to have more."

"You *were* the perfect mom," said Leo, because that was what she needed to hear. She waved him away.

"I tried so hard for so many years to show the world how perfect I could be. And then your father cheated on me! Honestly, we'd been having problems for years, and it didn't come as the biggest shock in the world. But it did shake my worldview. Like, how dare he? All I'd done, all the effort I'd made, and it didn't matter. No more kids, no more husband." She shrugged. "So I vowed to change. I told myself that if impressing the world hadn't worked, then I should just be happy. And I *was* happy, with you and my dad and my siblings in Michigan, and then you went off to college, and he died, and I got the opportunity to be selfish for the first time in years and years. So yes, I changed. I changed purposely, boldly, with the goal that your father would no longer recognize me." She paused, then added, a little wistfully, "I hope that doesn't mean you don't recognize me anymore, either. I've been selfish, and yes, that was my goal, but I hope I haven't drifted too far away from you."

Leo wasn't exactly sure what to say back to that because, honestly, she had kind of put herself out of his reach. But wasn't that her right? How much did she actually owe him as her child? And really, she was here right now. When his dad died and he'd called her, she came. So that's what he told her. She hugged him in response. "What are you really asking about, though?" she said.

"What are you talking about?"

They both watched Neptune snuffle at the roots of a bush before she said, "Were you really asking about me? Or are you asking about someone else? Your father?"

Hearing her mention his father brought that familiar twist of pain in his stomach, the one he kept thinking might lessen over the years and yet somehow never did. He'd heard somewhere that grief never actually got smaller; you just grew bigger to be able to keep it all inside you, and he thought maybe that was true. "No, Dad definitely changed," Leo said and surprised himself again by realizing that was true, too. His dad *had* grown and changed and become a better man, which was part of the tragedy of it all, that Leo had been given only a few years with that better man. "And I'm glad he did."

"Then who are you wondering about?" she asked. "Emily?"

Her name didn't stab him in the heart the way it used to (which was fortunate, considering approximately one in every four women his age was named Emily). He didn't make a habit of looking her up online, but last he'd seen, she'd gotten together with a coworker. He wished her well. "No, that came to its natural end," he said, though *natural* was a stretch given all the crying. "Do you remember our old neighbor? Shira Levinson?"

Her snort was a piece of art. "Of course I remember Shira Levinson," she said. "She was your best friend up until we moved. Every time we got into a fight in Michigan, that was what you threw in my face. I guess you felt too guilty to bring up your dad's cheating, so you'd tell me you hated me because I moved you away from your best friend."

"Oh," Leo said. He had no memory of that. To be fair, the whole divorce-and-move thing had been so traumatic that most of his memories were of the weirdest, simplest things. The look of his bedroom wall, pockmarked with ghostly pale afterimages of the photos and posters that had once hung there, right before he left that house for what he thought was forever. His grandpa's wife's face when she came to meet them at the airport in Michigan, one of her eyebrows drawn on crookedly so that even when they pinched together in worry, she looked as though she were smirking. "Sorry. I know it wasn't your fault."

"Thanks for the apology so many years later," she said. "But it's okay. I knew you didn't actually hate me. You hated the situation. And I hated that you'd never actually get to realize you were in love with her the whole time."

Leo choked on air. "Excuse me?"

"Boys and girls can't actually be that close of friends without something else bubbling up," his mom said, which was problematic in all sorts of ways, but it was hard to call her out, considering that in this case it was true. "I could tell with you two that it was only a matter of time." She squinted at him, veering into his path so that both he and Neptune had to stop short. Neptune's leash wrapped around Leo's ankles, literally binding him in place. "You were asking about her, huh? You guys reconnected, didn't you? I remember you telling me that."

He couldn't exactly dodge the line of questioning when he couldn't move, and despite a nudge with his foot, Neptune was content to lie down and spread his paws in the sun. So he spilled the whole story from the beginning, him kissing her and then her kissing him and then . . . whatever they were now.

"Well, you can't let this be it," his mom said immediately. "What kind of love story would that be?"

"Maybe it isn't a love story," said Leo.

"Of course it's a love story," she said impatiently. "Get it together. You've loved her your whole life." He didn't love her the last few years, not while he was with Emily. It seemed important to remind her of that because he wasn't a cad who'd tie up someone's life while pining for another woman, but his mom just snorted again. "Of course you were in love with Shira the whole time. Why else do you think you hesitated so much at the thought of getting married and having kids with Emily? Emily was perfect for you. You clearly cared about her. But you can't give someone your heart when you've already given it to someone else."

He wanted to protest, but it was true, wasn't it? He hadn't intended it. But it was what had happened. He'd been unfair to Emily. But at least he hadn't married her, he told himself. At least he'd realized it before tying her down. "But Shira didn't think I was good enough for her."

"You've both changed," his mom said. "Has she changed enough? I don't know. I don't know her well enough to say that. But look at me, Leo." She gestured up and down, and Leo had to laugh. Extra years aside, she looked about as different from her past self as possible. No more dieting away the hips. No more close-lipped smiles. No more muted colors or pale-pink nails. "I can tell you with certainty that I've changed. You admitted yourself how your father changed. You should at least give her the chance to show you what's different about her, too."

His body lightened and not just because Neptune stood up from where he'd been lying on Leo's foot. She was right. If change to the degree of his mother's was possible, Shira could absolutely have changed sufficiently to think he was enough for her now.

Now he just had to determine how to reach out to her. Because she'd kissed him last, right? So the ball was in his court. Neptune stretched his legs, as if giving him permission to go.

Of course, his leash was still wrapped around Leo's ankles, something he didn't realize until he was already falling. He was weightless for a moment, the hard concrete of the sidewalk looming before him—ready to break a tooth or worse—but then his mom was there, catching him, holding him up. He was surprised for a moment that she was strong enough, but then, hadn't she been strong enough this whole time?

Embarrassingly, tears pricked his eyes as he disentangled himself from his mom and then from the leash. "Thank you," he said, and he hoped she knew he wasn't just talking about saving him from a face-plant.

When they got back to his building, they stopped so he could grab his mail, which he handed to his mom to hold so that he wouldn't have to juggle the stack of envelopes and junk magazines with the dog leash and his keys. Once inside the apartment, he motioned for her to put the mail down on his counter while he poured Neptune some fresh water from the pitcher in the fridge (the spoiled dog would only drink it cold; Leo himself tended to drink from the tap), then plopped down on his couch and pulled out his phone. Opened his messages app. Stared at that perfunctory Thanks! Took a deep breath.

Hey, long time no talk. Was wondering if there was a Hanukkah party this year? I've really got a hankering for some latkes and Manischewitz. He paused before hitting send. Hope you've been well. Before he could talk himself out of it or get all in his head, he hit the button. The little whoosh said his message was off to its intended target. Leo let out his deep breath and turned his phone over, sliding it onto the countertop. It was done. He'd reached out. He'd done what he could.

"Hey, Leo, did you see this?" His mom brandished an envelope at him, because of course she was snooping through his mail. He squinted at the envelope. It was a big fancy one, light blue and sealed with a gold sticker on the back, like a wedding invitation. *Shira's*, he thought with a flash of panic, then realized that was ridiculous. He would know if Shira had been dating someone long enough to get married, and she hadn't been dating anyone last Hanukkah, right? Shira wasn't the type of person to throw caution to the wind and marry someone after dating less than a year.

"It's from Shira," his mom said, and he jumped up from his seat, making the dog prick his ears. His heart pounded as he crossed the steps into the kitchen and took it from her. His shoulders relaxed almost immediately at the doodle on the envelope. It was a menorah, with him standing behind it, ready to light it, his mouth open, ready to sing. Doodle Leo was a cartoon, so Leo couldn't say for sure how he knew it was him, but Shira had captured enough of his essence in the way the doodle was posed for him to tell. Something about the hesitation in his mouth because he was never one hundred percent sure that he was pronouncing the Hebrew words correctly.

He slit the envelope open with the side of a finger, careful not to ruin the drawing–he kind of wanted to hang it on his fridge. He slid out the piece of sturdy cardboard inside: an invitation. To the Hanukkah party. "Very fancy," he said, eyes scanning the invitation. It was hand-painted, covered in tessellations of blue and white and gold, neat cursive spelling out the details of the event. He would be there, he knew even before checking his calendar. After skipping last year's and spending the night at Aunt Ellen's, sitting morosely on the couch, petting her cat while all her friends cooed and clucked over him, he never wanted to miss another Hanukkah party again.

Wait. He squinted at the words. It wasn't just an invitation to the Hanukkah party; it was also an invitation to . . . an art show? For Shira's work? It had to be, right? Who else's would it be?

He was slightly devastated the event was more than a week away. He wanted to see whatever there was to see now.

Please RSVP to Shira Levinson. You know the number. Now he felt silly for the text he'd sent her before. He went back for his phone, stopping only to scratch Neptune behind his ears.

He had a whole volley of texts. From Shira.

You didn't get my invitation?

I sent an invitation. By mail. In case that wasn't clear.

It must've gotten lost. Curse your mailman.

I actually worked really hard on it! I'm slightly devastated.

. . .

He went to respond before she could spiral further. Sorry, sorry, I never check my mail because it's always junk. I got it! It's a beautiful piece of art. Sent. And then, because he realized he hadn't actually RSVP'd, he typed, I'll be there. Can't wait.

She replied immediately. Neither can I.

"Why are you smiling like that?" his mom asked, popping a chocolate into his mouth. Where had she even gotten it?

It was only then that he realized he was grinning like a fool.

24

SHIRA HAD FIGURED THAT ONCE SHE'D HEARD BACK from Leo, she'd be able to relax a little bit because clearly the fact that he couldn't wait to see her and come to the party and look at her art meant that he didn't hate her, and that her kissing him hadn't ruined everything forever. They could still be friends. Even if they never became more than that, that was okay. He would still be part of her life. Because she'd lived a life without Leo David in it already, and she never wanted to do that again.

But no, there was no relaxing. Which she probably should have figured because, one, her name was Shira Levinson and Shira Levinson did not ever really *relax*, and two, now she could go from stressing over whether he'd show up at all to stressing about what he'd think of her paintings, which she planned to hang all down her house's hallway, since they weren't due at the gallery in Philly until January. What if he hated them? Or worse, what if he thought it was super weird that she'd incorporated so much of their childhood into her art, that it was kind of sad and pathetic that she was clinging so much to the past while he was moving forward fearlessly into the future?

Ugh. She wiped a trail of sweat that was, despite the cold weather, snaking its way down her forehead.

As a distraction, she threw herself headfirst into prep for the Hanukkah party. With no job to do and her paintings finished, it was the only thing she really had to occupy herself with. Especially with Talia not at home anymore and her parents busy. It was weird, being at home for so long that her parents weren't taking time away from work or book club or bird-watching group to be with her. Who even knew her dad had gotten so into bird-watching? She'd let him bring her to one of their sessions to show her off and brag about her art, and she'd trailed after the group of sixtysomethings with binoculars strung around their necks and goggled at her father as he spoke authoritatively about something called a Swainson's thrush, but Shira wasn't entirely sure whether it was a bird or a disease.

It turned out one of the other bird-watchers was Jewish and had the most epic idea for the Hanukkah party: a latke bar. Shira couldn't believe she'd never thought of it before. "So of course you have the latkes, but then, in addition to applesauce and sour cream, you have a whole bunch of other different toppings people can try," she told Talia on the phone later. She still couldn't entirely believe she was talking to Talia on the phone, much less while walking the aisles of another dollar store where she'd stopped to see if they had anything new and fun for Hanukkah. "I went online for people's favorite offbeat latke toppings and jotted down some ideas. I'm going to get duck sauce, mango chutney, cranberry sauce, ranch dressing, peanut sauce, sauerkraut–"

"Ketchup?" Talia interrupted.

"Ew, no," Shira said. "That's just wrong."

"Ketchup and fried potatoes are a match made in heaven."

"Not with latkes," Shira said, though she hoped nobody would ask her to explain why.

"Whatever," said Talia. "Make sure you have kimchi and goat cheese. That's the real GOAT. Anyway, did you hear back from Leo yet?"

"I did," said Shira. She took a deep breath. "He's coming."

"Of course he is," said Talia, which was extremely irritating. "How are you feeling about it?"

"Good, I guess," Shira said. She picked up a dreidel garland and considered it. It was cute, but she already had about fifteen dreidel garlands at home. Still, this one was *shiny*. "Can we not talk about it?"

"Why not?" asked Talia.

Shira ground her teeth together in frustration and threw the dreidel garland into her cart. Now she'd have sixteen dreidel garlands. That was eight times two, which was good Hanukkah luck, right? "Because I'm stressed-out about it and I want to think about it as little as possible. What's going on with you?"

"Nothing too much," said Talia. "Oh, Anjali and I got engaged. That's why I was calling, actually."

Shira shrieked out loud in the aisle of the dollar store, but it was fine because nobody could probably even hear her over the row of plastic singing Santas some kid had just set off. "What? You're engaged? Oh my god, mazel tov!"

"Thanks," Talia said casually. "Anyway, be my maid of

honor? I wanted to go to city hall and elope, but Anjali wants to do a big Jewish-slash-Indian wedding, so turns out I need one of those."

"I'll try to ignore that you didn't ask me the proper way with a box and a bottle of wine with a handwritten note," Shira said. "Ideally with calligraphy."

"You don't even like wine."

"So?"

"So why would I give you wine?"

Shira sighed. Her sister was really the worst. "I would be honored to be your maid of honor. Unless . . ." The latter part of the wedding detail hit her. "I've seen videos of all the bridesmaids doing Bollywood dances at Indian weddings. I'm not going to have to do that, am I?"

"Oh man, Anjali just got home with the groceries," Talia said brightly. "I gotta go. Bye!"

Shira sighed again as her sister hung up. The *worst*.

The shock began to wear off as Shira wandered through the aisles of the store, turning into a mixture of delight for her sister and also, a little embarrassingly, surprise for herself. She'd never imagined her younger sister getting engaged and even married while Shira herself was still single. It wasn't like it was a bad thing—it was . . . well, it just felt weird. Thank goodness they weren't back in the day of Leah and Rachel.

It was great, though, because officially being Talia's maid of honor gave Shira one more thing to obsess over that wasn't what Leo would think of her art. So she spent the next week creating list after list not only for the Hanukkah party but for Talia's bridal shower, bachelorette party, and wedding prep. She didn't share any of them with Talia yet because Talia would think she was insane for preparing a list of games for the bridal shower when Talia probably didn't even want to have a bridal shower (Shira would convince her). But it kept her busy, so the day of the Hanukkah party rolled around to only a few frazzled nerves.

She gathered her parents in the kitchen that morning to give them their instructions. "Mom, you're on drinks duty," she said. "I have a list of suggestions here, but if you see something's on sale and you think it's an equivalent option, I hereby give you permission to wield your coupons."

Her mom rubbed her hands together gleefully as she took the list. "Just wait till you see how much money I save."

"Dad, you're on deli duty, and it would also help if you could swing by the—"

"I can hit up the bakery."

Shira almost jumped out of her skin at the sound of her sister's voice. She turned to see Talia sitting on the counter like a kid, legs swinging at the knees. Talia grinned, probably at Shira's expression of shock. "Talia, when did you get here?"

"I've been here the whole time," Talia said. "And by *the whole time*, I mean the twist is that I'm actually a ghost."

"If you were a ghost, we wouldn't be able to hear you," said her dad.

Talia shuddered. "God, what a punishment for all of you." She leaped off the counter, landing neatly on her feet. "Anyway, I'll go to the bakery and pick up the doughnuts. I owe you after not doing it that one year and turning you into a common thief."

"What?" said her mom and dad in unison, turning to pin Shira with their eyes.

"Nothing," Shira said hastily. "Thanks, Talia. Go, everybody! Off with you!" She made shooing motions with her hands, pausing only to let her mom run off to pee, until her family had gone. Then it was time to decorate: She hung garlands; dragged tables up from the basement and cloaked them in paper tablecloths; arranged chairs in a maze that would allow the maximum number of people to sit down while also making space for them to move.

And then, because she'd left it long enough: the gallery. She removed all the framed photos from the hallway, where school pictures and graduation photos of her and Talia usually hung in chronological order—anybody who used the hall bath could see their college and high school graduation photos beaming, but only those invited down the hall to the bedrooms could see their gap-toothed preschool photos—and hammered some stronger nails in the spaces where the pictures usually hung so that her parents wouldn't see the new holes for years, by which time it would be too late to yell at her about them.

And then she hung her work. By the time she was done, her shoulders were aching and one of her fingers throbbed from catching it between the frame and the nail and the wall. She stuck that finger into her mouth and surveyed the walls with a huff of pride. It had been a while since she'd set up an exhibition.

She was proud to finish with this one, the most meaningful one of them all.

Her family returned home soon, too, Talia with all the ordered doughnuts plus a few extras she couldn't resist ("this one looks just like a tomato!"), and her dad arranged everything perfectly in the fridge in his own little art show, and her mom came bearing the news that she'd saved them almost twenty dollars (which, as it happened, was about the amount Talia had spent on the extra doughnuts).

Assured that so far everything was going according to plan, Shira disappeared in a puff of steam to primp and polish and dress, emerging a couple of hours later with her hair in perfect curls, a rare occurrence because it not only required a fresh wash and a whole lot of creams and gels but almost an hour standing by the mirror with the diffuser nozzle on the hair dryer and the patience to use it. Her eyelashes were highlighted with mascara and her lips with a shiny gloss, and she'd donned a shimmery blue cocktail dress that accentuated the curve of her waist and hips and flattered the bump of her stomach. Most of her guests would not wear anything as fancy, but Shira was the hostess. She was allowed fancy.

And then, as the sky darkened, the guests began to arrive. Shira greeted them all at the door, her heart leaping every time it cracked open, then thudding when it was just the couple down the street or the lady whose cat she used to watch when she went on vacation. Shira smiled at them all, of course, shook hands, said "Thank you" when they congratulated her for moving to Philly, because obviously her parents had already told everyone, though to be honest she didn't know why it deserved a congratulations. The congratulations should really go to her parents, who had been working toward this goal for years.

When Leo finally came, he didn't give a knock, not even a cursory one. He pushed the door open, and there he was. Shira's face was still frozen in a smile from greeting the Yorks, who had spent their few minutes of greeting warning her that anywhere she went in Philly she'd probably get shot or stabbed, but it relaxed into a real, warm one when she saw him there.

He'd changed a bit over the past year—his hair now curled to that sharp spot where his jaw met his cheek, and he wore glasses, wire rims, though she'd never seen him wearing them before—but he was still him, in that plaid-checked shirt and well-fitting dark jeans and the intoxicating aroma of wood and cut grass and soap. "Shira," he said, and the way he said her name warmed her from the inside out more than a cup of hot cocoa taken as a shot. "It's good to see you."

"It's good to see you, too," she said breathlessly, and peered behind him. "Is your mom coming?"

Leo shook his head, still standing in the doorway. "She said to tell you thanks for the invitation and she wished she could make it, but she's busy. That's not true, she's not busy. She just didn't want to come." He gave her a sheepish smile. "Said too many of the neighbors knew my dad was cheating on her before she did and she was still mad at them."

"Understandable," Shira said. A gust of frigid air from the open door hit her in the face, and she stepped back to usher him inside, more out of worry for her hair than her body temperature, honestly. Perfect curls were a hard-fought accomplishment, and it was all too easy to ruin them. He shut the door behind him. The wind made it slam, and they both jumped, then laughed at themselves.

As much as she wanted to go show him her paintings right away, she decided to let him come in, relax, and put something in his stomach so he'd be poised in the best possible position to love them. She placed a hand on his shoulder and was a little surprised to feel the muscle corded beneath; he still looked lean from the outside, but these months of working on houses had clearly had an effect. "We have a new feature this year," she said, then cringed a little because it sounded like she was talking about a new iPhone. "A latke bar. Come explore its wonders."

His shoulder flexed under her hand, as if he wanted to make absolutely sure she felt the muscle there. "I'd like nothing more."

A half hour later, their stomachs were full of latkes and a motley assortment of toppings—kimchi, sour cream, mango chutney, smoked salmon—that sounded disgusting all together but had been quite delicious individually, along with one latke cocktail each. Feeling a little warmer and a little more relaxed, Shira placed her hand back on his shoulder. "Can I show you my paintings?"

"I'm excited to see them," said Leo. She steered him around the clusters of people hovering around the latke bar—it was very popular; she was definitely doing it again next year—and into the hallway, which was quiet because nobody was waiting for the bathroom. She dropped her hand from his shoulder so that he could move at his own pace from painting to painting.

And she held her breath.

Then stopped holding her breath because she didn't want to pass out, and he was taking an awfully long time studying the first painting. And then—after what felt like forever—he cracked a smile. "This one is me," he said, looking over at her. "Kind of? Maybe? I know there's no person in the painting, but it feels like me."

"I based this one on our childhood," she said. The painted cup was a plastic one—you could only really tell from the subtle difference in the shine of light upon it, something the gallery owner had specifically called out to praise—and it overflowed with Pokémon-like creatures fighting with one another, skinned knees, sharp pencils, and eraser dust. The candle poised on top was full and strong, unburnt, not even lit. "To be fully honest with you, I started out making this series for myself, as a kind of therapy. I didn't think I was going to sell them. But then I finished up, and figured, hmm, there's something here."

He was already moving on to the next one, reaching out as if to brush it with his fingertips before dropping his hand at the last second, probably hearing Shira's voice in his head. *Don't touch the art.* "And this—this is when I left."

Shira hated to brag—okay, that was a lie; she loved to brag, though hated to be *perceived* as bragging—but she thought this one was her finest of the series. The painting overflowed with emotion, everywhere from the water spilling from the cup to the uneven brushstrokes that left everything feeling slightly off-kilter. The candle was leaning to one side, just sparking to life, as if she were preparing to remember.

The rest of the series continued apace. Each one centered a stage in her life and the things that were most significant during them, the things she wanted or didn't want to remember from each one, along with the development of the memory candle itself: As more time passed and the cup filled with more things, losing some and gaining others, the candle burned farther and farther down. In the last one in the series, the candle was out, a puff of black smoke indicating that it had just happened.

They were very different paintings from what she'd done before, from the sort of things Danica was doing. She hated that she still thought in terms like that, but she couldn't help it. And yet she thought it was okay. She didn't have to be edgy, experimental, profound. She could just be *her*.

Shira took a deep breath. She'd thought for a long time about how she was going to say this next part. "You're in all of them," she said. "In case you haven't noticed. Even in the one from my college years, when we were apart. Because you helped build the foundation of who I am. I don't totally know who I am without you, and I'm grateful for it." She reached out and took his hand. If he tensed at all, if he displayed any sign that he didn't want her touching him, she'd drop it immediately.

But he didn't. He squeezed. Emboldened, she went on. "So much has changed over the past . . . how many years has it been since we reunited? Six?" She knew perfectly well how many years it had been but didn't want to be weird about it. "I've certainly changed. I've grown a lot. But you'll always know the core of me. You'll always be part of the core of me. And I hope we'll always know each other."

He was studying her like she was a book he desperately wanted to finish, to know how it ended. She coughed to dislodge the sudden lump in her throat. "Anyway, there wasn't room on the wall for all the paintings, so the final one is in the closet there."

He didn't question her, just opened the door to the linen

closet. And nearly fell over. "Jesus Christ," he wheezed, clutching his chest. Shira was alarmed for a moment until she realized he was smiling. "Are you trying to kill me?"

"No," she said. "But he might be."

The maniacally grinning Mensch on a Bench, dug up from the depths of her closet, leaned forward from his perch among the hand towels, almost as if he were about to dive forward and rip out Leo's throat with his teeth. Leo shuddered, slamming the door. "I can't believe he didn't figure into your memory candles."

"Our relationship is too private for that," Shira said. The Mensch on a Bench had defused some of the tension in the hallway, making it easy to move again. But Leo's face sobered as his eyes focused on hers once more.

"I have to show you something too."

"Okay," she said.

"It's in my car."

"Okay."

It was still frigid outside, but Shira was somehow warm as she scurried after Leo across the front lawn, her footsteps crunching in the layer of ice atop the sparse brown grass. Leo turned around halfway through and offered her his jacket, which she gladly accepted, not so much because she was cold but because she knew it would smell like him.

Leo was parked down the street, almost in front of his old house, which was blinking with multicolored Christmas lights. They tinted his face green and blue, red and white, as he unlocked his trunk and pulled it open. "Look at this," he said, stepping aside.

"You're not going to push me in there, are you?" Shira joked, but he only shook his head, eyes shadowed and intense, which made her even more curious. She leaned in, pulling aside a layer of tissue paper that crinkled like the crackling ice underfoot. She squinted at a sudden bright light, then realized Leo was shining his phone flashlight into the trunk to compensate for the dim streetlight down the block. "Oh, thanks."

It took her a minute to realize what she was seeing inside the trunk. At first it was just light, shining bits of color reflecting back at her, but then the shining bits of color crystallized into petals, a bloom, a stem, rays of light gleaming pure white in a clear blue sky behind the flowers. "Oh," she said, surprised. "Is that a stained glass window?"

He moved around her, brushing close enough that the heat of his body scalded her even through his coat, and lifted up the window so that the light of the phone could shine through it, making it come to life, dazzling and sparkling like the sun in all its glory was on the other side. Shira could only imagine how it looked when real sunlight was actually shining through: It must be magnificent. "To be exact, it's a stained glass window from a 1929 Tudor house near Philadelphia that was demolished several years ago to make way for some ugly millennial gray box," he said. The sound of laughter drifted from Shira's house, ghostly in the winter air. "I found it in a salvage shop in South Jersey, where it was covered in grime and caked-on dust. It took ages to clean it without harming it."

"It's beautiful," Shira said sincerely. Something tugged in her chest whenever she looked at it. If she believed in past lives, she'd think she'd once lived in that 1929 Tudor.

"It is," agreed Leo. He wasn't looking at her; he was gazing at the stained glass fondly, like it was his child or at least his beloved pet. "I have a whole stockpile of stained glass now. Because I put one window in every house I work on. It's kind of become my signature."

"Why?"

Now he looked at her, and his eyes were blazing like the sun was behind them too. "Because you said you wanted to live in a house with a stained glass window someday. All the homes I work on: They're all for you."

Something cracked in her chest just then, but not in a way that broke her. It was more like she'd broken open, and now the sun was shining through her too. "It sounds a little like you're saying 'I love you,'" she said like she was joking, but she knew she wasn't joking, and from the intensity still in his gaze, she knew he knew she wasn't joking, either.

"Your paintings sounded a little bit like you were saying 'I love you,'" Leo said. Had his eyes always held that hint of green? So many years of knowing him, and still there were surprises. "Am I wrong?"

"No," she said breathlessly. "No, you're not wrong."

Nothing had ever been more right, in fact, than the way their lips met. She didn't kiss him, and he didn't kiss her—this time it was a true meeting in the middle, both of them leaning in and crashing warm lips into warm lips. Warm turned to hot against the cold air, and somewhere deep in Shira's mind she wondered if they were steaming or smoking or burning.

Let them burn. Let it all burn, if it meant being bundled in Leo's arms like this. If it meant his eyelashes brushing against hers, his nose bumping against hers, the heat of his tongue tangled with hers. His heart beat against her chest, echoing her own, and they fell into each other's rhythms, his hands in her hair, pulling her closer to him.

When she finally broke free, it wasn't to go far, just to rest her forehead against his. "I love you," she said. "I hope it's not weird to say that and that it doesn't scare you off. I don't mean, like, in a romantic way. Not yet. But I love you, I've always loved you, and I want to love you more and more every day."

"I love you, Shira Levinson, more than I love latkes," he said, which made a giggle bubble in her throat. A giggle. When was the last time she'd giggled? "I don't think I have a passion for work or for art in the way that some people do. I don't think I'll ever find my life's meaning or my life's purpose in a job." He reached for her hand. It fit into his like it had been made for that one purpose, a key and a lock. "I think maybe my passion in life is you. I think maybe my life's meaning and my life's purpose is the family that we build together."

She caught the flash of panic over his face when he had to be afraid he'd come on too strong; she wiped it away with another kiss, then rested her head against his shoulder. She was filled with such a pure, strident happiness that it made her almost afraid. Out of the corner of her eye, she caught another package in the back of the trunk. "What else do you have in there?"

"Oh, that?" Leo stepped back just far enough to move the box into the light. Shira was pleasantly surprised to see a standard brass menorah inside—one decorated with curling vines—along with a small pack of candles. "I found it at the same salvage shop where I found the stained glass window and couldn't leave it behind. I thought maybe we could use it tonight, except then I got so nervous going in that I forgot."

Shira glanced over her shoulder, at the lit-up house and the shadows of people moving past the windows inside. An idea sparked. "Let's not go inside yet." She grabbed the menorah and the candles, which meant leaving Leo's immediate circle of warmth, but she was secure he wouldn't be going far. "Do you have a lighter?"

"Yeah, I think so."

"Then come on."

She grabbed him by the hand and led him back behind his old house—nobody would notice; its current occupants were at the party—and into the woods. She was a little nervous until she laid eyes on it: the old swing set. She actually laughed out loud with relief. "It's still here."

"Of course it's still here," Leo said. "You know how deep my dad sank this thing in? I still remember my mom out here worrying that I'd swing too hard and uproot it, and each time she said something he'd dig it in deeper. It's attached to the land by, like, tons of cement. That swing set is going to be here long after the houses are gone and we're all dead."

"A beautiful thought," Shira said dryly. She placed the menorah in the little cabin right above the slide; she and Leo clustered next to the swings, with her tucked close against his side. "You ready?"

He flicked on the lighter. "Born ready."

In the candlelight, his cheeks were pink, and she knew hers were rosy, too. Together, they set the candles into each arm of the menorah, before he picked up one last candle to serve as the shammash. Gently, he touched the flame to its wick and handed it to her before letting the lighter go out and tucking it back into his pocket. "You do the honors."

As she opened her mouth and sang the blessings, he sang along with her, and she swore that their two distinct voices sounded like a chorus: a chorus of years, a chorus of loves, a chorus of all the people and all the things that had brought them finally, finally together. And then, as the nine tiny lights twinkled against the stars in the sky, it was like all the lights in all the universe were shining upon them.

From Shira Levinson's sent-emails folder:

FEBRUARY: *The reviews are in! Painter Shira Levinson's long-awaited second show has received almost universal acclaim from Philadelphia critics. Don't miss her show at the . . .* FWD: Hey fam—here's the newsletter my gallery sent around about my show! They're obviously exaggerating for their own benefit ("long-awaited"? That's one way of putting it, lol. And there are only like two actual art critics in Philadelphia, and nobody in NYC or LA cares what they think) but it's exciting anyway. Who knows how many pieces I'll actually sell, but fortunately I'm not that worried about it anymore . . .

AUGUST: Hello, Talia's friends! For those of you who don't know me (I assume that is zero, considering how open and sharing Talia is 😉), I'm Talia's beloved older sister, Shira. I'm getting the ball rolling on her bachelorette party this fall. She insisted on doing something within driving distance that wasn't too expensive, so I'm thinking a Jersey Shore beach house (off-season, so we save money! Our mother would be very proud) or a drive up to Maine. Please let me know what you think about these options, or if you have something else in mind, I'm all ears . . .

From Leo David's email inbox:

APRIL: Hey Leo! Great to hear from you, man, though I haven't stopped missing you at the desk next door (your replacement smells like everything bagels, and while you may think that's a good smell, imagine smelling it all day, every day). I took a look at your new game as you requested. I loved it, but it might be a little too arty for us—hard to imagine teenagers playing it in waiting rooms or twentysomethings bingeing it in a weekend, you know? . . .

OCTOBER: Dear Leo, Thank you for letting us know about your decision not to renew your lease. While we will miss you in the building, I'm glad to hear you're moving in with your girlfriend. She's been lovely every time we've crossed paths, and I wish you two all the best . . .

Epilogue

Year Eight

HANUKKAH MIRACLE NUMBER ONE: EVEN THOUGH Leo arrived late to the bakery to pick up the doughnut order, he and Shira didn't have to break in again. The owner was locking up the back door when Leo hopped out of his car, panting and apologizing, and was kind enough to open the place back up so he could get his order.

"You look familiar," said the owner, squinting, as Leo checked to make sure everything was there. Everything was—not a miracle; the bakery was just good at their job—so Leo turned his attention to the owner. Sure enough, the owner looked familiar, too. Leo clapped his hands together.

"Theo Kanelos! How are you, man?"

It took Theo a second to remember Leo's name, but it turned out he did remember the daring chalk graffiti they'd left on the middle school blacktop (mostly penises). They spent a few minutes chatting and catching up, and when Leo checked his watch and told him he had to go, Theo slapped him on the back and threw in an extra dozen doughnuts for free.

HANUKKAH MIRACLE NUMBER two: When Shira had moved last year, lots of stuff had gone missing or gotten lost in transit. That included the Mensch on a Bench, who, even though he hadn't had to cross the entire country, had somehow gone into hiding; Shira assumed that someone had seen him sitting on one of her boxes and thought it was funny or that maybe her parents had taken advantage of the chaos of the move to toss the creepy old thing. She'd tried to find a similarly unnerving one online, but no luck. Apparently he had only been sold by a few dollar stores for a short period of time and whoever was "lucky" enough to pick him up didn't want to part with him or couldn't part with him, thanks to some kind of curse, who knew. So she'd resigned herself to her creepy uncle not attending the party.

And then, this morning, she'd opened Talia's old closet in search of past years' decorations, and there was the Mensch, at eye level, grinning horribly in her direction with all his teeth—had they always been so pointy?—on display. Shira jumped and clutched her chest, nearly falling over, before she remembered she'd stuck it there after last year's Hanukkah party to scare whoever went in next.

"Serves you right," Talia said a few minutes later. She was sitting very still in the kitchen so that nothing would jar her wet nails (she'd insisted on black, but Shira had convinced her to stud a few with tiny fake diamonds and pearls to look more elegant).

"Yeah," Shira said, sighing. She hadn't painted her own nails despite the occasion; she didn't like the feeling of polish on her fingers, and so what if people would judge her in the photos? She didn't care.

HANUKKAH MIRACLE NUMBER three: Despite the eruption of a minor volcano somewhere in Southern Europe, Leo's mom's flight was not canceled, only delayed, which meant that she arrived at the airport the afternoon of the party. Leo met her in the arrivals lounge, sweaty and frazzled, with the doughnuts in the car, and laughed a little to see his mother sail out all polished and breezy after ten hours in the air. "I'm so glad you made it in time," he exclaimed, kissing her on both cheeks in the way she'd come to expect.

She lowered her designer sunglasses and raised one perfectly manicured eyebrow. "It's just a Hanukkah party, darling. We could celebrate another night."

Leo exhaled a big breath of relief. "It's the eighth night tonight. There are no other nights."

"Still," his mother proclaimed, slipping her sunglasses back on and patting her lipsticked mouth as she yawned (elegantly, of course). "Hanukkah isn't an important holiday, you know."

"I know," Leo said and took another deep breath, kind of wishing she'd left her sunglasses down so he could see the look in her eyes. "But, actually . . ."

HANUKKAH MIRACLE NUMBER four: Despite all the latke and latke-topping taste testing Shira had done over the past few weeks, her dress still fit. She didn't even have to suck in her stomach while Talia zipped up the back. She smoothed the shimmery ice-blue skirt and ran a hand over her long side braid. "You're sure I don't look too much like Elsa from *Frozen*?"

"You do look like a winter queen," Talia said, brushing an imaginary piece of dust off Shira's shoulder. Shira had found the dress at a vintage shop and fallen immediately in love with the gentle shimmer of the fabric, the lace sleeves, the low neckline that left room for a dramatic necklace. "But no, Elsa is extremely skinny and blond, with a tiny button nose and enormous anime eyes. You look beautiful, but you look nothing like Elsa."

Impulsive hug time. Talia didn't even bother grumbling about it.

HANUKKAH MIRACLE NUMBER five: Everybody was actually on time! That included Aunt Ellen, who was escorting Leo's grandparents. It took them about twenty minutes to get out of the car and inch, very slowly, his grandpa with his cane and his grandma with her walker, up the shoveled front walk of Shira's parents' house. "I know it wasn't an easy trip for you," Leo said, leaning in to kiss all of them on the cheek. "Especially you," he muttered to Aunt Ellen so only she could hear. She widened her eyes like she was flashing a siren. She had been a firm no on the trip until Leo spilled the real purpose of this party, and then she grudgingly assented, though she grumbled the whole time.

You'd never know it from the smile on her face, though. "Wouldn't miss it for the world," she said, leaning in to give him a quick, brusque hug. He could feel the love in it, the sadness that she was the one here instead of his dad. And sure enough, Leo's heart squeezed with pain. He wished his dad were here, and it wasn't fair that he wasn't, and he would probably never stop feeling that way.

But if there was one thing his relationship with his dad had taught him, it was that life was short, and it was precious, and you couldn't count on it to be there forever, so you had to make things right with the people you loved when you still could.

And sometimes making things right didn't mean making up. It meant–

"What does this mean, 'Welcome to the wedding of Shira Levinson and Leo David'?" one of his former neighbors read in a quavery old-person voice. Shira's parents had set up the engraved placards by the door so that guests wouldn't be bewildered upon entering the living room and finding it filled with white plastic folding chairs, separated by an aisle leading to the sliding glass door. "I thought this was the Hanukkah party?"

Leo's face was threatening to split in two. *The wedding of Shira Levinson and Leo David.* He felt like he'd waited his entire life to hear that phrase. And what was that saying? When you knew what you wanted for the rest of your life, you wanted the rest of your life to start as soon as possible? Something like that. That was what they'd told Shira's parents and his mom, anyway, who were shocked given they'd been dating for less than a year. Leo wished again that his dad were there–he would've been so smug and full of *I told you sos*. "It'll be a full year by the date of the wedding," Shira had told them confidently, as if those extra few days made all the difference. "And we've been living together for months, and we've known each other our whole lives. We know what we're doing."

He hadn't been able to help it: He'd scooped her up and twirled her around and kissed her, right there in front of her family. They'd all applauded, which was good. And then her mom had asked, a little doubtfully, "And that's what you want? You want to get married at our house, during the Hanukkah party?"

"Not just that, I want it to be a surprise for everyone but family," Shira said. "You've seen those videos, right? Surprise weddings? They were viral for a while. That's what I want. Low stress, low expenses, and then we're going to go on an epic honeymoon and buy a house."

It was hard for Jewish parents to argue with saving money, though Shira's mom tried. "You're sure you don't want the big white dress and all your cousins doing the hora?"

Leo saw Shira hesitate, and he knew, despite all the work she'd done, what was going through her head. *What will people think about you getting married in your childhood home during a neighborhood party? Don't you want pictures to post?* But the work she'd done allowed her to shake her head and say with a smile, "I've always been afraid they'd drop me when I'm up on that chair. And it's not like I have so many friends out here yet that I want to invite."

"Who's Leo David?" asked the elderly neighbor now, squinting at the placard. Leo suppressed a sigh and the urge to say *I only mowed your lawn for all of high school.* Instead, he maneuvered his way over to his grandparents for misty-eyed hugs.

"I saved seats for you in the front," he said, turning to walk them that way.

HANUKKAH MIRACLE NUMBER six: Shira didn't trip as she walked down the aisle. She'd waited in her room with Talia and her parents, listening as Leo's mom first escorted him down the aisle to the prerecorded music of a string quartet. Then she took a deep breath and smoothed her skirt, leaving streaks of sweat behind.

"Are you getting nervous?" Talia asked. "It's not too late to back out. We're on the first floor, I can definitely get you out that window."

Shira let out what might have been a slightly crazed laugh. "I don't want to back out of the wedding. I kind of want to back out from wearing these shoes with this skirt, because I keep stepping on it."

Talia looked at her as if she were insane. "So change your shoes."

Shira regarded her high heels, which were barely poking out from under the slightly-too-long skirt of her dress (it had fit the rest of her body perfectly; she hadn't wanted to pay to tailor just the hemline). "But they go perfectly with the dress."

"You can't even see them under the skirt," said Talia, and damn it, she made sense.

And that was how Shira found herself walking down the aisle—thoughtfully carpeted with rose petals—in her shiny silver Converse. Talia had been right, Shira thought, looking at her sister's back before Talia turned around under the chuppah to face the audience because, as the family rabbi, she would be the officiant. You couldn't even see them under Shira's skirt.

And so she held her head high, standing between her parents, arms linked in theirs, as she walked toward her future husband.

HANUKKAH MIRACLE NUMBER seven: Leo didn't forget his vows. He thought he might as he watched his bride walk down the aisle, her eyes already shiny, her face glowing. Her beauty took over everything in his head, crowded out the rest of what was in there, even his sense of time, so that he blinked and she was thirteen, walking into his house all luminous with excitement over the latest Pokémon expansion, and he blinked again and she was beside him, and her parents were shaking his hand and giving him hugs and then sitting down, and then she was there standing across from him, her hands in his, her chest heaving with emotion.

Despite the location, they had a full Jewish ceremony beneath the chuppah, over which Leo had stretched his dad's tallit, which Leo couldn't remember his dad ever wearing but which he'd found all dusty in the back of a closet while cleaning out his house, so part of his dad was there in a way. Leo and Shira walked around each other seven times and repeated the Hebrew vows Leo didn't understand, and they stomped on the glass together, everybody cheering at the sound of the muffled smash.

Then it was time to say a little something. She went first. "This isn't love at first sight," she said, beaming at him. Her hands were in his. He squeezed them and thought, *I'm squeezing my wife's hands*. Incredible. "Or love at second sight or even love at a hundredth sight. It's better than that. This is a love that revealed itself slowly, layer by layer, piece by piece, so that once it was laid bare, it was impossible to miss."

Soon it was his turn. He actually improvised a little. "I think, for me, it was love at first sight," he said, to laughter from the crowd. "I just spent years pushing it away because I didn't think there was any way you could return it. And you couldn't, back then. It took years, and I'm glad we had those years to grow and change and turn into people who made each other better."

And the kiss. Though they'd kissed countless times over the past year, in bed and in public, long, passionate kisses that led to something else and quick pecks on their way out the door, this first kiss as husband and wife knocked the earth off its axis. Leo felt the world tilting under him, and he welcomed it.

❄

HANUKKAH MIRACLE NUMBER eight: doughnuts. Shira bit into one of the doughnuts they'd piled into a three-tier stack in lieu of a wedding cake and closed her eyes with bliss, the sweet cream and chocolate topping maybe the best thing she'd ever tasted.

Just kidding. The eighth miracle of Hanukkah was love, obviously. Doughnuts were great, but even the best doughnut in the world paled in comparison to finally, finally having found her person.

The sun had fallen. Everybody lined up in front of the menorahs. Shira and Leo took their place before the center one, which Aunt Ellen had purchased for them as a wedding gift. It was tall, grand, and fancy, plated with silver and gold, with pomegranate leaves twining off the branches and shaking delicately in the air. Shira sang the blessings, her heart full to bursting, and then she and Leo held the shammash and went from left to right, together. As they would always.

Leo's murmur stirred the hair over her ear. "You know, our whole relationship is a true Hanukkah miracle. Most couples get together soon after their first kiss, but it took us eight Hanukkahs."

Shira lit the final candle and then held the bottom of the shammash candle gently over the flame beside it, melting it just enough so that it would sit solidly in its cup without risk of falling over. Then turned to her husband, just halfway, so that she could see both his face and all nine candles blazing bright. The light shimmered over his face, turning it into gold. "Maybe it took us eight Hanukkahs to get here," she said, "and that's okay. We're not going to flicker out. We're going to be the eternal light."

His lips touched her forehead. She closed her eyes, but she could still see the flames burning bright.

Acknowledgments

Eight hundred thank-yous to my team at Berkley: Mary Baker, Kristine Swartz, Chelsea Pascoe, Elisha Katz, Christine Legon, Megha Jain, Colleen Reinhart, and Nancy Resnick. Petra Braun, thank you for bringing Shira and Leo to life on the absolutely stunning cover.

Eight hundred more thank-yous to my agent, Merrilee Heifetz, and the rest of the team at Writers House, especially Rebecca Eskildsen. Ali Lefkowitz, thank you for all your work on the film side.

Eight billion thank-yous to my husband, Jeremy. I wrote the first draft of this book sick and exhausted in my first trimester with our second baby while taking care of a toddler, and there's no way I could've done it without you. Miriam and Jonah: you actually make writing way harder, but I wouldn't have it any other way.

EIGHT WAYS TO SAY I LOVE YOU

AMANDA ELLIOT

READERS GUIDE

Discussion Questions

1. The book is told in two points of view: Shira's and Leo's. Did you find one more engaging than the other? Why or why not?

2. Do you think there is such a thing as a dream job? How have your thoughts on what you want out of a job or career changed throughout your life?

3. Do you agree with Shira's sentiment that friendship breakups often hit harder than romantic breakups? Why or why not? Have you experienced a friendship breakup that affected you the way Shira's breakup with Danica affects her?

4. Set in suburban New Jersey, the story depicts the suburbs mainly in a positive light. Do you agree with these positive depictions? Do you think you'd enjoy living in Shira and Leo's neighborhood?

5. Told over eight years, the book checks in with both main characters once a year during the holidays. How do you feel

about this structure? Would you have chosen to tell the story a different way?

6. With the exception of text or email interstitials, we only get to know the characters while they're home with their families. Do you think they're different the rest of the year? How do you think they might behave differently?

7. Leo's relationships with his parents are both rocky in different ways. Do you agree with how he handles those relationships over the course of the book? Why or why not?

8. Imagine a bonus chapter that takes place five years after the epilogue and features all the main characters. Where do you picture the characters' lives at this future point?

KEEP READING FOR A PREVIEW OF AMANDA ELLIOT'S

LOVE YOU A LATKE

AVAILABLE NOW!

OUTSIDE THE PICTURE WINDOW OF THE CAFÉ, SNOW drifted to the sidewalk in big fluffy flakes. Sleigh bells jingled on the speaker overhead, not quite covering up the burbling sounds of the machines behind me. Scents of gingerbread and mint drifted through the air. And, in my head, a Category 2 headache was pinching the area between my eyes and radiating back toward my ears.

There are five categories in ascending order of least to most severe, in case you're wondering.

"Sir, I don't know how many more times I can say it," I told the beet-faced man on the other side of the counter. He wore flannel like most of the other people who stopped in for coffee or a pastry, but he wasn't a local. It was easy to tell who was and wasn't a local when there were only a few hundred of them. "I can't give you a refund when you drank the entire thing. I can give you a new coffee. For free. For your trouble." *So you'll get out of here and leave me alone.*

The man glowered at me like I'd told him his beard was patchy. "I could barely taste the gingerbread. It didn't fulfill the expectations I had of a gingerbread coffee. I don't want a free mediocre coffee. I want my money back."

Excuse me, my gingerbread coffee was not just far from mediocre; it was excellent. I'd spent days perfecting the exact blend of ginger, cinnamon, allspice, cloves, and nutmeg to flavor the coffee without overpowering it. I'd even added a pinch of crushed red pepper flakes in the mix to mimic that gentle burn a good gingerbread cookie gives you in the back of your throat. Whenever I finished stirring a new batch of it up, it smelled exactly like I'd dropped a warm, fresh-out-of-the-oven cookie into a vat of coffee. The first time I'd tasted it I'd literally pumped my fist in the air—that glorious sensation of achievement that comes from creating some excellent piece of art. Yes, fun drinks were art. "Then you should have said something after your first sip or two," I said. "It couldn't have been *that* bad if you drank the whole thing."

"I wanted to see if it would get better as I went on. Maybe all of the syrup had settled at the bottom."

I had to hold myself back from rolling my eyes. Except fuck it, that was a really eye roll–worthy thing to say. I rolled my eyes. My brain was now throbbing. "I'm going to have to ask you to leave."

And then he said my absolute favorite thing problem customers said, the glorious seven words that made the throbbing in my head shrink into glee. "I'd like to speak to your manager."

I drew myself up so that, despite our height difference, our eyes were level. And I smiled. Not my fake, stretched-out customer-service smile, either. A real, true, toothy grin. "Sir, I *am* the manager."

I could've gone on from there. Because I wasn't just the manager. I was the owner. Well, technically the renter. But either way, I was the one in control of this warm, cozy space and the apartment above it. Another thing that had given me a glorious sense of achievement: running my own business at the age of twenty-eight and not having to answer to anyone else about how I spent my time or what drink specials I wanted to put on the board or how I wanted to talk to my customers. I didn't think I could ever go back to working for someone else again.

"Whatever," the man grumbled. He shook his head. "If this is how you treat your customers, you won't be in business much longer." He pointed at the menu board. "If your gruesome drawings don't put you out first."

I turned to look at my menu board, where I'd written all of our seasonal specials in chalk. Next to the gingerbread coffee listing I'd drawn a cheery gingerbread man going for a quick dip in a hot tub–esque cup of coffee. Though looking at it now, the gingerbread man did kind of look like he was screaming. (I was about as good at drawing cheer as I was at faking it. In other words, not very.) And you could possibly interpret his raised arms as flailing with panic.

The man was already storming out, but I wasn't going to let him have the last word. I called after him, "It's a festive doodle!" The door slammed shut with the tinkle of a bell.

I took a deep breath. His words rang in my head. *You won't be in business much longer.* They were just the nasty words of an aggrieved customer, I told myself. Not prophecy.

Though you didn't need to be a prophet to read what the profit margins of the last few months were saying.

No matter. I didn't have time to waste stressing over it or feeling sorry for myself. I turned my attention to the next customer in line, who was bound to be annoyed after the long wait. "Good morning, how can I help you?"

As I realized who I was speaking with, that Category 2 headache slammed back into my skull so hard it flipped right into a Category 3, which would ache at least as long as the person who caused it was in the vicinity. As long as *he* was in the vicinity, I should say. Because Category 3 headaches were reserved for one special customer.

"Beautiful day today!" said certain customer chirped, beaming a mouthful of very white teeth in my direction.

The snow had stopped falling, leaving a murky gray sky behind. The temperature was supposed to hover at that sweet spot between freezing and not freezing, so that what snow was left on the ground would turn into a nasty wet slush and anything that came down the rest of the day would be a sleety, icy rain. "It's supposed to be wet and rainy all afternoon."

His smile didn't waver. "Who said rain can't be beautiful?"

Ugh. When I closed the café at four and walked outside, I'd probably find him singing and dancing as the water poured around him, his tap shoes somehow magically not slipping in the slush. "What can I get you, Seth?"

It was truly a shame he was so annoying, because if not for the whole personality thing, he'd actually be handsome. I'd perked up the first time I saw him walk through my door, his green flannel setting off broad shoulders beneath dark hair that curled around his strong cheekbones.

And then he'd opened his mouth. Something he insisted on doing way too often each time I saw him. Now, instead of just telling me that he wanted a pumpkin spice latte with whipped cream—what he gets from October through December each year—he said, "Man, I wonder what that guy before me was going through. It must really be a lot for him to act like that."

I should have known better than to take the bait. I really should. But the man's words were still smarting, like poking at an already aching bruise. *You won't be in business much longer.* "Or," I replied, already mad at myself, "maybe he was just a jerk."

"Maybe he was tired and somebody rear-ended his car yesterday and his head hurt and he just wanted to feel like someone was taking care of him," Seth said.

"Or maybe he was just a jerk," I said. "Lots of people are. What do you want, Seth?"

"To continue believing that humanity is generally good, and that people who behave badly usually have a reason for it," he said. "Also a pumpkin spice latte, please. With whipped cream."

"Latte coming right up." I felt a little better as soon as I turned my back to run the machine, breathing in the sweet steam bath of coffee and sugar. He probably assumed I drank my coffee black and strong, but I actually loved a good pumpkin spice or vanilla or hazelnut cream latte. See? Just because I saw humanity as it really was didn't mean I was some sad, bitter person who snubbed anything sweet and indulgent.

Not that he'd gotten to me, or that anything he could say would ever get to me. I was one hundred percent right, and he was one hundred percent wrong. If he thought there weren't plenty of people out there who weren't jerks just for the sake of being jerks, he clearly hadn't met very many people.

As the machine was finishing its magic, I held the cardboard cup underneath the spout to let it fill. The moment I pulled it away, steaming and topped with a thick layer of pale foam, Seth said, "I like your drawings, by the way. They're funny. I mean, it's not like you drowned a *real* gingerbread man. Or like gingerbread men are real and can drown."

I gritted my teeth. "The gingerbread man isn't drowning. He's soaking in his hot tub of coffee."

"Oh. Well, it's up for interpretation. All good art is, right?"

"It's not art," I said, just to be contrary. "It's supposed to be fun." Bah humbug. I was never making a festive doodle again.

I spun around as soon as Seth's cup was finished filling to find him looking at me with what appeared to be sympathy. "I never like to assume people are just jerks; I like to think they're having a bad day and they feel bad about it afterward. Have you ever read Anne Frank? 'In spite of everything I still believe that people are really good at heart.' I try to live by her example."

I set the cup on the counter for Seth to take. Irritation boiled inside me. Why did people always need to bring up Nazis as a rhetorical talking point? They weren't rhetorical. My great-grandmother had lost both her parents and her sister to them as a child. "Yes, I've read *The Diary of Anne Frank*. I wonder if she still would've said that after the people she was talking about killed her."

Seth frowned. I thought he'd come back with something else about the Holocaust—good luck to him; my Hebrew school education might not do me much good in this land of Presbyterians and Methodists and hard-core atheists, but I could out-knowledge anyone about the Holocaust any day. Instead, he said, "What about the whipped cream?"

"We're out," I said. It was an asshole thing to say, especially considering it was making my business look bad and I couldn't afford to lose even my most annoying customer, but I couldn't help but feel a muted sort of joy as he looked sadly down at his cup. See, Seth? Some people really did just like being mean. At least to people who deserved it. I waited for him to protest that he could literally see the whipped cream can behind me, to call me out, to do something, anything—

His lips rose in an infuriating little smile. "That's probably for the best," he said. "I should be watching my sugar intake anyway. Have a wonderful day, Abby!" He grabbed his coffee and strode off whistling. *Whistling.*

The whistling alone made my headache throb at a steady Category 3 for the rest of the morning and into the afternoon, as I wound down the coffee orders and took some time to swipe crumbs off tabletops with a damp rag, then ran into the back for a sorely needed bathroom break. I washed my hands carefully for sanitary reasons, because I was *good* at what I did, damn it, and stared at myself in the mirror. My cheeks were even hollower than usual, and the bags beneath my brown eyes hung heavy enough to hold a croissant each. Or maybe the lighting was just super unflattering in here since the bulb directly above me had gone out.

I'd go with that, I thought, making a mental note to replace it and at the same time knowing there was at least a fifty percent chance I'd forget by the end of the day. It would be so much easier if I still had an employee or two I could ask while I manned the counter, but I'd had to let go both the teenager who helped out on weekends and the retiree who came in on weekday mornings for some extra cash and socialization. It was either that or take a pay cut myself, and I literally couldn't cut my pay any more without skipping meals or getting behind on rent.

My stomach clenched, as it did every time I had these thoughts. Maybe I wasn't as good at what I did (damn it) as I thought, because if I was, wouldn't I be making enough money to keep a couple part-time workers? As it was now, I could barely pay the rent, and that was with me praying that the bakery a few towns over continued to be generous enough to sell me their baked goods at cost in exchange for strategically placed advertisements. What was the point of them advertising in my café, after all, if there weren't enough people stopping in to see them? Now my stomach unclenched and rolled. If I lost my café, I'd have to start all over somewhere else. I wouldn't have the capital to start my own business again.

I could practically hear Seth's irritating chirp. *Look on the bright side! You get so much extra time to brainstorm Christmas coffee specials and draw designs on the menu board.*

My foot hurt. It took me a moment to realize it was because I'd kicked the counter.

Sometimes there was no bright side. Sometimes things just sucked.

Author photo by Cassie Gonzales

USA Today bestselling author **Amanda Elliot** lives with her family in New Jersey, where she experiments with homemade ice cream flavors, tries her best to grow vegetables in her tiny garden, and writes mysteries under the name Bellamy Rose.

VISIT AMANDA ELLIOT ONLINE

AmandaElliotBooks.com

AmandaElliotBooks